for Terri Lynn
my Soulmate and Best Friend

Marbeck

Abeloft

Stonekirk

Westhaven

Helkirk

Durness

Statmyr

Torgue

Odryssa

Contyn   Eglyn

Avnoch   Kinlich

Abynee   Glenloc

Orc's

Bane

A GameLit Adventure Series
(BRIDGE QUEST Book 2)

pdmac

Orc's Bane is a work of fiction. Though actual locations may be mentioned, they are used in a fictitious manner and the events and occurrences were created/invented in the mind and imagination of the author, except for the inclusion of actual historical fact. Similarities of characters or names used within for any person – past, present, or future – are coincidental except where actual historical characters are purposely interwoven. The actions, thoughts, and dialogue of the historical characters featured in this story are fictional and not meant to reflect actual personalities and behavior.

Published by Trimble Hollow Press, Acworth, Georgia

ISBN: 978-1-946495-18-1
eISBN: 978-1-946495-17-4

Cover design by Trimble Hollow Concepts
Cover art by James Esquivel

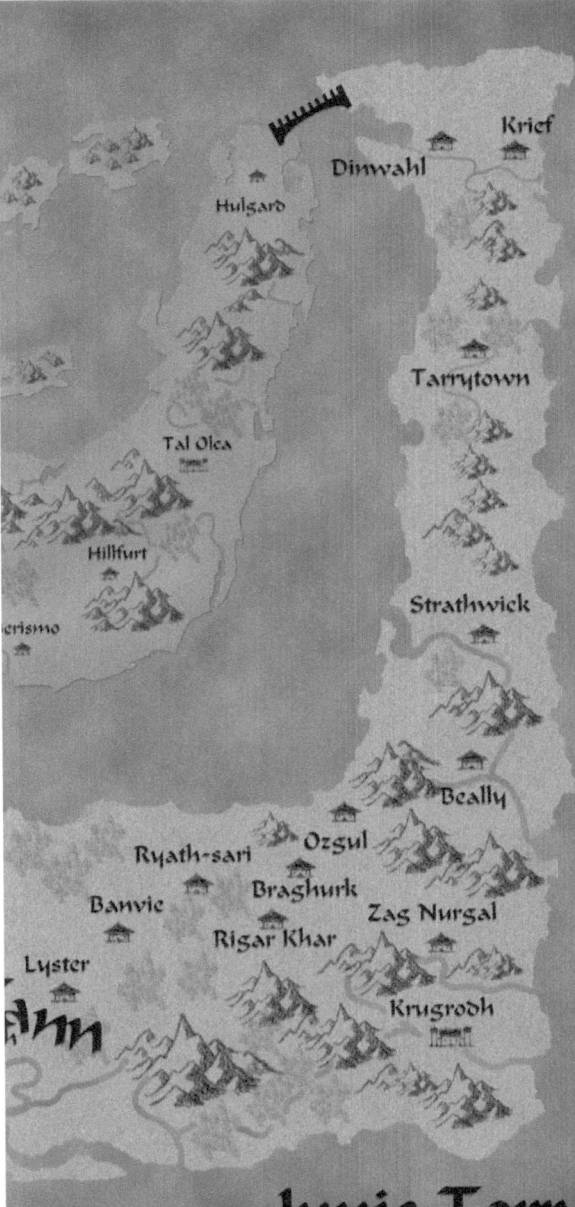

Krief

Dinwahl

Hulgard

Tarrytown

Tal Olca

Strathwick

Hillfurt

erismo

Beally

Ozgul

Ryath-sari

Braghurk

Banvie

Zag Nurgal

Rigar Khar

Lyster

Krugrodh

Innis Torr

Contents

Chapter 1

Karl paused in the middle of the bridge that connected the Misted Isle to the island of Innis Torr. Wind flapped his borrowed clothing as he peered over the side. Below, a churning and frothing sea made him thankful the bridge railing was of solid stone.

To his left, now obscured in an ocean mist, lay the gate to the Misted Isle, guarded by a land giant whose parting words of 'You may not return' contained more than a veiled threat. Karl wondered if anyone had ever actually attempted to return. If so, after the giant crushed, destroyed, and ripped apart the unfortunate victim, where would he or she respawn? If a player was not allowed to return, logically he or she would most likely end up at the last point of exit, which meant on the bridge, naked. Then he remembered what Hans had said in the beginning of his adventure inside the game about bind spots and the bridge: *Your bind spot will automatically move to the end of the bridge on the next island should you forget to move it.*

But did that take into account someone wanting to go back?

Maybe the fool would reappear at the point and place where he or she was killed, which meant a repeat performance by the land giant... which meant the poor slob would endure repeated painful deaths either for eternity or the giant became distracted.

Karl shuddered at the thought. One death was enough for him and though there were good memories back on the Misted Isle, there were certainly enough problems to remind him that he was glad to be on the bridge. Besides, his true friends were already on Innis Torr, and it was time to find them.

Turing to his right, he resumed walking, the bouquet of salt air refreshing. Though he was anxious to find Raquel

1

and Annabeth and the others, his thoughts lingered on the final vision of Gillien standing beside him on the bridge as she fizzled and vanished. The terrified look in her eyes as she disappeared haunted him. It was the same look a dying comrade had given him, a look that cried out for a second chance.

It caused him to once again wonder if the same had happened to Dieter's Elena. Had she come to that same spot and dissolved into thin air like Gillien? And Dieter, who was obviously head over heels in love with the NPC, was he inconsolable? Did he try to go back? Was one of the ripped apart bodies scattered around the land giant all that remained of the berserker?

Shaking his head, he knew the answers lay before him. It was time to move on.

As the bridge crested and began its descent to the other side, Karl's musings were interrupted by the presence of another land giant, standing in the middle of the distant gate. Activating the gaming screens, he read the creature's stats: *Hill Giant, Level 50.* He didn't bother reading the rest of the stats. What did it matter? Yet he chuckled. When they said you weren't allowed to return to previous islands, they really put some teeth into it.

Approaching the gate, he was taken aback at the size of the monster now facing him for the beast stood even taller than the one guarding the Misted Isle side. Like the giant at the other gate, this one held a long broad cudgel in his hands, the thick wooden head studded with jagged and bloodied marble shards.

Standing before the gate, the creature held out a palm, causing Karl to stop. When it spoke, the voice was ominous like thunder.

"You have crossed the bridge. You may never go back. If you attempt to return, I will kill you. What is the key?"

"Innis Torr," Karl replied.

The giant studied him for only a moment before stepping aside. "You may pass."

"Have others passed through here recently?" Karl asked.

The giant scowled at him. "You will pass or die. The choice is yours."

"I'm going, I'm going," Karl chirped as he hustled past the looming monster.

It was when he had bustled past the giant and through the gate that his consternation mounted. It wasn't the scattered piles of human remains littering the area surrounding the gate, nor the buzzards feasting on the half-eaten cadavers. It was the sudden awareness that there were three roads leading into the forest, and he hadn't a clue which one his friends had taken.

Pulling up his game screen, he saw that Innis Torr was shaped like a fat snake in the shape of a 'U', wrapping around the Misted Isle. The little highlighted arrow at the top right of the 'U' pinpointed his location. Three roads diverged from the bridge, each following a separate path until they connected at a town called Beally at the opposite end of a large forest called Dubhcrann. Occasional crossroads connected the main roads.

The map showed Innis Torr to be heavily forested and mountainous with numerous rivers and streams. What concerned him was the lack of town names and locations. Except for a single town shown on each of the roads leading away from the bridge, the rest of the map was blank concerning habitation.

"Go," the voice boomed behind him.

Momentarily ignoring the giant, Karl struggled to think which way Raquel would choose. He waffled between 'Right is right' and 'Hey diddle diddle, straight up the middle.' Discounting the road and town on the left as having no clever jingle, he tried pulling up information on the two remaining towns only to be rewarded with just their names: Dinwahl and Krieff.

"Be gone," the giant threatened, taking an earth vibrating step towards him.

Deciding the road to the right appeared to hug the coast and looked to be the shortest route to Beally, he headed off towards Dinwahl, silently offering a prayer to Freyja that his friends were there.

After three uneventful hours of walking through the forest, Karl emerged into a wide-open space. The walled city of Dinwahl lay ahead, situated on a small knoll, and surrounded by farms. Stone walls lined the road, separating it from the farm fields on both sides. As Karl headed towards the city, he observed farmers using wheeled plows, furrowing the rich dark earth in long strips, while others plucked the last remnants of an early harvest.

Traffic on the road was mixed, with farmers driving wagons pulled by oxen, peasants shouldering their meager possessions walking towards the city gates, monks and a few lowly priests holding private conversations, and warriors, lots of warriors in all shapes and sizes. They paid him suspicious attention, very few returning his polite smile of greeting.

His stomach began to growl, and he realized that he was hungry. It was as he passed a small hovel by the road that he smelled a delicious aroma wafting in the air. It smelled of roasted meat, causing his mouth to water. Deciding to play upon the pity of a stranger, he pushed open the flimsy gate and approached the solid wooden door.

The door yielded to his knocks and groaned open. Crossing the threshold, he stepped into a room dimly lit by the fire in the hearth in the corner. A small cauldron of something bubbled over the flames. Two spits jammed into the wall above the fire contained chunks of meat that sizzled and provided the tantalizing aroma. Yet there seemed no one at home.

"Hello?"

The door closed behind him, and he spun around to see a hunched over crone, dressed in black tattered clothes and a threadbare shawl, her silver hair done in a bun at the back of her head. Her bright expectant eyes gazed intently at him.

"I've been expecting you," she said, shuffling to the cooking pot. She flipped a hand at the table as she passed by. "Sit down. Knew you'd be hungry. It's almost ready."

His hunger pushing away his wariness, Karl pulled a stool away from the table and sat. His legs too large to fit under the table, he spread his knees and squirmed to get comfortable.

4

"Smells good," he complimented, wondering why she had been expecting him and if she might be a little light in the head. Though she was small, crazy people were unpredictable and his next thought was the food might be poisoned.

Ladling the stew into two small bowls, the old woman placed one before him, a spoon already inserted into the bowl. She then fetched the skewers of meat and placed both across his bowl.

"You need strength," she said before turning away to fetch two steins of ale.

Returning to the table, she placed a large stein next to his bowl. "Eat. Drink. You need to be strong."

"Thank you." He hesitated, looking up at her.

Cocking her head to the side she grinned and snorted a laugh. "It's not poisoned, dearie. See?" She thrust a spoon into her bowl then held it to her lips and blew the steam away before plopping it into her mouth.

Waiting until she swallowed, Karl lifted the spoon and dipped it into the steaming bowl filled with bits of meat and vegetables. Gingerly tasting the hot stew, he was surprised at the flavor. "This is delicious."

"Of course," she replied as though obvious. She sat across from him and ate quietly, an occasional slurp interrupting the silence.

Karl dug in and finished his meal before the old woman was halfway through.

"You eat too fast," she chastised, pausing to narrow her gaze at him. "Not good. Will it be the same when you start your quest? Everything too fast?"

"I was hungry," he lamely replied, knowing she was right. He had a tendency to eat quickly, a trait he developed during basic training when mealtimes were a race to see how much one could stuff inside one's stomach before being chased out of the dining hall and into formation. When he left the military for academia, he had forced himself to slow down and enjoy meals. Had Raquel and Annabeth been here, it would have been a leisurely meal.

"Hunger makes a man careless. How do you know I am not an evil witch, that your food wasn't poisoned?"

"You said it wasn't. I watched you eat some."

"Suppose I was lying? Suppose I secretly put poison in your bowl?"

"If you did," he answered, "it was the best tasting poison I've had in a long, long time." He stared at her over the rim of his mug, inhaling the bouquet of the thick full-bodied stout.

The corners of her lips curled into a smile. "You have the sort of recklessness that might save you. But you'll need more than that. Luck. You'll need luck too."

"I don't believe in luck," he replied. "Things happen for a reason."

"Oooh," she mocked. "Have all the answers do we?"

"Not yet. But I'm hoping you can answer some questions. Have you seen others like me pass through here? A Ranger and a sorceress, both quite beautiful, a tall berserker, a –"

She cut him off with a raised palm. "You have failed to ask the important question."

"And that is?"

"Why was I expecting you?"

"I was getting to that," Karl replied. "And don't worry, I can pay for my meal."

"It is not your gold I need," she sniffed in disdain.

Karl regarded her a moment. "OK. I'll bite. Why were you expecting me?"

"Because I could tell from the start that you were different." She leaned in and lowered her voice to a whisper. "You look like a man who has crossed a bridge."

"I did," he answered, more curious than puzzled.

She leaned back with a triumphant grin. "I knew it. You are the promised one, the one I've been waiting for."

"Me?" he objected. "Surely there have been others who have crossed the bridge before me."

Ignoring him, she focused on him with an intense stare. "My name is Elanda. I once was a powerful wizard, a white wizard. It's a long story, but the short of it is that I was defeated by the dark sorceress Eleris."

"Eleris?" Karl said, puzzled. "Man or woman?"

"Woman, a beautiful woman," she replied with a frown. "Don't interrupt. Like I was saying, I nearly died, but escaped to this town to gather my strength and powers. Sadly, while I have regained some simple spells and incantations, my former strength eludes me. Why? Because I need the Delf Stone to help me. Without it, I am condemned to spend my days here, brooding and waiting for a deliverer. Now that you are here, my prayers have been answered."

"Where's the stone now?" he asked, wondering how he could extricate himself from this crazy woman.

"My son has it."

"Your son? Why doesn't he just come here and give it to you?" He slid his eyes to the left, judging how far the door was. Crazy people always freaked him out.

"He is held captive by orcs who have bound him with chains imbued with a magic that keeps him captive."

"How do you know he still has the stone?" He nonchalantly scooted his chair back, positioning himself to bolt when the time was right.

"I don't."

As Karl pondered her story and wishing Raquel and Annabeth were here to lend sanity to the situation, a Quest box appeared.

Quest Alert: Rescue Elanda's son and retrieve the Delf Stone.
Reward:
1. Increased relationship with white sorcery.
2. Magic abilities increased 10 points.
3. Weapons strength increase: 15 points.

Surprised, Karl's first instinct was to punch the 'X' icon and close the annoying prompt. Ye the fact that the alert activated at least gave credence to the crazy woman. But, he had other priorities at the moment. "I really need to get my team back together," he apologized by way of explanation. "They crossed the bridge before I did as I was... uh, tied up at the time. Once I have my team together, I'll be happy to accept your quest. With them with me, it'll go a lot faster."

"Where are they?" she asked.

"That's the problem. I don't know. I was hoping you may have seen them. Like I said, one was a Ranger, a beautiful woman with long auburn; an equally beautiful sorceress with long raven hair –"

"A sorceress?" Elanda brightened. "How strong?"

"Strong?"

"Yes," she frowned at him. "Is she powerful?"

"Uh," he hesitated, knitting his brow, "she's a Level 10 player with level one or two sorcery skills."

"Bah," Elanda huffed, folding her arms, unimpressed. "You'll need more than her to get the Delf Stone."

"I have more than her," he not so patiently replied. "There's also a giant of a berserker, you can't miss him; a mage who is also an attractive woman with blond hair and emerald-green eyes, though a bit shorter than the other two women; and an assassin who most likely you wouldn't see."

Elanda's stared at him for an uncomfortable moment before she stood up and took his mug to refill. "While I have seen some of your kind though they were elves, no one as you describe has passed by my hut."

"Damn," he muttered. "That means I'll have to retrace my steps or go on and cross over and backtrack to Krieff."

"While you are wasting time searching for your friends," she retorted, "a kingdom lies in balance. Already the dark powers are spreading. Who knows? Perhaps they have already enslaved your friends."

"This all sounds like the plot of a B movie," Karl mumbled.

"A what?" she said, pursing her lips.

"Nothing," Karl said, shaking his head.

"Why not do both?" she suggested, her sour attitude suddenly changing. "You can look for your friends on the way of your quest. When you find them, as you say, it will go faster."

Karl pondered her idea, deciding she had a point. He had no clue where they were and at least a quest would give him something to do along the way.

"OK," he reluctantly agreed. "I suppose I can accept."

Quest Alert: You have accepted Elanda's quest.

Karl expected a gush with thanks and when none materialized, he asked, "How many were there before me who accepted your quest?"

"None," she mumbled as she walked over to a small chest on top of a narrow bureau against the wall. Prying the top open, she withdrew a small handkerchief.

Walking up to Karl, the top of her head came just above his shoulder though he remained seated. "Here. Take this." She held up the piece of silk cloth. It was embroidered and edged in gold thread.

"What am I going to do with that?" Karl scoffed.

"You need it to undo the magic in the chains. Simply wipe the cloth on the chains and the spell is broken. Do as much of the chain as possible to break the entire spell. Rub it over the lock and the lock will open."

Karl took the handkerchief and opened it. It felt soft and fine in his hands. The writing on it was in runes. "What does this say?"

"If you can't read it then you don't need to know," she curtly replied. "And here, you need these too." She held up a PC storage belt and bag.

"Where'd you get those?"

"None of your business. Do you want them or not?"

"Of course." Karl answered, taking the belt and bag, securing the belt around his waist. "How do I find where your son is?"

"He is being held at the Orc stronghold in the mountains, in a city called Krug-rodh. He is inside the Chieftain's great hall. Where that is, I don't know. You will have to discover that yourself."

"How do I get there?"

"Go through the town and continue south through the forest called Dubhcrann. The orc kingdom lies beyond the forest. From there Krug-rodh will be easy to find."

"Why?"

She sniffed at his ignorance. "There will be lots of Orcs there."

Karl pulled up his game screen map. The Misted Isle was merely a name at the end of the bridge symbol. To the south of Dinwahl, a dot with the name 'Krug-rodh' appeared, surrounded by mountain symbols and the word 'Kingdom of Krug.' In between Dinwahl and the orc kingdom was forest that spread the width of the island. Karl noted the three roads leading out from the bridge converged just before the borders of the orc lands, disappeared within the kingdom then reappeared on the other side as a single road before splitting again into three distinct roads.

When she turned back around, he asked, "Why don't you go yourself? You're a wizard."

"Can't," she replied without rancor. "Don't have the strength. That's why I need the Delf Stone. Now go. The longer you stay here, the longer I'm stuck here."

When she tried physically pushing him towards the door, he chuckled and strode through the door and into the lane heading towards the town.

Striding along the main road towards Dinwahl, he observed that traffic was thinning as the afternoon slipped into evening. Passing by the two burly guards at the gate, who gave him more than a cursory glance, he noted their Level 8 skills and gave them a cheery smile, reminding himself not to mess with the guards, at least not yet.

Once through the gate, the vista broadened to numerous single-story cottages and a wide marketplace where the bouquet of spices and food overpowered the vendors hawking leather goods, jewelry, pots and pans, potions, and of course meat pies and ale. Above the cacophony of merchants peddling their wares, he heard the bark and growl of an animal in anger.

Pushing through the hubbub of the marketplace, he caught the eye of a baker selling meat pies and he smiled as he remembered the first time he met Annabeth in the marketplace in Marbeck, just after he had turned down the offer of a meat pie from Baker Chesel.

Thinking Karl's smile was for him, the baker moved towards him then abruptly stopped when Karl waved him away. Unfazed, the baker smoothly turned to other shoppers.

As Karl worked his way past the vendor stalls, the snarling and yapping of the animal grew louder. It wasn't until he was at the opposite side of the marketplace that he saw the cause of the commotion.

In a clearing between several taverns, a wolf, the size of a small bus, was chained to a stake while being attacked and tormented by half a dozen men, obviously in their cups, who egged each other on. The wolf howled and snapped, baring its teeth with each parry and thrust. A few unlucky revelers had already met their demise and their bodies lay bloody on the worn earth. He watched as one body vaporized and disappeared.

Great Gray Wolf: Level 30
Life: 85 points
Strength: 150
Intelligence: 45
Unpredictable and ferocious

Part of him said to simply move along, he had a quest to accomplish. Yet another part was irritated that this animal, no matter how dangerous it was, could not defend itself, that it had been chained to be tormented until it died. What kind of sicko would do this? Sure, the one who finally killed the beast would reap whatever benefits it held, but what benefits could there be? For some reason, the more he watched, the angrier he grew.

He watched a bit more as one man, an archer with leather sheaves and crossbow, positioned himself to get a side shot. Karl noticed a gaping wound across his chest then glanced up to see the man's Life trait in the red zone. Apparently, his over confidence had caused him to wander a little too close to the wolf, which caused Karl to wonder why an archer would get close to his prey. The NPC was a Level 6, so it wasn't like he didn't know what was going on.

The archer raised his bow to take aim. That was too much for Karl and he leaped across the distance between them, thrusting his sword into the man's chest. The archer quivered in astonishment then anger before collapsing into a heap on the ground.

To Karl's surprise, the other five men attacking the beast paid scant attention to him other than to watch him rummage through the archer's belongings. So intent on striking at the wolf, they didn't notice him pick up the crossbow and three bolts then calmly walk about ten paces away. Noting that a bolt was still in the bow, he positioned the remaining bolts close by, intending to get off as many shots as possible before he had to defend himself. In all probability that would be one more shot. He aimed the first shot at a Level 7 samurai. Squeezing the trigger, he didn't have to wait to see the result as the bolt crashed through the samurai's head.

Jamming the cocking stirrup on the ground, he stuck a foot in and pulled back the bowstring, sliding another bolt onto the frame then sent another bolt speeding to the samurai who had turned to face him, his face screwed up in anger.

By the time the Samurai raised his sword to begin his attack, Karl had reloaded and took aim, causing the samurai to attempt a weak dodge, only to receive the third bolt, this time through the heart. The samurai wobbled before falling on his side.

Racing over to the samurai who had forced himself up to his hands and knees, Karl snatched the sword from the man's hand and swung in one hard arc, slicing the man's head off.

The Samurai's sudden demise alerted the other animal attackers and they turned in unison, only to face a Viking threatening with a crossbow and a samurai sword.

"Stay right there," Karl commanded as he aimed the bow at each of them in turn.

A Level 11 knight, arrayed in tattered armor, sneered. "A PK."

"PK? Preacher's kid?" Karl responded, confused.

"Very funny," the knight retorted then addressed the others though still watching Karl. "C'mon. We can take him."

Karl noted the armor then quickly surveyed the other three. One was a Level 10 berserker with a battle ax. The second was a Level 8 phalanx soldier with Roman sword, while the third was a Level 10 thief with a pole ax that seemed beyond his capability to wield.

Deciding the knight presented the greatest problem, Karl aimed at the thief who stumbled back far enough to fall within the sharp teeth and claws of the wolf. His screams of pain and terror momentarily distracted the others, giving Karl enough time to shift his aim to the knight who was in the process of turning back to face his opponent when the bolt impacted into his helmet, sending him reeling backwards and into the slashing jaws of the wolf who ripped his head off his body and spit it out so that it rolled in between him and the remaining players.

Dropping the crossbow, Karl twirled the samurai sword in his hands, liking the feel and length of the razor-sharp blade.

The phalanx soldier stared at Karl then took to his heels and fled, leaving Karl to fight the berserker whose wicked grin said he was confident of the outcome.

"Do we really want to fight each other?" Karl said, his blade ready. "You get no benefit from killing me. Why not just split up what we find from the others?"

"How about I just take it all?" the berserker taunted.

"I'm not gonna let you do that," Karl calmly replied.

The berserker studied him for a bit then asked, "Who are you?"

"Does it matter?"

"Just want to know a little about my victims," he sniffed in disdain.

"You first."

"OK. My name's Blood-axe."

"That's your real name?" Karl was both surprised and impressed.

"Of course not. It's my avatar name."

"What's your real name?"

"Chet."

"What do you do for a living, Chet?"

Chet grinned a wide smile. "I'm an accountant. Your turn."

"My name's Karl."

"What's your real name?"

"That's it. It's a lot easier to remember."

"And what do you do, Karl?"

"You ever hear of the Tiwanaku War, the Widow-makers?" he said, wanting to end this standoff though frustrated he had to resurrect his past.

"Yeah."

"I'm Lieutenant Colonel Heston."

Chet's confidence wavered. The name was famous. Heston's legend was that of ruthless and efficient death. Yeah, this was a game, but this guy was too fluid and fast. "You just get in to the game?"

"Yes."

"Surprised you're not farther along by now."

"Never played this game before."

Chet nodded, lowering his ax. He wasn't fooled one bit. The man was a pro. No wonder he was so fast. "You a PK?"

"Preacher's Kid?"

"PK. Player killer." Chet warily regarded him. If the man was a pro, he should know the term. Then again, perhaps he was toying with him. And then the thought occurred; every other PC he'd met in the game was a newbie like himself. This Viking here wasn't acting like a newbie, and if he really was Heston, Chet would be wise to leave well enough alone.

Understanding swept through Karl as he remembered Hans telling him to be careful of other players and characters whose sole purpose seemed to revolve around killing other players. He shook his head.

"No. Just don't like chained animals tormented. Would've left you alone had it been a fair fight."

"It's just a game," Chet replied. "The wolf's an NPC. You're supposed to kill them."

Deciding he was wasting time, he shrugged. "Whatever. Are we going to fight or be sensible?"

Chet took stock of his opponent

"OK. We split 50-50. Deal?"

"Deal."

They were both startled when the limp body of the thief was tossed in between them. Karl turned his head to gaze at the wolf who regarded him with fierce eyes. Keeping a wary distance from the wolf, they collected the weapons and coins and were pleased to discover the thief had enough gold to satisfy both of them.

"I'll keep the sword," Karl said.

"You can have it," Chet answered. "Got no use for the crossbow."

"Then I'll take it." Karl figured if he couldn't use it, he could always barter it sometime later. But he'd keep the sword. It felt good in his hands.

"That's twenty-two gold apiece," Chet announced, "half of that coming from this guy. Wonder how the little twit managed to get ahold of so much."

Karl shrugged. "He's a thief."

"There's three bracelets," Chet said. "I'll give you five gold for the odd one."

"Deal."

"There's five stones, all of 'em precious stones. You can have the odd one for the five gold back."

Karl chuckled. "I see your accountant skills come in handy."

Once the goods were divided, Chet asked, "Where you headed?"

"Looking for some friends of mine who got here before I did. Did you see another berserker come through here?"

"Nope. There's only a couple of PCs here and you killed two of 'em, which pretty much leaves me as the last one. I got a quest looking for a key to unlock the door holding a warlord's daughter. Where you headed?"

"South towards the mountains. The roads converge just before the orc kingdom. I figure if I don't catch up with them along the way, there's a good chance they'll stay put there. You?"

"I'm headed to another town. Thought I'd stop here and see if I could add some levels, but this monster," he ticked his head at the wolf, "was too much." Giving a last glance around the littered yard, he gave Karl a respectful nod. "Maybe we'll connect up again. I'm not a PK, so you can trust me when you see me." He held out a hand.

Karl returned the handshake. "If you decide you want to join a team…"

"I prefer to work alone," Chet replied with a shrug. "A lot less headache that way."

"I understand. Good luck to you."

Waiting until Chet was gone, Karl turned to the wolf who cocked his head and warily regarded him.

"Not sure how you got here" he said, speaking in soothing tones, "and I'm not sure what I'm about to do is the smartest thing in the world, but I can't stand to see an animal chained like this. And the more I think about what I'm about to do, the crazier it seems."

In an overt act of demonstration, Karl placed the sword and other weapons on the ground and took a hesitant step closer to the huge animal. When the wolf didn't react, he took another step closer then another step until he was within the circle of the animal's reach.

Karl pointed to his neck and then to the chain that was locked around the wolf's neck. "We need to get that off you." At first, he had no clue as to how he was going to remove the chain until he remembered the handkerchief in his pocket.

By now, he was within arm's length from the massive beast. Reaching up, he heard the low throated growl and closed his eyes, praying he wouldn't be eaten. Opening his eyes, he jerked back slightly as the giant head had swung around to face him.

"I'm just gonna see if this will work," he said, pulling the handkerchief out. He held it up for the wolf to see and was surprised that after the beast sniffed it, he lowered himself so that Karl could reach the lock.

With focused attention, Karl wiped the iron lock and breathed a sigh of relief when the shackle popped open. Quickly unhooking the chain, he pulled it off the wolf's neck, noting the discoloration and matted hair.

He was about to fold the cloth and stick it back in his pocket when it disintegrated in his hands.

"Oops." Karl quickly glanced around praying Elanda wasn't there to see what just happened. Why didn't she tell him it only worked once?

"Hey you," a voice called out. "What do you think you're doing?"

Karl turned to see four guards come rushing up only to jitter to a halt when the great wolf let out a triumphant howl.

"O my God," the sergeant clamored and fled, the other three on his heels.

Congratulations: You've freed the Great Gray Wolf.
Reward: Unyielding loyalty.
Reward: Speech +6.

Karl turned to face the wolf who was in the process of shaking his body and stretching, thankful to be free. The wolf approached and lowered his head to sniff Karl, the nose within centimeters of Karl's face.

Karl reached up and tenderly scratched the wolf's cheek. "Think we better get a move on. I have a feeling those guys will be back, with reinforcements this time."

The wolf lowered himself to prone and nudged Karl to his side. *Get on.*

Karl heard the voice, causing him to pause and rapidly look around. It took another second more before Karl realized the animal was prodding him to clamber up. Shaking his head, he assumed the voice he heard was his own.

"Yes, it does make sense," he said with a smile, collecting the sword and crossbow. Grabbing handfuls of hair, he climbed up to sit behind the head. It was as he was getting in position that he again heard the voice, a warm baritone. *Hold on.*

Frowning, his first thought was that he was merely talking to himself. But this voice sounded much different.

The wolf moved off in an easy trot, and Karl had to hold in his mirth as the people fled when they saw him riding by. By the time enough brave villagers found the unlocked chain, Karl and the wolf had ridden through the south gate and were on the open road.

"I need to give you a name," Karl said aloud.

I already have a name.

Karl startled and leaned to the side to gape at the wolf's face.

Yes, I'm the one talking to you.

"But I'm not hearing any sound," he objected then heard what sounded like a sigh.

I'm the great gray wolf. You rescued me. Part of the benefits of rescuing me is that we can communicate using only our minds.

"It didn't mention that in the dialogue box."

There you go again giving sound to your thoughts.

Sorry. It didn't mention that in the dialogue box.

Did you check your stats?

No. Karl called up the player screen and checked his stats, reviewing them several times. *It doesn't say anything about telepathy.*

Odd. Still, we are speaking, are we not?

Yes, Karl chuckled. *What is your name?*

Uafas. It means 'terror.'

I like it. How did you come to be chained in that town?

Long story. The short version is that I was placed there by a dark mage to be tormented by anyone who happened to walk by. The mage commanded that the people must feed and water me. At first, the town was terrified, but once they realized I was on a leash, they took to throwing things at me. Then word spread and you saw what's been happening since I was chained.

So what exactly did you do to piss off a mage?

A dark mage, Uafas corrected. *I killed one of his apprentices.*

Why?

18

She deserved it.

Karl thought about the response as he took in the countryside that spread before them, wide and verdant until the farmlands ceased and a tall forest in the approaching distance encroached the road leaving it more a narrow path than a thoroughfare.

Why did she deserve it?

Practicing magic without a brain.

Huh?

The fool of an apprentice was using spells that she couldn't control. I warned her more than once. I warned the mage about her. He wouldn't listen. When she decided she'd rather have a cat than a wolf and thought to use magic to make the change, I eliminated her.

And he was mad about that?

Let's just say the apprentice in question was rather attractive for a human and the mage had more than a passing interest.

Ah. I understand.

By the way, where did you get that cloth to unlock the chains?

Uh, Karl sheepishly replied, *I got it from a sorceress named Elanda. Her son is being held captive by orcs. She gave it to me to use on the chains and locks to free her son.*

And you used it on me instead.

I didn't' know you could only use it once.

Silence settled for a bit before Uafas spoke. *I imagine she wouldn't be very happy if she learned what you did.*

Probably not, Karl chuckled. *But I don't regret using it.*

Thank you. I am in your debt. By the way, where are we going?

South to find my friends and rescue a sorceress' son.

As they approached the edge of the forest, he did a quick scan of both sides of the road.

Once entering the forest, the wolf's pace slowed to a cautious lope and Karl appreciated Uafas' wariness, for it allowed him time to scan both sides of the road. As they travelled, Karl shifted his concentration to the thickening forest, especially the intertwining branches overhead where a man could hide and get off a shot, causing enough of a distraction while the flanks were attacked by the rest of an outlaw band.   Placing a hand on his sword, reassuring himself, he reached into his bag and withdrew the crossbow and three bolts.

The entwined and overlapping branches grew thicker, blocking out the late afternoon sun and casting a dismal darkness.

"This place smells like an ambush," Karl mused aloud.

The wolf abruptly stopped and sniffed the wind then sidled to the edge of the road and into the trees. *Gnolls.* He sniffed again. *Something is not right.*

Like what?

Gnolls are night creatures.

Karl glanced around the darkening forest. *It's dark enough to be night in here. So what do you want to do?*

Kill them.

OK, he grinned. *Do you know where they are?*

Upwind to the right.

How far?

Uafas sniffed again. *The scent is weak but consistent, which means they are waiting in place for someone to come by on the road. I don't know how far.*

Karl thought for a moment. *Let's take the battle to them. If they're hunkered down by the side of the road, we move deeper into the forest then come up from behind them.*

You do not know how many there are, the wolf reminded him.

If there are too many, we'll simply continue sneaking past.

That's easy for you to say. You may have noticed that I'm a bit large when it comes to sneaking.

Karl analyzed a bit more before saying, *I don't see any way around it. We need to take the battle to them. Hit hard then run like hell. We do what I said to begin with. We go deeper into the forest then come up from behind.*

As you wish.

Karl dismounted then led the way deeper into the forest, working his way through the underbrush, using whatever cover was available. His stealth skills refined in the military, he was pleased at how quiet he was before reminding himself that the wolf was just as quiet. More than once he looked over to see the wolf silently gliding through the trees, amazed that a creature so large could be so quiet.

When he felt they had gone a sufficient distance, he paused and did a slow scan of their surroundings. The forest was growing darker. If they were going to have the element of surprise, they would have to strike now, before night swallowed up the forest, increasing the danger of travel.

Let's see what we can find. You can see and smell better than I can. Sing out if you sense something.

Bending low, Karl worked his way back towards the road, the wolf a short distance behind him and to his right. It was as he could see a break in the trees where fading sunlight barely penetrated the overhead branches above the road that he heard voices. Edging closer, he positioned himself behind a low copse and peered out. About ten meters away, three gnolls lay in wait, apparently bored that nothing had come by. He was surprised at how large they were, far larger than he imagined and his marvelous plan of a crushing hit and run suddenly developed flaws.

He strained to listen and understand but all he heard was modulated grunts and low whines until the one on the far left turned to the middle gnoll and spoke, his voice low and raspy.

"I ain't understood a word you said for the past half hour. Speak common tongue."

"That's 'cause you ain't smart enough to understand."

"You sayin' I'm stupid?"

"I ain't sayin' it. You are."

"Will you two shut up," the third gnoll snapped. "It's no wonder nothing has come by with you two yapping all the time."

"He said I was stupid," the first gnoll complained.

"Well you are," the second snorted.

"I've a mind to show you how stupid I am," the first gnoll snarled, leaping to his feet.

21

The third gnoll let out an exasperated sigh as the second gnoll jumped up and went for his companion.

While the two commenced to reigning blows on each other, Karl readied a bolt in the crossbow, took aim and fired at the gnoll watching the two combatants. The bolt plowed through its head, propelling him forward.

Unaware of their companion's dilemma, the two antagonists continued their battle. The wounded gnoll forced himself to his knees, staring dumbly up and down the road then reached up to feel the blood gushing out of the cavity in its head. By now, Karl had notched another bolt and sent it speeding through the gnoll's back and out through its chest, causing it to momentarily waver before keeling over.

Ready Uafas?

Ready.

You start on those two while I finish off this one. Then I'll help you with the other two. On three. One. Two. Three.

Karl leaped forward, samurai sword hand while the wolf rose like a giant menace emitting one biting bark that froze the two fighters. Karl raced over and in one quick downward slice chopped off the gnoll's head.

Ignoring the *Congratulations, you just killed a gnoll* prompt, he turned to help Uafas only to see the giant wolf's sharp teeth wrapped around a gnoll, tossing him around like a rag doll. The other gnoll lay dead under a massive paw, its head ripped off its body. In one final ignominious gesture, the wolf flung the body onto the road.

Karl quickly collected another battleax and a short bow with arrows, stuffing everything into his bag. He then remembered he needed money and started searching their clothes. He was disappointed to discover the gnolls carried little money and he collected a total of five silver and perhaps a dozen copper coins.

"We need to move out," Karl observed. "There may be more close by."

Uafas pushed through the underbrush and stood waiting on the road. *Climb up and hold on. I'll pick up the pace.*

Gnolls have excellent dark vision. If we move fast enough, we can avoid them.

By the time Karl clambered aboard, night had settled, immersing the forest in an inky darkness.

"You can see OK?"

Again, you give sound to your thoughts. If we are to avoid them, we must be quiet.

Sorry, he sheepishly replied. *I keep forgetting.*

Well don't. Our lives depend on it.

Once Karl settled, Uafas set out on a controlled trot, his great legs gobbling up the road in long strides. As the great wolf loped along, Karl stared intently ahead, concentrating on sounds and any movement ahead. After some time, his mind wandered, and he found himself again wondering where Raquel and Annabeth were and whether they missed him as much as he missed them.

His musings were interrupted when he felt Uafas slow down. In the far distance, he saw faint light and as they drew closer, the light separated into separate torches atop stone walls surrounding a closed city gate. It struck him odd that here in the middle of a forest populated with gnolls and other dangerous creatures, there would be a town. His first thought was whether it was populated by humans.

Sensing his hesitation, the wolf said, *Gnolls don't live in towns in the open. They prefer dark places.*

Remaining in the shadows a distance away, they waited until they saw a guard manning the wall parade by. He was human and he carried a cross bow.

Karl suddenly felt tired and hungry. *We're gonna need a place to spend the night.*

I can't go in there. You saw what happens when humans get a look at me.

I need something to eat and a place to sleep.

You go ahead. I'll find a place out here.

You sure?

Of course I'm sure. I don't want to end up like I did before.

I'll be back at first light.

Be careful. You know nothing about this place.

23

I didn't know anything about the other place, Karl pointed out.

Just be careful. Uafas turned and faded into the night.

Karl activated his screen and pulled up the map. The town was labeled Tarrytown with no other additional information. Puzzled that he could learn nothing about the town, not even a brief history, he waited a bit more then approached the gate when he saw the guard abruptly stop when he noticed movement outside the gate.

"Who are you?" he demanded, pointing the crossbow at Karl.

"I'm just passing through," Karl calmly replied, holding up his empty hands, "looking for a place to get something to eat and spend the night."

The guard didn't answer but instead focused into the darkness behind Karl. "You alone?"

"Yes."

"How'd you get past the gnolls?"

"I killed them."

"You did?" The guard was surprised and impressed. "How many?"

"Just three. They were waiting in an ambush a ways up the road from here."

"How'd you know they was there?"

"I could smell them," Karl chuckled. "They were upwind. Not very smart. We gonna chat here or can I come in?"

The guard eyeballed him one last time then disappeared. A moment later, a small door within the larger gate opened. "C'mon then."

Karl had to bend down to enter. "Thank you." Standing erect, he gazed down at the guard. He was a wiry, middle-aged man missing several teeth.

"You're either brave, crazy, or damn lucky mister. Few folks make it through the forest at night."

"Let's just call it lucky. You recommend a place where I can get a meal and spend the night?"

"Chicken Gizzard's got the best food, but the rooms ain't as good as Hog and Whistle."

"Chicken Gizzard?" Karl snickered.

"Yeah," the man replied with a frown. "What's so funny?"

"Nothing. Uh, how do I get there."

The guard raised an arm and pointed down the main street where candle lit streetlights sporadically interrupted the darkness. Two- and three-story stone houses, shuttered tight, edged the street.

"Stay on the main street here. You'll see the first place on yer left. The sign's in the shape of a gizzard."

Karl snorted a laugh.

"What's so funny?"

"Nothing," he replied, *just that the developers of this game have a weird sense of humor.*

Cocking a suspicious eyebrow at him, the guard said, "Hog and Whistle's a little farther up to the right."

"Let me guess. Their sign is a hog and a whistle."

"Yup."

"Much obliged," Karl smiled and headed off.

"Remember what I told ya," the guard called out after him. "The food's better at the Gizzard, but the rooms're better at the Hog and Whistle."

Karl waved without looking back and headed up the silent street. The smell of hearth fires mixed with the tempting aromas of evening meals. Up ahead, creaking in the light wind, the irregular shape of what he guessed was a gizzard, suspended above a wide door. Pushing open the door, the darkness and silence of outside evaporated in the overlapping chatter of garrulous patrons and the glow of a low fire in the hearth.

Heads turned when he entered, and the chatter momentarily dropped then just as quickly resumed as guests and serving girls continued their nightly rituals. A plump man wearing a kitchen apron and with thinning hair that he parted just above the top of his left ear and combed the thin strands over the balding dome, bustled up. He had hard eyes and a scar on his cheek.

"Welcome stranger," he said, his warm voice a contrast to his darting eyes. "What'll you have?"

"What will dinner and a room cost me?"

"Dinner is four coppers not including drinks. A single room is one silver, or you can share a room from one to five copper depending on how many share it with you." He wiped his hands with his apron.

"I'll take a single room then," Karl responded glancing around for a table, "and dinner. What's to drink?"

"Ale of course," the man sniffed, "the best in town."

"Is it cold?"

"Of course."

"Good." Karl made his way to a table near the wall by the hearth, positioning his chair so he could take in the entire room.

A gorgeous, flaxen-haired, buxom serving wench with low cut peasant blouse that invited ogling her ample cleavage, sashayed over and plopped down a pewter mug of ale.

"Dinner will be along in a minute or two." Her voice was sultry, and she winked at him.

"Thank you." He grinned at the woman and the whole ambiance of the tavern. All the serving girls were gorgeous to the point of cliché: long legs, narrow waist, toned body, beautiful faces, and of course overly endowed chests. *The game developers definitely have a sense of humor.* Suddenly an aroma he had not inhaled for some time pierced his senses.

"My God, is that coffee?"

"Yes," the serving girl replied, staring at him as though the answer intuitively obvious. "Would you like some? Usually, folks prefer ale with the meal."

"Yes, yes, please," Karl said with urgency.

The girl returned with a large mug of steaming coffee, handing it to the overwhelmed Viking who paused to luxuriate in the bouquet of roasted coffee beans.

"Thank you," he sighed, leaving the girl to smirk as she sauntered away to fetch the rest of his fare.

Savoring the dark brew, Karl uttered a contented moan and gazed around the room. The rest of the tavern was the typical medieval montage of farmers, merchants, warriors, and priests. Yet there was a subtle sinister feeling to the place that he couldn't quite place.

The serving girl brought the meal, a bowl of thick stew with ample portions of meat, a demi-loaf of bread, and a small wooden board with a slab of farmer's cheese. Digging in, he realized he was starving, and the guard was right, the food was delicious.

"What brings you to Tarrytown, handsome?" the girl asked, batting her eyes at him.

"Just passing through."

"I haven't seen you in town before." She leaned on the table to expose more cleavage.

"Just got here tonight."

"Tonight?" She stood up straight. "They let you in after the gate was closed?"

"Yeah."

"You made it through the forest?"

"Yeah. Why is that such a big deal?"

"You meet any gnolls?"

"A few." He paused and looked around, noticing the conversations had stopped and everyone was staring at him.

"What did you do?" a farmer at a table close by asked.

"I killed them."

"How many?" another farmer at the same table inquired.

"Just three," he shrugged and sipped his ale.

'Just three," the first farmer mimicked then grinned. "You must be a mighty warrior. How'd you manage to kill three gnolls at once?"

"Just lucky, I guess." Karl returned his attention to his meal.

"You think you can beat me?" a guard sergeant at a nearby table challenged.

Karl looked at the man's bar, noting a Level 12. "You won't get any benefit by fighting me. It's like picking on someone smaller than you. If you win, you're a bully. If you lose, you're a schmuck."

Another non-com at the table laughed and slapped his partner on the back. "Got your number."

"Bah," the sergeant snapped and turned back to his meal.

Thankful to be left alone to finish his meal in peace, he was sopping up bits of stew with the bread when he found his attention beginning to wander. Shaking his head, he couldn't get rid of a light-headedness. Suddenly his world dimmed and before it went black, he saw the taverner close by, wiping his hands on his apron and grinning wickedly.

Chapter 2

Awareness crept into Karl, and he found himself sitting on a cold stone floor. His face felt funny, and he smelled of stew. When he went to scratch his cheek, his arm was heavy with something hard wrapped around his wrist. He lifted his wrist closer only to discover that he was chained to a wall. In fact, both arms were chained though his legs were free. Focusing in deep concentration, the last thing he remembered was eating stew at the Chicken Gizzard.

"You're awake," a voice quietly said.

Karl looked around, but all he could make out in the darkness of the cell were vague outlines of wall edges.

"Where are you?"

"Right across from you," the voice replied.

"I can't see you."

"No kidding. That's because it's dark," the voice mocked.

"Then how do you know where I am?"

"I was dragged down here about the same time you were."

"Why?"

"Got caught stealing some silverware."

"Why were you stealing silverware?"

"I'm a thief. That's what I do. I was working on my stealth skill when I got caught."

"Apparently you're not very good at it."

"Oh yeah? Like you got room to talk? You're the big mighty warrior. You should've seen yourself. One moment you're eating and talking like normal then plop. You're face down in your stew bowl. When they drag you down here, there's still stew on your face."

"Point taken," he chuckled then tugged on the chains. "Why am I here?"

"It's called Tarrytown for a reason."

Karl pulled up his personal screen and using a finger, typed in 'Tarrytown.' "Just great," he complained as the screen lit up with a short paragraph. "So now I get the info. Where were you before?"

Tarrytown: also Clachdur, a town in the Black Forest, a day's journey south of Dinwahl. Tarrytown (original name Clachdur) was built by dwarves during the middle kingdom as a trading center. During the Clan Wars, the town suffered numerous attacks, changing hands at least a dozen times before finding itself in the middle of the no man's land between the dwarven kingdoms and the troll domains. With the subsequent arrival of orcs and the growth of the surrounding forest, Tarrytown was left to fend for itself. It has become a refuge for the castoffs of various clans who specialize in procuring contraband and slaves.

"Slaves." Karl sighed then tugged on one hand and noticed a subsequent movement with the other hand. He repeated the motion in a see-saw method then pushed himself to standing to discover the chain connecting the two wrist shackles ran through a single rusted iron grommet in the stone wall. The grommet was wide enough to pass a hand through it. As he felt around the grommet's base, he heard the chains of his fellow prisoner rattle.

"What are you doing?"

"I'm trying to see if I can figure a way out of these," Karl replied.

"Good luck with that," he scoffed. "I've already tried. I think they make the ring base rusted on purpose, luring prisoners with the false hope that they might have a chance and break it. Trust me. It ain't moving."

"You're a thief," Karl said over his shoulder as he studied the grommet and his chains. "Aren't you supposed to be some sort of expert picking locks?"

"I am," he protested. "It's just that I can't reach my tools."

"Where are they?"

"On the floor by the door," he moaned. "They took them from me when they locked me up."

"I'm surprised they're still here." Karl wrapped the chains around the grommet, attempting to work an angle of leverage and twist it.

"They're in my bag. I had a mage friend of mine use a binding spell and bind them so only I can use them. When they realized they couldn't trade them, they kept the rest of my loot and tossed the bag on the floor, the scum. Those tools are expensive."

Karl positioned himself then grabbed hold of the chain just above his wrists and using his weight, yanked hard. He swore he felt a tiny yield, but when he felt the base of the ring, he couldn't be sure.

"What's your name?" Karl asked as he wrapped the chains in the opposite direction.

"Noble."

"Noble?" Karl chuckled. "An unusual name for a thief."

"Yeah, I know," he smirked. "I'm Noble the thief, or I'm a... Noble thief. Get it?"

"Yes," Karl smiled. "Clever." The chains positioned, he yanked and strained with no result. "Is that your real name?"

"Naw. My real name's Lester, but in here I'm Noble."

"What did you do in real life, Noble?"

"I was a general mechanic."

"What's a general mechanic?"

"I can fix any machine you can think of, from cars to computers to HVAC to you name it," came the proud reply.

"How'd you end up here?

After a heavy pause, Noble said, "I can fix machines, but no one could fix me. Got cursed with a case of terminal plague or some such. Doctors gave me minutes to live, and I decided being here was a lot better than the other option. So what's your name?"

"Karl."

"Karl? Karl the Viking? That doesn't sound like it's going to impress anybody. How come you're not Eric Bloodaxe or Asgar the Orc-slayer or some really cool name?"

"Because my name's Karl. I'm not out to impress anyone."

"Well you certainly won't with that name. So what did you do in real life, or I-R-L as they say."

"I was a university professor."

"A teacher?" Noble just about sneered. "And now you're a Viking. Oh that's a good one. Talk about living beyond reality."

"You didn't let me finish," Karl said. "Have you heard of the Tiwanaku War, the Widow-makers?" he said, thinking this response was going to get old after a while.

"Yeah."

"I'm Lieutenant Colonel Heston."

The silence grew thick before Noble let out a soft whistle followed by a "Damn. Honest?"

"Yes, honest."

"I take back everything I said, Colonel."

"I'm not a colonel anymore."

"Sure, sure. How'd you end up in the game?"

"Like you, I was diagnosed with an incurable disease."

"Just damn," Noble chuckled. "Imagine me, sitting here in a cell with Colonel Heston of the Widow-makers."

"Listen, Noble, you can be impressed all you want later. Help me think of a way out of here?" Karl rewrapped the chains to the other side and again yanked, strained, and tugged.

"What do you expect me to do? I'm a thief, not wizard."

"Then maybe you should just keep quiet while I try to figure this thing out." Karl again groaned against the immoveable iron ring.

"Oh dear. My apologies, your Highness. I'll just keep my yap shut while you bang your head against the wall over there. Don't mind me, poor peasant that I am."

For the next hour, Karl struggled against the grommet while Noble rambled about his game progress so far and why he got caught followed by his plan to get himself killed so he could respawn at his bind spot which was far enough away but the problem was how could he take his tools with him, especially as they were expensive and were spell-bound to him so why would anyone else want to use them?

Karl let him ramble, tuning him out like he was background noise. Then, just as he was tired enough to call it quits, there came a loud snap and the grommet popped away from the wall.

"What was that?"

"I'm free," Karl matter-of-factly replied.

"My God," Noble blurted. "You did it?"

"Yes. Where are your tools?"

"By the door. Hurry."

"Where's the door."

"To my left."

Karl moved to his right, treading carefully, his hands stretched out before him. As he passed a wall edge, he saw light to his left, coming from the gap between the prison door and the floor. To the side of the door was Noble's bag. Retrieving the bag, he was retraced his steps to stand beside the thief.

"You're amazing," Noble gushed. "No one's ever escaped from here."

"There's always a first time."

Noble fumbled though his bag, found his lock pick and in mere seconds, four wrist shackles lay on the ground and the two prisoners now stood by the door.

"Now what do we do?" Noble asked, rubbing his wrists.

"We have two options. We stay here or we leave."

"Thank you Captain Obvious.," Noble said, rolling his eyes.

"What I mean is, we can stay here and try to overpower the guards and hope we can get a clean escape, or we slip out of here and do our best to evade notice. You're the thief. You know how to make things disappear. Can you use your skills to make us invisible?"

"I'm a thief not a magician," he sourly replied. "Besides, look at you. You're like a sequoia in the middle of a pigmy pine tree farm, or table lamp misplaced with the desktop lamps, or a –"

"OK. I get it. We'll wing it. But I need to do something first."

"What?"

Ignoring him, Karl silently called out. *Uafas? Are you there?*

"What are you doing?"

"I'm calling a friend."

Noble cocked his head to stare at him, uttering a slow drawn out, "Riiight."

After several tries, Karl shook his head. "Nothing."

"What *are* you doing?"

"I have a friend outside the town. I was trying to talk with him."

"Like IM?"

"I don't think we have that capability. At least I haven't seen it."

"So how you communicating?"

"Telepathy."

Noble stared hard at him, deciding the man believed what he said. "I suppose it could happen. After all it's just a game."

Karl recognized the condescending doubt. "I thought the same thing…"

They heard feet scraping outside the door then stopping, followed by muffled voices.

"Think we should check on 'em?" a voice said.

"Why? They ain't goin' nowhere," came a gruff reply.

"There's still that bag o' tools in there."

"Leave 'em. They got a mage comin' in the mornin' to unbind the spell on 'em."

"Damn it. How come we never get some of the loot?"

"'cause we're guards, that's why. 'sides, you'd only spend it on that whore at the Painted Pony."

"That's my sister," the voice growled as it rose in volume, "an she ain't no whore."

The other voice barked an obscene laugh. "Yer sister? Man, that girl went ten rounds with an ugly stick and lost."

The growl burst into anger as Karl and Noble listened to the melee on the other side of the door. Karl placed a finger against his lips, his ear cocked almost against the door. He smiled as he heard what had to be furniture scraping and crashing. Finally, after nearly five minutes of mayhem, silence reigned.

Karl waited a little longer then motioned to Noble. "Can you unlock the door?" he whispered.

"Gimme a sec," Noble softly replied then opened his bag and pulled out a long flat bar about two centimeters wide, slipping it in between the door and the frame. Jiggling the bar, he pushed the door at the same time. A moment later, it silently swung outward.

Karl slowly pried the door farther open to peek out then opened it wider and stuck his head out as Noble hung back.

"C'mon out," Karl said, stepping into the room. "It's OK."

Noble emerged and saw the carnage. One guard lay on his stomach, a knife protruding out of his back. The other sat against the wall, a knife in his chest. A wooden table and two chairs were in pieces and scattered throughout the guardroom.

Karl gazed down at his cellmate. Noble was short, a little taller than a dwarf and he looked young like he was a teenager. His mop of dark hair reminded Karl of Moe from the Three Stooges.

"Lock the cell door," Karl ordered, scanning the room for a weapon better than a knife. He was rewarded with two Roman swords in their scabbards that hung on pegs by the exit door. He then yanked out the knives stuck in the two guards, wiping the blades on the guards' clothing.

"Gross," Noble said, curling a lip.

"They're good blades and I can use them." Keeping the one sword out, he placed the other three blades in his otherwise empty bag. "C'mon. We need to move. You know the way out?"

"Sure do," he grinned then led the way down the long dimly lit corridors, passing by other occupied cells.

"Hold on," Karl said, his voice low.

Noble skidded to a halt and turned. "What?" he whispered

Karl leaned over to a door and slid the peephole open then peered into a small cell to see a large man slumped against the wall, chained like he and Noble had been.

"How long would it take you to unlock his shackles?"

"Too long," he snipped. "You want to escape or what? We stop to free every prisoner here and we'll never make it out."

"Just this one."

"We don't have time," Noble fussed.

"Just do it."

"Damn it all," Noble groused and popped the door open, causing the berserker to jerk his head up and frown as the thief stalked over and undid his shackles. Seeing Karl standing in the doorway he gave him a half-grin. "You look familiar."

"So do you. Chet?"

"Karl?"

"Yeah. C'mon."

"Thanks man." He leaped up and followed them into the hallway. "I don't have any weapons. They cleaned out my bag."

"Here, take this." Karl dug in his bag then handed him the other Roman sword.

"Sweet," Chet grinned. "I owe you."

"You two can indulge your bromance when we're out of here," Noble grumbled.

"Where'd you find the leprechaun?" Chet deadpanned.

"Oh that's real funny," Noble grumped.

"He's a thief," Karl explained, "and he's fast with picking locks. And he also knows the way out of here."

"That's good, because I don't have a clue as to how I ended up here."

"Are you two finished?" Noble quietly demanded, hands jammed on his hips.

"Lead on McDuff," Karl said with a wave of his hand.

Fortune smiled on them as dawn had yet to arrive and all decent folk were still in bed. Noble led them through the labyrinth of hallways and past the various levels of security to finally emerge through the front doors of the prison and into the darkness of early morning.

As they hung back in the shadows, Noble said, "Now what's the plan?"

"I don't intend on staying here," Karl replied.

"Me neither," Chet agreed.

"However," Karl added, "I think someone owes me for all the trouble they've caused. I had some money and other things when I arrived and now my bag is empty."

"I completely agree," Chet grinned.

"What should we do?" Noble asked, rising to the quest.

"I think we need to recoup for our losses and then some. And I think the first place we ought to start is the place where it all began."

"Suits me," Chet said, twirling his sword.

Arriving back at the Chicken Gizzard was easy as no one was out this early in the morning. Noble led them to the back door, picked the lock and opened the door leading into the kitchen.

"You guys guard the door while I help myself to the silverware."

"Slow down, Noble," Karl cautioned. "We'll have time for that in a minute. We're gonna need your help in a minute."

"What's your plan?" Chet asked with an eager smile.

"A certain proprietor has our money, and I intend to get it back. Where's his bedroom?"

"Upstairs above the front door," Noble answered.

"How do you know that?" Chet asked, cocking an eyebrow.

"I cased the joint before I got caught."

Chet twisted his head to give Karl a skeptical look. "Are you sure about him?"

"He's fine. He just needs practice, that's all."

"I got here to this island, didn't I?" Noble retorted as he led the way.

Standing outside the door, Karl stared at Noble who was frustrated with his inability to open the door.

"It's got an iron slide bolt on the inside, and I don't have anything that can open it from here." His shoulders slumped when he suddenly smacked his forehead. "What an idiot I am." Reaching inside his bag, he withdrew a small powerful magnet and placed it against the door opposite the bolt lock. Pulling the door tighter against the frame, he began sliding the magnet horizontally across the door, feeling the bolt move with it. A few silent moments later, he pushed the door open.

Slipping past him, Karl heard the snoring of a man in deep sleep. A low candle on the nightstand by the bed cast soft flickering light on a wide four post bed.

"Isn't that cute," Chet intoned. "He sleeps with a night light."

"Looks like he's not alone," Noble whispered.

Beneath the covers, next to the plump proprietor was one of the serving girls, a pretty brunette lying on her side, her mouth open with a tiny bit of drool spilling onto the pillow.

"That's not his wife," Noble snickered.

"Light another candle while I wake our host," Karl said, walking over to stand by the side of the bed.

While Noble lit another taper, Karl gazed down at the slumbering man, noting the man's thin strands of hair that would normally be carefully combed over the bald pate were now lying limp on the pillow. With a wicked grin and using the flat of his sword, he smacked the man on the forehead.

"Ye-ouch. What the hell?" The proprietor bolted upright, a hand to his forehead, causing the covers to yank off the serving girl who likewise jerked upright at the loud exclamation, much to the satisfaction of the three men who caught a vivid though fleeting vision of the woman's firm breasts before she snatched the covers back up, shielding her nakedness.

Her frightened doe eyes shifted between Karl and Chet and the swords in their hands, noting their attention had settled on the man in bed with her. "I probably should go," she said, hoping they would pity her and let her leave.

38

"Stay where you are," Karl commanded. "We'll attend to you in a moment."

Panic replaced the fear in her wild eyes as imagined degradation invaded her thoughts.

A sword point pricking the proprietor's neck, Karl said, "You poisoned us to sell us into slavery. That wasn't very nice. Not only that, you stole everything we own. We're here to collect." Grabbing him by the throat, he forcibly lifted him out of the bed and plopped him sitting on the edge. "Noble. Watch the girl. If she moves, slice her up."

"O my God," the girl cried. "I won't move. I promise."

"You," Karl growled at the proprietor. "Are you right or left handed?"

"What?"

Karl tightened his grip on the man's throat and pressed the sword point deeper into the flesh. "Answer the question."

"Right handed," he croaked.

"Good. You have a choice. I'm going to ask you questions, and for each answer I don't like, my berserker friend here will hack off one of your fingers, beginning with your right hand. I warn you though; the blade's a little dull and it may take him a couple of whacks before the finger is separated from your hand."

The man's eye's widened and he began to perspire.

"Do you have our belongings?"

"Yes," the man rasped.

"Are they here in the tavern?"

The man hesitated until Karl said "Chet."

Chet grabbed the man's wrist, raising his sword at the same time.

"Yes, yes," the man warbled.

"Good. See? You're doing well so far. Now, where exactly are our things?"

The man swallowed hard, shifting a glance to Chet who still had a firm grip on his wrist.

Karl stared hard into the man's eyes then looked up at Chet. "I believe he thinks we're bluffing."

"Easily solved," Chet smiled. While Karl pinioned one arm behind the proprietor's back, Chet jerked the man's hand up, grabbing hold of the pinky. "This is just an appetizer," he grinned, and in one quick motion, twisted and bent the little finger until there was an audible snap.

The man yelped in pain and tears streamed down his cheeks. "Downstairs," he gasped. "Downstairs in the basement."

"Wait," Noble chimed in. "Is it guarded?"

The proprietor shot him an angry glare.

"Do it Chet," Karl snarled, shaking his head.

Chet fixed the man's hand against the bed post, aligning the bent pinky and swept the sword in one smooth arc, chopping the little finger off. Blood gushed out, dripping over Chet's hand as well.

The proprietor howled in pain and he writhed, trying to free himself, but the two players held him fast. "You bastards," he seethed. "I'll kill you for this. Your lives won't be worth two coppers when I'm through with you. I'll sell you as slaves to the necromancers and you'll never see the light of day."

Chet gave him a wry grin. "You're threatening us?"

Karl shifted attention to the girl. "Do you know where our things are?"

"Yes," she replied without hesitation.

"What's guarding them?"

"A fire minion."

"Bitch," the proprietor snapped.

"Now, now," Chet admonished. "Don't interrupt when a lady is speaking." He balled up a fist and cold-cocked the man in the jaw. "Ouch," he chuckled, shaking his hand. "That hurt, though it did feel good."

"Do you know where he keeps his coinage?" Karl asked.

"Yes."

"Is it guarded?"

"Only at night. During the day, it's only locked?"

"Where is it?"

"The bedroom above us."

"I'll sell you too, you slut," the man spat.

"You're beginning to get on my nerves," Karl warned. "One more outburst from you and..." he paused and cocked his head. "I think I might have an idea." Turning to the girl, he said, "What's your name?"

"Julie."

"We'll need your help, Julie. Go ahead and get dressed."

Julie hesitated for only a moment, then relaxed, deciding to make the best use of her assets. Flipping the covers off, revealing her luscious body, she took her time sashaying over to pick up her skirt and top from the chair in the corner, enjoying the overt ogling of the three men.

Karl watched her saunter across the floor, taking her time, ensuring everyone got a long lingering peek. Like all the other barmaids, she was nothing like he had ever seen in real life: long legs, narrow waist, flared hips, large firm breasts, and long brunette hair that fell to the middle of her back. Karl shook his head to refocus his attention as she seductively bent over to step into her skirt.

Waiting until she slipped the top over her head, Karl said, "Find something to wrap around his hand, get him dressed then tie him up and gag him."

"With pleasure," she answered, giving the proprietor the evil eye. "It's about time you got what's coming to you, you pig."

"Why do you sleep in his bed if you hate the guy?" Noble asked.

"I don't have a choice," she scowled. "My family was killed in the Orc attacks ten years ago. Though he took me in, if I don't obey him in everything, he'll toss me out and I have nowhere else to go."

"Have no fear," Karl gallantly spoke. "We'll make sure no harm comes to you."

Quest Alert: Rescue the serving girl and return her to the House of Rhyeem.
Reward: Enduring friendship with the House of Rhyeem.
Do you accept? Yes No

"What the hell?" he frowned then tapped 'Yes' without thinking. "Anyone know anything about the House of Rhyeem?"

"They're supposedly one of the most powerful houses in the Kingdom of Mann," Noble replied.

"How do you know that?" Karl asked, puzzled.

"It's in the resource part of the gaming info."

"What?"

"Just pull up your map and you can see for yourself," Chet said.

"There wasn't a whole lot on it the last time I checked," Karl replied. Bringing up the game screen, he discovered more of the map filled in. The Kingdom of Mann was to the southwest of the orc kingdom. Noticing a red flag at the top the Black Forest, he tapped the screen and spread his fingers to make the map larger and larger until it showed the flag pinned to Tarrytown.

Recognizing the flag showed him his present location, he pinched his fingers on the screen to make the map smaller and then shifted it around until he saw where he was in relation to where he needed to go. Taking the girl to the Kingdom of Rhyeem required going through the Orc domains. Closing the screen, he shook his head. *Why is it now I find out about what I need to know?*

Deciding he had more pressing priorities, he glanced back to see the proprietor bound and gagged. With an evil grin, he said, "Let's go see if we can eliminate a pesky minion."

"Excuse me, Sir," Julie interrupted.

"Yes?"

"He does keep coinage here in the bedroom as well."

The proprietor growled in rage as Julie led them to a place on the floor where a carpet covered the wooden floor. Using her foot, she pulled back the carpet to reveal a trapdoor.

"He keeps a small chest here also."

Karl looked up at the man who eyes filled with loathing.

Dropping to his knees, he lifted the door, reached down and oomphed as he pulled out a small heavy chest. "Damn. You got lead in this?"

Opening the top revealed a chest filled with gold coins.

"Bingo," Noble exclaimed, eyes bright.

It took another ten minutes before the gold was apportioned out among the three players, each storing them in his player bag. Replacing the chest beneath the floor, Karl closed the trapdoor and replaced the carpet.

Turning to Julie, he grinned, "Anything else in here?"

"No Sir."

Karl then addressed the other two. "Do either of you know how to handle a fire minion?"

Chet pulled up his screen and did a quick search. "Minion, fire. Fire minions, and all other minions, are restricted to the magician class unless given as a gift. Fire minions excel in shooting fireballs at their targets and are extremely accurate. Damage is assessed based upon location and accuracy of hit. They are capable of hurling fireballs at the rate of 60/minute until their resources are depleted. They are among the weaker magical beings and require inactivation in order to heal. They only obey voice commands of their masters."

"Damn," Noble muttered.

"Any ideas? Karl asked Chet who was calculating the rate of fire and his ability to duck.

"Excuse me, Sir," Julie spoke.

"Yes?"

"It seems to me that if they only obey the voice commands of their master, if their master is gagged, he can't give them any orders."

Karl's head swiveled from staring at her to focusing on the gagged proprietor. "That's brilliant. All we need to do is make sure he can't speak. Tighten his gag even tighter. I don't care if he can't breathe."

"Before we begin," Noble spoke up. "Do we really need to get our things? As far as I'm concerned, the other stuff I had to have was my thief tools. With the gold I have now, there's nothing down in the cellar that I can't replace."

Chet thought a moment. "What about the chest of money upstairs?"

"Now that's another matter," he answered with a wicked grin.

Chet looked at Karl. "You?"

43

Karl shrugged. "It's not like I have a lot of stuff. The only thing of value was my samurai sword. What about you?"

"I've got my armor and weapons down there, but truth be told, I got more than enough to buy a better set without having to sell the stuff downstairs."

"Upstairs then?"

"Agreed."

Satisfied their prisoner was securely bound and gagged, Karl and Chet frog marched the man down the hallway then up the stairs to stand in front of a narrow door.

"This it?" Karl asked Julie.

"Yes, Sir. The minion is most likely asleep but will wake as soon as the door opens."

"You wait here," he said, gently touching her arm.

"Yes, Sir. Be careful." Her warm eyes seemed to say more than giving a simple caution.

He turned to the thief. "Noble. Do your thing."

Folding his arms, Noble studied the door and the two clasp locks, while noting the absence of visible hinges. With the air of a professional, he intoned, "Door opens to the inside. The locks are the typical Rouse and Buehler type."

Reaching in his bag, he withdrew a lock pick and in mere seconds, both locks were open and positioned neatly on the floor by the door. With a bow and a wave, he said, "After you, Messieurs."

Karl leaned in to the proprietor and whispered, "Do you value your life?"

Despite the man's cold stare of hatred, he dipped his head 'Yes.'

"Good. Because if you fail to do exactly as I say, I will slit your throat. I won't bother cutting off fingers, toes… or your nuts, though I might do the last part just because."

The man stiffened and he again nodded.

"Good." He pulled back so that the rest of the team could hear. "We're going to take off the gag and he's going to tell his minion to disappear. He's got two seconds to do that before I slit his throat. If he does anything other than what we tell him, whoever is close enough will cut off his nuts then slit his throat."

Towering over the man, Chet grinned wickedly. "I look forward to it."

Karl stood behind the proprietor, gripping the back of his nightshirt with enough force to force the man to stand on his tiptoes before thrusting his sword between the man's legs and lifting it tightly against the crotch. He smiled with only his lips. "Please screw up, 'cause I've been waiting for payback."

Noble turned the handle and pushed the door open. There in the middle of an otherwise empty room was a large wooden chest with two more locks. Atop the chest was a minion whose bored expression morphed to one of anger then confusion as his master was pushed into the room.

The minion reminded Karl of a smaller and skinnier version of Noble, with differences also in the hooked nose and wider eyes. The minion twitched back and forth as he waited for his master to tell him what to do.

With the edge of his sword pressing into the man's crotch, Karl reached around and pulled the gag out of the proprietor's mouth, adding a warning. "Remember what I told you." He lifted the sword edge higher as a reminder.

Chet strode across the room, sword in hand, to stand close to the minion, while Noble slunk around to the opposite side.

"What's going on, Master?" the minion asked, his nervous hands wanting to make a fireball but unsure of this situation.

The proprietor cleared his throat. "Remember when I said that there may come a time when you'll have to act fast?"

"Yes," he frowned.

Karl knew what was about to happen and grabbed the man by what was left of his hair and jerked his head back. "Time's up." He quickly nodded at Chet while raising his sword, causing the man to involuntarily prance on his toes.

"Attack," the proprietor shouted, fully expecting to die, but with the satisfaction that they would not be able to open the money chest without the right spell.

Startled into action, the minion lifted his hands and curled his fingers like he was making a snowball, but he was too late. In one sharp swing, Chet downward sliced through the air and cut off both hands.

The minion let out a howl of pain and dumbly stared at the blood gushing out of the two stumps then looked up at the man and whimpered in anguish, "Master." That was the last word the creature spoke before Chet cut off his head.

The body collapsed and the head rolled towards the proprietor who was desperately back peddling in shock despite the sword at his throat. A moment later, the body and head fizzled then disappeared.

Karl turned to Noble. "Before I slit his throat, see if you can open the locks."

"They're spellbound," the proprietor blurted.

"If they're spellbound," Noble said as he approached the chest, "I can't do anything. I don't have the magic to break the spell." He bent down to examine the locks then tried one of his tools. After a few tries, he stood back up. "Nope. No can do."

Karl spun the proprietor around to face him. "Looks like you may be useful after all."

"Go to hell," he spat back.

"What for? This is far more fun," Karl mocked. "Will you open the chest for us?"

"No."

"That's what I thought you would say."

Sheathing his sword, he grabbed the man by the shirt. Lifting him up, he kicked his legs out from beneath him then thrust him down hard to land on his back with an excruciating 'umph,' knocking the breath out of him.

As the man gasped for air, Karl and Chet stretched the man's arms out and stood on his wrists. Chet reached down and twisted and broke another finger.

"We're gonna break each finger first then we'll cut them off one by one then we'll castrate you. But we won't kill you immediately. We're simply gonna let you bleed to death. It's a slow, very painful process. But we have plenty of time."

Noble walked over and whispered in Karl's ear, "Dawn's about an hour away. We need to hurry."

Nodding, Karl looked down at the man, his breaths in labored panting. "I'll ask you again to open the chest. Any time you answer incorrectly or don't answer, we break a finger, followed by you know the rest. So. Will you open the chest?"

The proprietor, sweat dripping from his face, shook his head.

Chet reached down and broke another finger.

The man yelped in pain.

"We'll wait a moment for the pain to subside before we ask again," Karl grinned with nonchalance. "Don't want you to have all the fun all at once."

"Excuse me, Sir." Julie's sweet voice interrupted his taunts.

"Yes," he smiled and frowned at the same time, twisting his head to gaze at her.

Walking over to him, she pointed to the chest. "Though the locks are spellbound, the rest of it isn't."

"Shut up, you bitch," the proprietor seethed.

Ignoring him, Karl stared at her, not understanding. "What do you mean?"

"Look at it. The chest is old. The wood is brittle. Why not take an ax to it and get the money that way?"

"She's right," Noble exclaimed, focusing on the wood of the chest. "I was so worried about the spells on the locks that I didn't even think there could be another way. He walked over to Chet. "I'll take your place. You're stronger than I am. Go see if you can bust it up."

Chet strode over to the chest and lightly rubbed his fingers over the wood, stopping when he found a suitable spot. Using the sword pommel, he whacked it hard against the spot and felt a satisfying break in the board. After the fourth whack, the board broke loose and gold coins gushed forth.

Karl flashed a warm smile at Julie. "You're a genius."

"You're gonna pay with your life for this," the proprietor sneered at her. "I won't forget this. I'll track you down wherever you are."

"Bold words from a man in your position," Karl chuckled.

A half hour later, with the gold divided three ways and safely tucked away in their individual bags, Noble glanced outside and said, "We got maybe half an hour before the town really wakes up. We gotta get going."

"You won't get past the guards," the proprietor threatened. "All of this will be for nothing."

"We'll see," Karl scoffed, refitting the gag then pushing the man ahead of him.

Though dawn had yet to arrive, the night skies were thinning, and the once inky darkness of evening was slowly creeping away as Karl and the others made their way to the front gate.

"If only we had horses," Chet mused. "We could make our escape all the faster."

"Too late for that," Noble fretted, worried now about the gnolls who patrolled the lands surrounding the town. "How're we gonna get through the rest of the forest?"

"No worries," Karl calmly replied. "I've got a friend waiting on the outside." *Uafas. You awake?*

Of course. I'm surprised you're awake already.

Long story. I'll tell you about it when we get outside the town.

We?

Like I said, long story. Meet us on the south road on the other side of the town.

Take your time. I haven't eaten since yesterday.

No problem. I think I can help.

You? I doubt it.

Karl chuckled and cast a sidelong glance at the proprietor. *Oh, I don't know. Let's wait and see.*

Then hurry, because I'm hungry.

See you in a bit.

The proprietor was dismayed while the others were pleased to see there was no one at the gate when they arrived. Chet did a quick peek into the guard room and smiled to see the guard, feet on the desk, hands folded across his stomach and his head back, mouth open, contentedly snoring.

"All good," he whispered.

Unfortunately, the hinges of the small door groaned loudly causing the guard to startle and pop up. He was out the guard room in time to see the proprietor being pushed out the gate door.

"Hey. What're you doin'?" he demanded.

"C'mere.   Let me show you something," Chet said, excitement in his voice.

"What?" The guard hastened over to the door. By now, only Chet remained on the inside.

"See here?" Chet placed a hand on the guard's shoulder and leaned over the bottom edge of the door.   When the guard leaned over, Chet thrust his sword into the man's gut then dragged him outside the door before closing it.

Leaving the dying guard curled up on the ground, Chet hurried after the others, catching up to them as they skirted the northern wall of the town.

By the time they reached the south side of the town, dawn was beginning to crest. It wasn't until they were on the road and out of sight of the town that they relaxed.   That lasted until a massive wolf leaped onto the road.

"O my God," Julie screamed while Chet thrust his sword in front and Noble frantically searched for a place to flee and hide. Even the proprietor jumped in fright.

"Relax," Karl smiled. "This is my friend, Uafas."

"That's the wolf from Dinwahl" Chet barked, nervously eyeing the great beast and hoping he didn't recognize him.

You befriended one of my tormentors?

I needed him to help me escape. I was drugged and imprisoned. They were going to sell me as a slave.

Welcome to my world for the past years. Can I eat him?

Not yet. But the other fat one is yours if you want. I can slit his throat and save you the time and trouble of having to chase him.

That would be fine
Where would you like to dine?
Follow me.

The wolf turned and entered the forest.

"Follow him," Karl commanded.

Julie immediately scooted up and grabbed hold of Karl's arm.

"It's OK," he soothed. "He's my friend."

"Your friend's a giant wolf?" Noble sputtered.

"Yes. And if you know what's good for you, you don't want to get on his bad side." He shot a knowing look at Chet.

"You rescued the wolf and now he's your friend?" Chet asked, silently kicking himself for not thinking of it himself.

"Yup. Once you took off and I was left alone, I figured he needed to be free. The rest is, as they say, history."

They came into a clearing to see the wolf sitting on its haunches staring at each of them in turn.

"Everyone take a seat," Karl said. "We'll be here for a little bit. We can rest up before we get started."

"Started for where?" Chet asked.

"Well, for one, I still need to find my friends."

"You sure they're here?"

"They crossed over the bridge before I did."

Chet frowned. "What happened?"

"I was… um… sort of tied up," Karl hesitated, reluctant to spend the time retelling the story, "and they crossed and were supposed to wait for me. Unfortunately, it looks like I took the wrong road out from the gate."

"Ah," Chet nodded in understanding.

"We also have to deliver Julie to the House of Rhyeem."

"Why?" Chet inquired.

"I accepted a quest for her."

"When did you get that quest?" Noble asked, puzzled.

"When we were in the fat guy's place," Karl replied. Turning to Chet, he said, "I know you like working alone, but you're welcome to tag along for as long as you like."

"Thanks. I just might do that."

Turning his attention to Noble, Karl said, "What about you? You up for hanging around for a while, go on a quest?"

Noble glanced around at the forest and assessed his circumstances. "Yeah, sure," he grinned with a pleasant shrug. "Got nothing else going on at the moment."

Are you going to feed me, or what?

Sorry.

Without a word, Karl took the gag out of the proprietor's mouth then cut the bonds around his wrists. "There, that should be better."

Breathing a sigh of relief, the man stared at his mutilated hands and vainly rubbed his wrists. He was about to make a snide remark when Karl jerked his head back and slit his throat then pushed him forward towards the wolf.

The others watched in horror as the wolf growled and leaped on the man who had dropped to his knees and began ripping the body apart in a ravenous devouring.

"O my God," Julie sputtered, taking several fearful steps backwards and turning away.

"You coulda warned us," Chet sourly complained.

"You didn't think we were taking him with us, did you?" Karl said.

"Of course not," Chet answered. "It's just that… you, know, it's sorta gross to offer him up as a meal to your overgrown pet."

"Uafas was hungry and despite eyeing you as the most suitable snack, I figured he was the most expendable."

"Very funny," Chet replied, wondering if it was such a smart idea teaming up with a gigantic varmint who might want to dine on him at the first opportunity.

Aghast at the sight, Julie buried her face in Karl's chest. Noble continued to watch with a distracted curiosity.

Karl watched for a moment then turned to Chet. "How'd you end up in the cell?"

"When I left you, I continued on with my quest. Had to come through Tarrytown."

"You didn't meet any gnolls along the way?"

"I have a horse, or rather, I *had* a horse. I figured there were critters along the way, and I wasn't in the mood to stop and add XP, so I raced that little thoroughbred as fast as I could to get here."

"Guard tell you to eat at the Chicken Gizzard?"

"Yup."

"And to stay at the Pig and Whistle?"

"That's Hog and Whistle," Noble corrected.

"Whatever."

"Yup."

"So what happened?"

"I was eating some stew and the next thing I know is that I'm waking up in a dark cell, chained to the wall. Then you and your kid show up and here we are."

"We shoulda left you back there," Noble groused.

Karl looked at the mutilated carcass in front of Uafas. Other than the shredded clothing, all that remained were bones and bloodied organs. *You about ready?*

Yes.

Can you ride four?

I will take three. The tall one you call 'Chet' can walk.

I understand.

Turning to Julie and Noble, he said, "You two will ride." Giving Chet a bemused smile, he said, "You ready to run?"

"I'm a berserker. I don't run," he crisply replied, cocking an eyebrow. "That's why I have a horse."

"Had a horse," Noble pointed out with satisfaction as he climbed up to sit behind the wolf's head.

When Julie hesitated, Karl took her gently by the elbow. "It'll be OK," he soothed. "Uafas is a gentleman and will take great care of you."

"Yeah, c'mon up" Noble agreed, suppressing a leer as he expected her to sit behind him and press her body against him. He sighed in heavenly glee when she climbed up and wrapped her arms around him for security.

"Why don't we all ride?" Chet objected.

"Someone I know still hasn't forgiven someone else I know for the previous abuse," Karl answered.

Chet blinked then shut his mouth. "I can't run fast or far," he pointed out.

"Do your best," Karl encouraged.

"Yeah, big guy," Noble jeered. "You're tough. Let's see how tough you really are."

"I'd watch my mouth if I were you, midget man."

"Enough," Karl commanded. "Move out."

Uafas loped in a smooth graceful gate. Noble grabbed a handful of hair and held on, reveling in the Julie's tight embrace.

Not so tight.

"Not so tight, Noble," Karl cautioned, running comfortably beside them. "Uafas knows how to carry you."

"Sorry."

They had not traveled three kilometers before Chet began lagging behind. Karl told Uafas to slow down until Chet caught up then pushed the pace again. The yoyo effect lasted for another two kilometers with Chet lagging farther and farther behind before Karl's single-minded focus was beginning to wonder if he should just leave him. But then his team's motto of leave no one behind kicked in and he slowed the pace once more.

Slow down. Let's wait for him to catch up again.

I thought he was supposed to be a berserker?

"We're never gonna get anywhere if we have to keep waiting for him," Noble fussed, taking a measure of the sun in the sky. "At this rate, we'll be stuck in the forest when night comes."

Karl was about to ask Uafas if he wouldn't reconsider so they could at least get out of the forest when he heard distant shouting behind them. Whirling around, he ordered, "You two get down and stay here."

Nobel and Julie quickly slid down and scurried over to hide in the brush by the edge of the road as Karl and the wolf raced back, the wolf ducking into the forest.

Rounding a bend in the road, Karl came upon Chet fighting a losing battle against five guards and two townsmen from Tarrytown. Arrows protruded from his back and chest while another had pierced his thigh.

"There's the other one," one of the guards shouted and pointed a sword at Karl.

Two guards detached from the struggle with Chet whose strength and life points had fallen to the point that he could neither flee nor defend himself. With one last effort, Chet cast a frustrated glance at Karl then lifted his sword for the last time as a guard plunged a sword through his chest. Chet crumbled to the ground, dead.

Triumphant with the kill, the remaining guards and townsmen followed after the other two guards who had yet to confront an angry and determined Viking.

"He's one o' them that killed Bryen," the trailing guard called out.

A loud and vicious growl emerged from the woods causing the Tarrytown men to jump and turn as Uafas burst through the trees and attacked. The two townsmen dropped their weapons and fled for their lives. The remaining guardsmen were not so lucky as Uafas tore and ripped flesh and heads from bodies.

As soon as the wolf appeared, Karl carried the attack to the two guards before him, their attention diverted to the monster on the road. In one wide arcing sweep, he struck the one guard, the force of his blade cleaving through the collarbone and down to the ribs.

Knowing his fate was certain, the remaining guard threw away his sword and fled up the road towards Noble and Julie.

"Get him," Karl shouted.

Uafas took off in an instant and before the man could get forty paces away, the wolf descended on him, ripping him apart.

Karl placed a foot on the guard's chest and yanked his sword free, wiping it clean on the man's clothing. He then collected six swords, carefully examining each one and keeping the best and placing the others in his bag. He looked over in time to see Chet's body briefly fizzle then disappear.

Looking farther down the road, he saw horses tethered at the side of the road. His first thought was to collect them and ride, but when they suddenly turned skittish, he turned and watched Uafas come padding up. Recognizing the horses would be uncontrollable with the wolf so close, he sighed at leaving them, knowing the wolf was far more beneficial than the horses.

Good job. Let's get back to the others. Karl started walking up the road then abruptly stopped. "What am I doing?"

Quickly turning around, he backtracked to where Chet's belt and bag lay on the ground.

"No sense leaving this for someone else to find." He emptied all of Chet's gold into his own belt then collected the weapons.

You ready finally? Uafas said.

Yeah. Karl looked once around then headed to where Noble and Julie waited.

Can't say that I'm disappointed he's gone.

I understand.

You're not mad at me, are you?

Why would I be mad at you?

Because I waited until I knew for sure he was going to be killed.

Karl swore he heard a faint chuckle. *No, I'm not mad at you. Besides, he was holding us back.*

That's right, he was.

Karl felt the hot breath on his shoulder and stopped and turned. Reaching up, he scratched the wolf's cheek and head. "I'm glad you're here."

Me too. It's a lot more fun than Dinwahl.

Julie and Noble emerged onto the road when they saw Karl and the wolf approaching, their gait relaxed and casual.

"Where's Chet?" Noble asked.

"Dead."

"Bummer," Noble replied with a shrug that said he was glad Chet was gone. "Wonder where his bind spot is?"

"Haven't the faintest idea. We need to keep going. It's likely they'll send another group when they find out what happened."

"What happened?" Julie asked, sidling close to Karl and causing Noble to scowl.

"Chet was attacked by a group from the town. By the time we got there, it was too late."

"How many were there?" Noble inquired.

"Just seven. Two got away. The others are dead. I'm surprised they were able to catch up so soon. I figured it would have been a while before the gate guard was discovered. And how did they know we were the ones responsible?"

"Probably one of the wall guards saw us," Noble offered, "when we were headed south. Besides," he added gazing up at the wolf, "he's kinda hard to miss."

"Perhaps you're right," Karl nodded. "We better get going."

"I thought he was a berserker," Noble said, looking back down the road. "Isn't he supposed to be some sort of battle demon?"

"We were pushing the pace hard," Karl answered. "He was probably exhausted by the time they arrived, and they had horses, so they were fresh for battle."

"Horses?" Noble brightened? "Why didn't you bring them?"

"Thought about it then accepted the fact that horses and wolves don't mix and in the overall scheme of things, I'd much rather have Uafas with us than horses. Besides, I consider Uafas part of the team."

Noble stared down the empty road and heaved a sigh of disappointment.

"We better get moving before they send reinforcements."

Noble looked up at the wolf, its size alone enough to intimidate anyone. Add the wolf part to the equation and you get real terror. "You really think they're gonna come back this way when the tale is told about a giant wolf?"

"Maybe, maybe not, but we don't need to be here to find out." Karl felt his stomach rumble. "We need to find something to eat soon." Lifting his head to Uafas, he said, *Ready?*

Climb aboard.

Two hours later, they emerged from the forest to wide fields that once had been verdant farmlands but were now overgrown with thistles and weeds and sporadic trees. Uafas stopped just inside the tree line.

"I think this is where I'll get off for a while," Noble said, sliding down.

"You going to walk?" Karl frowned.

"Naw. I was thinking I'd check out Lyster for a bit, work on some skills."

Karl pulled up his game map, noting Lyster was about ten kilometers due east at the edge of the forest while Strathwick, the next town south, was about thirty kilometers from where they now stood.

"I was thinking you guys could hold up in Strathwick for a couple of days, gimme some time to practice without distraction. Say three or four days. I'll find you in town."

Karl looked at Noble who pretended to be absorbed in the map, knowing the thief would be a no show. "Sure. See you then."

With a cheerful wave at Karl and a sigh of lust at Julie, Noble turned and headed along the edge of the forest towards Lyster.

"Looks like it's just us," Karl sighed then looked up at Uafas. *We're going to need a plan. I seriously doubt you're going to get a warm welcome when we get to the town.*

Don't worry about me. I'll meet you on the other side of the town.

OK. Karl reached up to wrap his arms around the wolf's neck. *Be careful. I don't want anything to happen to you.*

Nor you. It's not yet noon. It's still a long walk to the town. Give me a little bit. Perhaps I can find you something to eat.

Something not people, OK?

Spoilsport. The wolf turned and plunged back into the forest.

"Where's he going?" Julie asked, her nervousness showing.

"He's going to find us something to eat."

"Why did Noble leave?" She folded her arms across her ample chest, hugging herself as she stared at the small thief disappearing over a knoll.

"I think he realized hanging around with us was dangerous to his health," Karl chuckled, though disappointed.

He enjoyed the little man's irreverence. "While we're waiting, why don't you tell me about you and the House of Rhyeem."

"I... I don't know much about it," she hesitated. "In fact, I don't know anything about it."

"Then why do I need to take you back there?"

"I don't know."

Karl stared at her. She was gorgeous and even sexier when she appeared helpless. "How long have you been in Tarrytown?"

"For as long as I can remember."

"You've never lived anywhere else?" He studied her mannerisms when she answered the questions and knew she was telling the truth.

"I can't remember anywhere else. Sometimes I dream of another place and it's always the same, but I know it's just a dream because the house is grand and bright and I'm happy."

"Do you want to go back there?"

"To Tarrytown?"

"No. To Rhyeem."

"How can I go *back* when I've never been?"

"That doesn't make any sense," Karl frowned then rechecked the quest.

Quest Alert: Rescue the serving girl and return her to the House of Rhyeem.
Reward: Enduring friendship with the House of Rhyeem.

Why would the ruling house of Rhyeem care about a serving girl, no matter how stunning she looked? But more importantly, what were Annabeth and Raquel going to say when he showed up with Julie? He was quite sure they were not going to be happy.

Uafas silently slipped out into the open, a large hare in his jaws.

I found a place back in the woods where you can have a fire and still defend ourselves if necessary.

"Smart thinking," Karl said causing Julie to give him a puzzling stare.

Of course it's smart thinking. I'm a wolf.

"I didn't say anything," Julie remarked.

"I was talking to the wolf. C'mon. He's found a place for us to set up a temporary camp to cook the rabbit."

"How do you know?"

"He told me."

Deciding to wait until later to ask how, Julie followed closely behind Karl as they trailed behind the wolf who led them a distance into the thick forest until they came to a rock outcropping that provided some protection. While Karl gathered dry wood and tinder, Julie expertly butchered the hare. When she saw Karl remove a string from his shirt to make a bow drill, she stopped him.

"I have a flint and steel," she smiled, reaching into her satchel.

Karl chuckled. "You carry a flint and steel? I've heard of strange and unusual things in women's purses, but never a flint and steel."

Julie smiled back at him. "I started carrying them when I worked in the kitchen. The cook was a man who hated working there. He had a habit of letting the fires go out and then blame me. So I started carrying a flint and steel ever since. I don't really use them anymore. They're more like good luck charms now."

"You're full of surprises," Karl acknowledged, dipping his head in thanks. "Not only are you beautiful, but resourceful as well." He saw her blush then smile.

Accepting the flint and steel, he bent down and after three strikes, the tinder caught and a short while later he had joints of rabbit roasting over the open fire.

Accepting that Julie was the far better cook, he kept a careful watch on the surroundings while Uafas scouted the perimeter, far enough away to be silent and unseen.

"How is it that you can talk to the wolf?" Julie asked, poking the meat.

"We talk with our minds," he replied over his shoulder.

"I thought only mages could do that." She gazed at him with newfound respect.

"I wouldn't know," he shrugged then looked up at the sky. "We're going to need to eat pretty soon if we're going to make it to Strathwick before nightfall."

"It's done," she announced, bring him a thigh jabbed on a charred stick.

Karl tore into the meat, surprised at the flavor. It was juicy and tender, far better than he could have expected had he been doing the same thing on maneuvers at Ft Bragg or elsewhere. He remembered the time he had captured a rabbit during training. He shared it with his team. The meat had been tough and stringy, probably because of the haste to cook it and the low fire, which tended to dry out the meat.

Glancing back over his shoulder, he saw Julie daintily holding a rabbit leg with two fingers from each hand, and taking small nibbles. Unaware of his fascination, she looked innocent and almost shy, and absolutely fetching. Shaking his head, he turned back to surveil the forest. He heard her walk up and turned to look up at her.

"Here's a nice breast for you," she said, holding out a large chuck of cooked rabbit.

Karl looked over his shoulder at her chest then up at her face and smiled, causing her to blush. "Thank you. Have you eaten enough? Make sure you've eaten enough. You need your strength just as much as I do."

"That's OK. I have another breast –" she began when he snorted a laugh. "Oh," she huffed and stamped her foot, though fighting a smile, "you men. You're all alike. Your minds are always on one thing."

"Really?" he said, turning fully to face her. "And what would that be?"

"You know as well as I do what that is." She stood before him, hands jammed on her hips, trying to look serious but the smile destroying the attempt.

"You only have yourself to blame," he replied, turning back to his surveillance duties. "They get one look at you and what do you expect them to think? Though you know how to use your sex, you don't. You're genuinely a nice person. A rare combination for someone so beautiful. Men fall in love with you because they see you as the epitome of their desire, gorgeous vixen and the girl next door." *And you're just an NPC, which makes my lust all the weirder, although Gwen certainly didn't disappoint.*

There was a long pause before he heard her quietly reply, "That was sweet. No one has ever said something like that to me before."

"I find that hard to believe."

Put out the fire. The wind has carried the smell into the forest and woken gnolls.

Karl jumped up and kicked dirt over the fire then stamped on it. "We need to go."

"Why?" she asked, sensing his urgency.

"Gnolls."

"O my God."

"We'll be OK," he reassured her as Uafas raced in.

"Up you go, my dear," Karl smiled, helping Julie climb up to sit behind the wolf's head. Karl leaped up in time just as five gnolls came crashing into the clearing.

Uafas let out an angry growl followed by a loud bark, causing the gnolls to jitter to a halt. By the time they collected themselves to give chase, Uafas' speed and size had stretched the gap between them. Bursting out of the forest and out into the open, they were already half a kilometer down the road when Karl looked back and saw them halt in the deep shadows at the forest edge, shaking their swords at them in frustration.

You can slow down now.

Karl studied the terrain. The rolling fields that had certainly been fertile at one time, stretched all around them. The occasional tumbled down farmhouse stood amidst the ruin. Pulling up his map, he noted the red flag and the distance between it and Strathwick. He guessed the distance to be roughly twenty-five kilometers. Also, as far as he could tell, the land was open between here and there, which meant there was no place for Uafas to hide.

We're going to need to split up pretty soon. The rest of the way to the town is like this.

OK. Where do I meet you?

Karl concentrated on the map. *Looks like there's a bridge across the river beyond the city that way.* He pointed straight ahead. *The road across the bridge leads south and it's surrounded by forest. Meet us on the other side of the river as close to the bridge as you can.*

OK. Try to stay out of trouble this time.

I'll do my best.

Tomorrow?

Day after. Hopefully we'll be there early.

What about the little one? He said he'd be there in three or four days. Not sure I can hide that long.

I don't expect we'll see him again. I think he wants to work on some thief skills with us not around.

Pity. I was beginning to like him.

The wolf eased to a halt and the two riders slid down.

You'll need to head back to the forest and take it north before crossing the open fields tonight, Karl advised.

You did notice that I'm a wolf? Despite your doubts, I can take care of myself.

Didn't look that way in Dinwahl.

That's because I pissed off a dark mage. You do the same thing and see what happens to you.

"Let's hope that never happens," Karl said, scratching the wolf's cheek. "You take care of yourself."

We've been through this already. Go.

"May I hug him?" Julie asked.

Of course. Besides, she smells a lot better than you do.

Grinning, Karl nodded. "He said that would be fine."

Julie hugged him around the neck. "Thank you for saving our lives."

Anytime. Uafas looked at Karl. *I like her. She's going to need protection if we're to take her to Rhyeem.*

I know where you're going with this. I'll take care of her.

Good. Giving them one last look, Uafas turned around and headed back to the forest.

Karl watched him until he disappeared into the distance then turned to see an anxious Julie. "Don't worry. He'll be fine."

"It's not him I'm worried about."

"We'll be fine. You're with me, remember?"

"Yes," she replied with a nervous smile, taking his hand in both of hers. She leaned forward and kissed him on the lips. It wasn't a deep kiss nor a light brush of the lips, but a kiss full enough to let him know there was more where that came from.

Momentarily caught off guard, Karl cleared his throat, reveling in the woman's touch. "We better get moving," he said with a smile. "We've got a lot of ground to cover."

Karl was surprised at Julie's endurance as they covered the distance to the town. Not only did she not complain about the pace, but she matched him step for step. Along the way, he learned more about her.

"I worked in the kitchen until he noticed that I was growing into a woman. I was thirteen when he first took me to bed."

"Thirteen," Karl repeated, disgusted. "Glad I fed him to the wolf."

"Me too."

"Then what happened?"

"After that, he took me whenever he wanted, threatening to kick me out if I complained. I had nowhere else to go. Besides, I'd seen what happened to those who had no protector." She shivered. "Then he took a shine to some of the other girls and I got a break. As often as I could, I pretended to be sick. When the other girls did the same thing, he knew what was happening. He got real mad and kicked one of the younger girls out. It was enough to scare the rest of us to give into his demands."

"What happened to her?"

"No one knows, but they said she was left outside the gates one night and never seen again."

"What about the hustle with the stew and slavery and all?"

"He was one of the inner circle of the slave trade. That's how he got so rich."

"Rich?" Karl cocked an eyebrow. "No offense, but that place wasn't all that grand."

"He liked it that way," she nodded. "Made others think he wasn't doing all that well."

Karl hefted the coins in his pouch, amazed both at the amount the pouch held as well as the amount that spilled out of the treasure chest. Now he could afford to buy better weapons... and some decent clothes. Hopefully Strathwick would have a smithy and swordmaster. As they passed one of the deserted farmhouses, Karl slowed down to stare at it. It looked like all the other lonely, dilapidated homes they had passed.

Glancing up at the afternoon sky, he said, "We got time. Let's check out one of these homes."

Julie froze. "Are you sure? Don't we need to hurry to get to the town on time?"

"You're stronger than I expected," he complimented, "so we're making good time. Just this one then we'll move along."

"I... I suppose." Grasping his left hand with both her hands, she marched alongside him, their shoulders touching.

Walking up the path towards the house, Karl studied the building and the surroundings. The house was made of stone and a thatched roof that was partially caved in. The single window on the front was still shuttered, but the shutters for the window on the side hung loose and swung lazily in the gentle wind. The area around the house lay open then abruptly transitioned to weeds high enough to hide a dwarf.

It was as they drew closer that he curled a lip. "It stinks around here." No sooner had he made the comment that he felt Julie jerk to a halt. When he looked back at her, he saw the terror in her eyes. "What's wrong?"

"It smells evil."

Karl momentarily frowned. "It smells like sh –" He caught himself and cleared his throat. "Evil, huh? Are you sure?"

"Yes I'm sure."

"What say we find out." After a quick scan, he opted for a sizeable patch of weeds by the path. "Give me five minutes."

"O God, please don't leave me here by myself." She clutched his hand.

"Five minutes," he firmly replied, wondering why she was so frightened. As far as he could tell, except for the smell, there was nothing else here. But why then, if there was nothing here, was it so important that he determine it so? It was more than curiosity. It was the needing to know the layout of the land, the potential dangers. Why was the house and surrounding land deserted?

She hesitated only an instant then stepped up beside him. "Then I'm coming with you."

He was about to argue when he saw her look of determination. "OK. Stay close." When he felt her pressed against him, he added, "Not that close."

The closer they came to front door, the stronger the foul odor, as well as an increase in the number of scattered bones, now bleached from the sun. Karl cast a studious gaze at the various bones and decided they looked to be animal bones, probably tossed out after meals.

But the smell... he couldn't' figure out why the smell. Standing by the front door, he looked at Julie and held a finger to his lips then cautiously opened the door.

Stench poured out along with a swarm of flies causing Julie to dry heave while Karl ducked. Pushing the door all the way open, he saw the two decaying orc bodies. One leaned against the fireplace, his legs splayed out in front. Half his head was missing, and flies had gotten to the remaining eye. The other orc lay sprawled on the floor next to him, a dagger still in his back.

Covering his mouth with his hand, Karl stepped into the cottage, conducting a rapid appraisal. The room contained a rough-hewn wooden table and two chairs. The remains of two other chairs were scattered on the floor. A cooking pot on a swivel arm stood inside the long dead fireplace. There was little else of importance. Then he saw the curved orc blade in the boney grip of the orc leaning against the fireplace.

Crossing the room, he tugged the sword away from the dead orc then yanked the dagger out of the other's back. Just as he was about to check for anything else of value, he saw a small vial filled with a colored liquid by the leg of the table. Retrieving the vial, he stepped back to where Julie waited just outside the door.

Without a word, he led the way back to the road then exhaled and took a deep breath. "Phew that stinks in there. Didn't realize orcs smelled so bad." He held up the vial, noticing the liquid inside was a light purple.

Congratulations: You've gained a speed potion. Speed potions allow you to move very quickly without suffering ill effects or impacting your health, mana, and strength. Potion lasts for 10 minutes.

Reward: Orc scimitar, common only in Orc domains, Damage: 10-18, Durability: 90/100.

Reward: Orc curved razor knife, common only in Orc domains, Damage: 9-16, Durability: 90/100.

Karl jabbed the 'X' to close out the screen. Though not liking the constant intrusion, in this instance he appreciated the info. He gave a quick glance at the weapons and potion in his hands then tucked them into his belt and bag, keeping one of the blades out just in case.

"The sooner we get to town, the sooner we can have a bath, a nice meal and a place to spend the night," she said with a poignant stare.

Karl's gaze took in the entire woman standing before him. Even with the hasty departure, flight through the forest, and the escape from gnolls, she looked just as desirable as the first moment he saw her, especially when she traipsed naked across the room. Once again he had to remind himself that she was an NPC. And once again he reminded himself that so was Elena... and so was Gwen.

It was then that he puzzled at the image of the decaying orc bodies. Why were they still there? By all rights, after they died, they should have fizzled and disappeared. Glancing at the vial in his hand, he shrugged. *Maybe they're there permanently for folks like me to find this potion.*

Deciding he had more important things to worry about, he did a quick scan of the area and the position of the sun. Activating his game map, he calculated the distance and the time to Strathwick.

"You're right. We better get a move on. I figure another three-and-a-half to four hours by the time we get to town, providing no interruptions along the way."

Slipping a hand in his, she flashed a warm smile. "I'm ready."

Chapter 3

The gates were still open when Karl and Julie arrived. The first thing Karl noticed was that Strathwick was much larger than Tarrytown, with high walls made of smooth sand-colored stone and city gates made of iron, broad enough so that two merchant carts could comfortably pass each other.

Another thing Karl noticed as he and Julie joined the throngs of citizens and visitors passing by the gate guards, was that there seemed to be little traffic going out of the city. In fact, the only folks leaving Strathwick were a troop of soldiers, resplendent in armor, some with halberds, others with swords and battle axes.

Karl stepped to the side to let them pass, noticing the stares of approval he received when the soldier caught sight of the orc weapon. He watched as the troop came to a halt just outside the gate and a large burly man, the only one wearing a helmet, came from around the front of the formation and marched towards him.

"You there. Hold fast."

Karl stood waiting, Julie at his side, as the man strode up. He was a bit shorter than Karl, but his broad shoulders and thick arms made him appear larger.

"I'm Sergeant Hemlin. Where did you get that sword?" he demanded.

"About four hours up the road from here towards Tarrytown."

"Four hours, ya say," Hemlin frowned. "What were ya doing there?"

"We left Tarrytown this morning intending to come here," Karl explained. "Ran into some gnolls along the way. Managed to shake them when we hit the edge of the forest and out into the open. It was all quiet on the road. Didn't see a thing except abandoned cottages. Decided to take a look in one and found two dead orcs. Looks like they might have had a disagreement. They'd been dead for a while. So I helped myself to this." He held up the sword as evidence.

"Dead how long?"

"Can't really say for sure. Flies already got to them and they stunk pretty awful. No more than a couple of days I'd say."

Hemlin nodded. "Anything else?"

"I did surveillance scanning along the way and saw nothing except a circle of buzzards to the south. Other than that, all quiet."

"Much obliged. Where you headed?"

"Rhyeem."

Hemlin's eyes widened. "Rhyeem? You'll have to go through orc territory once you cross the river."

"I know."

Hemlin cast a disapproving eye at him then ticked his head at Julie. "You takin' the missus with you?"

"Yup."

"Don't be a fool, man. Stay here. You'll only be diggin' yer own graves."

"Why is all the land here so barren?" Karl asked, changing the subject.

"Easy," Hemlin sniffed. "Orcs. They began layin' waste to the land three years ago. Killed most everyone who lived 'tween here and the forest. Strathwick was a powerful city back then. Now we send out the few farmers we have left to tend farms close by. We go out in the morning, and all come back in the evening. It's a good thing you came when you did. When these gates are closed, they won't open for hell or high water."

"Appreciate the info."

Hemlin gave him a quick look then said, "If yer gonna go through orc territory, the least ya oughta do is get yerself a decent blade, one that will last against orc steel. Go see Grimmar the gnome on Broadchurch street. He's the best. Then get yerself some potions from any of the mages. Hopefully ya got enough to pay fer it. Otherwise, yer just askin' to be killed."

"Thanks for your sound advice, my friend," Karl said with a respectful dip of his head. "What time will you be back?"

"We do patrols fer an hour."

"Then perhaps you will allow me to buy you a drink after you return."

Hemlin's eyes brightened. "Yer a decent fella –"

"Karl."

"Karl," he nodded with a grin. "I accept."

"I know you have to go, but perhaps you can recommend a place to stay that has both good food and good ale."

"That would be the Feather's Nest. Ask anyone. They'll know where it is. It's not cheap though."

"As long as the food is good, the ale, strong, and the beds soft," Karl replied with an impish smile.

"Haw," Hemlin barked a laugh.

"An hour or so then." Karl gave him a courteous bow and watched as the man happily made his way to the front of the formation. Leaning over to Julie, he whispered, "Hopefully they won't drug me this time."

Passing through the gates, the guards merely nodded at the two newcomers. Having witnessed the exchange between Sergeant Hemlin and Karl, they assumed the two new arrivals were certified as safe.

As Karl came beside one guard, he asked, "Where can I find Grimmar the gnome on Broadstreet?"

"Straight on this road through the city until you come to the Blacksmith Guild portion. He's halfway down in the middle."

"Much obliged."

The city was indeed grand, for a half hour later, Karl and Julie found themselves in the middle of the service merchants quarter, passing by jewelers, physicians, bankers, and others before finally coming to the blacksmith guild, delineated by a sign of a crossed hammer and sword. Working their way through the passing crowds, Karl saw Grimmar's sign, an artfully carved plaque of fancy swords, hanging from a post. Karl paused outside to study the array of swords, knives, battle axes and other weapons in the window display and was impressed with the quality and design. Opening the door, he tripped a small bell to tinkle, announcing a customer had entered.

Grimmar looked up from behind the counter, placing the book he was reading on the countertop. His face was the color of tanned leather, edged with a short, carefully trimmed beard of white whiskers. Beneath bushy white eyebrows, his sapphire blues eyes merrily appraised them.

"Good day to you, my most excellent Viking and his lovely companion," he smiled.

"Wife," Julie not so subtly corrected.

"Wife," Grimmar repeated, his smile widening in amusement, especially when Karl looked at her with surprise. "How may I help you?"

Karl laid the orc blades on the counter. "Sergeant Hemlin said you were the best weapons man in Strathwick."

"Ah," he nodded at the name. "Hemlin's a good man. Honest and dependable as the day is long." He gazed with approval at the sword in Karl's hand. "That's a fine orc blade. Where did you get it?"

"On the way here from Tarrytown."

Grimmar regarded the Viking with newfound respect. "I can tell you're not from Tarrytown. How did you manage to escape?"

"Long story," Karl answered, not interested in having to repeat the details. He was hungry and getting tired. "I need a blade that will defeat these kinds of swords and daggers. Hemlin said you'd have what I needed."

"Why? You're safe here in Strathwick. Why not stay? They could use a man like you."

"I'm heading… uh, we're heading to Rhyeem."

"Through orc territory?" Grimmar frowned in consternation. "Why?"

"We have business in Rhyeem, and we need to get there the quickest way."

"Quick isn't always the smartest way," he quipped. "Why go through a place you know is dangerous when you can go another way that isn't?"

"I have additional business with the orcs."

72

Grimmar raised a suspicious eyebrow. "Oh?"

"They're holding someone hostage and I intend to free him."

Grimmar leveled his eyes at him for a bit then shook his head. "You're either exceedingly brave or raging crazy. However, I do have something you can use, but it's expensive." Scooting off the high stool, he motioned Karl to follow him towards the display windows.

Pointing to a sword near the front of the display, he said, "That one."

"That one?" The sword reminded Karl of a 17th century basket hilted rapier. "That's it? That blade will break the first contact with stouter blades."

"Go ahead. Pick it up."

"Why don't you just hand it to me?" Karl frowned, noting the gnome was closer.

"I can't."

"Why not?"

"It's too heavy."

"What?" Karl reached in and, using two fingers, lifted the sword out of the case.

"By the gods," Grimmar exclaimed, his mouth gaping open. "You're the one."

"I'm the one what?" He flicked the sword side to side. "What am I supposed to do with this?" He started to put it back when the gnome stopped him.

"Wait a moment." Grimmar strode across the floor to the counter, reaching up to retrieve the orc sword. "Now defend yourself." Without warning, he attacked.

Karl instinctively jumped back, his blade high as the dwarf, holding the sword with two hands, swung at him. Instead of the ping of blade hitting blade, Karl's thin rapier sliced through Grimmar's sword like a knife through soft butter, cutting it in half, the top part of the blade falling to the floor.

"My God," Karl blurted. "That's incredible. How much?"

"Fifty gold."

"Will it do that to other blades?"

"That is the sword called Orc's Bane. It was crafted by an elven bladesmith when Strathwick was but a mere trading post."

"How did you come by this?" Karl sliced through the air several times and marveled at the balance and lightness of the sword. It was as if he held a feather.

"That's my business," Grimmar replied with a stoic grin.

"Why hasn't anyone else bought this?"

Grimmar paused before answering. "First, the sword responds to the swordsman. Perhaps you noticed that I told you to get the sword instead of me."

"I did find that odd," Karl admitted.

"That's because the sword recognizes the sword master. Every other man, woman, gnome, orc or whatever, will find the blade more than cumbersome and heavy... too heavy if you know what I mean. You are the first person to have ever held the sword with one hand. The sword has chosen you."

Karl parried and thrust, awed by the delicate lightness of the blade. "And the second reason?"

"Fifty gold separates those merely looking from the serious buyer. And third, knowing the blade like I do, I would not part with it unless I know the person and sword are meant to be together."

Karl chuckled. "That almost sounds like some magical mystery story I'd read in fairytales."

The dwarf grimaced and let out a long-suffering sigh. "Give it to your wife. Go on."

Karl looked at him then at her and shrugged, using two fingers at the handle, and holding it out to her.

Julie reached for the sword and immediately felt an immense weight, causing her to use two hands while struggling to hold it up. Feeling the weight increase, she lowered the sword to the floor then looked up at him with frowned wonder.

"Pick it up," Karl said.

"I can't," she complained, dropping to her knees and grasping the sword by the handle.

"She won't be able to," the dwarf patiently commented. "In fact, neither can I, for the sword will now only recognize

74

the rightful owner. And that's a pity if you don't have the fifty gold, for the sword will stay there as a permanent fixture."

Karl bent down and again using two fingers, retrieved the sword.

"Thank you," Grimmar said with a sigh of relief. "I'd hate to think that every time a customer came in he'd have to dance around the sword on the floor and I'd end up having to relate the tale of why it was there."

Karl placed the sword on the counter. "I'll take it." Reaching into his belt, he pulled out handfuls of coins until there were five neat stacks of ten gold coins each.

Grimmar smiled with satisfaction, scooping up the coins. "I'm glad to have finally found the rightful owner. Guard that sword with your life. Treat it like it was part of your body and never let it out of your sight. Should you lose that sword, it will take you a lifetime to find it again."

Congratulations: You have received Orc's Bane, exceedingly rare, one-of-a-kind; Damage: 45-60, Durability: 150/100.

Karl stared at the durability, at first wondering how something could be more than the maximum durability points then reasoned the sword could cut through everything it encountered.

"What about me?" Julie interrupted. "Don't I get a sword or something?"

"I have just the thing for the missus," Grimmar smiled, and pulled out a replica of Karl's sword, though just a bit smaller. "It too is an elven blade, but not like Orc's Bane. However," he added when he saw her disappointment, "this blade will hum when it feels an orc presence. Watch."

As Grimmar brought the blade closer to the orc dagger, it began to hum a low resonating tone, increasing in volume and pitch the closer it came to the dagger.

"What's the benefit of a humming sword?" Karl asked, cocking an eyebrow.

"The noise disorients orcs, and the pitch causes them pain."

"How close do you have to be to for it to work?"

"You see how it hummed and this is just an orc weapon," Grimmar said, pointing at the orc dagger. "The sword will react if a real orc is within 100 meters. The closer it comes, the higher the pitch until you can't hear it, but it drives orcs crazy." When he saw Karl's skeptical look, he added, "So I've been told."

Karl took the sword and balanced it in his hands. It was light like Orc's Bane. "How effective is it in a fight?"

"It's not Orc's Bane if that's what you mean," Grimmar replied. "But it is an elven blade, which means it is quite durable and effective."

Karl handed the sword to Julie who immediately brightened as she swung it around in a clumsy imitation of Karl's sword handling. "How much?"

"It too is not cheap. Twenty-five gold."

Julie turned to face Karl, giving him a child-like pleading look complete with protruding lower lip. "I'll make it worth your while."

Karl smirked as Grimmar snorted a loud laugh.

"How can you say no to that?" the gnome chortled.

"I can't," Karl agreed with a wide smile. "What'll you give me as trade for my weapons?" He brought out the rest of the weapons and laid them out on the counter. "I'll keep the crossbow and bolts and take some more bolts if you have them."

Grimmar looked at the lot and did a quick calculation. "I'll give you twelve gold for the lot, including the orc blade cut in half. I figure I owe you on that one."

"Done. Add in another dozen bolts for the crossbow if you have them."

"A dozen is too few, especially when you're in battle. You can carry more than that now that you've unloaded the weapons out of your bag. I sell a dozen bolts for one silver. You also can use a new crossbow."

"What's wrong with this one?"

"It's a beginner's crossbow. Feel the weight. Now try this one." He walked over to a display hook and pulled down a small finely crafted pistol grip crossbow. "This fires a smaller bolt, but the speed is faster, and the damage is the same or better." He handed the crossbow to Karl who marveled at the lightness and balance.

"How much?"

Grimmar did another mental calculation. "A new sword for the missus, new crossbow and three dozen bolts... thirty gold, and that's with a discount because Hemlin sent you."

"Done." Karl once again reached into his belt and counted out thirty gold pieces.

"Pleasure doing business with you, Viking," Grimmar said, sliding the coins across the countertop and into his waiting hand.

"The name's Karl," he said.

"Karl the Viking," Grimmar repeated with a wry smile. "No offense, but that's not exactly a name that's likely to strike terror into an enemy's heart."

"It soon will," he replied, wondering what happened to his reputation as local hero and folks knowing who he was.

"No offense."

"None taken. You're a good man, er... gnome, Grimmar. Whenever I come through here again, I'll be sure to give you my business."

"Tell all your friends," the gnome enthused.

"Will do. Now, where's a good mage or apothecary who deals with potions?"

"The best for your money is Lucinda. It's called Heaven's Elixir. You passed it on the way here."

Karl nodded, remembering a quaint shop that looked straight out of a Victorian movie set, complete with bay windows and ornate sign. With a friendly wave, Karl and Julie were back outside and heading towards Heaven's Elixir. Julie matched him stride for stride, both hands holding his left hand, proudly wearing her sword at her side.

"I've never had this much fun in my entire life," she gushed, feeling the sword slapping against her thigh. It gave her a feeling of power.

"It's the least I could do for the missus," he replied with half-lidded eyes.

"I'm sorry," she contritely said. "I didn't know what else to say. I didn't want him to think I was some silly woman you took a sudden fancy to."

"You are hardly a silly woman." He shifted his glance to once again take in her overwhelming beauty. "We need to get us some traveling clothes. And supplies, we'll need supplies."

Ho Uafas. Can you hear me? When no reply came, he tried again. *Uafas. Can you hear me?*

Faintly.

Where are you?

Heading towards the bridge crossing the river.

We're going to need another day. I need to get supplies. I should have thought about that sooner.

I understand.

Give us another day.

Same place?

Yes.

Bring me something special.

Karl chuckled. *Like what?*

Something sweet.

Anything in particular?

Use your imagination.

OK. See you day after tomorrow.

Standing outside Lucinda's shop, he turned to Julie. "We need to find something sweet for Uafas. Any ideas?"

"Apples are sweet."

"I guess," he replied, unconvinced an apple was special.

Opening the door to the shop, he allowed Julie to enter first then followed into a quaint store with shelves upon shelves of vials and powders and jars filled with herbs and poisons. Lucinda was busy helping an elf couple, both rangers, dressed in elven armor who appeared to be frustrated over their present financial resources.

Lucinda was an attractive middle-aged Halfling, with curly black hair that was held back with butterfly shaped barrettes. She wore a loose skirt and frilly blouse.

"I'll be with you in a moment," she said, her voice lilting and melodious.

"It's too much," the male elf said in a low voice to his partner. "We still need to find a place to stay and food to eat. And we still need supplies."

The woman elf pursed her lips and nodded. She was a tall shapely woman with long golden hair held back by an intricately tooled leather headband.

"Where are you headed?" Lucinda politely asked.

"Rhyeem," he answered.

Julie squeezed Karl's hand.

"How are you getting there?" Lucinda inquired.

"We were gonna go through the orc lands, but we don't have enough protection," the woman elf replied. "Looks like we're gonna have to take the long way around."

Julie twisted around to whisper in Karl's ear. "Do you think we ought to have them join us? The more of us there are, we'd have a better chance to get through."

Karl pondered the idea and squeezed her hand. "Pardon me," he said, causing the elves and Lucinda to turn look at him. "We're also heading to Rhyeem. Perhaps we should join forces."

The male elf shot his companion a glance that intimated he wasn't thrilled with the idea.

Lucinda shifted her gaze down to the sword on Karl's hip. "By the gods of the heavens and earth," she exclaimed, "you're wearing Orc's Bane." She strode over to stand before him, looking him all over. "You're the one." She reached out a hand and touched his face, causing a 'get-your-hands-off-him' scowl from Julie.

Ignoring Julie's penetrating look, Lucinda turned to look at to the elf couple. "You'd be fools not to take his offer. He's wearing Orc's Bane."

"What's Orc's Bane?" the woman elf asked, her hesitation of forming a group fading.

"It's a sword that only one person can wield. But more importantly, the person who wields the sword will rescue us from the depredations of the orcs." She studied Karl with overt approval then smiled. "Grimmar sent you here."

"Yes.   He said you were the best apothecary in Strathwick."

"It's true," she replied with self-assurance. "If you're looking for mana potions, antidotes, healing and even throwing potions, you've come to the right place."

"I'll wait 'til you're finished with them," Karl said.

Lucinda gave him another look of satisfaction then returned to the two elves. "Have you decided?"

"Almost," the woman elf replied then focused her attention at Karl. "How long do you expect it will take to get to Rhyeem?"

"Don't know," he shrugged.

"Before the orcs came, it was a three-day trip," Lucinda said, "by wagon. Now?" She shook her head. "If you can evade the orc patrols, it will take you four days or more... if you survive."

"The larger the group the harder it is to conceal," the male elf asserted, "and she doesn't look like much of a fighter." He cast a disdainful nod at Julie.

"Looks can be deceiving," Karl responded with a condescending chuckle. "For instance, I thought elves were supposed to be smart."

The male elf stiffened and glared at Karl. "What do you mean by that?"

"I don't *mean* anything by it. I'm merely stating a fact. Elves are supposed to be smart, correct?"

The male elf was tall and well-armed with a long bow and double swords and turned to face Karl. Curling a lip, he sneered, "Why should we team up with a Level 12 Viking? You're only one level higher than us. You and her would only hold us back."

Instead of taking offense, Karl grinned. "But we have a secret weapon."

"Like what?"

"If we told you, it wouldn't be a secret, would it?" Karl said, a not-so-subtle mocking in his tone.

"Bah," the elf retorted then turned his back on Karl and directed his attention to his companion. "Let's go find another apothecary," he contemptuously said, "one who is not so expensive."

"Remember the old adage," Karl interrupted, before Lucinda had a chance to reply. "You get what you pay for."

The elf snapped his head to scowl at Karl then glanced rapidly at everyone else. "We're done here," he announced and marched to the front door. He was half-way to the door when he realized his companion hadn't moved. Whirling around, he fixed her with an intense gaze.

"Well?"

"I'd like to hear more about his plan," she calmly replied.

"What?" he exclaimed. "I thought we were a team. He's got nothing we need. I could tell that as soon as he walked in. I got this covered. I know what's best for us."

"I said," she replied more firmly, "that I wanted to hear more about his plan."

"No," he tartly answered. "We've heard enough and we're leaving." He began to turn when she held her hand up, stopping him.

"No, *we* haven't heard enough. I said that I'm staying to listen to his plan. You said *you* were leaving."

The elf's mouth slacked open. "Are you kidding me? Caryn? You're really siding with him?"

"It has nothing to do with siding –"

"You got a choice to make right now, right this instant," he said, his anger rising. "You stay where you are and we're through. You understand? We're through. Finished. You come with me, right now, and I'll forget this whole thing happened." He folded his arms and waited.

"Goodbye Frank," she said, in a tone that Karl swore sounded relieved.

"What?" Frank stiffened to full height. "You're actually choosing that loser over me?"

"Goodbye Frank." She turned her back to him, pretending to examine the vials in the display case.

Frank remained in place, his shock morphing to hatred. "You'll pay for this, bitch. And you too," he threated Karl. "I'll see you again."

"Have a good day," Karl grinned, adding a cheery wave.

Frank spun around and stalked to the door, casting a final, "You all can go to hell," over his shoulder.

When the door slammed shut, Caryn stood up and sighed with a mixture of resignation and relief. Turning to the others, she gave them a weak smile. "Sorry. That was rather embarrassing."

"Only for him," Karl reassured her. "So your name is Caryn?"

"That's my real name. I have an elf name, but I suppose that really doesn't matter at the moment."

"Who was he?" Julie asked.

"He is… or was my boyfriend."

"Ouch," Karl winced in sympathy then frowned. "You both were diagnosed…?" He left the question unfinished.

"I was. He volunteered to come with me with the understanding that he could opt out at any time."

"Has he ever done it?"

"A number of times," she quietly replied. "The last time he was gone for a week. When he came back, he wasn't the same. He won't tell me what happened, but now when he tries to punch out, it doesn't work. Now that he's stuck here, he gets mad when things don't go his way. I mean *real* mad, like hissy fit mad. To me, this is my life and I've come to embrace it for all it is, a new adventure."

Karl stared kindly at her, debating whether he wished he could just 'punch out' and go home. Part of him said it was the rational thing to wish for. The other part said he was having a lot more fun than he could ever expect IRL.

Caryn's melancholy lasted only a minute more before she asked, "So what's your plan?"

"Well," he said, looking at her then Lucinda. "I came here on the excellent advice of a wise gnome to purchase as many potions as I can carry."

Caryn's eyes burst wide. "You have money to do that?"

"Yes. What ones were you looking at, Caryn?"

"I was looking at a mana potion and an agility potion," she said, casting a wistful glance at the vials in the display case.

"Which ones?"

"Those two there." She pointed at one vial with a sparling liquid and the other containing a pinkish liquid.

Karl turned to Lucinda. "I'll take three of each, plus I'll need a belt for Julie."

"Naturally," Lucinda said, dipping her head with satisfaction. She selected level appropriate vials of each potion and placed them on the counter then went to fetch Julie a belt.

Karl picked up two vials and handed them to Caryn. "Here ya go."

"I can't afford these," she blushed awkwardly.

"I've got it," he casually remarked then turned his attention back to the other potions.

"But... but..."

Karl gave her a warm smile. "You can pay me back some time later, if you feel you have to. If we're a team, we need to take care of each other."

Caryn stared at him then looked past him to Julie whose unmasked joy at being with Karl was almost comical. "Is he always like this?"

"For as long as I've known him," she replied with a wide smile.

"How long you two been together?"

"Oh, a couple of days," she brightly replied.

"A couple of days?" Caryn blinked, not getting the joke.

Lucinda returned with a belt for Julie who wrapped it around her harrow waist and pirouetted around the room in search of a mirror. Finding one towards the front door, she preened and clapped her hands.

"I'm beginning to look like a warrior."

"Yes, you are," Karl laughed. "Now come back here and help us finish. We still have to get you some clothes before we meet Sergeant Hemlin for a drink."

"You know Sergeant Hemlin?" Lucinda said, surprised.

"Met him on the way into the city. He struck me as a decent fellow."

"That he is.   He's one of the finest warriors in Strathwick, and one of the more trustworthy men in the city. You've done well to be friends with him."

"Can't say that we're friends yet, but I hope to remedy that."

By the time he was finished, Karl had potions for mana, speed, strength, endurance, agility, fire, and freeze in place. The total came to 42 gold.

"Can you recommend a place to outfit my charming warrior here?" he asked Lucinda.

"Wendell's Warrior Warehouse," she immediately answered.   "You passed it on the way here from Grimmar's place."

"Yes, I remember" he chuckled, recalling the store front with manikins ill fitted in men's and women's armor. "Also, where is the Feather's Nest?"

"The Feather's Nest?" she said, cocking an eyebrow. "You're going to stay at the Feather's Nest?"

"That's the plan."

"It's awfully expensive."

"So I've heard."

"The staff there is rather snooty."

"We'll manage."

She shrugged. "It's your money."

"Do you know a better place?"

"The Feather's Nest does have the best food and ale and the beds are unmatched," she admitted. "But if you're willing to eat good food and good ale and sleep in a good bed, there are other far cheaper places."

Karl twisted his head to gaze at Julie whose beaming face said she really didn't care where they were, as long as she was with him. "No. I'd rather we had the best place."

Lucinda saw the exchange and chuckled. "When are you leaving?"

"Day after tomorrow."

"Make the most of it then. Once you cross the river into the orc lands, you'll wish you had never left the city."

Karl gave her a confident grin and the three companions stepped outside.

"As you heard," Karl said to Caryn, "we're going to get her outfitted then spend the rest of the day dining with a friend and then to bed. We still need supplies but will do that tomorrow. You're welcome to join us for shopping and dinner, unless you have other plans. Otherwise, meet us tomorrow at the Feather's Nest, say around ten o'clock?"

Caryn thought for a moment. "While I'd like to take you up on your offer, I have a feeling I ought to get back and disconnect from the ex-boyfriend."

"I understand."

"I'll see you tomorrow at ten." With that, she ambled away towards the food market.

"She's not a very happy elf," Julie observed as Caryn walked away.

"You wouldn't be either if you were with him," Karl said, gazing after Caryn. Watching her walk away, he pondered what Annabeth and Raquel were doing at this very moment. A twinge of guilt pulsed when he cast a sideling glance at Julie, wondering how he was going to explain her when they finally caught up to the rest of the team. *I'm just getting her back to Rhyeem.*

He felt her hand slip into his and he felt his desire quicken followed immediately with an ominous foreboding that this former servant woman was going to be a problem.

She gazed up at him, devotion in her eyes. "Thank you for saving me. No one has ever escaped Tarrytown who was exiled into slavery. You're the first."

"Well," he said, looking up and down the thriving street. "It had to happen sometime. C'mon. Let's get you outfitted."

"You too," she smiled.

By the time they selected Julie's clothing and appropriate Viking garb for him then found their way to the Feather's Nest, Hemlin was standing outside waiting for them.

"Was beginning to wonder if ya stood me up," he grinned.

"Had to do a little shopping," Karl said, his arms full of wrapped packages. He tipped his head at Julie, whose arms were also full.

85

"Haw," Hemlin barked a laugh. "Say no more. C'mon. Let's get you settled." He was about to start up the steps when he saw the blade at Karl's side. "By the gods, you're wearin' Orc's Bane." He stuttered to a stop and studied Karl with newfound respect. "You're the one."

"Everyone keeps saying that," Karl muttered. "Why?"

"I'll explain over an ale. C'mon."

The Feather's Nest was a grand affair, four stories tall made of white granite with a wide portico supported by six Corinthian columns. Karl noticed the clientele gliding up the marble steps were the elite of the city, condescendingly arrogant to the staff who in turn were condescendingly arrogant to anyone they deemed unworthy of even standing on the steps of the upper crust establishment.

"I got a cousin who works here," Hemlin said, marching up the steps. "Tip folks whenever you can," he said out of the side of his mouth. "Usual tip is a silver."

"That's quite a tip," Karl observed, touching the money pouch of his belt with a reassuring pat.

"That's the kinda folks that stay here," Hemlin replied, sliding his eyes at a pompous woman in fur marching up the steps, two servants overloaded with boxes and clothing, struggling to keep up.

The doorman at the top of the stairs cast a haughty look at the approaching group until he recognized the man in front.

"Good day to you, Cousin," he said with a warm smile.

"Hullo Jared. Lookin' sharp as ever. These are two friends of mine."

Jared gave Karl a noncommittal appraising glance, while barely acknowledging Julie. "Welcome to the Feather's Nest," he said, his tone officious. "Will you be staying the evening?" The question implied that he doubted they could afford the drinks, let alone a room.

"Probably," Karl offhandedly replied. "Though I would have liked something better, a little more elegant, this will just have to do."

He brushed past the man whose pursed lips said he was not amused, especially when Hamlin smirked then cleared his throat.

Karl paused at the doors, waiting for a doorward to step lively and open a door for him. Instead, the doorward, a young man dressed in the gilded gold and white livery of the Feather's Nest, stood immobile, a look of bored disdain permanently fixed upon is face.

Karl stood only a moment longer then held a hand out to stop Hamlin from opening the door. Towering over the doorward, Karl fixed him with a hard stare, smiling at him with only his lips. "You have a choice, friend. You can either open the door for us, or I reach down your throat and rip your heart out."

Gaping up at the imposing Viking, the doorward slid around him and grabbed the door handle, yanking it wide open.

Karl reached into his belt pouch and fished out a silver coin, flipping it in the air at the doorward whose quick hands snatched the coin mid-air.

"I want to get a room first," Karl said over his shoulder to Hemlin before walking up to stand in a short queue in front of the wide receptionist desk. Casting glances around the foyer, he was impressed with the opulence. Tall marble colonnades supported an arched ceiling decorated in pastoral frescos. It was as he was admiring the suspended candelabras that he heard the voice.

"My how their standards have fallen," a woman staged whispered. "They let any of the riff raff just walk in off the streets."

Karl looked to his left to see a woman dressed in a finely wrought silk gown, her shoulders draped with animal furs, gazing at him with overt hauteur.

"I know," Karl sighed audibly. "I was wondering how you made it past the doorwards."

The woman's stunned shock was too much for Julie who started giggling. Hemlin turned away so as not to be recognized as he bit his lip to stop laughing.

Ignoring the vain aristocrat, Karl stepped to the desk when the well-dressed couple, assisted by two young porters struggling under the weight of the travel chest, moved on to their room. The receptionist, a clean-shaven slender man in his mid-thirties, dressed in a crisp white shirt buttoned to his neck, gave a slow disapproving gaze at Karl and his companions.

"Surely this is some sort of prank." He leaned to the side to stare past Karl as though searching for the person responsible for placing these indigents in the line.

"Listen Tinkerbell," Karl growled leaning on the table. "I want a room, one with a nice large bed and a bathtub big enough for two."

"My word, how crude," the aristocratic woman blurted.

"You stay out of this, bitch," Karl snapped, narrowing a hard glare at the receptionist. "I've spent the past week or so killing orcs, goblins, giant spiders, and gnolls, so I'm a little testy right now. I want a room and I want it now." He was going to add succubi but thought better of it.

The man stiffened in fright when Hemlin stepped up and pointed to the sword on Karl's side.

"He's wearing Orc's Bane."

A hush descended on the room until a voice suddenly uttered, "He's the one."

"Is that really Orc's Bane?" the receptionist asked in awe.

Karl pulled the sword out and placed it on the counter. "Pick it up."

The man gaped at it a moment before reaching a hesitant hand and wrapping his fingers around the hilt. With a grunt he tried lifting it to no avail. Using two hands, he could not budge the sword.

"I can't," the man declared with glee.

"Here, let me try," a burly man in expensive jacket and leggings declared, pushing his way to the desk. Shooting a quick glance around the expectant faces, he positioned himself by the sword. A hand shot out and he grasped the hilt. Expecting the sword to yield, he jerked at it only to feel a spasm in his back when the sword remained locked in place.

"My God, I've injured myself," he moaned, hunching over, holding his arm close to his chest. "Get me a physician," he snarled at the receptionist.

With a bemused smile, Karl gazed at the rest of the onlookers. "Anyone else?" When no one else moved, he picked up the sword with his thumb and forefinger and placed it back in the scabbard.

Turning back to the receptionist, he said, "Now about that room."

Fifteen minutes later, Karl and Julie joined Hemlin who waited patiently outside the door to the bar.

"I thought you'd have a significant head start by now," Karl teased, ticking his head at the posh bar.

"Not my kind of people," Hemlin replied, rolling his eyes then gazing in at the bar where a number of well-heeled guests were chatting, occasionally casting supercilious glances at the doorway. "There's another bar in the hotel here were the lesser folk go."

"Nonsense," Karl breezily answered then pushed his way through the bar.

The barkeep, seeing him approach, shot him a haughty glare and purposely moved away to another part of the bar to attend and chat with a patron.

Smacking his hand on the counter, Karl called out, "Hey you, shit-for-brains, we'd like some service."

"Watch your tongue," an older man wearing an expensive fur vest reprimanded.

Karl smiled at him. "Nice vest. What is it? Roadkill?"

As the man's mouth gaped open in shock, the barkeep hurried over. "I advise you to watch your language," he snapped. "This is a respectable establishment."

"If it's such a respectable place, how come you're working here?"

"I don't have to take this," he coldly taunted then stalked over to the edge of the bar, flipped open part of the counter and bustled out, returning quickly with the hotel's enforcer, a large broad-shouldered man with brooding eyes. Pointing to Karl, the barkeep testily demanded, "I want him removed."

The enforcer took look at the tall muscular Viking and then at the sword at his side. "Is it true?"

"Is what true?" Karl carelessly replied.

"Is that Orc's Bane you wear?"

"It is."

The enforcer turned to the barkeep. "Treat him well. Give him whatever he wants. Put it on my account."

"There's no need to do that, friend," Karl amiably said, "though it is a considerate and kind gesture. We can pay for our own drinks. All we ask is that shit-for-brains here treat us like he would any other patron."

"See what I mean?" the barkeep whined.

The enforcer's lips tightened before he spoke. "I would ask that you refrain from such colorful language."

"Because you asked it," Karl gallantly answered, dipping his head, "I will be happy to oblige. I will call him 'Dung-for-brains' from now on. Is that better?"

The enforcer smirked then resumed his serous demeanor, returning his attention to the barkeep. "As I said, treat him well." With that, he gave Karl a polite nod of respect and departed.

"Now that we're all buddies" Karl cheerily said, smiling at the barkeep, "my friends and I would like a drink."

With a baffled stare at the disappearing enforcer, the barkeep turned back to the grinning Viking and politely asked, "What may I get you?"

"I'll take a mug of your best ale."

While Hemlin ordered the same and Julie ordered a glass of sweet white wine, Karl led the way to a table offering more privacy. Once seated, he turned to Hemlin.

"So what's with all the deference because I have a sword?"

"It's not just a *sword*," Hemlin emphasized.

"Yes, I get it," Karl interrupted. "It's Orc's Bane. What else is it?"

Hemlin stared at him for a fleeting moment. "There is a prophesy associated with the sword. It is said that the one who can wield the sword will rid the land of orcs and unite the separate kingdoms into one nation. He and his sons will rule for a thousand years."

"That's quite a tall order," Karl opined, wondering not only how he would accomplish that, but how the game developers would incorporate PCs having children and if that was even possible. Casting a side glance at Julie who sat demurely sipping her wine, he admitted that if they could make sex with an NPC possible then they probably could generate children. He frowned in thought, trying to remember if he had seen any pregnant NPCs and none came to mind.

The real question was, why would they even want NPCs reproducing? It served no purpose that he could see. Besides, the entire game was a sort of suspended animation. No one aged. Even the children who gamboled in the various town and villages would remain children forever.

Momentarily lost in his thoughts, he didn't notice two officious looking men enter the bar, scan the occupants then make a beeline towards his table. He glanced up when he felt their approach.

"Are you the one called Karl the Viking?" the older of the two men asked. He wore a vest with a gold and crimson chest patch of the Strathwick crest of a double headed hawk clutching a bundle of arrows in both claws.

"I am he," Karl replied, deciding not to be flippant.

"Burgrave Eljyn desires the presence of your company."

"Burgrave Eljyn?"

"The city magistrate," Hemlin explained.

"Why would he want to see me?" Karl politely asked.

Instead of replying, the man glanced down at the sword on Karl's side.

"Ah yes," Karl chuckled. "How could I forget." Standing, he placed a firm hand on Hemlin's shoulder while looking at Julie. "I leave you in the capable hands of our friend here. You two enjoy yourselves until I get back." Turning to Hemlin, he said, "Drink to your heart's content. Make sure Mister Dung-for-brains takes good care of you. I'll settle up when I get back."

Hemlin snorted a laugh for at that very moment, the barkeep approached the table, his sour look revealing he had heard the comment.

Twenty minutes later, Karl stood in the reception hall of the city's Burgrave. The room was large and tall with a wooden ceiling resting on thick wooden crossbeams. Finely woven tapestries of hunting scenes hung over smooth stone walls. Seated at the far end of the hall on a raised platform, a grand fireplace behind him, sat the Burgrave, a somber man who rarely smiled. He wore the chained medallion of office around his neck. Otherwise, his clothing was nondescript as though he were just an everyday average merchant.

He looked up when Karl and his escort entered. Beckoning them forward, Karl strode confidently across the floor, the two escorts hurrying to keep pace.

"You wished to see me m'Lord?"

Though flattered at the appellation, the Burgrave politely demurred. "I am not a lord, good Sir, but merely the servant of the people." He motioned for the two escort to remain in place. "I have asked you here to inquire if the news is true."

Understanding, Karl unsheathed his sword and placed it on the floor before him. "Ask either one of these fine gentlemen to pick it up."

The Burgrave twisted his head to stare at the younger of the escorts, a wide shouldered young man in his prime. "You, sir, if you please."

The young man bent down, grasping the sword by the hilt and struggled to lift it, eventually using two hands then down on his knees, straining to move it even a fraction.

"I can't, Burgrave Eljyn," he grunted, finally yielding and standing.

"Shall I try?" the older escort offered.

"No need," the Burgrave replied, shaking his head.

Karl bent down and with two fingers lifted the sword and placed it back in the scabbard.

The Burgrave nodded. Whether he was pleased or impressed was impossible to tell. Addressing Karl, he intoned, "The resources of the city are at your pleasure.

Anything and everything you need or desire is yours for the asking."

"In return for what?" Karl demanded.

"In return for fulfilling your destiny," the Burgrave answered, as though there was no doubt as to why. "The sword has claimed you. You have no other choice."

Quest Alert: You have been bonded with the sword called Orc's Bane. To use the sword requires that you accept this quest, which is to destroy the orc kingdom of Krug and unite the various kingdoms and the separate and independent cities on the island into a unified nation.

Reward: Unlimited access to supplies, scrolls, potions, and weapons currently in the town; you and your descendants will rule the nation for the next 1000 years.

Do you accept this quest? Yes   No   Failure to accept this quest renders the sword inoperable. Neither you nor anyone else can use the sword unless or until that time you accept this quest.

"Well that sucks," Karl muttered. "I'm stuck anyway I look at it." With a longsuffering sigh he pressed the 'Yes' icon.

Waiting patiently, the Burgrave shifted his attention to the older guard, handing him a scrolled parchment. "Our Lord will need supplies, additional weapons, and victuals. There may be a few who are hesitant. This will allay their reluctance."

Standing, he descended the dais and dropped to his knee in obeisance. "The city is yours to command, m'Lord. All I ask is that you remember my years of faithful service when you assume the throne."

Startled, Karl frowned wondering how much of this charade he was expected to play, though the thought of ruling a kingdom sounded inviting. Still, if the object of the game was to get to the last island, why was this even an option... unless there was some other twisted reason for it.

Realizing the man was waiting for direction, Karl gently touched him on the shoulder. "Get up. I'm not a king yet."

The Burgrave pushed himself to standing.

"But there is one other thing you can help me with. I'm looking for some friends of mine. We got separated a few days ago. One of them you can't miss, a big hulking berserker."

"There have been few strangers here, m'Lord. The most recent are two elves, not quite husband and wife, but together, if you understand my meaning."

"I do," Karl grinned, "and I think they might not be as together as they let on. I'd keep an eye on the male elf. Something about him that I don't trust."

"Yes, m'Lord. And the woman elf?"

"She's OK." Karl quickly punched up his personal screen, frustrated that the map still only provided the barest of details. "Maps. I'll need the best maps you have."

"Of course, m'Lord," the Burgrave dipped his head. "How many of the city's warriors would you like to accompany you?"

"None," Karl replied, much to the Burgrave's relief. "Once I reconnect with my team, we'll take it from there. Oh," Karl added suddenly remembering Uafas. "I have a rather unique friend outside the city walls. I don't expect any trouble with him, but you should warn your soldiers when they do their patrols that should they see a wolf the size of a small tavern, to leave him alone. He's my friend."

The Burgrave's eyes blinked wide. "Yes m'Lord."

"Thank you. Is there anything else you needed from me?"

The Burgrave hesitated before saying, "My position here, m'Lord?"

"What about it?"

"Do you wish me to continue?"

"Of course. Why wouldn't I?"

The Burgrave visibly relaxed. "Not everyone is happy with my decisions."

Karl studied the man then grinned. "Sounds to me like someone might be vying for your position."

"You have immediately surmised the problem," the Burgrave smiled for the first time.

"Tell him to stand down. Tell him I said so. Tell him that if I find out he's creating problems, I'll come back here and skin him alive."

"Yes, m'Lord," the Burgrave replied with satisfaction.

The door thrust open and a fashionably dressed, handsome man of obvious wealth strode in. His dark wavy hair came down to his shoulders. Unlike many in the city, he was clean-shaven for an overt display of his chiseled face.

"So you're the one everyone's talking about," he said, his voice a rich baritone striding up as though one in charge.

"Who are you?" Karl asked, immediately not liking the man.

"He's the one I was telling you about, m'Lord," the Burgrave confided.

"Spreading lies again, Eljyn," the man dismissively replied. Turning to Karl he ticked his head in begrudging respect. "The name's Ronyn. Hopefully I've arrived in time to dissuade you from making a perilous mistake."

"And what mistake would that be?"

"Keeping this tiresome individual as Burgrave. What the city needs is new blood, new ideas, and a new man to implement those new ideas."

"And what new ideas do you have in mind?" Karl quizzed.

"I'm glad you asked," he replied with enthusiasm. "The first is that the tax base is far too low. Raise the taxes, I say, and use the money for the indigent and poor."

"Interesting," Karl said, feigning curiosity. "Would everyone pay taxes?"

"Naturally," Ronyn suavely answered.

"So let me see if I understand your proposal." Karl stoked his chin as if in deep consideration. "You would raise taxes on the poor and indigent so that you could give them back their own money. You would tax merchants more causing them to raise prices to maintain their previous profits."

"Um," Ronyn waffled, "perhaps we should raise taxes on those who can afford it."

"The rich you mean? So you're willing to raise your own taxes? By how much?"

"Uh… Well that it, I, uh."

"Come, come, good sir," Karl challenged. "What say you to ten percent more? Surely that should provide ample income to pay for the poor and indigent." Karl turned to Eljyn. "Do we not have a listing of every citizen in the city?"

"Yes, m'Lord."

"Excellent," Karl grinned. "Let's see what support good Ronyn here has for his fiscal ideas. Inform everyone whose income is anywhere near Ronyn's that he demands they pay another ten percent of their income for the good of the city."

He turned back to Ronyn. "When would you like to begin your tax hike? Shall we say at the beginning of next month?"

Realizing he had been out-maneuvered, Ronyn graciously smiled. "Perhaps my plan was not fully developed."

"Nonsense," Karl admonished. "Your motivation to help the poor is commendable. Therefore, I charge you to convince your peers that it is likewise in their best interests to raise their own taxes. When do you think you will accomplish this? Is a week enough time?"

Ronyn stiffened. "I… I'm not sure they will be receptive."

"Now how can that be? Surely you've convinced them that you ought to be burgrave. I imagine you've offered them ample promises to gain their support. Now show me that you can run this city by getting them to agree to raise their taxes. And now that I think about it, ten percent does not seem to be sufficient. I think twenty percent is a more appropriate amount, don't you?" Karl folded his arms and leveled a stern stare at him.

Ronyn's eyes widened. "They'll never agree to that."

"Then you are wasting my time," Karl snapped. "Either you convince them of a twenty percent tax increase, or you go about your business and leave the affairs of the city to Burgrave Eljyn."

"You have no right to do that," Ronyn huffed.

"He does," Eljyn countered.

In one smooth motion, Karl slid Orc's Bane out of the scabbard and tossed it at Ronyn, hilt first.

Expecting to easily catch the sword, Ronyn was shocked when the weight of the sword crashed in on him, knocking him off his feet. Before he could raise himself off the floor, Karl had already retrieved the sword and towered above him, the tip of the blade pointing close to where he lay.

"Get out of here," Karl threatened, "before I forget I'm a gentleman."

Ronyn scrambled to his feet, brushing off his clothing in the process. His first instinct was to verbally lash out, but his self-preservation took over and he humbled himself. "Of course, m'Lord. I apologize for my behavior. It will be as you wish."

"That's better," Karl relaxed and smiled, sheathing his sword. "Good day to you."

"Good day, m'Lord." With a respectful bow, he turned and briskly paraded away.

Waiting until he was gone, Eljyn said, "Well played, m'Lord, though I wouldn't trust him."

"I don't," Karl chuckled, "which is why you'll need to keep an eye on him."

"I will, m'Lord."

"Now, if you've got nothing else for me at the moment, I really should return and rescue my friend Hamlin from the boorish behavior of those at the Feather's Nest."

"Hamlin?" Eljyn repeated. "He's a good man, m'Lord. Trustworthy and smart. If you ever need a future leader, he'd be my choice."

"I'll take that as sound advice." Giving Eljyn a reassuring pat on the shoulder, Karl strode confidently back to the waiting Hamlin and Julie.

"Well?" Hamlin asked with a curious smile. "Everything OK?"

"Absolutely," Karl answered, sliding into a chair next to Julie. "I like him. He's a good man." Twisting his head to gaze at Julie, he frowned to see her staring at him all googly eyed. "How many has she had?"

"That's her fourth glass," Hamlin smirked.

Karl smiled and shook his head. "Looks like I probably need to get her upstairs."

"Need any help?"

"Naw, I'll just toss her over my shoulder."

Hamlin guffawed and stood up, imagining what the proper folks in the hotel would do if they saw a Viking with a beautiful woman thrown over his shoulder, marching up the steps to his room.

"Have a good night," Hamlin grinned. "Thanks for the drinks."

Chapter 4

Karl lay on his back, hands behind his head, physically exhausted, wishing he was asleep, frustrated his mind wouldn't settle down. Beside him, curled on her side, lay the beautiful Julie, her breathing shallow as one in deep sleep.

He smiled despite his tiredness. Even as tipsy as she was, the woman had been voracious and exquisitely satisfying, on par, to say the least, with Raquel and Annabeth. And that's what caused his present sleeplessness. How could an artificial character, a NPC, cause him to feel such pleasure? How was it possible for her to display all the traits of a flesh and blood human? After all, she was merely the creation of some character designer. Yet if he were to place Julie next to Raquel and Annabeth... or Gwen, he would be hard pressed to say who was more human than the others.

Then he remembered his initial game briefing when Hans said, *NPCs are every bit as human as you are. Though they are computer generated, they have emotions and feelings and everything else, just like you.* It abruptly occurred to him that in his present condition, he was not much different from Julie or Gwen. The only difference was that he had a past, memories.

Then he wondered if an NPC could have memories? If so, they had to be artificial beyond a certain point. Julie would probably "remember" her past in Tarrytown. But how much of a past did she have beyond then? When the character designer developed her, he certainly didn't begin with her at birth. And if that was the case, that meant the connection to the House of Rhyeem was artificial, contrived.

Karl let out a sigh of frustration. *Go to sleep, damn it.*

He rolled over and tried to get comfortable. *What does it matter if it's contrived? The whole damned game is contrived. Julie is merely another quest, another challenge to keep me occupied, an entertainment of sorts... not much different than real life.   We all run around looking for gratification, entertainment... and power.   Sort of like what Hobbes says in* Leviathan; *the inclination of all mankind is the perpetual and restless desire of power after power that ceases only after death.   Is that what I'm doing here?   And in the end does it really matter?*

Karl rolled onto his back, huffing in irritation. *So now I'm pretending to be a philosopher.*

Slipping the covers off, he scooted out of bed and crossed to the windows that overlooked the wide boulevard, silent now in the dark hours before dawn.   Flickering streetlamps lined the edges, eventually fading and disappearing in the distance.

Do I miss my old life, my real-life life?   He stared absently at a streetlamp. *Not really.   I'm having far more fun now than I ever did in real life.   And I'm still alive.   I don't know how it works, but I'll take it.   Weird that a part of me hopes they never find a cure.   But I do miss Raquel and Annabeth and the others.*   He looked over his shoulder at Julie. *Wonder why the House of Rhyeem is so interested in her.*

Yawning, he padded back to the bed and slipped under the covers.   For some reason the battle in Westhaven solidified in his thoughts.   Overlapping images of the tunnel, the night raid on the enemy camp, the next day's fighting, and Gwen morphed into his journey to the bridge and Gillien and he was soon asleep.

The smell of coffee permeated his dreams, and he blinked his eyes open, momentarily at a loss as to where he was. Sunlight poked through the gap in the window curtains. As Julie tiptoed past the bed towards a small side table, clarity coalesced. He watched her as she did her best to be quiet, holding a tray with a coffee urn, cups, cream, and sugar.

"Good morning," he said, rubbing his eyes. "What time is it?"

"Middle of the morning, sleepyhead," she replied with a sweet smile. Pouring a cup of coffee, she sashayed over to where he sat on the edge of the bed. "Hamlin came by and I told him you were still asleep. He said he'd come back later."

A knock on the door caused their heads to swivel towards the offending sound.

"Now what?" Karl grumbled.

Julie opened the door to a solemn Burgrave Eljyn.

"Is he available?" Eljyn quietly asked.

Casting a glance over her shoulder, Julie saw Karl hurriedly donning trousers and a shirt. Waiting until he was somewhat presentable, she turned back to Eljyn. "Yes. Please come in."

Eljyn strode across the room to stand before Karl. "My apologies, m'Lord, but terrible news."

Taking a sip of coffee, Karl motioned for Eljyn to sit while he sat on the edge of the rumpled bed. "What."

"A family to the south of the city were killed yesterday, most likely in the afternoon or later after the patrols went through. Hamlin discovered the bodies this morning."

"How many dead?"

"Five. Mother and father and three children."

"Orcs?"

"Most likely, m'Lord," Eljyn replied, his face stoic. "We've seen an increase in activity recently. This family refused to use the shelter of the city. They've paid a heavy price for their desire of freedom."

"Any others?"

"A few still harbor the belief that they are safe behind the locked doors of their homesteads."

Another knock interrupted their discourse and Julie bustled over to let Hamlin in.

"Just the man we were talking about," Karl smiled at him. "Tell me what happened."

"Looks to me like they were surprised," Hamlin said, eyeing the coffee urn.

"Help yourself," Karl chuckled. "Eljyn?"

"I'm fine, thank you, m'Lord."

"The door wasn't forced," Hamlin explained, pouring a cup of coffee, "which means they hadn't yet settled for the night."

"Your thoughts?" Karl asked.

"They probably got hit in the early evening. From the mess of it, the parents were killed... butchered might be a better word. No sign of the children which means they were probably taken as slaves. What cattle they had are also gone." He took a savoring sip of his hot brew.

Karl turned to Eljyn. "Spread the word of what happened to this family. Tell those who refuse to use the refuge of the city that they are now on their own. We will no longer send patrols out to secure their safety."

"M'Lord?" Eljyn sputtered, aghast.

"My guess is that once they hear the news, they'll be more likely to reconsider their choices. Secondly, how many warriors, fit enough to do battle, does the city have?"

Though Eljyn knew the answer, he looked at Hamlin.

Before Hamlin could respond, a pounding on the door interrupted, causing Karl to frown. Julie was halfway out of her seat when the door thrust open, and a tall well-built middle-aged man strode in. Shooting a quick glance at the occupants, he scowled when he saw Hamlin.

"You're dismissed, sergeant."

As Hamlin was about to place his coffee cup on the table, Karl held out a hand for him to stop.

"And who are you?" Karl asked, smiling with only his lips.

"This is General Lennach," Eljyn answered for him.

Karl took in the man. Lennach was not as tall as he was, though he had the same muscular arms and legs. He wore the dress uniform of an officer, complete with epaulettes. Lennach's dark hair was cut short as was his beard. He had the aura of one used to being in charge. Karl did notice though that despite the vigor, the man had the beginnings of a paunch. He had seen the same before when he was with the Widow-makers, men used to battle pushed up to higher positions of responsibility, which meant they became desk-bound, their once taught and fit bodies sloughing off the hardness as inactivity robbed them of their strength.

"Then you can answer my question, General," Karl said. "How many warriors, fit enough to do battle, does the city have?"

Giving Hamlin a stern glare, Lennach said, "I gave you an order, sergeant."

"And I told him to remain," Karl said, his voice calm though firm. "Now answer my question, General."

Lennach stiffened and gave Hamlin an evil snarl before turning to Karl. "You may have fooled some around here, but you don't fool me. We'll settle this man-to-man."

"Lennach," Eljyn snapped. "Think what you are doing."

"It's alright," Karl said with a smile. "When and where?"

"The sparring circle in the barracks compound. One hour," he answered with a haughty sniff.

"I'll be there," Karl grinned then turned to Eljyn. "Ensure the entire city is witness, or at least as many as possible."

"Yes, m'Lord," he somberly replied, rising.

Karl then twisted his head to smile at Hamlin. "You better go, for now. We'll talk more after this is over."

"You assume too much," Lennach scoffed. "We fight to the death."

"Yes," Karl impatiently retorted, "I got that. If you've nothing else to contribute, perhaps you can stop wasting my time. I'll see you in one hour."

Lennach's lips pursed as he straightened to full height, spun around and stalked out, calling over his shoulder, "Sergeant."

As Hamlin hustled to follow the general, Eljyn warned, "Be careful, m'Lord. Lennach is the city's best fighter. He's crafty and dangerous."

"Thanks for the warning. It'll be fine. You'll see."

"Yes, m'Lord," he answered, unconvinced.

The crowds surrounding the sparring pit overflowed and people jostled for a better view. The second story balconied walkways of the barracks surrounding the pit were likewise jammed with some sitting on the ledges while others stood shoulder to shoulder. Eljyn stood in the center waiting for the combatants.

Lennach was the first to enter. He was bare-chested and carried a sword and buckler.

Karl stood behind the crowd, two vials in his left hand. Uncorking one, he downed the contents of the speed potion, followed by the entire contents of the strength potion. Handing the vials to a frightened Julie, he smiled with self-assurance.

"Don't worry. It's all good." Already he could feel the speed potion coursing through his body.

"I hope you know what you're doing," Caryn said as she walked up.

"Like I told her, it's all good," he replied with a confident smile.

Caryn glanced down at the vials and smirked. "Don't make it too obvious."

Knowing he had ten minutes until the effects vanished, he gave Julie a quick kiss and pushed through the crowds, forcibly slowing himself down then stopping opposite Lennach.

Frustrated, Eljyn shook his head, but proceeded. In a loud resonating voice, he said, "The rules are simple. You fight until one of you is dead... or the champion agrees to spare your life."

"It won't happen," Lennach snarled.

Karl replied with a flippant shrug.

"You may not fight outside the circle," Eljyn continued. "If one of you is forced outside the circle, the other must move to the center and wait for the opponent to return before resuming the contest. Questions?"

The two combatants shook their heads 'No,' impassively staring at each other. Eljyn exited the circle to stand at the edge of the sparring circle where the rest of the council stood.

"Begin," he commanded.

Lennach attacked first, leaping high and fast, his shield swinging outward to ward off counterblows while simultaneously striking overhand and slicing down. Karl moved at the same time and Lennach was shocked to find no one in front of him. Instead, he felt pain as Karl's sword entered the side of Lennach's ribs, penetrating about a knuckle's depth. Blood immediately began flowing.

Surprised he had been wounded so soon, Lennach spun around to face him, his eyes hard with anger. Ignoring the pain, he focused his attention on the Viking, gazing at his eyes, but keenly aware of his sword and posture. Suddenly sensing Karl's guard down ever so slightly, he leapt again.

Instead of falling back or dodging, Karl was on him in an instant and instead of a clashing of swords, Karl's thin blade sliced through Lennach's hardened steel blade cutting it in half, the top half falling to the ground amidst the startled and loud "ooh's" of the crowd.

Shocked, Lennach stared at the half blade then at the Viking who held back. Sensing Karl wouldn't attack, he impatiently yelled, "A sword."

A moment later, another sword was tossed out into the pit.

Karl backed up, allowing Lennach to collect the new blade then in a blur met him head on. Bucklers clashed with loud viciousness and once again Lennach's sword was sliced in half. But this time, he felt tingling numbness from the impact of the bucklers.

While blood oozed out of his wound and down his hip, Lennach's confidence began to wane as he felt his strength and stamina diminishing. Looking at his opponent, doubt crept in as to the wisdom of his challenge. Before him, Karl balanced lightly on his feet, gauging and measuring him. For a moment, the thought passed that the Viking might be toying with him. Anxiety passed into anger that he was giving into fear.

Lennach leapt again, but in an eye-blink sooner, Karl too had launched himself into the air so that the force of his power and strength came crashing against Lennach's buckler. The crowd heard it, an audible snap. Lennach felt the surging pain as his arm went limp and he stumbled to his knees. His arm was broken, the buckler slipped from his hand into the dirt.

Stepping inside the circle, Eljyn implored the General. "You are in no condition to continue. Do you really wish to die like this?"

Lennach scowled at him. To yield now was to admit defeat. Where was the honor there? Without a word, his broken arm hanging limply at his side, he forced himself to stand. Snarling, he defiantly raised what remained of his sword and pressed the attack.

Karl easily parried his thrusts and jabs, truly making him angry, for now he *was* playing with him. Standing at the edge of the circle, Lennach panted like a wounded animal, staring at the Viking as he patiently waited for him to continue the contest. Intently focusing on his opponent, an odd thought emerged; perhaps he had been wrong. Perhaps the Viking really was the promised one. Yet his mind raced with what to do. To yield now would be to publicly admit he was wrong. To continue meant death. Casting a sharp glance around the training arena, he saw the crowd watching him the thrill of the fight dissipating. They almost seemed bored.

Inhaling deeply, he made his choice and straightened to full height. Slowly spinning his half sword, he moved towards Karl, his wary approach announcing his intentions. His resolve stiffened when he saw the Viking shake his head at him, his disdain obvious.

"Do you really want to die?" Karl taunted, standing firm and aloof. "Think about what you are about to do. Is your pride worth that much?"

Lennach swallowed, staring at the man, silently debating his own future. He would no longer be general and would thus live in embarrassment the rest of his life. The answer was made for him.

Karl saw the decision and instead of waiting for him to attack, he carried the force of his strength against him, driving him back to the stones that marked the edge of the match circle, finally forcing him to step out. Calmly watching him, Karl walked backwards to the center, waiting for him to reenter.

That he had been forced out fueled Lennach's frustration and anger. Jerking his foot back in, he quickly approached and attacked, only to find himself again yielding ground under the weight of Karl's attack. Repeatedly he was pushed outside the circle.

Exhausted by now, he panted heavily, his left arm broken, his right arm a dead weight. His body a sheen of sweat, he felt light-headed. But his will would not allow him to yield. Stumbling forward, he again attacked.

Karl easily parried his weak blows, the effect of the potions beginning to wane. Then, deciding enough was enough and using the last bits of extra speed and strength, he zipped in and in a crashing arc, smashed the loop guard of his sword against Lennach's skull.

Out of the corner of his left eye, the General saw the sword basket sweeping towards his head and pain burst before the world went black.

Karl stood over his opponent. Instead of killing him, he had delivered a powerful stroke and knocked him out. Now the once proud general lay at his feet, a crumbled destroyed man. Sighing with disappointment, he turned and casually strode to where Eljyn stood.

"That was too easy," he said as though genuinely let down.

Cheers erupted and the crowds poured onto the sparring circle, carefully avoiding the prone general.

"You let him live," Eljyn observed. "He would not have been so generous had the roles been reversed."

"It seems a shame to kill an able-bodied fighter. The city still needs all its soldiers. However, he can no longer command them." He scanned the crowd until he found Hamlin, whose face reflected relief at the result. "Sergeant Hamlin, would you please come here."

Pushing through the crowd, he hurried to Karl's side. "Yes, m'Lord?"

Karl was about to utter a complaint of "Not you too," but decided to leave it for now. Maybe being a king wasn't so bad. Everyone wanted to be your friend.

"Assemble the military leadership in the Burgrave's office."

"Yes, m'Lord." He was gone before Karl had a chance to explain what to expect.

Now that the challenge was over and the winner declared, the crowd drifted away to retell the story, embellishing it to the point that Karl virtually became invisible he moved so fast. Several soldiers lifted the limp general and carried him to a physician, his severed blades already claimed as souvenirs.

By the time Karl and Eljyn returned to his office, Caryn and Julie in tow, Hamlin had assembled Strathwick's army leaders, which consisted of ten captains, five of whom were regimental commanders, the others staff officers. They stiffened to attention when Karl and Eljyn entered.

Karl scrutinized them. "Who are the regimental captains?"

Five held up their hands. Of the five, one was a woman and she actually looked the part of a battle-hardened leader. Yes, she was obviously attractive, tall and well-proportioned with long auburn hair held back in a ponytail. Her deep blue eyes held his as though anticipating his commands, wanting to be free of the confines of an office.

The others? While they looked somewhat fit, it was obvious to Karl that they led from the rear. They had the softened look of comfort. The rest of the staff fared worse. They were a mix of roly-poly officers who obviously received their positions from influence rather than talent.

Sergeant Hamlin stood by the door, hoping that Karl wouldn't notice him so he could stay and eavesdrop on the proceedings.

"What's your name?" Karl asked the woman captain.

"Rhan, m'Lord."

Karl already knew the woman's name, having pumped Eljyn for information on the walk back to his office.

"You are now General Rhan," Karl announced. "You are now the commander of Southwick's army."

"Yes, m'Lord." Though she tried to remain stoic, a smile of accomplishment flitted across her lips.

"Sergeant Hamlin is promoted to Captain Hamlin and will take over as captain of your regiment."

"Yes, m'Lord." If she was surprised or disappointed, it didn't show. Hamlin on the other hand was more than stunned as his mouth gaped open.

However, the announcement met with some resistance among the remaining officers whose low murmuring bubbled up.

Karl was about to tell them to shut up when Rhan interjected a firm commanding, "Silence. The matter is settled. When our Lord has released us, I want a status report from each of you."

Karl slid his eyes to Eljyn effectively telling him his advice on the new commander was more than appreciated.

"That's all I have for now. General and Captain Hamlin, if you would remain behind please."

Once the other officers filed out of the office, Karl addressed Rhan. "I sense some of these fine gentlemen need reassigning. Go through your leadership. Make changes where you believe necessary. Promote and demote as you see fit. I want a combat force ready by the time I get back. How many combat ready soldiers do we have now?"

"Each regiment has three cohorts of one hundred men and women," Rhan replied. "So theoretically, we have supposedly fifteen hundred battle ready soldiers. However, I can only speak for my regiment at this moment. I have two hundred eighty-seven battle ready soldiers. Thirteen are either with infirmities or on leave."

Karl smiled at the efficient report. "Get the rest to par. Do whatever you believe necessary. I want admin and supply folks also trained to combat readiness."

Rhan grinned. "With pleasure, m'Lord."

"You said 'when you get back'," Hamlin interrupted. "When will that be?"

"Hopefully no more than a couple of weeks... maybe longer." Turning his attention back to Rhan, he said, "Your mission, until I get back, is to eliminate orcs and any other problems in the surrounding areas. I'll explain future operations when I return."

"Yes, m'Lord."

"Is there anything else for me?" Karl asked.

"Are you sure you don't want additional forces with you, m'Lord," Rhan asked, "when you cross orc lands?"

"No," Karl answered, "not yet. For now, I want all of Strathwick's forces clearing the surrounding lands of orcs. I'll have follow-on missions when I return."

"Yes, m'Lord."

"Anything else?"

There was a pregnant pause before Hamlin said, "Are you sure I'm the right choice?"

"Yes," Karl smiled with kindness. "It's sort of like Eisenhower in World War Two."

"Who?"

"Uh, never mind. Just know that it was a sound decision. Now go and make me proud."

Hamlin grinned in reply. "Yes, my Lord."

It seemed half the city was there to send him off. Burgrave Eljyn stood at the front, content in his authority.

"If you need anything, m'Lord, we are at your service."

"I know, Eljyn. Thank you. I'll be back." Karl wasn't sure why he said that, nor if he even would ever be back, but it sounded sincere. With a final wave, Karl turned and headed down the road towards Beally, the last fortified city before the Orc kingdom. They were half a kilometer away from the city when Karl remembered and turned to Caryn.

"I forgot to tell you that we're meeting a friend along the way."

"I forgot all about Uafas," Julie innocently smiled.

"Uafas?"

"He's our wolf friend," she explained.

"You have a wolf as a friend?" Caryn sputtered.

"Not just any wolf," Julie proudly stated. "He's as big as a house. He's so big that the three of us can ride on his back."

Caryn regarded Karl with newfound admiration. "My God, so that's your secret weapon."

"Not all of it," Karl replied with an evasive smile.

"There's more?" Caryn marveled.

"He has friends," Julie interrupted. "I haven't met them yet. We have to find them first before we attack the orcs."

"Slow down, Amazon girl," Karl chuckled. "Let's enjoy this time of peace while we can. I have a feeling it's not going to last long. Let me see if I can find Uafas." *Uafas. You close by?*

I was wondering when you were going to show up.

Got delayed a bit in the city.

I sense the presence of another individual.

That's Caryn, an elf. She's coming with us. Where are you?

Other side of the river. Be cautious. There have been a few orc patrols scouting the area.

Karl turned to Caryn. "Uafas says that orcs are in the area."

"How'd you learn that?" she frowned.

"Telepathy."

"Sweet," she nodded with a smile.

I can see you, Uafas said. *When you cross the bridge, work your way to the tree line to your right. There's a clearing just inside between where the large tree spreads its branches over the road and the cluster of rocks.*

Once inside the clearing, Caryn stutter stepped backwards, bumping into Karl when Uafas emerged.

"My God, he's huge," she blurted.

"But he's sweet," Julie affirmed, walking over to give the wolf a hug.

Ignoring the comments, Karl walked up. *What's the status?*

Last orc patrol went through here a while ago, headed away from the river. They stayed inside the trees.

How many in the patrol?

Three.

Karl was about to tell Caryn about the orcs when he saw Uafas twitch his head and sniff the air. *What?*

I smell orc.

The same patrol from a while ago?

How should I know? All orcs smell the same.

They headed this way?

Uafas paused. *Yes.*

"We got company," Karl announced. "Orcs headed this way."

"What do we do?" Julie fretted, scooting closer to Karl.

"Get out of the way."

"Hide?"

"Until we see how many there are," Karl replied, noting that Uafas had already disappeared. Ducking into the bushes, they hunkered down and waited.

They heard them before they saw them. Karl noted that for a patrol, they were careless, loud, both by talking and the nonchalant way they stepped on dried branches and leaves. A child could have heard them.

There were three of them, emerging into the clearing.

"I sez we stop here," a grizzled orc with matted hair growled. "Ain't nuthin' happenin' around here."

"Orders sez we patrol and report back," another said. He wore a leather vest with shoulder plating.

"Orders don't say we gotta keep walkin'," the third orc, a smaller one with large lower tusks, argued. "We been goin' in circles. I sez we stop and eat. I'm hungry."

"Me too," the first one agreed, casting a slow look around the clearing. Satisfied, he unshouldered his pack and pulled out some rabbit jerky. Ignoring the other two, he sat down and started eating, laying his falchion within easy reach.

The smaller orc wasted no time and plopped down next to the first orc. Digging into his pack, he pulled out a dried leg bone.

"Where the hell you get that?" the orc seated next to him asked.

"Left over from yesterday," he grinned.

"Aw hell," the standing orc grunted. "Might as well join you. Ain't nuthin' gonna happen 'fore we get back." He sat next to the smaller orc, placed his falchion across his knees and opened his pack.

As the three orcs munched and talked, Karl looked at Julie and motioned her to stay put then focused on Caryn and her bow. By means of hand signals he made her understand that she was to take out the small orc in the middle.

Uafas. You there?

Yes.

You close by?

Yes. I am looking at their backs.

Caryn is going to take out the one in the middle. I'll take out the one with the shoulder armor. You can have the other one.

OK. When?

Let Cary shoot first then we attack.

I'm ready.

Karl locked his gaze on Caryn and nodded.

Notching an arrow, Caryn silently rose, pulled back the string and let fly.

The orc was mid-chew when the arrow pierced his throat and he gurgled and choked, dropping the leg bone. No sooner had the first arrow found its mark that two more arrows whizzed in and impaled his chest, thrusting out the back.

It happened so fast that his two companions watched him flop onto his back, quite dead before they saw the Viking leap out of the woods followed by a bone chilling howl behind them. Grabbing their falchions, they leaped to their feet, one facing Karl while the other turned to face the growing terror in the forest.

When Uafas burst out of the tree, the orc gave a yelp, backing up into his companion who was vainly trying to parry the Viking's sword only to discover his hardened steel blade sliced in half. Yet neither of them was aware that a ranger elf was merely biding her time for another shot.

Waiting until Karl had dodged a weak parry, Caryn sent an arrow speeding to its target, piercing the orc's head just above the ear and coming out the other side. The orc wavered a moment then crumbled.

Unaware of his partner's fate, the remaining orc stumbled backwards over the dead orc and into the range of Karl's deadly sword, which flicked out and severed the head off its body.

Uafas cocked his head to gaze at the dead orcs. *Do you mind if I eat? Don't know when I'll get the next chance.*

Help yourself, Karl chuckled, waving a hand at the corpses.

"O my God," Caryn blurted as Uafas tore into the flesh. "I forgot about that part."

"We move out once he's done. Nice shooting, by the way."

"Thanks," she sheepishly replied. "I know it would've been an easy kill for you. I just thought it would be a good idea to get it over with as quickly as possible."

"I agree. While he's dining on that one, let's check for anything of value on the others."

They were disappointed with the results as the collection totaled little more than four silver. Karl stared briefly at the remains then back up at the forest before activating his screen and pulling up the island map.

"It looks like it's about a day or two to get to Beally. Providing we have no more encounters with orcs and other things that go bump in the night, we should get there tomorrow, probably afternoon sometime. "

Caryn activated her personal screen, likewise pulling up the island map. "If the orc kingdom is beyond Beally, doesn't it seem like the orcs are far beyond their own territory?"

"I know," Karl answered with a nod. "I was thinking the same thing, which means we need to be extra cautious on the way to Beally. Everyone ready?"

Chapter 5

Listening on the earpiece, Felix paced the office, waving for Gerard to come as he concluded with a "Yes, Sir."

Gerard quietly opened the door and scooted over to plop into a comfortable overstuffed chair. He was a confident young man in his late twenties, dressed in designer jeans and polo shirt, and brown penny loafers. He looked like a model for some yacht advertisement.

Felix tapped the earpiece to end the call then gave Gerard a nondescript smile. "Talk to me about the second island and this whole prophecy thing. This is the first I've heard about it. Why is that even in the game? It seems intuitively counterproductive if we expect them to move from one island to the next. What's the incentive for Karl to leave if he's going to live in peace for a thousand years?"

"That's just it," Gerard answered. "He's in the game for the rest of his life, which is going to be a lot longer than a thousand years. What's the point in getting to the next island and the next one and the next one? At some point in time, he's going to say, 'I've had enough for a while. I'm just gonna stay here.' Why not let him make that decision? Besides there's going to come a point in time where he's going to get bored staying in one place and he's going to move on. This also gives the AI time to add more islands and deal with variables."

"Then what's the whole point of the game?" Felix frowned.

"Just like any other game," Gerard said, "adventure, mystery, surprises, excitement, and more. Real life is boring. Where are the dragons in real life? Where are the trolls or elves or magic swords? Where are the quests that give real purpose to a man or woman's life? That's the whole problem with real life. Mankind intrinsically yearns to be the hero or heroine, accomplishing quests against insurmountable odds.

115

Why else would Virgil's *Odyssey*, written thousands of years ago, still be the basic playbook of quest and adventure? Or how about *Beowolf?* Mankind hasn't changed. We still yearn for that thrill of danger."

Felix held up a hand to stop him from his over-enthusiastic explanation. "I get it. So why is Bridge Quest restricted to so few players?"

"MMORPGs can be unwieldy," Gerard explained. "Besides, with the plethora of games, there's no longer a need for so many MMORPGs. Think about how many games there are now… thousands upon thousands of them fulfilling anyone's fantasy, from the sublime to the kinky. And then, since a person can only get immersed into one game for life, they're being choosy in what game they select."

Felix frowned at him. "That's still doesn't answer my question. What makes Bridge Quest different from any other game? Why is it restricted to only a certain number of players and why the super-secret shroud over the whole game?"

Gerard stared at him for a moment, "You don't have a need to know."

"The hell I don't," Felix flared. "I just got off the phone with Landon. He wants me to personally brief him on the progress of Bridge Quest. Now either you tell me what's going on or I call Landon back and let you talk to him."

Gerard shook his head. "You are not cleared for the information."

Felix swung around his desk and pulled up his computer screen, twisting it so that Gerard could see it before tapping the connect to Landon's office. In a moment, Landon's secretary's visage appeared on the screen.

"Yes?" she politely said.

"If Mister Landon is available, I need him to settle a question of access to the Bridge Quest program."

"What seems to be the problem?" she asked, wanting clarification before bothering Landon.

"Mister Helm here refuses to give me the information I need to brief Mister Landon day after tomorrow, claiming I don't have a need to know."

The screen changed and Mister Landon's stern face filled the monitor. "I've got this Miss Whitmer."

"Yes, Sir," she said, though her avatar remained on the screen, indicating she was still listening.

"Mister Helm."

"Yes, Sir," Gerard replied with a gulp.

"Give Felix everything he requires," he said, his voice steely.

"But Sir, he doesn't have clearance –"

"Did you not hear what I told you?"

"But Sir –"

"Leave us," Landon commanded. "I will speak with Felix privately."

"Yes Sir," he meekly replied before scuttling out the door, closing it firmly behind him.

Landon waited until Felix nodded. "Get rid of him."

"With pleasure, Sir."

"Wait until after you've milked him for everything you need."

"Yes, Sir."

"Make it permanent."

Felix grinned. "I look forward to is, Sir."

"My apologies for not realizing this sooner. I'd forgotten some parts were still restricted. Now bring him back."

"Yes, Sir." Felix caught Gerard's attention, curling his fingers telling him to come back in.

Gerard approached the monitor so Landon could see him.

"I am the one who determines who gets access to everything in this organization. If I say Felix, or anyone else in this company needs this access then you give it to him. If I want the koi in your pond to have access to company information, you give it to him. Do you understand?"

"Yes, Sir." Gerard looked like a beat cur, wondering how Mister Landon knew he had a koi pond.

Landon looked back at Felix. "Any other concerns, Felix?"

"No Sir," he replied, thrilled that Mister Landon had called him by his first name in front of another employee.

"Carry on then," he smiled then the screen went blank.

Felix gave Gerard a hard stare. "You were saying?"

Gerard took a deep breath and settled himself. "Since Mister Landon commands it, I will do so, but I want written notification that I am doing so under his directive and not of my own volition."

"So be it," Felix said, pressing the record button on his console. "Per directive of Mister Landon this date and time, Gerard Helm is authorized to give Felix all information regarding Bridge Quest." Pressing the button to play the notation back, he looked up at him. "Satisfied?" He picked up his coffee mug, inhaling the piquant aroma.

"Yes. So, as instructed, Bridge Quest was originally designed as a means to assemble assassination teams to carry out hits in the real world."

"What?" Felix choked on his coffee.

"Why are you so surprised?" Gerard frowned with condescension. "It's not like we're the only ones who thought of it. Who do you think took out French President Babineaux?"

"We did?" Felix replied, aghast.

"Of course not," Gerard replied, shaking his head. "We're not there quite yet. The Russians did that. Quite proficiently if you ask me. It was a brilliant hit. By the time the police were called in, the Russian team was already back in their game."

Felix sipped his coffee, absorbing this latest bit of news, wondering how it was that he could be the CEO of a company and not know what's going on. But then, he was a relatively recent hire selected to manage an organization that was already fine-tuned. Still, the fact that he was just now learning ITL's mission concerned him. Perhaps that was why Landon wanted him plugged into everything.

"So how did we choose the folks who are in the game? What criteria did we use?"

118

"We focused on people we believed would work well together, who didn't have big egos, but were still confident in themselves. It was a quirk of fate that the ones we were most interested in were non-gamers. So we developed a game around them."

"Then how did Kevin end up in the game?"

"Kevin was one of the spoilers to help refine the team," Gerard explained. "There are a few other players who serve the same function. Between them and the actual game, we figured we'd get a good team out of the process."

"Why do we need an assassination team?"

"Initially it was because the governments were becoming too involved and trying to tax and over-regulate everything. You remember how it was just three years ago? The European Union passed legislation regulating who could totally immerse, specifically excluding police, firefighters, medical and military personnel, and finally government personnel. A year later, when they realized everyone they prohibited was a government employee and that the overwhelming subscription to total immersion had reduced the tax base, they then upped the regulation to selected individuals approved by the government."

Felix nodded, remembering the riots and mayhem that followed. "Why not simply kidnap and immerse the problems, one government at a time?"

Gerard flashed an impish grin. "We've already been doing that, along with the Russians and Chinese."

Felix dipped his head in a slow nod of understanding.

"We take out the low-level individuals first, secretaries, drivers, security personnel, other government functionaries."

"Military?"

"They're a little harder, but again, we start at the bottom. At the same time, we're immersing military age individuals, all very public and on the up and up, effectively eliminating any pool of potential replacements for the military."

"So that's why the European Union is imposing even tougher restrictions on immersion," Felix said.

"The EU is still living in the twentieth century," Gerard dismissively replied. "Russia and China are so far ahead in immersion practice that it boggles the mind. China and India have reduced their populations to less than 300 million combined, and that's without our help. Russia is down to less than 50 million and getting less every day."

"So what's to prevent the EU from attacking and over-running Russia?"

"For what purpose?" Gerard said. "Despite the hesitancy of the EU leadership, the youth of the EU are flocking to immersion. In time, only the old and dying will remain. What does Russia have to fear?"

"Hacking?"

"That's always possible," Gerard admitted, "but with advanced AI that continually reinvents itself, that's almost impossible to do. Besides, what's the point? You hack a game and the AI discovers the hack, it simply shuts down the game, fixes the hack and resumes. With the independence of each game, it's virtually impossible to shut down the system. And then, with immersion, how's a hacker going to hack? He or she is in the game, subject to the parameters of the game itself."

"That brings me back to my original question – why is Bridge Quest restricted to only a certain number of players?"

Gerard shrugged. "I asked the same question and was told that it was an experimental game, one designed with a future in mind."

Felix's brows furrowed. "A future?"

Gerard splayed his hands. "My take on it is that with the thousands of games out there, each one is designed to maintain a struggle, a quest, at the expense of someone else. Bridge Quest has that same thing, but with a twist, especially with the 1000 years of peace. Can you imagine? All the races living in harmony. It's never been offered before."

"But to point out what you said," Felix countered, "after a while it's going to get boring and someone will want to shake things up."

Gerard again shrugged and shook his head. "That's about the only thing that makes any sense to me. I'd say, 'we'll see,' but with each of us in different games, we'll never know."

"Which brings me back to my original question; why the secrecy surrounding Bridge Quest if no one is ever going to know its original purpose?"

"Truthfully, I don't know. You'll have to ask Landon about that."

"Landon?" Felix frowned in surprise.

"Yeah. He's the one who imposed the classification levels on the game."

Felix silently mused then said, "Anything else I need to know?"

"I can't think of anything at the moment," Gerard replied, ready to be someplace else. He never did care for Felix. Not that he hated the man, but he was too corporate, too management. That he was just now trusted with some of ITL's secrets showed that they still weren't sure of him. Besides, even with the EU blocking immersion, it was just a matter of time before they came on board. Most of the rest of the world was already immersed. Hell, Africa was almost one huge ghost town.

"Thank you," Felix said, with a grand smile, already thinking of creative ways to deal with Gerard.

The travel to Beally was uneventful, despite their overly cautious movements, and it was with great relief that they emerged from the forest with Beally in the near distance.

The land surrounding the walled city of Beally had been cleared to the distance of three kilometers. Beyond that, the forest grew thick and ominous. Every day, woodcutters, protected by a troop of soldiers, went out to keep the forest at bay simultaneously cutting enough wood to supply even the poorest among them with enough wood to cook and keep warm when the winter snows arrived. The cleared land was then put to use in fields of billowing grain, grazing livestock, or simply left fallow.

Though not as large as Strathwick, the solid stone walls surrounding the city were higher. Six no-nonsense and very alert guards manned the gate, which was wide enough for a single large wagon to pass through. They had monitored

Karl and the two women as soon as the travelers appeared on the road from Southwick, the guard in the high tower having alerted them.

"Welcome," a tall guard greeted them, his attention focused on Karl. "You are Karl the Viking?"

"Yes," Karl replied, his puzzlement solved when the guard pointed through the gate.

"Your friends await you at the Fist and Hammer. It's a large tavern in the middle of the city." Glancing at the two women, he said, "I see you brought two more with you, though this one," nodding at Julie, "seems more suited for the bedroom than the battlefield."

"Looks can be deceiving," Karl smiled as Julie bowed up with indignation. Grasping her elbow and guiding her away before she gave the guard a piece of her mind, Karl whispered, "He was just fishing."

"Fishing?" she frowned, glancing back over her shoulder to the guard still watching her.

"Looking to see if you might be interested in a little you-know-what," he grinned.

"What?" she exclaimed, casting an evil eye back at the unsuspecting man. "The nerve."

Annabeth was the first to see him when they walked in.

"Karl," she yelled, leaping up from the table where the rest of the team sat eating. Racing across the room, she grabbed him in a tight hug, kissing his passionately, much to Julie's annoyance.

The kiss lasted longer than Julie could tolerate, and she cleared her throat in obvious irritation. "This must be one of your lady friends you were telling me about," she acidly stated. Only to find a beautiful Ranger sauntering up and tapping Annabeth on the shoulder.

"May I cut in?" Raquel sweetly asked.

"Of course," Annabeth grinned then stepped aside for Raquel to grasp Karl's head with both hands and plant a long deep kiss, causing Julie's jaw to clench.

Raquel pulled back to stare into Karl's eyes. "We've missed you. We were beginning to get worried."

"Who are your friends?" Annabeth chimed in.

"This is Caryn. Met her in Strathwick."

"Level 11," Annabeth said with a respectful nod then frowned when she studied Julie. "An NPC?"

"I'll explain later," Karl said.

"He rescued me," Julie proudly asserted. "He's taking me to Rhyeem then he's going to unite the kingdoms and rule for a thousand years, with me by his side."

Annabeth grinned at Karl. "Obviously lots happened since we were together last."

By now the rest of the team surrounded Karl, expressing their relief and joy at his safe arrival. Caryn's eyes widened when Dieter approached.

"I see you have more than one secret weapon," she said with awe. "He's almost as big as Uafas."

"Uafas?" Annabeth queried.

"His pet wolf," Caryn explained.

"He's not a pet," Julie corrected. "He's a friend."

"Where is he?" Annabeth asked, eyes bright.

"He's outside the city," Julie answered before Karl had a chance to open his mouth. "He doesn't like cities and we felt it would be best if he stayed away, especially as the people here would probably not take to him too well."

Annabeth noted the repeated use of 'we' and smiled before observing the sword at Karl's hip. "What do you expect to do with that?"

"Oh, that's Orc's Bane," Julie knowingly replied, wanting to emphasize her place in Karl's life. "It can cut through any blade and because the blade chose Karl, he's going to defeat the orcs and unite the kingdom and rule for 1000 years."

There was as pregnant pause before Karl uttered a slow sigh. "There's a lot to explain. Let's sit and I'll tell you all about it and by the way everyone, Caryn is joining our team. And this is Julie. We're taking her back to the ruling house of Rhyeem." He frowned when he realized two of the team were missing. He cast a quick analytical glance at Dieter, noting the big man seemed relaxed, even though Elena wasn't there, which seemed extremely odd, especially with the way the man felt about her.   Maybe he was able to reconcile that she had to stay behind. Deciding to cautiously probe, he asked about the other team member.   "Where's Carole?"

"She didn't cross," Raquel answered.   "Decided she'd rather stay there and hook up with the others."

Karl nodded without surprise. He had expected as much. "It's probably for the best."   Seeing Caryn waiting for an explanation,   he   said,   "Carole   was,   uh,   is   an   elf. Unfortunately, she was bitten by spiders and nearly died. We were able to save her, but she was never the same after that, very nervous and fearful."

"Perhaps you should have let her die and respawn," Caryn suggested.

"Have you ever had that experience?" He asked, cocking an eyebrow.

"No."

"It's not something you ever want to, trust me."   Turing to Raquel to avoid asking about Elena, he said, "Which way did you take to get here?"

"We tried thinking of which one you would take and eliminated the left route figuring the other two had more to recommend them in the 'right is right' and 'hey diddle diddle straight up the middle.'   We flipped a coin and the middle route won."

"Any problems," he asked as she led the way to the table.

"Not really," she shrugged.   "Rather an easy trek to here. We were going to wait in Krieff, but after you didn't show up in a reasonable amount of time, we figured you had taken another route.   Since all three of the routes end up here, we decided to wait here."

Ordering another round of ales, they scooted around the table and for the next two hours, Karl regaled them with his adventures.   Outmaneuvered for a seat next to him, Julie sat across the table and glared at Annabeth and Raquel who blithely ignored the daggers in her eyes.

"Think we'll see Noble and Chet again?" Sakura asked.

"Hard to say," Karl replied.   "Don't know where Chet's bind spot was. My guess it was back in Dinwahl. Noble was headed to Lyster. Unless he's got himself in trouble again, there's a chance he might end up here, though between the two, when it comes to a fight, I'd rather have Chet."

"Tell me about the 1000 years thing again," Raquel said. "It seems an odd quest for the game."

"Game?" Julie frowned.

"Just a word we use for this whole thing called life," Karl fudged, wondering if NPCs knew it was just a game and if they did, did it matter?

"Oh," she slowly nodded, unconvinced.

Turning to Raquel, Karl said, "I don't understand it, especially within the context of island hopping, but I believe our more immediate concern is getting Julie back to Rhyeem through a kingdom of orcs." Remembering his obligation to Elanda to rescue her son, he added, "And to rescue a certain son of a white sorceress held by the orcs."

Annabeth gave him a wry grin. "My, my, we have been busy."

"You have a plan, Boss?" Dieter asked.

"Not yet. I wanted to reconnect with you all first and make sure we were all still committed as a team."

Dieter did a quick glance around the table. "I think I can speak for the team here, Boss. We're with you all the way." Staring at Caryn, he said, "I won't put words in your mouth. I know he said you were joining us, but you can still opt out. But know this, if you do stay with us, we're more than a team; we're family. We stick together no matter what."

"I like that," Caryn said with a heartfelt smile.

"You didn't ask me," Julie fussed.

"You're the reason we're going to Rhyeem or whatever town we have to go to get you back," Dieter answered. "Until we know why you have to go back, you have no reason for a permanent commitment to the team." He wanted to add that she was nothing more than a serving girl who, despite carrying a sword that she couldn't truly use, she would be of little value, but then he remembered Elena and decided to leave well enough alone.

"I don't know why I'm supposed to go there," she pouted. "Suppose I said I didn't want to go back, that I wanted to stay with you?" She gazed longingly at Karl.

"It doesn't work that way," Karl gently answered. "There's a reason you're going back. We'll find out what it is when we get there."

"That's not fair," she whined.

"Life's not fair," Dieter pronounced as an end to the discussion.

Annabeth turned to Caryn. "You're awfully quiet."

"I'm the new person to the team," she shrugged. "Don't have much to say."

"Other than dumping your boyfriend, which sounds like a smart move, tell us about yourself. What did you do before you immersed?"

"I was a Highlander Scout."

Jovial conversation around the table came to an abrupt halt.

"You never told me that," Karl admonished.

"You never asked," she answered, holding his gaze.

"What's a Highlander Scout," Julie piped up.

"They're like the Widow-makers," Dieter replied.

"Not quite at that level," Caryn corrected.

"Still very lethal," Raquel stated.

"What are widow-makers," Julie frowned in confusion.

"I'll explain later," Karl impatiently said, still looking at Caryn. "I'm even more pleased you're part of the team."

"How'd you end up with loser boyfriend?" Annabeth asked.

Caryn chuckled, giving Annabeth a warm smile. "I like you. You say what's on your mind. Wish more people were like that. But to answer your question, I wanted a love interest and figured it ought to be outside of my profession. Saw him and you know what they say about opposites attract. It wasn't until I immersed that I saw him for what he really was."

"A jerk?" Annabeth concluded for her.

Caryn laughed and nodded.

"Think he'll show up here?" Sakura asked.

126

"No," Caryn replied, shaking her head. "When I told him we were finished, he left."

"Where'd he go?" Raquel frowned.

"Don't know," she replied with a shrug. "All I know is that as soon as I told him to take a hike, he called me some choice names and stormed out."

The door to the stairwell leading up to the bedrooms opened and an attractive woman emerged, giving them all a warm smile.

"Elena," Karl exclaimed. "But how..." he stammered as she came up to stand next to Dieter, placing a loving hand on his shoulder.

"I know," Dieter sheepishly grinned. "I was worried too. But thank the gods, nothing happened." Seeing Karl's confounded frown, he explained, "I know it said we weren't allowed to, but I gave her the password anyway."

"And you had no problems crossing the bridge?" Karl's frown deepened as he wondered why Elena and not Gillien.

"Piece of cake," he grinned. "Once she gave the password to the land giant, he stood aside and let her walk across with me." He patted Elena's hand.

"I don't understand any of this," Julie complained.

"Best leave it alone for now," Karl said, deciding to squelch his curiosity and leave Gillien in the past. Turning to the group, he said, "We need to come up with a plan to rescue a man from the orcs, deliver Julie to Rhyeem, defeat the orcs, and unite the kingdom. Think about it. I'll take any and all input. In the meantime, you all need to meet Uafas. We'll do that tomorrow morning. Now, what's the situation in the city here?"

No sooner had Karl asked the question when the front door opened and two guards stalked in, casting a suspicious eye over the tavern's patrons. Seeing Karl, they headed straight for him.

"You are Karl the Viking?"

"Who's asking?"

"The Bargrave would like a word with you," the younger guard haughtily demanded.

"Then he knows where to find me," Karl replied with a yawn.

"But… but, the Bargrave demands to see you," the guard sputtered, much to the amusement of his fellow guard, a middle-aged man who was more interested in the serving girls than carrying out his orders.

"Like I said, he knows where to find me." He pretended to turn to Raquel for conversation, waiting for the man's reaction.

"You… you… you can't ignore the Bargrave just like that." Bowing up to full height, he used his voice of authority and said, "Karl the Viking. You are ordered to accompany me or I shall be forced to make you obey."

Karl slowly turned his head to gaze up at the man before bursting out in laughter, the rest of the table joining in, even Julie whose forced laugh showed she had no clue as to why they were laughing.

"And how do you expect to force me?" Karl said, his mirth subsiding.

The guard glanced around the table, his eyes pausing as he took in Dieter whose evil smile implied he'd like nothing better than to rip the man apart.

Glaring at Karl, he threatened, "You'll pay for this," and stormed out, his partner silently mouthing 'sorry' as he followed him out.

"Was that wise?" Raquel asked.

"If I'm to be lord of the realm," Karl sniffed, "they better start treating us nicer." He flashed her a silly grin then refocused on their future. "I think we need to prioritize our missions. The first is to get Julie to Rhyeem. The second is consolidate a power base."

"How do we do that, Boss?" Dieter asked.

"I'm supposedly the one who's going to rule this entire island, if this whole Orc's Bane sword stuff is true. But to do that, I've got to eliminate the orcs as a threat and unite the kingdom. Somehow I don't think my welcome is going to be so warm when whoever's in charge of Rhyeem or the present kingdom of Mann finds out who I am and why I'm there.

Still, my swag is that there will be some who will follow us because of the prophecy."

"Swag?" Annabeth frowned.

"S-W-A-G, silly wild-assed guess," Caryn explained with a grin.

"Swag," Annabeth repeated with a smile. "I'll have to remember that one."

"This all sounds iffy," Raquel pointed out.

"A big iffy," Karl agreed. "For now, I think we ought to keep me and this whole sword-prophecy thing to ourselves until we can get a lay of the land, so to speak. What I propose is to get Julie back to Rhyeem and kill some orcs along the way. After that, who knows."

The tavern door flung open and the Bargrave stormed in, followed by a squad of guards. The younger guard from before thrust a finger to where Karl and company sat.

As the Bargrave, a plump man of inflated self-importance, stalked over to stand imperiously in front of Karl, the tavern's cacophony froze to silence. Jamming his hands in his hips he called out in a loud commanding voice. "I am Giblick, Bargrave of Beally."

"Did he say giblets?" Annabeth stage whispered to Raquel, causing her and several others in the tavern to giggle.

"That's Giblick," the Bargrave snapped, giving her a cold stare. Returning his attention to Karl who sat impassively waiting, he growled, "You were ordered to come see me."

Frowning, Karl twisted his head to look at Dieter. "Was that an order?"

"I thought it was more of a request," Dieter offered.

"No," Annabeth joined in. "It sounded more like an invitation. Wouldn't you say so Raquel?"

"Ah," she pensively nodded, "invitation sounds close, but the way it was phrased gave it more umph, you know, like you're begging but you don't want to appear like you're begging. What do you think Caryn?"

"Oh, don't ask me," she said, flipping her hand. "I wasn't really paying attention, though I thought him approaching on his hands and knees was a nice touch."

"I never," the guard sputtered with indignation.

Smirking, Karl looked back at the Bargrave whose face was turning red. "You were saying?"

"You think you're amusing?" the Bargrave sneered. "Let's see how amusing you are when you find yourselves in gaol."

"And how do you intend to make that happen?" Karl leaned over to gaze pointedly at the six apprehensive guards who were with the Bargrave.

"I'll bring in an army if I have to," he growled.

"Why not save a lot of trouble and lives by simply telling me what you want?" Karl grinned. "After all, here you are and here we are." He spread his hands then motioned to an adjacent table. "Pull up a chair. Kick off your shoes and set a spell. The ale's pretty good here."

Hearing the titters, the Bargrave stood up to full height, his gaze piercing down at Karl. "You think this is funny? Do you know who I am?"

"Yes. You already told me. Your name is giblets."

"That's Giblick and I will not be mocked in my own town by you or anyone else." He cast a daring eye around the room.

"Then sit down," Karl said, his voice suddenly turning hard, "before I make you sit."

"What?" the Bargrave indignantly retorted. "Who do you think you are?"

"I am Karl the Viking," he replied with equal force. Waving a hand at the rest of the team, he added, "And these are my friends. We've killed goblins and orcs and gnolls and giant spiders, by the thousands." He then leaned forward and stared at him. "We haven't added a Bargrave yet."

The Bargrave's eyes bolted wide, and he began edging backwards. "You... you can't come in here... I mean... surely you don't mean to, uh... what I'm saying..."

"I said 'sit,'" Karl commanded, pointing to a chair at the nearby table.

Dieter stood up to make space for him, reminding the Bargrave how large the berserker was.

The Bargrave glanced rapidly around the room, quickly realizing not only would no one come to his aid, they were all enjoying the spectacle. Telling himself that they would all pay for their treachery, he meekly maneuvered around the table to sit. Once he sat, cacophony in the tavern resumed.

"Now," Karl regally said, "what is it you wanted to see us about?"

"It was you I wanted to see," he said, gaining some of his nerve back.

"About what?"

"I received a message from Burgrave Eljyn that you were coming."

"If that's the case, then you know who I am and why I am here."

"That's just it," Giblick replied. "All he said was that you were coming, but no more as to who you were or why you were here."

Karl pulled out Orc's Bane. "Do you recognize this sword?"

Giblick studied it a moment before shaking his head. "No. Should I?"

"It's Orc's Bane."

As soon as he spoke the words, the tavern hushed.

"Is it really?" Giblick said in awe. "I've heard of that one."

"Go ahead. Pick it up." When the man hesitated, he gazed around the tavern. "Any of you are welcome to pick it up."

There was an awkward pause before several patrons scooted chairs back and approached the table to stare down at the sword. One impetuous young man shot a 'what's-the-big-deal?' at the others and reached for the sword only to grunt when he couldn't move it.

"It's a trick," he complained, using two hands as he struggled to budge it.

"Here," a large burly man spoke, "let me try."

Smacking then rubbing his hands together, he positioned himself near the sword, grasped the grip and tugged... and yanked and tugged some more, all to no avail.

"It's a trick," the young man repeated, dropping to his knees to inspect under the table.

"No trick, youngster," the burly man soberly replied. "It's magic."

"That's what I said," the young man retorted, screwing up his face.

"A trick is not magic," the burly man stated. "Any simpleton can learn a trick. It's merely a slight of hand. True magic comes from wizards and the ancient ones. This sword is soul bonded. Only one man can wield it."

Turning to Karl, he bowed. "My Lord."

"Why are you doing that to him?" the young man said, his tone verging on a sneer.

"Because of the prophecy."

"What prophecy?"

The burly man sighed and shook his head. "The ignorance of youth. Pity that brain of yours is wasted. The prophecy says that the man who wields Orc's Bane will unite the kingdoms and rule in peace for 1000 years." He twisted his head to cast a disparaging eye at the Bargrave. "But you knew that, didn't you Giblick." It wasn't a question.

"I had my suspicions," Giblick said, nervously rubbing his hands.

"But you still came in here like some high-and-mighty city ruler and treated him like a commoner."

"Just because Eljyn said he was didn't mean it was necessarily true," Giblick whined. "You know how he is."

"What I know is that he is an honorable man," the burly man said.

"How did you know about me?" Karl asked.

"Bird messenger, m'Lord," the burly man replied.

"And you are?" Karl said with a polite smile.

"Neylin, m'Lord. I'm a smithy by trade and an advisor to the Bargrave by consent of the people."

Turning to Giblick, Karl asked, "And what were you before you became Bargrave?"

"I was an apothecary."

"Were you good at it?"

"The best," he proudly answered.

"I wouldn't go that far," Neylin countered.

"Then perhaps you should stick to what you're good at," Karl intoned. "Just how did you become Bargrave?"

"I was chosen by the city council," he stiffly replied.

"How long ago was that?"

"Ten years ago," Neylin answered for him.

"And the city council? How long have they been in power?" Karl asked, anticipating the answer.

"Also ten years," Neylin responded. "I was elected a year ago when one of the members died."

Karl nodded with a smile. "So I suspected." Then in a move that surprised even himself, he said, "Effective immediately, Neylin is the new Bargrave of Beally. Elections for a new city council will be held a week from today. All taxpaying citizens of Beally are eligible to hold office."

A cheer burst inside the tavern. Several patrons wormed their way through the throng and pushed out the door to tell the rest of the city the good news.

"You can't do that," Giblick cried out. "You have no authority here."

The uproar in the tavern died down so they might listen.

"Do you deny the prophecy?" Karl challenged.

Giblick hesitated, quickly scanning the crowd only to see they had deserted him. "No, I don't deny the prophecy," he mumbled.

"I didn't hear you," Karl said.

Giblick's lips tightened before he said in a voice loud enough for all to hear, "No, I don't deny the prophecy."

"Then you accept me as the rightful ruler of Beally and the rest of the kingdom?"

This time Giblick paused and sighed.

"What about the rest of you?" Karl called out to the assembled crowd. "Do you accept me as ruler of this kingdom?"

The response was an impressive 'Aye' and Giblick knew his days lining his pockets as Bargrave were over. He was about to slink out when Karl stopped him and pointed at the medallion of office suspended from the chain around his neck.

"You can leave that here," Karl commanded.

Glowering, Giblick hesitated for an awkward moment then slowly removed the medallion and chain and handed them to Karl, pointedly ignoring Neylin. As he slithered his way through the numerous patrons, many gave him a knowing sneer, and realization pierced through his funk that he had few friends in the city and those who said they were would probably abandon him as soon as the new council was elected.

Once Giblick pushed out the door, Karl handed the symbols of office to Neylin. "You are now the Bargrave of Beally. Do well. Make me proud."

"Thank you, m'Lord," he gravely said. "I will serve with honor."

"I know you will. I'll give you a week and then want a report of your findings and impressions."

"A week?" Neylin replied, flustered.

"I know it's not much, but my friends and I are looking to take off soon and go kill some orcs. All I'm looking for is general impressions. You can give me a full report when I return... whenever that will be."

"Yes, m'Lord," he said.

"Well then," Karl smiled, "I'm sure you have work to do while I coordinate our future with my friends here."

"Yes, m'Lord." With a respectful bow, he turned and passed through the parting crowd who slapped him on the back and offered their congrats.

Turning to the assembled patrons still fascinated with the turn of events, he grinned and announced, "Drinks are on me."

The cheer was louder this time as the crowd mobbed the barkeep.

Sakura regarded him with a curious smile. "Interestingly played. Am I to assume that we will be on this island for quite some time?"

"Who knows," Karl said, shrugging. "Right now we need time to think and plan. I figured a week should be more than enough time. In the meantime, I need some sleep and tomorrow we'll go meet Uafas."

Yawning, he glanced over to Julie who was slumped back in her chair, scowling, her hands crossed over her chest.

"She's not happy," Annabeth explained, "once she learned that she has to share and that we have first priority."

"You never told me they were *that* kind of friends," Julie snapped.

"You never asked," Karl replied with a tired sigh. He had anticipated this reaction yet hoped she would recognize her place and accept it. From the look on her face, he saw his hope was in vain.

"Raquel and I flipped a coin," Annabeth said with a cheerful smile, "and luck was on her side, again, so she has you tonight and I get you tomorrow." She twisted her head to gaze at Julie. "I suppose we might let her have you the third night, but I don't know if I can wait three days."

"What?" Julie sputtered, sitting up straight.

Karl rolled his eyes and shook his head. "Are you sure you two aren't succubuses?"

"That's succubi," Annabeth corrected with a grin, placing a tender hand on his cheek.

Felix stood in Mister Landon's office, waiting for Mister Landon to finish his present task, which was composing a response to a news inquiry. Why Landon was composing the reply instead of his PR department surprised him. Though to be honest, Landon's attention to minutia was well known throughout the company.

While Landon's attention was on his response, Felix's eyes wandered around the large room that comprised Landon's office. Stretching the entire width of the building, the room seemed tall and deep enough for a three-putt hole on the golf course across from Felix's own offices, also in Chattanooga, a little over three miles away. Yet in stark contrast to Felix's all-business office, Landon's office was replete with furniture, sculptures, antiques, artifacts and antiquities, oil paintings, drawings, plants, and bookshelves crammed with tomes that lined an entire wall. The office seemed more of a living room than the brain-center of Landon Limited.

Felix's gaze wandered back to where Mister Landon looked to be finishing up. For a man who was reputed to live in his office suite, Landon was tanned and fit. Felix wondered if the man had a tanning bed hidden somewhere. The joke was that the only time Landon ventured out was in the dark when vampires ruled the night.

Landon cleared his throat and looked up. "Thank you for your patience, Felix." Sliding his laptop to the side, he narrowed his gaze at the CEO of Immersion Technologies. "Talk to me about the transition of staffing."

"Sir?"

"Your reduction in staffing," Landon repeated. "How is it proceeding?"

"Quite well," Felix replied. "HR is completely automated as is Finance and Corporate Affairs. Overall, we're about 60% automated."

"And where have they been placed?"

"We've developed a new game called 'Corporate CEO.' Many employees and their families are now immersed in the game, though more than a few have chosen other approved games instead."

"Tell me about Corporate CEO," Landon said with a polite smile.

Felix stared at him a moment, knowing full well the man knew all about the game. "It's pretty much the same as in real life. A player is put into the game with the ability to form his or her own low-level company, or by joining an already established small company. By forming alliances, players work to make their company stronger as they climb the corporate ladder to become the ruling CEO of the game."

"Sounds boring," Landon observed.

"I suppose to some it might be, but there are almost an infinite number of companies and intrigue with the usual murder and betrayal. So far we've had excellent feedback."

"And the employees with children? How did they react to loss of their position with the option of immersion?"

Felix almost laughed when Landon said 'option.' There was no choice. Either accept immersion or face the consequences. When word spread like wildfire that one employee who chose to go his own way met with unfortunate circumstances involving him and his entire family, it only took two more incidents of unfortunate "accidents" to remind the others of the consequences of going against the company's wishes. Besides, with the latest programming advancement allowing children to age, the resistance, from the children's perspective was virtually eliminated. In fact, the youth's demand for immersion was loud and vocal, many times choosing games that did not include their parents or siblings.

"Those families with children are the most supportive," Felix said. "That reflects more on the children's knowledge of technology advancements than the parental concerns."

"Good," Landon nodded without smiling. "Now tell me again why we have a game like Bridge Quest? None of the players have any gaming background."

"That's exactly it," Felix replied, remembering Gerard's comment that Landon was the one who initiated the clearance levels for Bridge Quest, which meant the man already knew what he was about to tell him. Still, he needed to demonstrate to the big Boss that he knew what he was doing.

"Not everyone is a gamer," Felix explained. "We needed a game where newbies can experience the benefits of gaming without all the associated minutia that active RPG players are fascinated with. For example, a true RPG player wants to know all the how and why of point allocation, when and where to use various quest objects, MMORPGs, actual character role playing, things like that. Non-gamers find that boring. They get overwhelmed with the amount of skills, attributes, and spells say a sorceress has as she levels up. That's especially true with older non-gamers. They've eschewed the gaming world as a waste of time. Now that they're in the game, we didn't want to overwhelm them. What Bridge Quest does is give them the rudiments of gaming while giving them an adventure."

"Why then the charade of terminal illnesses?"

Felix smiled yet remembered that Karl and the others were immersed with the sole purpose of putting together an assassination team. "No non-gamer in his right mind would ever agree to immersion unless that was the last choice."

"I believe this Raquel woman has children."

"That one slipped past us," Felix admitted. "The one responsible has been dealt with. We're looking at options right now as to what to do with them."

"Why not put them into the game?"

"We're looking at that," Felix replied. "It would require some modification to the present game, allowing the children to age. And then there's the shock of discovering her children are in the game. We're not prepared to make that adjustment quite yet. In the long term, it may be better to put them in another game. After all, they believe their mother is terminally ill."

Landon slowly nodded. "What about your Immersion Department? I believe we are far enough along to eliminate the human factor."

Felix blinked with foreboding at the statement yet expecting it. As it was, his headquarters building was half-empty, the parking lot almost abandoned, the dining hall reduced to vending machines. Though he knew the planned future, he wondered if computer generated golf would be as invigorating as a true golf course.

"Yes, Sir. The Immersion Department is at a point where all immersions are now handled by AI."

"Then you know what to do."

"Yes, Sir," he replied, wondering what he was the CEO of anymore. What had once been a company of almost 1,000 employees was now less than 400. Eliminating the Immersion Group would further reduce his staffing to less than 300, most of which were maintenance and support.

When Landon Limited had gone public with Immersion Technology several years ago, the demand exponentially exploded. And then Landon shared his technology, at a price, with other companies, even international ones. Once governments saw their collective powers vanishing in a flash, they reacted and outlawed immersion, but the lid to

Pandora's gaming box was already open and they were powerless to stop it. Their citizens simply went to where they could immerse. Admitting defeat, governments then sought to regulate it, which meant exorbitant taxes.

But it was too late. The populations of whole towns and cities disappeared overnight. Families simply abandoned homes and walked into the world of gaming, occasionally leaving pets behind, despite the ability of taking the supposedly cherished pet with them.

It was the same throughout Chattanooga and elsewhere. Felix silently chuckled that he never had a problem now getting a tee time on a golf course.

Yet not everyone was enthusiastic. There were those holdouts who rejected the better world of gaming where players never died. And of course, the various governments were still searching for ways to regulate and dominate gaming. Yet progress could not be stopped.

Computers were ruling human lives and the world was becoming a large ghost town.

"Before you go," Landon spoke, interrupting Felix's thoughts, "Tell me about the latest collaboration with the North American Union."

Felix silently stared at Mister Landon for just a heartbeat, but with that time, decided to throw caution to the wind and said, "Sir. May I ask a question?"

Landon's visage hardened, piercing Felix with a cold stare before relaxing. "Yes."

Taking a deep breath, Felix blurted, "Since you already know what I'm about to tell you, why ask me to repeat what you already know?" Expecting a harsh rebuke, he was surprised when a smile curled the corners of Landon's mouth.

"I have led this company for the past twenty-eight years, and you are the first person to ever ask me to explain myself. Well done. I've been waiting for someone with the cojones to speak his mind." Landon pointed to his computer. "Why am I composing a reply to a news inquiry? Because my HR department is filed with linguini-spined 'yes-men' who refuse to think for themselves. They'll spend man-days in meetings debating what they think I want, instead of simply asking. I'd fire them all, but it's easier now just to put them into a game and be done with them."

Standing, Landon walked to the tall windows behind him, beckoning Felix to come along. Landon pointed to the buildings surrounding his headquarters.

"See that? A testament to man's genius. We conquered the physical dimensional world. And now we've conquered time." Turning around, he pointed to a painting of an elderly man with a conquistador type helmet. "There is an original Rembrandt, or so they once thought. It used to hang in the Staatliche Museum in Berlin. Or that Remington sculpture over there by the far bookcase. It's called 'The Bronco Buster,' or 'The Broncho Buster' when it was first sculpted. That one was originally given to Teddy Roosevelt."

He then escorted Felix around the office, pointing out the provenance of each work of art or artifact.

"I've spent years collecting history only to realize that I am a rare person who sees the worth in maintaining history. Sadly, this too shall pass. When all the world is finally immersed, none of this will matter."

Felix dutifully followed Landon around the office, listening politely as Landon explained each item, thrilled that the great man was giving him so much time, though not sure of the point of it all. They ended up near the far window with Landon explaining the history behind a beautiful Tang dynasty Sancai horse.

Landon paused, his attention distracted by a drone that buzzed past the window. With a sigh, he turned back to Felix.

"To answer your question, I ask you for your explanation for two reasons; first, so that I see you know what you are talking about, and second, to verify what I've been told. So, now it's your turn. Tell me about the latest collaboration with the NAU."

Felix warmed to the man's confidence. "Yes, Sir. It's a new game called 'Gang Lord.' In a concerted effort by the member states of the NAU, gang and cartel members are rounded up and forcibly immersed into the game. With no one to inform those still in real life, the numbers and influence of gangs and cartels has been significantly reduced."

"What about the bodies?"

Felix grinned. "They're immediately cremated. It saves time and money. No unnecessary and wasted cold storage. The game's designed so that no respawning occurs. A player dies and that's that. Quite effective if you ask me."

Landon frowned. "I'm surprised no lawyers have questioned the permanent disappearance of their clients."

"That's the beauty of it," Felix replied. "The individuals are immediately transported to an immersion center before any lawyer gets a chance to spring them, though a few have gotten through to their lawyers."

"What happened?"

"The lawyers were immersed into the game."

"Seems rather harsh, doesn't it?" Landon asked, peering intently at Felix.

"Not my call," he shrugged. "The NAU determined that any lawyer willing to represent the dregs of society deserves the same fate."

Landon mused for a moment. "What's your take on the PR fallout when it's discovered?"

Flattered and surprised that Mister Landon would deign to ask for his opinion, Felix paused to wisely consider his reply. "I think that the overwhelming majority of honest, law-abiding citizens would be supportive. Those who believe that the rights of the gang member supersede the rights of the victims will be the ones against it as well as the most vocal in their opposition. But quite honestly, with the way things are going with immersion, it's going to be a non-issue. By the time anyone complains, the problem has disappeared."

Landon listened attentively, nodding agreement. "Well spoken." A ping sounded and he frowned with mild frustration. "I've an important call in five minutes. Thank you for stopping by, Felix. If it is convenient for you, perhaps you might like to share dinner with me. Tomorrow night at seven?"

Felix's mouth slacked open and he quickly closed it. *My God. He's asked me to dinner.* "I would enjoy that. Thank you, Sir," he said, straining to control his glee. In all the years he had worked for Mister Landon, he had never heard of him inviting anyone to share a meal.

"Excellent. Then I'll see you tomorrow."

Giddy with excitement, he stopped by Alyson Whitmer's desk in the outside office. "Mister Landon invited me to dinner tomorrow night at seven."

Alyson jerked her head up to frown at him. She was about to chide him for his silly attempt at humor when she realized he was telling the truth. "He did?"

Felix smiled at the woman's obvious shock. "Yes, he did."

Alyson blinked a few times then smiled back, as though reappraising him. "I'll make note of it. Remember to be on time."

Felix felt his heart give a quick flutter and he found himself thoroughly captivated. Not only was she beautiful, her smile radiated with a sort of innocent charm. *Be on time?* He chuckled as he pushed through the tall double doors. *What made you think I wouldn't be? Especially if I get to see you again.*

With a light-hearted strut, he walked down the hallway to the elevators, passing by offices now permanently empty, wondering how long it would be before no one worked here anymore.

Chapter 6

It was midmorning by the time they finished breakfast, Sakura pleading just one more cup of coffee, and headed out the city gates. Flanked by Annabeth and Raquel, Karl led the way along the outside of the city walls, as the team leisurely made their way to the open farm fields to the south. Julie walked two paces behind them, angrily frustrated that she was shunted off to insignificance while those two hussies monopolized Karl's attention.

Stewing as she relived the morning's failed attempt at reinserting herself into Karl's orbit of focus, she pondered how she might learn combat skills sufficient enough to impose her own will, like Raquel did this morning.

It was early, before most folks were up or awake when she knocked on Karl's door, louder perhaps than the hour permitted. Raquel answered the door, a thin gossamer wrap doing little to hide her voluptuous and strong body, though the sword in her hand intimated she was ready for the unexpected.

"What are you doing here?" Raquel frowned. "It's not even daylight yet."

"I want to see him." She craned her neck to peer inside the room then made to brush past the ranger only to feel the strength of a firm hand pressed against her chest, holding her in place.

"You're going to have to learn your place," Raquel intoned, slowly but solidly pushing Julie back into the hallway. "You'll get your turn, but you need to learn the rules first. Whoever has him, has him from the evening until after the next morning's breakfast." Casting a slow glance around the darkened hallway, she intoned, "And breakfast is still a few hours away." With that, she closed the door in Julie's face, but not before giving her a smug wink.

Julie swore she heard the woman snicker before silence reigned and she thrust her ear to the door, straining to hear his voice, but was met with nothing but quiet. Storming down the hallway back to her room, she envisioned the shenanigans going on in the bedroom as they probably waited for her to go away before resuming their romping. She vowed then to learn the craft of the warrior so that she could be in the position to tell Raquel what to do, and Annabeth too.

Now here she was, trailing behind the group, pondering and maneuvering how to get him back.

Karl wasn't oblivious to her disenchantment; it was that he had other more important things to worry about. About a kilometer past the edge of the city, he again tried contacting Uafas. Concerned with no response, he picked up the pace.

"Something wrong?" Raquel asked, noting the focus and forward progress.

"Uafas hasn't responded. It's not like him." Though staring straight ahead, he ordered, "Spread out and stay alert. Something's not right."

They were coming to the end of the farms and the forest spread wide before them. Karl tried again to contact Uafas, but the wolf beat him to it.

I could use your help right now.

Where are you?

I'm in the forest south of the city, heading your way.

What's wrong?

You'll see.

Uafas burst through the trees to the right, causing a collective gasp amongst those who had not yet witnessed the size of the beast.

Get ready, Uafas warned as he came charging up.

They heard the guttural shouts coming from the woods, the hunters excited for the kill.

"Orcs," Karl warned. "How many?" he said aloud to Uafas.

I stopped counting at about a dozen, but probably not many more than that.

144

"There's probably fifteen to twenty," Karl announced. "We attack as soon as we see them. Sakura, you disappear and hit them from the rear."

"Got it." In a dozen or so long fluid strides, she vanished in among the trees.

"Annabeth," Karl continued. "You stay put and throw out as many spells as you can."

"Roger dodger," she grinned and saluted.

Smirking, he turned to the remaining members. "Raquel, you're with me. Caryn, you're with Dieter. Be sure to give him space. Uafas is wherever he wants to be. Once the battle is done, we assemble back here. We destroy them all. No survivors."

He then turned a stern eye at Elena and Julie. "You two find some place to hide. Quickly."

"There." Dieter pointed to a tumbled down farmhouse behind them. "Hurry." When Elena delayed, his voice softened. "Go. I'll get you when this is over."

"Yes, Dieter." Heaving a worried sigh, she motioned for Julie to follow.

"I want to stay here and help," she nervously offered.

"Go," Karl commanded as orcs burst through the trees. "Now."

"Hurry," Elena demanded, grabbing Julie's hand and tugging her towards the farmhouse.

As more orcs piled out of the forest, the two women fled to the safety of the house.

Rapidly assessing the enemy spilling out of the woods, Karl grimly smiled. "Let's do it."

The first orcs emerging from the forest were surprised at the humans and elf to their front. They were even more surprised when those same humans and elf along with the giant wolf launched an immediate attack.

Yet the orcs were confident in their superior numbers, even with the presence of the wolf, the former prey now predator, and they pressed forward as more and more orcs appeared from behind.

Karl leapt forward, his sword swinging in deadly slashes. He startled his first opponent when Orc's Bane sliced through the orc's falchion reminding Karl of the old adage of a knife and warm butter. Yet Karl gave the orc no pause and in the back swing sliced off a hand, causing the orc to howl in pain. The pain was brief as Karl twirled and severed the head from the body.

While Karl engaged two more orcs, Dieter's berserker lust had erupted and his double ax swept fast and furious, hacking limbs, severing parts of arms and legs, and crushing skulls.   Behind him, Annabeth busily cast a variety of conjurations and evocations: flare bursts, which temporarily blinded and disoriented everyone within a three-meter radius, and frost rays, which froze single orcs in place. Then she rediscovered her Spark evocation, grinning delightedly when clothing caught on fire, laughing as the orcs jittered in fear, trying to put out the flames.

Raquel and Caryn notched arrow after arrow, dispatching flaming orcs and those on the flanks, as Uafas prowled the edges of the battle, ripping apart any orc trying to escape.

And then, like a finger snap, it was over. Piles of orcs lay in twisted agony, a few still clinging to life. Karl, Raquel, and Caryn prowled the dead and dying, finishing off those still alive. Dieter's bloodlust continued to rage when they heard Sakura call out from the depths of the forest.

"It's me, Dieter. I'm coming out."

Dieter's wild eyes began to relax as Sakura slipped out from among the trees.

"Well?" Karl asked.

"I took out about half a dozen back there," she said, thumbing over her shoulder.

"Any escape?"

"Not that I could tell."

I'll be back.

Karl watched Uafas bound back into the trees.

"Where's he going?" Annabeth asked, blowing the imaginary smoke from her imaginary six-shooter fingers.

"Checking on any survivors," Karl replied. "We don't want anyone knowing our presence just yet. Everyone OK?"

"It all went so fast that I didn't have time to get hurt," Caryn answered with a surprised frown.

"You've killed orcs before, right?" Raquel asked. "You had to. You're a Level 11 elf."

"Yeah, I did, but not like this. Frank and I usually killed orcs or goblins or gnolls in small groups or individuals. This is the largest skirmish I've been in in the game."

"Well you did great," Karl complimented. "I'm glad you're part of the team."

Caryn warmed to the praise, noting this was so much better than it was with Frank. The one thing missing was another elf, preferably a tall handsome male elf. Not that she had anything against humans, but from the way things were here, Dieter was preoccupied with Elena, and Karl... Well, Karl had enough woman problems of his own.

"I better check on the ladies," Dieter said.

Karl replied with a nod then turned his attention to the dead. "Cut off the left ear while you check for booty. We'll display those back in the city."

"I count seventeen here," Caryn said. "With the six Sakura killed, that makes twenty-three."

"Seems a rather large scouting party," Raquel observed, nudging one with her foot. "This one's got some sort of badge on his vest. It's different from the rest."

Karl walked over to take a look at the badge. It was a small circular metal badge of bronze, about two and a half centimeters in diameter. In the center were three raised diamonds, colored a dull red.

"I don't recall any of the other orcs we're killed having that," Raquel observed.

Dropping to his knees, Karl unhooked the badge and stood, studying the badge. "Maybe it's a rank designation of some sort." Looking up at the others rummaging through the dead, he said, "Take what we can carry. Leave the rest."

Dieter returned with the two ladies. Elena clung to his arm, her face flushed with relief. Julie rushed over to Karl, scrutinizing his whole body.

"Are you hurt?" she asked, tenderly caressing his cheek.

"I'm fine," he said, stiffening. "Why don't you help the others and collect what gear we can carry. Make sure we take all the coinage we find, even if that means leaving the weapons."

Sakura emerged from the woods, followed by Uafas.

Nothing moving south of here.

"Thanks," Karl answered then turned to Sakura. "What do you have?"

"I found this badge on one of the dead." She handed him a badge like the one Raquel found, except this had three raised cobalt blue diamonds.

"Don't know what it signifies," Karl said with a shrug. "I'm thinking it might be a rank badge."

"Don't remember something like this when we were in Westhaven."

"Might be nothing more than decoration," Karl offered. "You got your ears?"

Sakura lifted her hand to show him six ears strung on a bow string.

Karl turned to the others, noting Julie and Elena labored under the weight of the falchions they carried with both hands. Thinking this might cure Julie of wanting to be a warrior, he gave her a nod of recognition before saying, "We got everything? Good. Let's head on back."

"We didn't get much of a chance to meet the wolf," Annabeth complained.

"You'll get to spend time with him later," Karl admonished. *I hope you don't mind, but other than saying 'nice to meet you' I don't see a reason to spend too much time here out in the open.*

I agree.

How did you happen to get mixed up with the bad guys?

When I discovered them, I trailed them for a while, hoping to see what they were up to. Unfortunately, they spotted me when I got distracted by a rabbit. The chase ensued after that. Not only did I have to make a run for it, I lost my dinner.

I can come back with some food.

That would be nice. Any kind of meat would be good.

Karl paused a moment before asking, *You can use telepathy to talk to me. Can you do the same thing to the others?*

If I wish.

Is there a reason you don't?

You ever have more than one voice in your head? Now imagine two or more voices all demanding attention, all at once.

Say no more. You want me to come back, or can I send one of the others?

The woman ranger will suffice.

Karl turned to Raquel. "I need to get Uafas some food once we get back to the city. He says he would like you to come back here with it. I'll send Caryn along with you."

Hearing her name, Caryn perked up. "What am I doing?"

"We're coming back to feed the wolf," Raquel answered.

"Cool," Caryn grinned.

The reception back in the city was what Karl had hoped. Once word spread that they had wiped out a platoon of orcs, the rumor grew to where they had destroyed a whole army. Crowds gathered and surrounded them as they made their way to the park in front of the bargrave's residence.

Karl waited until Neylin pushed his way through the crowd, still wearing his medallion of office. Calling for quiet, it was only after Neylin shouted for silence that the cacophony subsided.

Karl pointed to the ground by his side and Dieter and the others deposited the orc hardware in a pile. Then, with a grand display for effect, Karl spoke in a loud commanding voice.

"Bargrave Neylin and the good people of Beally. Today, my friends and I present you with the ears of twenty-three orcs as well as their weapons as a gift to the good people of Beally."

A raucous cheer erupted and again it was some time before the noise subsided.

"As long as we are here, we will protect this city –"

Cheers burst louder this time and despite their best collective efforts, neither Karl nor Neylin could silence them.

"Let them cheer, m'Lord," Neylin leaned in and shouted. "They have had little to celebrate for too long."

"Let's talk," Karl shouted back.

Neylin nodded and led the way back into the bargrave's residence, parting the crowd who back slapped Karl and company so much that they were sore by the time they escaped into the large home.

Once safely inside, Karl s pulled Neylin aside. "We'll be leaving soon. We need no other force with us. Are you in contact with Southwick?"

"Yes, m'Lord. We use the bird messengers."

"Good. When the time is right, we will attack the orc kingdom and wipe it out."

Neylin's eyes blinked wide. "M'Lord?"

"I said when the time is right," Karl reassured him. "You will not be doing it alone. Strathwick will join you and you will attack from the north while I and my armies will attack from the south. Until that time comes, I want every man and woman able to weld a sword to be trained to fight. Most will be required to defend Beally."

"I understand, m'Lord."

"Good. I leave you to it then."

Back in the tavern, Karl held council. "With the addition of another ranger, albeit an elf ranger whose archery skills are exceptional, we are six combat players and two support individuals."

"I can fight," Julie objected.

"I'm sure both you and Elena can fight. The problem is that we need you both to do more than just fighting. Elena has fed us, taken care of our wounds, and has been a necessary and integral part of the team."

Elena preened, sliding adoring eyes up at Dieter.

"I can do that to," Julie affirmed.

"I'm counting on it, especially as we move through orc territory. Here's my plan."

For the next hour, Karl outlined his plan to get through Krug and subsequently deliver Julie to Rhyeem.

"The bottom line is that we act as though we are a recon unit. We observe and remain unseen."

"Might be kind of tough with the wolf," Annabeth pointed out.

"I know," Karl admitted. "I'll let him decide, though he's pretty handy when it comes to battle."

"You'd be surprised how quiet he is," Caryn said.

"I agree with Caryn," Sakura added. "He's even surprised me a couple of times."

"We'll let him decide," Karl replied. "If there are no other questions, we leave in the morning. I want us to slip out quietly, unnoticed. I don't want anyone to know how we're getting to Rhyeem. The less they know, the better for us."

"Don't trust the folks here?" Sakura said.

"No. I have a feeling Giblick is not happy with the way things turned out for him. So watch your backs."

Though Julie listened, her attention was on Annabeth and Raquel, so that when the meeting broke up, she hurried to make her claim. "I get him tonight."

"Sorry, Sweetie," Annabeth replied with a polite smile, "but your turn is tomorrow night."

"Tomorrow," Julie wailed. "But we're going to be gone tomorrow. We'll be in orc territory. It's not fair." She stamped her foot then attempted to thrust herself between Annabeth and Karl. "Tell her it's my turn tonight."

Karl extricated himself from her grip, shaking his head as he held up his hands, stating, "You all work it out," before heading off to his room.

Annabeth stepped in front of Julie and leaned over to whisper. "You behave or I'll cast a spell on you so that you'll have stag horns on your head and a pig's nose on your face."

Julie gasped in horror, plopped back down in her chair and turned her head to avoid looking at the sorceress.

Annabeth turned, caught Raquel smirking, and winked.

151

Felix walked down the deserted aisle, past the numerous cubicles where accountants, admin assistants, payroll managers, and numerous other middle and upper managers once quietly worked. Most of the cubicles and offices had been stripped clean of their former occupants' identities: photos of loved ones, favorite coffee mugs, framed wall decorations of college degrees and other accomplishments announcing the owner of the space. All that remained was office equipment: desks, chairs, filing cabinets for the backup paper copies despite the 'paperless' emphasis, computers, printers, phones, and trash cans.

That not all had vanished was evidenced by several offices still neat and tidy, though the occupants had gone home for the day. These tended to be upper management types, unhappily assuming all responsibilities and tasks for their departments, until the time of their own departure to the inner adventure of their chosen games.

Felix opened one of the massive double doors that reached floor to ceiling, which swung smoothly and easily for its size, and stepped into the inner sanctum, the front office leading to Mister Landon's abode, and walked up to stand before the secretary's desk.

Secretary. Felix inwardly smiled at the word for it was a throwback to another era long before he was born. But it was a title used by the woman herself whenever she called him. *I wonder if it bothers her to be called a 'secretary?'*

It was still a few minutes before seven when Felix approached Alyson Whitmer's desk. A tall curvaceous woman with long black hair and a penetrating stare, Felix had a feeling she wasn't too happy about his presence this evening. And then the thought occurred that perhaps she and Mister Landon had a thing going. After all, Alyson Whitmer had a gorgeous body and face, almost like one of the cliché serving girls in Bridge Quest... or was he thinking of Annabeth and Raquel? It occurred to him that perhaps she might be the prototype for the characters in the game – large firm breasts, narrow waist, long legs, thick long hair, flawless skin, pert nose on a captivating face, and bright eyes that were innocent, sensual, and resolute all at once.

Fascinated by the analogy, he continued his reverie while waiting for the anointed hour of his dinner. Surmising she normally had dinner with Landon, Felix decided that Landon wanted to keep their liaisons a secret, thus she was not to be included in tonight's affair. Most likely she'd pretend to go home then hang around somewhere close so that when he left, she would return for the goodnight kiss and frolic in the hay afterwards.

Felix wondered if she would follow Landon into his game or if she had her own passions. "I'm surprised to see you working so late," he said as though making conversation.

She looked up at him and frowned. "Why wouldn't I be here?"

"I don't know," he shrugged. "I'm sure you have a life outside of here."

"This *is* my life," she responded with a thoughtful sigh.

"Really?" Felix said with a smile that conveyed his pity. *Yup. She's sleeping with him. And she's pissed that I'm here tonight screwing up her normal evening routine. That sly old devil. All this time everyone thinking he was some sort of hermit. Wonder what she's like in bed? Hopefully a lot more fun than she is here and now.*

"Yes, really," she replied with the same detached countenance.

"You don't like to do other things like reading or music or exercise? It's obvious from the way you look that you take excellent care of yourself." It came out before he had a chance to think about what he said and he cringed, expecting her to chastise him for inappropriate remarks.

Instead, she softened at the compliment, making her even more fetching and Felix had a sudden epiphany of why the gaming world was so appealing. It was the rare woman who looked like Alyson Whitmer. Even with all the artificial enhancements, few women could match what Alyson had naturally. Hence the gaming world where everyone is beautiful.

Well... maybe not everyone for he knew some gamers chose hideous creatures as their avatars. There's always one weird one in any group.

"Yes I do have other interests," she said with a pleasant smile, effectively brightening the entire room. "I love music and play the piano."

"Ah," Felix nodded, "an evocative instrument. Who is you favorite composer?"

"Are you familiar with Debussy?"

"Claire de lune is one of my favorite works," he sighed contentedly. "The Impressionist period is perhaps my favorite era, though I confess that there are Baroque pieces I find equally enchanting."

Alyson's mouth gaped open. "You... you actually know music. So many around here are linear morons who couldn't tell Bach from Beethoven, whose grasp of music is whatever white noise is piped in."

Felix laughed at the analogy, remembering his own frustration at what passed for music to some of his own employees. 'Cacophony' was the word that came to mind.

"How long have you been playing?"

"I started lessons when I was four," she answered.

Felix stared at her and the epiphany hit. "It was you... at the World Music Festival and Competition in Vienna. You were what... sixteen or seventeen?"

Alyson blushed. "You were there?"

"Yes, on holiday with my parents. You were incredible. You blew away the competition with a Chopin nocturne among other pieces. It was a masterful performance. Forgive my asking, but how did you end up here? It seems a strange journey from concert pianist to corporate secretary."

Alyson uttered a heavy sigh and looked out the window. "It's a long story, one involving another musician and the realization that I hated performing." She paused to ponder how much she would relate when instead, her hand went to the earpiece in her right ear.

"Yes, Mister Landon, he's here. Yes, Mister Landon. Yes, Sir. Thank you. Yes, Sir. Good night." Tapping off, she smiled at Felix. "He's waiting for you. Enjoy your evening."

"Thank you." He paused and smiled kindly at her. "Perhaps one of these days you would allow me to listen to you play."

"Perhaps," she replied with a cryptic grin that made his heart leap. "You better go in. He doesn't like to be kept waiting."

When Felix and Landon walked into the dining room, the first thing Felix noted was the size of the table, large enough to sit thirty people. Thankfully the place settings were opposite each other at the far end.

"The table is from Louis XIV's furnishings," Landon explained. "I picked it up recently."

"It's beautiful," Felix complimented, caring little for the immenseness of the piece.

"I hope you like pheasant," Landon said, leading the way to the end of the table.

"Never had it," Felix admitted, "but I'm sure I will."

Seating themselves, Landon lifted a small bell off to his right, giving it a light jingle. A moment later, the door opened and the cook, a balding older man in crisp clean white smock and apron, emerged carrying a tray laden with the meal. Deftly placing the steaming plates before them, he then placed the tray on the sideboard and poured the wine. Leaving the bottle on the table, he curtly bowed and went back to the kitchen.

Landon lifted his glass. "Prost."

"Yamas," Felix replied.

"Ah," Landon winked and smiled, "a Greek response. Well done. Again, you're the first person to not only question me, but the first to actually know what I was saying." He shook his head. "What a world we've become where knowledge is a veneer found on the internet."

Felix glanced around the room at the various pieces of furniture, chairs, wall hangings and art. "What are you going to do with all this when you immerse? Seems a shame to simply leave it, especially after all the work it took you to collect it."

"That's exactly it," Landon said with a wistful sigh. "Everything I collect is either a one of a kind original or has a one-of-a-kind provenance.   While a game can make something rare, it can also negate that rarity by simply recreating another one. This table for instance was owned by Louis XIV. While someone could make a table just like it, it won't be the same table. Nothing can replicate one of a kind."

"So, what will you do?"   Felix sipped the wine, a delicious chardonnay.

"I've decided to place everything in a sealed warehouse… for posterity, that is if any future generations tire enough of the gaming world to want to return to the real world." He cut a small piece of pheasant and dipped it in the gravy spilling over the mashed potatoes.

They ate in silence for a bit before Felix screwed up enough courage to query, "Do you mind if I ask you a question, work related?"

"No," Landon answered with a chuckle.

"Bridge Quest was originally designed as an assassination team training ground."

"That's correct."

"If we assume the entire world will be immersed within a generation, why the need for an assassination team, and why the need to keep it secret?"

Landon chewed his food and swallowed, followed by a sip of wine before answering. "Initially, an assassination team was necessary because too many were interfering with progress. The only way to handle obstacles is to get rid of them."

"But we never developed the team," Felix objected. "They're all still in the game, and the obstacles we expected are being eliminated one by one."

"That's all very true," Landon acknowledged. "So tell me, once everyone is immersed, what's to stop someone from coming back and interfering in another game?"

"The AI controlling the game can prevent that," Felix argued.

"Who controls the AI?"

"Whoever programmed it. But returning also requires a body. While we advertise that everyone is cryogenically frozen, it's obvious to anyone who actually thinks about it that we have neither the storage capability nor the energy to cryogenically freeze the entire world. That's why we're now reprocessing bodies."

"A polite term for cremating and composting," Landon chuckled.

Felix dipped his head and smiled agreement. "Still, if we are eliminating bodies once they're immersed, there's nothing to come back into."

"Again, you are partially correct, for it assumes that all companies are playing by the same rules, reprocessing bodies once the subject is immersed. But we can't make that assumption. For example, we still have Karl's body, available any time we wish, as well as Annabeth's body, Raquel's, Dieter's, and Caryn's. We must assume that we are not alone doing this."

Felix noted the absence of another key member. "Sakura?"

"Unfortunately, hers had to be destroyed when it was discovered that she really did have an incurable disease. The pity of it is that she was the most promising. We're toying with finding another body for her."

"But that goes back to my point," Felix said. "If the AI can independently reason and recognizes the danger of resurrection, for lack of a better word, what's to say that fail-safes built into the system won't prevent the scenarios you've presented?"

"That's just it," Landon answered. "We can't know for sure. The only way to do that is to have the capability of someone returning on a regular basis, ensuring no one tampers with the gaming worlds."

"But why an assassination team? I would think a computer-slash-AI nerd would be a better choice, someone who understands the system."

"Once again," Landon smiled, "you are partially correct. Computer nerds can work wonders with the gaming worlds and all associated facets of them. Unfortunately, they are not as promising in real life. What I mean by that is the down and dirty of survival in the real world. Sure, a computer nerd can program building security, missile systems, and the like. But when it comes to basic survival, they are ill equipped."

"I don't follow you," Felix said, pouring them both more wine.

"Once everyone is in the world, what need do we have for computer nerds?"

Felix frowned as he pondered the question.

"They're all in the game," Landon continued. "Who's left on the outside… in the real world?"

"No one," Felix answered, "but if one was to return, he could wreak havoc."

"Agreed. But he would have to eat and sleep and find shelter and all the other basic requirements of life. Once the canned vegetables in the long disused supermarkets have expired and the frozen meats rotted, how will he survive?"

Felix blinked at the realization. Supermarket closings had accelerated as grocery chains consolidated. Farms followed suit and the mom-and-pop farms had all disappeared as governments took control of the farming industry. Food surpluses grew as fewer people remained to be fed. Cows, pigs, and other farm animals were butchered at a rapid rate to meet the reduced demand.

The same held true for oil fields as the demand for gasoline plummeted. The Middle Eastern nations, once among the richest nations in the world felt the impact of idle wells, now covered under the windblown sands of the desert.

As the demand for human essentials plummeted, there was an inverse demand for the gaming worlds. With the plethora of satisfying even the weirdest passions, people lined up to be immersed. New immersion centers opened faster than could be controlled, which meant the human penchant for making a buck off of any situation allowed immersion hustlers to charge for what was essentially a free commodity. Individuals simply signed over their tangible assets to the immersion company and they were in the game. It didn't matter if one was rich or poor. Immersion was an equal opportunity.

Well… that wasn't exactly true.

Felix remembered the first time he witnessed an immersion. He arrived at the immersion room a few minutes before the scheduled time for immersion. He was surprised at the size of the room, assuming that immersion was a small intimate affair. Instead, the room contained over 100 immersion beds, all filled with bodies waiting their departures.

The only corporate presence were two technicians, one to handle the control console and the other to walk the room double checking connections, a redundant job since everything was automated and controlled by AI. The man's ennui was too obvious as he mindlessly ambled in between beds, paying little attention to travelers or machines.

Close to the console, a late arriving family prepared to enter a game. The family had been on the lower end of the income spectrum. After turning over their meager assets, they were hyped to be entering the Lottery Game, 'Where everyone's a winner!'

Why anyone would want to spend eternity playing the lottery was beyond Felix's comprehension, but apparently there was enough demand to develop a game for them.

Felix stood off to the side and listened to the technician explain to the family, a man and wife in their early 30's with two teenage boys whose sole focus was on what they were going to buy with their winnings.

"Once you are in the game," the technician said, "you will be directed to your new home and given instructions on how to proceed."

"What about initial cash?" the father asked. He was a lanky pimply-faced man with a scraggly beard and crewcut, and darting eyes that looked like he was expecting to be busted for some transgression.

"Everything you need is in the home."

"Is it big?" the mother asked. She was an attractive, lithe and buxom woman with long strawberry blond hair.

Felix struggled to understand how she ended up married to Mister Paranoid.

"Your initial home is a three-bedroom bungalow, in the Craftsman style. To give you an idea, a comparable home here in the far outskirts of the Chattanooga area would run in the half-millions.

The woman sucked in her breath, an avaricious grin spreading across her face.

"An' we're gonna grow up like normal, right?" one of the boys asked.

"It's all programmed into the game," the technician reassured him. "Your parents will stay the same age, while you two will age until you get to an age you like and then you'll remain that age. If there are no other questions," he said, ready to be done with these folks, "go ahead and get on the immersion beds so we can connect you up and get you on your way."

Felix watched as the family positioned themselves on the immersion beds while the technician moved to the main control console. Removing their shoes and socks, they stretched out on the beds as electrodes attached themselves to their skulls, feet, and fingertips.

Once secure, the technician announced, "Ready?" over a loudspeaker then flipped the main switch.

What happened next surprised Felix. Expecting zaps, electric discharges, and other sounds of electrical activity, he was met with silence instead. After less than a minute, the technician pressed the release button and electrodes detached as beds raised at steep angles and holes in the floor yawned open. Bodies began sliding off the beds into the caverns below where the hum of conveyor belts broke the silence.

When the last body was deposited below to be carried off to the crematory, the floor closed, and the beds lowered. Felix guesstimated that they could immerse 100 an hour for 12 hours a day, yielding almost half a million immersions in a year, for this facility alone. ITL had immersion sites in all the major cities in North America.

He walked over to the technician waiting patiently for the beds to level into position. "So they're going into a lottery game."

"Yeah." The man shook his head and sniffed in derision. "Losers."

"Why losers?" Felix frowned. "They're going into a game they wanted."

"That's just it," the man replied, receiving a 'thumbs up' from the other technician. "They're going into a low-level game. They're gonna be bored in less than a year."

"I don't understand."

"The Lottery Game is one of the simpler games," the technician explained, "not a lot of data space required to run the program. You play the lottery, you win a little or a lot, you get stuff and that's the extent of the game. Because everyone's a winner, like the hype says, there's no challenge, no suspense. What makes the lottery so popular in real life is that so few people actually win. It's the thrill of being different, of winning and being able to gloat."

"Are there different lottery games?"

"Sure," he said, "but this is the one they could afford."

"Pardon?"

"This is the one they could afford. Let's just say that they weren't financially in a position to warrant immersion in another game, one with more variables. You get what you pay for."

"So the rich…"

"Get the golden egg," he grinned. "Why not? They're paying for it, and it takes money and time to develop really complex games."

"So when the rich come here –"

"Oh, they don't come to this room," he interrupted. "We have other suites for the uber rich."

"And the people who come here?" Felix curved a hand at the room that was now filling up with the next session of travelers.

"Pretty much everyone else. Their specific immersion games are already programmed into the beds. All I have to do is send them on their way. Now, if you'll excuse me, I

161

have to get this group settled. There's always one or two who get cold feet."

He stepped down from the console and headed to where the other technician was soothing an older woman and her husband.

Felix walked past the couple towards the main doors, overhearing the woman's plaintive plea.

"How do we know it's going to work? What if something goes wrong and we're sent to the wrong game?"

"Let's go to your beds and see what's programmed," the technician encouraged.

Felix was out the door by the time the couple arrived at their immersion beds. Walking back towards his office, he mused on the volume of annual immersions. The Chattanooga Immersion Center had been operating for the past three years, this current year seeing a significant uptick in applicants. Yet not all immersion centers followed the same ethical code that Mister Landon was so strict about.

The rapid increase in the number of legitimate immersion centers saw the concomitant increase of dubious locations offering immersions at cut rates operated by individuals who either didn't know the first thing about immersion or knew a sucker when they saw them – a fool and his money and all that. Too many folks discovered that instead of immersion into their expected game, they were still in the real-world sans their life savings.

That's when the immersion police emerged, sanctioned and controlled by agreement between the governments and the major immersion companies, like ITL. Funded mostly by the companies, yet controlled by the governments, the immersion police were effective in reducing, but not eliminating the back-alley immersion centers.

With a knowing smile, Landon patiently watched Felix ruminating on the question. "You were lost there for a moment."

"I was just thinking of the past year of immersion," Felix explained. "So much has happened in just the last year that it's sometimes hard to wrap my mind around the speed of things. But I still don't see the need for assassination teams, even if I accept that a computer nerd could not survive in the real world, though I think that point is still debatable."

Landon chuckled.   "I prefer to think of them as enforcement teams.   But to allay your confusion, you know that we are not operating independently concerning assassination squads, correct? What I mean by that is that the major players in Russia and China have already employed their teams. One would think that we here in the west would be the first ones to utilize hit teams. Sadly, we're a little behind the times for a number of reasons, the key one being negative publicity if the media ever discovered our plans."

Felix sipped his wine, waiting for Landon to continue.

"Each of the major players agreed to keep their operations within their own spheres of influence. In other words, Russian hit teams stayed in Russia and its satellite countries, likewise China and the others. The problem we've had here in the west is that once word got out, the subscription for immersion far exceeded anything experienced by other nations and hence the delay in putting together our own hit teams."

"So is there still a need?" Felix asked.

"Even more so now," Landon replied.

"Why?"

"It's called 'faith in humanity.'" Landon noted that Felix had finished eating and rang the bell.

The cook came in and cleared the plates.

"Delicious as usual," Landon complimented.

"Thank you, Sir," came the humorless reply.

"What game are you interested in?" Felix asked the cook who shot a worried glance at Landon.

"It's OK, Henri," Landon soothed. "I'm not going to stop you... when you're ready."

Felix immediately understood 'when you're ready' actually meant when Landon was ready.

"Go ahead and answer his question," Landon said.

The cook straightened, plates in hand. "I think I should like to be in a Pirate Harem game."

Felix blinked in momentary confusion before understanding swept through. "Not some cooking game, eh?"

"Anyone can cook," the man replied, "but few are good at it. I am a cook because I am good at it. Still, if I am to spend eternity doing something, being in the kitchen is not where I want to be."

Felix nodded with a smile. "A wise answer."

The cook shifted his gaze at Landon, waiting to be dismissed.

"Thank you," Landon said. "You may bring out the brandy." Turning to Felix, he asked, "Do you smoke?"

"No I don't."

"I understand. After dinner is the one time I enjoy a pipe. I hope you don't mind."

"Of course not," Felix reassured him, thinking it was his house and he could do as he bloody well wanted. "I like the smell of pipe tobacco. In fact," he grinned, "one time I worked for a gentleman who smoked a tobacco that smelled like chocolate. Anytime he walked the halls there would be a rush on the candy machines."

Landon laughed. "Sounds like a progressive company, allowing such vices as smoking and candy machines."

He scooted back from the table and led the way to the living room with two walls of windows that, during the daytime, provided a grand vista of the Gold Point Marina across the river and the mountains in the distance. Now, in the late hours of evening, all was an inky dark for the headlamps of cars on the highways that once disturbed the night no longer choked the roads and byways. Chattanooga was slipping away to nonexistence.

As they settled into two plush chairs positioned before the hearth, Landon filled the bowl of his antique Meerschaum pipe as the cook appeared with a tray containing two snifter glasses half-filled with a rich cherry brandy, as well as the bottle.

"It's actually a liquor," Landon explained, "from Croatia. I hope you like it."

164

"I'm sure I will," Felix replied, accepting the glass, swirling the liquor and inhaling the fruity bouquet.

Landon lit his pipe, inhaled a slow draw then breathed out the puffs of tobacco smoke. The aroma had a faint hint of berries. Taking another draw, he slowly exhaled while gazing wistfully at his pipe.

"I wonder if the gaming world pipe tobacco will be the same."

Once the cook deposited the liquor and departed, Landon said, "We were talking about the continuing need for our special teams, and you questioned whether the need remained. One area we have neglected to mention is the matter of those not wanting to immerse. What do we do with them?"

Felix sipped the sweet liquor, letting the thick liquid settle on his tongue before swallowing. "It is a matter that I've given some thought. We certainly can't let them remain to roam at will."

"Why not?"

"There's always the possibility of someone interfering with one of the AI centers."

"Hence the need for an enforcement team," Landon said with a triumphant smile.

Felix laughed. "You win."

"It's not a matter of winning," Landon replied with a smile. "It's a matter of control. We've programmed the AI to exercise complete control over every facet of all the games, including the ability of players to change games if they desire. We've created a real Shangri La for mankind. The fact that not all subscribe to this reality is troubling."

"There's always someone who refuses to accept progress," Felix agreed.

"We're getting to the point where the only ones left will be a few game developers, gaming managers, and certain government officials. Any one of them can cause problems. It's a question of do we trust the last man standing?"

"That means we need to be the last man standing," Felix stated.

"Exactly."

"What about those holdouts who head to the hills to avoid immersion?" Felix took another sip, hoping Landon would see fit to refill the glass when his was empty.

"We're already decided that anyone refusing to immerse either needs to be forced, or…"

"Eliminated," Felix finished for him.

"Exactly."

"You said 'We'," Felix stated.

"'We' as in the other corporate heads," Landon replied. "As you can see, we especially do not trust government, nor do we trust everyone remaining before total immersion. That's why certain individuals have been chosen to act as safeguards. Karl and his team are the ones selected for the North American continent."

"That's a huge area," Felix frowned.

"True, but it is not impossible, especially with the aid of technology. The AI is globally interconnected, though the likelihood of our team travelling overseas is nil, unless one of them can fly a plane or sail a boat across the seas. Still, with drones and cameras and the like, Karl's job will be made that much easier."

"When do you think this will happen?" Felix ventured.

"Soon," Landon evasively answered, "very soon." Noting Felix had finished his drink he motioned to the bottle. "Please, help yourself. Finish the whole thing if you like. I've plenty more."

Felix chuckled as he refilled his glass, holding the bottle up to see if Landon wanted more, pleased when Landon held out his glass.

"I noted that Gerard is still with us," Landon observed.

"I haven't thought of a suitable departure for him yet," Felix explained.

"Actually, that's good. When the time comes for Karl to be brought back to real life, perhaps Gerard should be the messenger."

Felix barked a laugh. "A wonderful idea."

"So are you still interested in the golf pro game for your immersion?" Landon asked.

"I'm leaning that way," Felix answered, suddenly realizing that the body he now inhabited would no longer be available once he immersed. Once he was in the game, his body would be cremated, his along with the rest of humanity, except for the select few enforcers.

"What's going to happen to our enforcers as time goes on?" Felix wondered aloud. "Every time they are brought back to real life, they will age. Also, they'll be susceptible to disease and even death by accident or something."

"True," Landon admitted. "That's why they need to be the best so that accidents don't happen."

"Even if they do survive –"

"Which could be a thousand years," Landon interrupted.

"OK, a thousand years," Felix agreed. "At some point in time, their bodies will age to a point where they will no longer be effective."

"By then," Landon said, "all those who are presently holding out will have long been dead."

"Unless they have babies," Felix pointed out.

"True, but even then, there is little chance that they will have evaded the enforcers for that length of time."

"And all this is controlled by AI," Felix mused. "To think, our lives are now permanently in the hands of computers."

"If you think about it," Landon said, "our lives already *are* in the hands of computers. You can't even buy a cup of coffee without the aid of computers."

"True," Felix solemnly nodded, "true." Taking a deep draught of the liquor, he held it in his mouth, letting the flavor permeant his tongue. Swallowing, he asked, "Have you finally decided on your game?"

Landon chuckled. "I thought I had, but now with the possibility of moving from one game to another, it certainly allows for more prospects. Still, my greatest joy is acquiring antiquities. The search, the discovery, the acquisition, those are what I enjoy. So, for the beginning at least, I'll immerse into one of the antiquities games."

"Wonder what game Alyson will choose," Felix said before realizing he said it out loud.

"That's a good question," Landon agreed, either unaware of Felix's more than passing interest or choosing to ignore it.

"She's quite an accomplished pianist," Felix said.

"She is?" Landon replied with a frown.

"Yes," Felix said, surprised that Landon didn't know that about his own secretary.

"How did you know that?" he asked, cocking an eyebrow.

"We were chatting briefly before I came in for dinner and I realized where I had seen her before. It was at the World Music Festival and Competition in Vienna. She was sixteen or seventeen. I was on a college break in Vienna on holiday with my parents. She won the competition."

Landon tilted his head and furrowed his brows as he pondered the news. "Interesting. When I hired her, it was on the recommendation of a friend. Her resume said nothing about music."

"Most likely not wanting to give the wrong impression," Felix opined. "You know how flakey artists can be."

"Did she tell you anything else?"

"Not really," he shrugged. "Didn't have enough time." *Maybe he's not sleeping with her.*

"Now you have my curiosity up," he said. "I'd appreciate any more information you might glean. I suppose I really ought to know more about my employees, though it seems rather moot now that we're all headed in different directions."

"You really didn't know?" Felix blushed when he realized that his question was too in-your-face.

"No, I didn't," Landon replied without malice. "I purposely do not create intimate relationships with close employees. It avoids all the potential problems of romantic involvement."

"A wise decision," Felix replied, thrilled at the news. *Wonder if she would consent to go out with me?* Felix glanced at his watch, noting it was almost 9:30 pm. Gulping the last of his liquor, he placed the glass on side table next to the chair. "Thank you for a delightful evening."

"Leaving already?"

168

"I… I don't want to overstay my welcome."

"Nonsense. You have somewhere else to go?"

"No," Felix chuckled and shrugged, "not really."

"Then relax," Landon expansively replied. "Have another drink. Now tell me about yourself."

Chapter 7

He was leaning against the city gate, his arms crossed, when Karl saw his diminutive figure and burst a greeting.

"Noble. You made it."

"It looks like just in time," he grinned, giving the ladies a more than glancing once over.

"Folks, this is Noble," Karl said by way of introduction.

"So, this is the great thief we all heard about," Annabeth said. "You've quite a reputation to live up to."

Noble's confidence wavered slightly as he decided against telling them he had been run out of town and barely escaped with the clothes on his back.

"I do my best," he lamely replied. "Where we headed?"

"Take Julie back, remember?" Karl answered.

"That means going through orc territory," he warned.

"Unless you can swim, that's the only way," Raquel said.

"You still wanna come?" Annabeth asked.

Noble hesitated, looked once over his shoulder and knew that it would only be a matter of a day or two before he was run out of Beally. He really needed to work on some thief skills.

"Yeah," he replied with a grin. "Might as well."

The road south from Beally ended at the edge of the farm fields. Where the road once continued, the path was now overgrown with trees and underbrush. Still, they could tell where the road led as the trees were younger than the surrounding forest. Surprisingly, one hundred meters up the unused trail, the congestion of trees and undergrowth vanished and a well-trodden road reappeared. A single footpath on each side of the road led away into the forest, apparently edging the border of the forest.

Karl halted the team and sent the two rangers to investigate. Caryn returned twenty minutes later.

"The trail stops about half a kilometer from here at what looks like an assembly area large enough for a platoon. There's a fire pit in the center. Looks like it was recently used, maybe a day or two ago."

Raquel showed back up and reported the same information, except the fire pit was still wet from dousing the fire, which meant the assembly point had probably been used yesterday evening.

Uafas? Anything out there?

Nothing on the road, though they've been here earlier. Their smell is still on the trail.

We're moving on. Give a shout if you see something.

That's why I'm here, isn't it?

Traveling silently, with Caryn and Raquel on point and Uafas continuing as roaming security, they continued up the road. Karl frequently checked his map, hoping to glean more information about the terrain and cities and towns. The dot locating Krugrodh, the capital, stood in the center of the area delineated as the Kingdom of Krug, which, by the map, appeared to be mountainous with plenty of rivers and roads. Their location was a red dot barely inside the boundary line. He was about to close the map when he noticed the icon for information on Krug active.

It's about damn time, he sighed with frustration. Clicking the icon, the screen opened.

The Kingdom of Krug was established by the petty tyrant Krug the Blind during the Islands Wars. Initially confined to the mountain regions around Krugrodh, subsequent rulers expanded the domain to its present boundaries. The present ruler, Magruk, also known as Magruk the Iron Fist, is a direct descendant of Vagruk the Brutal, a former guard captain who gained control in a palace coup 300 years ago.

Magruk is cunning, cruel, and paranoid, having survived several assassination attempts. He trusts only his closest friends, yet even they are not beyond suspicion, especially after his favorite nephew was discovered part of an assassination plot. The nephew and his entire family, including his parents (Magruk's own sister and brother-in-law) were executed.

The Kingdom of Krug is divided into four realms called tetrarchs, ruled by Magruk's most trusted allies, kept loyal by hostages from each ruling family.

Deciding that it was time to expand the kingdom's boundaries, as well as divert energies from another coup, Magruk has initiated raids into the south and north, in violation of the nonaggression pact signed by his great-grandfather, Zugaruk the Black.   Discovering little resistance, he has begun preparations for a full-scale invasion, stockpiling weapons and supplies in Krugrodh.

Recognizing that he can defeat only one enemy at a time, he has yet to choose which part of the island will bear the brunt of his forces – the Kingdom of Mann to the south, or the numerous independent city states to the north. Be that as it may, the stockpiling of weapons and supplies is drawing to an end and the choice will be made very soon.

Karl again skimmed the additional parts about orc society, religion, and relations, and was about to jump down to the stats chart when that same paragraph caught his eye.

Orcs view dwarves and elves with an odd mix of overt hatred, resentment, and caution.   Though orcs respect strength and power, they cannot fathom why these two races of inferior strength have kept orcs at bay for countless ages. As such, they never miss an opportunity to torment a dwarf or elf who falls into their hands. However, when it comes to full-scale battle, they proceed with caution unless certain of the outcome.   Orcs view humans as weaklings who, like sheep, blindly follow. However, even sheep can produce an obstinate ram. Thus, while they happily kill and/or oppress humans too weak to fend for themselves, they always keep one eye open for that human who will not back down.

He remembered the time in Abeloft when their ambush was almost discovered when an orc's keen nose had smelled the dwarves and elves, and he cast a quick glance at Caryn, wondering if it was such a good idea having her as point. Then he remembered Uafas who had a greater chance of being discovered by his sheer size alone. Though there were disadvantages to their presence, their advantages far outweighed the negatives. The same held true with Elena. Not only was she a superb cook, her medical skills had improved enough so that he didn't miss Kendra and Tina as much. Julie? *Um... let's just say she's the weak link in the group.* He caught her staring at him and gave her a self-conscious smile before returning to the information screen, dropping down to the combat stats.

Orcs are proficient with all simple weapons preferring those that cause the most damage in the least time, such as the falchion or the double axe. They like to attack from concealment and are proficient in setting up ambushes. Orcs will obey the rules of war (e.g., honoring a truce) only as long as it is convenient for them.

- *+4 Strength, -2 Intelligence, -2 Wisdom, -2 Charisma.*
- *Night vision: strong out to 50 feet.*
- *Light Sensitivity: Orcs prefer operating at night, in overcast conditions, or in the predawn hours. Bright sunlight affects their ability to wage combat. The same holds true within the radius of a daylight spell.*
- *Languages: Common, Orc. Additional languages: Dwarven, Gnoll, and Goblin, though these languages are not prevalent.*
- *Favored Class: Berserker/barbarian.*

He had read it all before, back in Abeloft when their battles with orcs were reduced to an almost comical adventure as the same three orcs kept reappearing only to be killed and return the next day. Thankfully, someone in the game controls must have seen what was happening and put a stop to it.

Realizing they had stopped for too long, he caught their attention, circling his fingers and pointing down the road.

They traveled silently. Karl had chosen to begin their venture using the road, assuming that any orcs they encountered would be less cautious as the likelihood of humans being this far south disappeared years ago. However, with the discovery of the two assembly areas, he wasn't so sure his plan was sound.

After an uneventful yet stressing two hours on the road, he ordered a halt and they moved into the edge of forest, far enough off the road to have ample cover and concealment, yet close enough to pick up the pace if necessary.

They had yet to settle when Uafas spoke.

Orcs coming.

Where?

On the road.

How many?

Don't know. I can smell them.

Take cover and count them if you can.

OK.

"Orcs coming," Karl said. "Noble, take Elena and Julie another hundred meters or so farther into the woods and find a place to hide."

Needing no other impetus, Noble flipped his hand at the two women. "C'mon ladies."

Casting a quick glance to see that the two women obeyed, Karl turned to the others. "Raquel and Annabeth are with me. Dieter, you take Caryn and Sakura to the other side of the road. We prepare for an ambush, but our first mission is to let them pass. We don't want to be seen if we can help it. If we're discovered, we initiate the attack. Wait for my signal."

With a nod of understanding, Dieter led the other two across the road and into position, ensuring he could see Karl.

I counted seven of them, Uafas said, *walking on the road. They are not very cautious for they are talking loudly. Once they are past, I will circle around to join you.*

No. Stay behind them on the road. I want to let them go by. We'll ambush them only if necessary. If that happens, I want to make sure none of them survive.

As you wish. They should be arriving soon.

They heard them before they saw them.

"… damn waste of time," a guttural voice complained.

"You been whinin' that same song ever since we started," another retorted.

"Well its' the damn truth. We was here just a couple o' hours ago. Weren't nobody 'round fer days. All them houses locked up tight. Everbody's gone to the castle city."

"Wull somethin' tripped the warnin' alarm," a third voice said.

"That stupid alarm is goin' off all the time. It's probably just a deer or some boar just like the last time," the guttural voice said with some exasperation. "I'm tired an' I ain't et since last night. I'm hungry. One o' you boys got somethin' t'eat?"

"Shoulda thought o' that 'fore you left, ya ignorant turd."

"Shaddup the both o' ya 'fore I brain the two o' ya," a gruff voice commanded.

The orcs rounded the bend in the trail and came into view. The front orc wore a mustard yellow sleeveless jerkin that revealed arms covered in tattoos of daggers and skulls. He carried a falchion on his left hip. On the left breast of the jerkin was a small circular metal badge of bronze, about two and a half centimeters in diameter. In the center were three raised diamonds, colored a dull red. Behind him lumbered the other orcs in careless watch, bored, tired, and hungry, their weapons still on their hips. One carried a halberd across his shoulders.

Peering through the gap in the brush, Karl caught Dieter's eyes and held a finger to his lips.

The orcs were midway past when one in the middle scrunched his face.

"I smell somethin' funny."

"That's 'cause yer sniffin' yer own stinkin' self," another retorted.

"Yeah, you smell like horse shit anyway," another joined in.

"Look who's talkin'," the affronted orc snapped. "Stop tryin' to be a smart ass, 'cause yer just an ass."

"Oh yeah? I was wonderin' how you got here. Someone leave yer cage open?"

Amidst the snickers of the other orcs, the lead orc simply shook his head and marched on, yet the insults continued.

"Yeah, well, if you was twice as smart, you'd still be stupid."

The voices diminished as the orc patrol moved on towards where the trail split to go to the two assembly areas. When they had disappeared down the trail, Karl signaled for Dieter and his team to come back across.

"We need to move, fast. Sakura, get Noble and the others."

Uafas appeared on the trail, blocking a good portion of it. *What's the plan?*

"We need to move down the trail as fast as possible to put some distance between us and the orc patrol. I'm going to send you and Sakura ahead to clear the way for us. We'll stay on the road for as long as we can." He pulled up his screen map. "We want to head west. According to the map, the road goes south for a while towards Krugrodh then splits off to head to Ozgul near the coast."

"The patrol is likely part of a larger unit," Raquel reminded him, looking at Uafas and knowing he was blocking his thoughts so that only Karl could communicate telepathically.

"Which means there's probably a military post somewhere close to here and this road probably goes through it," Karl acknowledged.

"It's not shown on the map," Caryn said.

"One of them said something about tripping an alarm," Annabeth interjected.

"You got something that can see it, a spell or whatever?" Karl asked.

"I think I'd have to be a lot closer than we are now, and besides, it's moot. Whatever we tripped is back there." She jerked a thumb up the road towards Beally.

"Good point," Karl said, silently kicking himself for not thinking about security systems.

Annabeth saw the look and read his intent. "You couldn't know," she soothed. "None of us had any idea."

"Now that we do know," Karl said, "we need to assume that the cities and military camps are likewise protected. Do you have something you can use to help?"

Annabeth pulled up her screen and quickly scrolled through her two levels of skills. "I've got a divination skill called 'See Invisible' that allows me to see things that are invisible as long as they're within my normal range of vision. Huh. It only lasts ten minutes… unless I had an 'Etched in Stone' spell.

"That's good enough for now." He turned to see Noble and the two women approach. "Where's Sakura?"

"She was with us a minute ago," Noble shrugged, glancing side to side. "What's the plan?"

"Once Sakura returns," he said, containing his irritation, "we move out. Fast." He impatiently scanned the area, wondering where she was. Turning to the group, he said, "We need to be especially cautious from here on out."

At that moment, Sakura appeared by his side.

"Where the hell have you been?" he acidly demanded.

"They're headed back this way," she replied, surprised at his tone.

"Damn it all," he snapped. "Everyone back in positions. Noble. Get those ladies out of here."

"Let's move, ladies," Noble urged while Dieter, Caryn and Sakura scooted across the road and hid.

Uafas. Head farther down the road just around the bend and cover us there.

In long galloping strides, Uafas was gone, disappearing as the trail curved.

Not more than five minutes later, the orc patrol returned, even more careless than before, and still grumbling.

"See?   Told ya," a voice complained.   "Every time somethin' triggers that damned alarm, we always gotta check it out.   Why doesn't some other squad check it out?   Why always us?"

"Yeah," another voice joined in.   "He's right.   How come it's always us?"

"Shut yer traps," the orc wearing the badge commanded.

"I'm hungry.   Think they'll still have hot chow when we get back t' camp?"

"Yer always hungry," another voice chided.

"Can't help it.   I start thinkin' o' some human flesh and I gets real hungry."

"Ain't had human meat ever since that last time we knocked down that door to that farmer's house.   Scared the shit out 'em so bad I nearly choked from laughing."

They were midway past Karl and the others when one orc spoke.

"There it is again, that smell.   I swear this was the same place I smelled it before."

"Yer always smellin' somethin' funny."

The orc in front held up his hand, causing the patrol to stop.   He tilted his head back and sniffed the air.   "I smell it too, now.   Smells like... like... smells like... elf."   He frowned and turned around to look at the others then twisting his head to stare into the forest on both sides of the road. "Don't make no sense.   Still, let's spread out and check it out."

"Why?" an orc complained.   "Ain't nuthin' here.   The smell's probably some dead skunk or somethin' else gone bad."

"Quit yer bitchin'," the leader fussed, "and just do what yer told.   Yer probably right that it's somethin' dead, but we better look just in case."

"Just in case what?"

While the one orc was busy demanding justification for delaying mealtime, Karl caught Dieter's eye and nodded, frustrated that Caryn had given them away through no fault other than being an elf.

179

He saw Dieter turn his head to alert Caryn and Sakura, and he did the same with Raquel and Annabeth. Narrowing his gaze at Annabeth, he placed his hands together by the side of his face, pretending he was asleep then pointed to the orcs.

Immediately understanding, she cast a sleep spell on the lead orc who responded by drowsily blinking his eyes, dropping to his knees then to his side, curling up in a fetal position, head on his arm, fast asleep.

"What the hell?" an orc exclaimed

"What's with him?" another spat.

One orc nudged the sleeping orc with his foot. "Wake up." When nothing happened, the orc shook his head. "We oughta leave the damn fool. Serve 'im right."

Karl looked once again at Annabeth who had the look of mischief in her eyes. He turned to watch as she cast another spell and an orc began leaping about, slapping at his arms, legs, face, and neck.

"Agggh, stingin' wasps. Git 'em off me, git 'em off me."

The others stepped back and watched, mystified as they could see nothing to cause the reaction.

Jittering in a spasmodic dance, the orc's anguish intensified until he fled up the road back towards their camp.

"Let 'im go," one orc said with a dismissive sniff. "He's kinda nuts anyway."

Karl suppressed a giggle, watching the orc jumping around. He looked back to Annabeth who held up a finger for one more opportunity. He nodded and gazed at Annabeth as she worked her hands as though rolling a ball between them then thrusting the invisible spell towards the orcs.

A moment later, a loud crashing came from up the road towards the assembly areas, causing the orcs to turn in unison only to see a giant centipede heading straight for them. In unison, they fled screaming up the road, leaving their sleeping comrade behind.

Ignoring the slumbering orc, the centipede gave chase, moving surprisingly fast for a creature with so many legs.

Uafas. Giant centipede coming your way. Stay hidden.

There was a pause before the wolf answered. *That thing is huge*, followed by a chuckle. *They ran past here in a panic, quite unlike the fearless orcs we're all told they are.*

Waiting until cries of panic dwindled in the distance, Karl emerged from the hiding spot, stepping onto the road, soon joined by the others.

"I thought the snoozing orc was nice touch," Raquel said. "Even had to contain my laughter at the one jumping around like he was bitten by bugs. But the last one just about scared the crap out of me. That thing was huge."

"How long does it last?" Sakura asked, casting a wary glance at the sorceress.

"Don't know," Annabeth shrugged with an impish grin.

"Can you control it if it comes back?" Karl hastened to ask.

"Yes."

"What do we do with him?" Raquel asked, casting a disapproving look at the snoozing orc.

"How long does it last?" Karl asked.

"About an hour."

"Leave him," Karl said. "We don't want anyone to know we're here."

Uafas came padding up and bristled when he saw the orc. *That one is still alive. I'd eat him, but orcs don't taste that good.*

"We're leaving him. Like I said, we don't want anyone to know we're here."

"I'm not sure we're too successful with that," Raquel observed. "After all, how many giant centipedes are there in these woods?"

"And he is an orc," Sakura pointed out. "We kill him now or we'll have to kill him later."

"Leave him," Karl ordered. "Go get Nobel and the girls. The rest of you, make enough of a mess around here to look like they tried to run away through the woods."

"Why?" Annabeth asked.

"They're going to come back here and look around. We want them thinking that our hiding spots were caused by them trampling here. Remember –"

"We don't want anyone to know we're here," Annabeth finished for him.

"Exactly."

Karl turned to the two Rangers who were busy trampling the lower brush. "Raquel and Caryn, one of you see if you can roust up a bird or two to act as scouts."

"There's not a lot of wildlife around here," Raquel said, gazing up to the sky.

"It's like no one wants to be around where orcs are," Caryn agreed.

When Julie arrived, she stutter-stepped backwards when she saw the orc. "He's still alive."

"Be careful. He bites," Annabeth deadpanned.

Julie took another step back, causing Raquel to smirk.

"What are you doing?" Elena asked, watching the others trampling the area.

"Making it look like orcs did this," Annabeth explained.

"Why?"

"That's good enough," Karl announced. "Let's move out. Uafas and Sakura in the lead. We stay on the road until it comes to a split. We take the road to the right. We move fast and silent. If we come upon orcs or anything else, we either hide or fight, the first option always being to hide."

Thirty minutes Uafas called back, *Orcs coming.*

How many?

Lots.

"OK folks," Karl urged, "follow me. Careful where you step. Leave no trace."

By the time Karl had his team sequestered a good fifty meters deep into the woods, the forward orc scouts were opposite them, their pace quick but guarded. A minute later, the main body of the patrol passed, all armed with falchions and the occasional halberd, moving in menacing silence.

Anymore?

No.

Keep a look out. Is Sakura with you?

No.

"Damn that woman," Karl muttered.

Waiting another few minutes, he motioned to the rest of the team. "Move out. We got to put some distance between us and them."

Leading them back to the road, he did a quick head count. "Caryn take point, Raquel take rear security."

"Where's Sakura?" Caryn asked.

"Don't know," Karl tersely answered. "We don't have time to wait for her. Move out."

An hour later, Sakura suddenly appeared next to Karl.

"Where the hell have you been," he growled.

"Checking on the orc patrol," she replied, wondering what he was so mad about. "Once they found the sleeping orc, they did an area search and now they're headed back."

"Who told you to do that?"

"I just thought –"

"Well you thought wrong," he snapped. "I don't give a rat's ass what they're doing back there. You had an assignment as point and your absence caused me to select another to do the job you were supposed to be doing."

"But I thought –"

"Dammit, just do what I tell you. Your absence jeopardized the entire team. No one knew where you were. For all we knew you could have been injured. And I don't care how great an assassin you are, at some point you're going to get hurt. If that happened here, you'd have been left on your own... in orc country."

"I'm... I'm sorry," she said, her initial indignation fading.

"I'm not trying to squelch your initiative," he continued when he saw her contrite expression. "But dammit, you gotta clear it with me first. I can't, we can't afford anything to happen to you. You're more important to this team than you realize."

"But how was I to tell you?" she asked, though pleased with his statement.

"You were with Uafas. He and I can talk. Remember?"

Sakura heaved a deflated sigh. "Sorry. I forgot."

"Well don't. Now get back up there and send Caryn back."

"Yes, Sir."

A few minutes later, Caryn drifted back.

"I see you found our lost assassin," she said. "Where was she?"

"Investigating what the orcs were doing."

"That was stupid. She could've compromised this whole operation."

Karl shook his head and rolled his eyes. "Civilians."

Caryn grinned. "Still, we do have a good team. Raquel is a really good ranger. And Annabeth in improving daily with her sorcery skills."

It was the way she said it, that caused Karl to note that she only mentioned the two women he was intimate with. Casting a surreptitious glance at her merely reconfirmed that she was a handsome woman.

We're at the road split, Uafas said, interrupting Karl's reverie.

Hold tight. We're coming.

Karl stopped, causing the others to likewise stop and wait until Raquel joined the group.

"Listen up folks," Karl warned. "We're coming to the split in the road. We'll be heading towards the coast to the orc town called Ozgul. My guess is that the closer we get to the town, the more orcs we're going to encounter, which means we'll be spending more time in the forest working our way around the town. We got another six hours of daylight, so we're going to make the most of it. Remember, we don't want to be seen."

Six hours later and ducking into the woods seven times to avoid orc patrols, Karl called a final halt for the day, and they entered the forest to find a place to spend the night. The forest seemed to thicken as they worked their way in a southwest direction, the canopy of trees almost shutting out the afternoon sun. Occasional bits of sunlight pierced the cover and illuminated the forest floor in long shafts. Every now and then they crossed a game trail.

Forty-five minutes later, Uafas froze and said, *There's someone upwind not too far away. I can smell him. He's not an orc.*

Holding up a clenched fist, Karl halted the team and they hunkered down in cover. Pointing to Sakura, he motioned her forward.

"Uafas says there's someone up ahead," he whispered. "Check it out."

With a nod, she was gone.

Karl turned back to the team and held a finger to his lips then patted the air, effectively telling them to wait in place.

Uafas. Anything?

Sakura went by a little while ago. Do you want me to check?

Not yet. How about doing a quick perimeter search, make sure nothing is beside or behind us.

OK.

Twenty minutes later, Sakura appeared beside Karl.

"There's a small campsite," she whispered, "within a cluster of large rocks that keep it well hidden. I managed to get inside the walls and saw a man squatted down by a fire ring, eating what looked to be dried meat."

"Anyone else?"

"Not that I saw. From the looks of it, he lives there alone. He's pretty scraggly."

"Weapons? Booby traps?"

"He had an orc blade beside him, and I saw a quiver full of arrows by the entrance of a cave."

"Got it. Good job. I want you to come with me in a moment." He pointed to the rest of the group, curling his fingers, telling them to come.

When all had approached and crouched down near him, he lowered his voice and said, "There's a man up ahead. We're gonna go find out what's up. I'm taking Sakura with me. Caryn is in charge while we're gone." He noted the indignation flash across Raquel's face, her lips pursed. "Questions? Then spread out."

Sakura led the way as they zigzagged through the forest. The undergrowth was thick and more than once, Karl felt the brambles tugging at his leggings. The terrain began a sharp incline and Karl scrambled after Sakura who seemed to barely touch the ground.

Cresting a steep hill, she paused and pointed. Across a sharp draw, boulders protruded in a protective wall, trees growing out from among the gaps and cracks. She then motioned for him to follow. Snaking her way down and across the draw, she worked her way up the short cliff and perched atop an outcropping, waiting for Karl to catch up. She pointed to a grouping of rocks and nodded.

Silently crossing the short distance, Karl was about to climb up when the man suddenly appeared, standing atop a tall rock, staring down at him. He held a staff in his hand. His dark wild hair fell to his shoulders while his beard fell to the middle of his chest. He wore an orc vest and leggings that were ripped and torn just below the knees.

"Well, c'mon then," he said, his voice gruff. "Tell me who you are and how did you find me?"

"Nice to meet you too," Karl replied with a smile. "May we come up or will you come down?"

"We?" His head twitched to scan the area. "I only see you. How many more of you are there?"

"Just her." Karl chuckled when Sakura appeared next to the man whose startled jump nearly dislodged him off the stone.

"An assassin," he exclaimed.

"Don't worry. We come as friends," Karl said. "Who are you?"

The man frowned at him for an awkward moment. "You better come in. Are you sure there's just two of you?"

"Actually, there's nine of us."

"Nine?" he said, his mouth dropping in wonder before musing to himself. "Imagine that. After all this time, nine have made it this far and at once." Turning, he dropped and disappeared behind the rock, only to emerge around the side.

"Well," he said, taking stock of the tall Viking, "you're welcome here."

"I'll get them," Sakura said and took off.

"She's good," the man said as Sakura vanished.

186

"Who are you?" Karl asked, staring at the wiry man who looked like he'd been living in the forest for most of his life.

"Name's Ben," he replied, turning around and leading Karl between the rocks to his camp. You?"

"Karl."

Karl stepped into a wide clearing surrounded by massive boulders with a canopy of intertwined branches from trees that surrounded the encampment. Opposite the single entrance was a cave with a fit pit in the entrance.

"How long you been here, Ben?"

Ben scrunched his face. "What year is it?"

"2037."

"Damn. Have I been here that long?" He shook his head. "Came here in 2035, the very first player inserted into the game."

"You've been in the game for two years," Karl marveled then added, "and this is as far as you got in two years," before thinking about what he said.

"Yup," Ben replied, unaffected, walking over to stir the coals in the fire pit.

"What happened?"

Ben blinked as he remembered then chuckled. "By the gods, lots happened. Met a girl on the first island, an NPC and we took a shine to each other. She was a tavern wench, good looking, if you know what I mean." He winked. "Well, I figured what the hell, they never said I couldn't take her with me, so we run off together and the next thing you know, we're caught up in this war between Gwen and her brother-in-law and the last thing I want to do is get stuck in some time warp of having to constantly refight the battles between the two, so Sweet Cheeks, that's the name I gave her, so Sweet Cheeks and I take off and evade all sorts of orc and goblin patrols. And so we get past Durness and on into Hillfort. I tell you, I hadn't met another player the entire time I was there on the island. So, we're heading for the bridge, and we get there only to discover I don't know the password and neither does she. So we turn around and spend the next three months trying to figure out who knows the password. Ended up all the way back in Durness. Luckily bumped into a guy named Nervel who told me the password like it was no big deal. What pisses me off is that the programmers could at least have given me a clue."

"So then what happened?" Karl interrupted, wondering if the man was going to take a breath.

"So Sweet Cheeks and I traipse all the way back to the bridge, doing a bunch of orc and goblin killing along the way and guess what happened."

"What?"

"I said 'guess.'"

"She didn't want to go?"

"Nope. Wrong answer." He snorted a strained laugh. "Guess again."

"You didn't want to go," Karl said, rolling his eyes.

"Haw," Ben chortled. "Not even close. Guess again."

"I give up," Karl, sighed.

"I'll tell you what happened. We get halfway across the bridge and poof, she was gone. Disappeared in a fizzling pop. Well you can imagine just how pissed I was. Here it was after all that time trying to find the damn password and then getting back only to have her vanish and no chance of me going back to get her." He snarled at the memory. "So I get here to this island and make it all the way to Beally and I tell you I'm not a happy camper. Despite the offers along the way, no one was like Sweet Cheeks. Anyway, I get to orc country and come to discover that I like killing orcs. Decided I just might stay a while and sorta work through my anger issues, if you know what I mean."

"How long you been here?" Karl asked, looking around the camp, noting it appeared permanent.

Ben scratched his cheek. "Don't rightly recall. Never bothered keeping track of the time. But I do keep track of my enemy. Here, lemme show you."

Ben led the way into the cave.

Karl was surprised at the size, initially wondering how it was formed, but those thoughts vanished as he took in the dwelling. It was well lit with oil lamps, which caused Karl to wonder how and where Ben found oil lamps. A table and two chairs made from twisted branches sat in the center.

Against the wall to the right was a wide storage shelf made from the same branches as the table and chairs. Neatly arranged on each shelf were various weapons: falchions, bows, quivers stuffed with arrows, daggers of all sizes, and a few swords. Several halberds leaned against the shelf. On the opposite wall was a replica shelf containing food: dried meats, vegetables, and pitchers for water.

Off in the corner and almost mid-calf high was a pile of orc ears.

Remembering how fast he had leveled up in Abeloft, Karl frowned when he studied Ben's stats. "You're a level 15? There has to be a couple of hundred orc ears there and you're still a level 15."

"Yeah, I know. Pretty good, huh?" he grinned. "Actually there's 106. I figure another hundred more and I should be close to level 20. Then I'll get off this island to the next one." He startled when he heard Sakura call out. "Damn, that spooked me. Forgot for a moment you had friends with you."

Ben hustled out and led the rest of the team back inside the camp, noting with some overt interest the pulchritude of the women in the group.

"What?" Caryn frowned at him when she found him staring at her.

"I've never seen an elf before, let alone such a gorgeous one," he candidly replied.

Mollified, she accepted the compliment. "That was sweet. You live here by yourself?"

"Yup," he answered, his attention diverted to the hulking presence of Dieter. His eyes drifted to Elena and Julie. "NPCs... good looking ones." He frowned in puzzled reverie. "Why didn't I think of that?"

'Think of what?" Noble asked.

"Find myself another Sweet Cheeks."

"Sweet cheeks?" Noble repeated, cocking an eyebrow.

"Let's do the introductions," Karl interrupted. "Ben, you remember Sakura. That one there is Nobel, our resident thief." He continued the introductions then turned to the group. "We have one more friend who doesn't like being cooped up so he's hanging around outside. At least I think he is."

I am.

Do you want to come inside the camp and rest? We'll post a watch.

Is there space?

Karl glanced around the encampment. *Not a lot.*

Then I'll stay where I am.

"Where is he?" Ben asked.

"I'll introduce you to him in a bit. But first," he said turning to the team, "this is Ben, the very first one inserted into the game. He's been in the game for almost two years."

The team stared at him with a mixture of wonder and surprise that this was as far as he had achieved, and that he was only a level 15. Annabeth was about to comment when Karl waved a warning hand at her.

"Let's hear how Ben's managed to survive for so long," Karl grandstanded, "and how he's been so successful in killing orcs."

Felix sat with his arms folded and listened as Gerard, standing behind a portable podium, used a laser pointer to highlight bullet points on the screen behind him.

"As you can see on the map here," Gerard said, pointing to a spot on the screen map, "Karl and his company are here, about twelve klicks from Ozgul."

"Klicks?" Felix said.

"Kilometers," Gerard explained.

"Why not just say kilometers?"

"Um… it's a military term," he replied.

"We're not in the military," Felix said with a firm stare.

"But Karl was, as was Caryn," Gerard replied with a not-so-subtle tone of condescension.

Felix stared at him, pursing his lips. "Continue."

"Like I said, Karl and company are here. They've met up with Ben, our very first insertion."

Felix blinked then frowned. "Ben? As in Benjamin Sawyer?"

"Yes."

"Are you sure? He's been in the game for almost two years."

Gerard stared at Felix for an awkward moment. "Uh... has no one briefed you on him?"

"Apparently not," he tersely replied. "Why is he still on the second island?" *And why hasn't Landon asked me about him?*

"Ben was an early beta tester," Gerard explained. "We put him into the game along with another individual."

"Allan Westlund," Felix said.

"Yes. We had to take Allan back out of the game because the man was incompetent." Gerard shook his head and rolled his eyes. "He never could grasp the concept of quests and leveling and all the other associated gaming requirements. I mean, sheesh, how many times do you have to respawn before saying, 'damn, this hurts' and figure out how not to get killed?"

"So what happened to him?"

"He was neutralized," Gerard flatly replied. "We couldn't let him –"

"I understand," Felix said, flipping a hand to cut him off. "Talk to me about Ben."

"We were concerned that Ben suffered from the same mental block as Allan. However, our fears were unfounded as Ben turned out to be a real killer, especially after we took away his lover when he crossed the bridge to Innis Torr. Unfortunately, all he wants to do now is kill orcs."

"His lover was an NPC?"

"Yes," Gerard smirked. "He called her 'Sweet Cheeks.' She was a tavern wench in Berismo. The problem was that we had only two beta testers at the start. We assumed that the simulation would be so lifelike that Ben wouldn't be able to tell the difference. Of course, we neglected to consider that players could tell the stats and class of everyone simply by pulling up a character's screen. We also didn't figure on the dependency of a player with other players. We assumed that by making NPCs as real as players, it wouldn't matter.

What we didn't count on was that a player would fall I love with an NPC."

"Like Dieter?"

"Yes," Gerard chuckled, "Like Dieter. Unfortunately, Ben fell hard and when the girl was prevented from crossing the bridge, he sort of went off the deep end."

"Why didn't someone simply allow the girl to cross?"

"Your predecessor was a stickler for gaming rules. 'Rules,' he said, 'are there for a reason.' We had the 'No NPC crossing the bridge' rule to prevent wholescale NPCs from roaming between the islands."

"I'm surprised Mister Landon didn't get involved."

"I think he decided to let us handle it," Gerard opined.

"And Ben? Mister Landon had no problem with leaving him where he is?" Felix's frown deepened.

Gerard shrugged. "Ben's sort of like a Robinson Crusoe stranded in the middle of orc Kingdom of Krug. His stealth and fighting stats are well above what he needs to survive in hostile territory."

"What class is he?" Felix interrupted.

"He's a swashbuckler."

"Swashbuckler?"

"Yeah," Gerard said with a soft chuckle. "He chose that because of the hero status attached to it, or at least so he thought."

Felix was silent as he sifted the information. "So what you're saying is that Ben isn't quite together, that unless something drastic happens to change his situation, he's going to remain where he is, doing what he's doing, for a long long time."

"Yes."

"Why not just send another femme fetale and rescue him?"

"We thought of that. We're hoping that one of the ladies with Karl will help."

Deciding to keep silent his opinion that none of the ladies with Karl would be interested in a man who wasn't all there, Felix asked, "Who's the farthest along in the game?"

"Ben."

"What?" Felix exclaimed. "No one has gotten beyond the Wildman?"

"When we pulled Allan out of the game, we had a break in insertions for a while until we hammered out some of the peripheral problems. But you saw how many are still in Marbeck waiting for their miracle healing."

"Yes," Felix grimaced, "I know. That looks to be a screening error more than a gaming error."

"I agree. The problem, as least as I understand it, is that most suitable candidates have been snatched up already. We're the proverbial Johnny-come-lately and are playing catch up. We were extremely lucky to get Karl and Caryn. Those two alone more than compensate for the others."

"The others are coming along quite nicely," Felix countered.

"Sure, but Karl and Caryn have actual combat experience."

"Point taken," Felix acceded. "So what's the prognosis for the near future? Do you expect Karl to take Ben with him?"

"We'll see."

"Don't waffle," Felix mildly scolded. "Give me an answer. Will he or won't he? What's your best guess?"

Gerard paused before saying, "I think he'll want to. Karl's a soft touch when it comes to maudlin hard luck tales."

Felix smiled at him. "I say that Karl won't. How about a wager? Loser takes the winner to a restaurant of his choice."

Gerard broke into a wide grin. "I accept, though there's not much choice of restaurants left."

The fire in the cook pit had dwindled to a rippling bed of coals, perfect for cooking freshly killed venison. Karl stood back watching Elena trying to coax Ben into letting her do the cooking.

"I'm sure you know what you're doing, Ben, but Elena is a superb cook. Why not sit back and enjoy having someone else do the cooking?"

Ben shifted a worried glance at Karl then to Elena then back to Karl before forcing himself away from the fire, leaving a relieved Elena to do things her way.

"I'm surprised you're able to cook and no one comes knocking," Caryn said, "especially with the aroma wafting upon the wind."

"I only cook at certain times," Ben replied, "when I know for sure that there are no orc patrols in the area."

"How can you be so sure?"

"While orcs can be unpredictable, they have their routines, especially in areas where they don't expect an enemy to be."

"Whaddaya mean?" Noble asked, walking up then looking over his shoulder at Elena who devoted her attention to the cooking.

"What I mean is that we're not that far away from Ozgul," he grinned, flicking his eyebrows. "In fact, we could be there in less than twenty minutes."

Noble's eyes bolted wide.

"Don't worry little man," Ben placated, "they won't come in here."

"Why not?" Noble asked, irritated at the condescending slight.

"Because when they're not fighting, orcs can be pretty lazy," Ben explained. "We're close enough to where they don't even bother scouting the area, though they do have a good sense of smell. That's why I eat the same times they do."

"From the pile of ears in the cave, I'm surprised no one has tracked you back here?" Karl observed.

"That's because I don't kill around here," Ben replied. "Orcs can be pretty good trackers. I take my kills far from here and overlay my tracks with theirs. And I only hit when I know for sure I can hit quick and clean. Take the ear and get out of there without being seen."

"And no one suspects anything?" Noble said with obvious doubt.

Ben cackled with a twinkle in his eyes. "Orcs are mistrustful as it is. I've heard them arguing that it's one or more of their own. Some figure it's a blood feud and the ear taking is copycat to throw off suspicion. Haw," he gleefully chortled. "I've got them fighting among themselves."

Karl nodded thoughtfully. "Well done," he complimented, thinking Ben would add to his own quest of conquering the island. "How far do you range? In other words, how well do you know the territory?"

"I've been all over Krug. Know just about every inch of the place. Been studying orcs ever since I got on this island."

"So what are you?" Noble challenged. "You look like some wild man."

Ben stiffened and stood to full height. "I, sir, am a Swashbuckler."

"A what?" Annabeth chimed in, leaning back from her conversation with Raquel.

"A Swashbuckler."

There was an awkward pause before Julie innocently asked, "What's a swashbuckler?"

Ben's irritation dissolved when he saw Julie's child-like gaze at him. With a professorial tone, he explained, "A swashbuckler is a fighter who prefers either light or no armor, relying instead on cunning, daring, agility and brain power rather than brute force. He is suave and oft times flamboyant, and also very gallant. Think of the heroes in Dumas adventure novels or Errol Flynn movies of the 20th century."

Julie's eyes blinked in vacuous ignorance before she turned to Karl. "I don't understand any of what he just said. What's a movie?"

"They're –" Noble began.

"Hard to explain," Karl interrupted then changed the subject. "Can you get us to Mann without us being seen?" he asked Ben.

Ben gave him a 'duh' look. "What do you want to go to Mann for?"

"He's taking me back there," Julie piped up, "so that he can become king and we'll rule Mann for a thousand years."

Annabeth rolled her eyes. "Slow down Cinderella. We don't even know why we're taking you back. And there's a 'to do' list that's a kilometer long along the way."

"What do you want to go to Mann for?" Ben repeated, shifting a puzzled glance from Julie to Karl. "Stay here and kill orcs with me. It'll be fun."

"We can't," Karl replied. "We've accepted a quest to return Julie to the House of Rhyeem."

"And then he's going to become king," Julie beamed, "because he wear's Orc's Bane and the prophecy about the one who can wield the sword."

With a subtle look of condescension, Ben glanced down at Karl's sword. "No offense, but is that the sword, the one she call's Orc's Bane?"

"Yes," Karl smiled, noting the mocking doubt in his tone. He withdrew the sword and held it out to Ben. "Here. Tell me what you think."

Ben cocked an eyebrow at the weapon. "That's Orc's Bane?" he repeated with a disdainful sniff.

"It's a magical weapon," Julie exclaimed. "You won't be able to lift it."

Ben studied the thin blade before reaching for it, only to feel an abrupt heaviness as soon as his hands clasped the handle. When Karl let go, the weight of the sword forced him to the ground.

"Damn," he blurted, using two hands in a vain attempt to lift the sword.

Karl reached down and casually picked up the blade and sheathed it.

"A magic sword," Ben marveled, standing. "Who'd of thought…"

"You're not a gamer, are you," Raquel observed with a chuckle.

"Nope. Probably the last man on the planet who never got into role-playing games. Had too much other stuff I enjoyed doing."

"Welcome to the club," Noble quietly mused.

"How long would it take to get to Mann?" Karl asked, getting back to the topic.

Pondering as he scratched his bearded cheek, Ben said, "You could get there in less than two days, three if you want to be sure you're not seen."

"Will you guide us there? We can kill some orcs along the way if you want."

Ben's eyes brightened. "Now you're talking. We can leave tonight... after dinner that is."

Chapter 8

It was midnight when Karl and company followed single file behind Ben as he led them away from his camp. Acting as roving security, Uafas silently patrolled the two flanks and the rear.

The night was warm and moonless, which meant it was dark enough that they had to follow closely behind one another, pausing occasionally to take up the count, starting from the last person in the column.

Relegated to the tail end did not please Raquel, especially when she saw Caryn's elevation to Karl's most trusted second-in-command. Yet she found it difficult to harbor resentment against Caryn for the elf went out of her way to be a subordinate member of the team, even volunteering for rear security or any other menial task. Still, Raquel knew why Karl looked to Caryn. They both shared the same combat experience, something Raquel never had or desired to have.

And then, unlike Julie who made no effort to hide her emotions concerning Karl, Caryn never intimated she wanted anything more that to be a part of the team. Still… she was rather attractive, and the elf ears gave her an almost exotic aura. It was just a matter of time before she'd want her share of Karl.

Raquel puzzled as she silently followed behind Noble. Why was it OK sharing Karl with Annabeth, but not anyone else?

Her thoughts were interrupted when Noble stopped and whispered, "Pass up the count."

"Two," she whispered back.

"Two?" Noble startled. "You're the last in line. You're number one."

"If you know that, why are you asking me?"

"Because you're supposed to do it right. You're supposed to say 'one.'"

Shaking her head at the silliness of the frequent head count, she said, "You just like me tapping you on your butt every time we have to take up the count."

"Never said otherwise," Nobel grinned. "You gonna pass up the count? They're waiting."

With a silent sigh, she playfully swatted him on the butt. "One."

Noble turned and tapped Julie on the butt, whispering "Two."

The process repeated until Caryn tapped Karl on the butt and whispered, "Eight."

Karl turned to Ben. "OK. Move out."

"It's gonna take a lot longer if we have to keep stopping," Ben groused.

"I'm not leaving anyone behind," Karl firmly informed him. "We'll take as long as necessary to get everyone safely to Mann, you included."

"Who said I was going to Mann?" Ben replied before taking up the lead.

An hour later, he motioned a halt to confer with Karl.

"We're getting close to a village, straight ahead. It's a small one, but there's an old orc who doesn't sleep much and takes to walking at all hours. She's old, which means she doesn't move fast, but she's mean as a snake. I've seen her chew out big and nasty orcs. Got a feeling she may be a priestess or something. Tell that wolf of yours to scout around to the east side of the vil."

Uafas.

Yes.

Ben says there's a town up ahead. We need you to scout the east side of the village.

Which side is the east side?

Left.

That doesn't help.

Karl pulled up his map and did a quick visual. *There's a small river with a bridge over it on the east side coming down from the mountains.*

200

Got it.

Ten minutes later they heard a shrill voice shouting followed by clanging on an alarm gong.

Some old hag has seen me and she's raising a ruckus.

"How big is the town?" Karl demanded.

"I don't know," Ben answered in a rush, "twenty or thirty maybe."

Karl whirled around. "Pass the word. There's a village with about twelve houses, approximately twenty to thirty orcs. The houses are close together lining both sides of the road that runs through a common area. We attack. No survivors. Take out the orc making the noise first. Noble stays with Elena and Julie. Assembly area is at the bridge crossing the river on this side of town. Let's move."

"Hot damn," Ben chortled. "This will add a whole bunch of ears to my count."

As Noble hustled the two NPCs away from the action, Ben led the way and they hunkered down at the forest edge just in time to see about twelve male orcs, half-dressed, a few with weapons, stagger out or their homes, growling for the infernal noise to stop. The orcs glanced around, noting the lack of a threat, many shaking their heads in irritation as they assembled on the commons.

Karl motioned for Sakura. "Go put an end to that racket."

She was gone in an instant and thirty seconds later, the clanging gong stopped.

One orc, larger than the others and gripping a falchion, barked an order at another orc and pointed to where the hag had been raising the alarm.

"OK folks," Karl whispered, "you know what to do." Just as Ben was about to launch the attack, he grabbed his arm and hauled him back down. "Let's let our resident sorceress have some fun first."

Standing in the darkness of the forest, Annabeth cast her first conjuration, a combustion spell that caught a bored orc who had already turned to go back in and burst him into flames. No sooner did his howling erupt that she flung another spell, freezing the large orc in place.

"Now," Karl shouted and leaped out of the forest.

The shock momentarily stunned the remaining orcs, but they quickly recovered only to quaver when they saw Dieter and his raging blood lust.

The initial battle was over in mere minutes with Annabeth continuing to hurl spells while the others cut down the remaining orcs. Dieter decapitated the large orc, the job made easy as the orc remained frozen in place. All that was left was to clear out the houses of whatever orcs were still alive. But this meant killing children and women.

"Kill them now or kill them later," Ben reminded them as he kicked in the door to a house.

"Do it by twos," Karl ordered. "Protect each other. Raquel's with me, Annabeth with Dieter, Sakura and Caryn. No survivors."

There were no cries or screams or begging for mercy. In fact, the battle to clear the houses reminded Karl of urban warfare. The women fought back, and the children snarled and snapped, tossing anything within hands' reach at the intruders. By the time it was over, just about every member of Karl's team had bruises or scrapes.

Karl watched as Ben went orc to orc, slicing off an ear and thrusting it into a bag at his side. Uafas came trotting up.

Caught a couple of them running off. Don't mind saying, orc tastes terrible.

Which way were they headed?

Opposite the direction we were going. There's a road heading out of the town.

How many?

Two.

Warriors?

One was. The other was a woman.

Karl turned to Ben. "Uafas said he killed two more on the road heading back the way we came. You sure this isn't going to complicate things for you? Why not come with us?"

"Not ready yet," he said, peering down into the bag, doing a silent count. "Besides, we're far enough away that they won't know where I am."

"Where's your bind spot?"

Ben's head snapped up and his brows creased in a deep furrow as he struggled to remember. "Back in Beally... I think."

"You may want to be sure," Karl counseled.

Sakura appeared at his side. "All clear."

Karl studied the damage in the little village for a moment before turning to Ben. "Is there something we can do that would confuse anyone stumbling in here?"

Ben thought for a moment. "Yeah. Let's line them up in rows on the commons according to size. Place them neatly in position with their hands on their chests. That'll cause some confusion."

"Why?" Annabeth frowned.

"What would you think if you came upon a village and all the people in it were neatly laid out in a respectful way, and they're all missing an ear?" He flashed a grin.

"I see your point."

"It won't take long," Ben said, sensing Karl's itchiness to get going.

It took almost forty-five minutes to haul the bodies out and arrange them, beginning with dragging the largest orc to his place and on down to the smallest orcs, two children that looked to be around three to four years old. Once in place, their hands were folded upon their chests. Karl noted that Ben had severed the left ears of all the dead.

"I've got to do one more thing," Ben said with a sly grin. "I'll be right back."

"Where you going?" Karl snapped as Ben took off through the town on the road toward the way they came.

"Be right back," Ben called over his shoulder.

"Damn it," Karl fumed. "Let's get ready to move out." He was checking his game map when Ben returned, holding an ear in his hand.

"Forgot to get the ears of the two your wolf dropped. Also left a clue for those who come by later," he explained, holding up the ear. "Left one of these farther up the road."

Karl immediately understood, but also recognized their need to keep moving. "Daylight's coming. We need to find a secure spot to settle for a couple of hours."

"Already got a place in mind," Ben replied with a wink. "Follow me."

Ben led them along the road out of town and across the bridge, the pace at a double-time. They stayed on the undulating road that seemed to gradually rise until they approached an orc settlement then took to the forest to bypass the town, repeating the deviation for each town.

An hour later, just as dawn's tendrils spread across the sky, Ben slowed the pace then stopped, bent his head to listen then turned to Karl.

"We need to be extra careful from now on. The closer we get to Mann, the more vigilant orcs become. We stay here until nightfall."

Karl scanned the surroundings. All he could see was thick forest. "Lead the way."

Ben leaned back to gaze at the rest of the group. "Stay close," he warned, "and watch where you step."

Ducking into the forest, he carefully threaded his way among the trees, the rest of the team using his same foot placings. A little more than 200 meters later, he stopped and motioned them to come up. Huddling close by they saw the reason for his cautiousness for not more than two meters away, the forest ended at the edge of a precipitous cliff.

Annabeth sidled close to the edge and glanced over. It descended to a rocky gorge where a strong current river gurgled and frothed to the far distant sea.

"That's a looong way down," she intoned.

"There's a cave part way down the cliff," Ben said. "The path down is narrow, very narrow," he added, staring at Dieter. "You might have a problem getting down there."

"I can help," Annabeth said. "I've got a Spider's Touch spell I can use on him. He'll be able to walk on walls or ceilings if he wants." She smirked. "Pity we can't use that in an ambush. Be sort of fun to see the look on their faces when he dropped down from the ceiling."

"We need to move," Karl reminded everyone. "We need some rest."

Ben stood up and led the way along the edge until they came to an outcropping of rocks that hung over the edge. On the other side, a narrow trail about the width of Elena's shoulders went down and under the outcropping.

"Watch your step," Ben cautioned. "It can get slippery, especially after a rain."

"Are you sure this is a good idea?" Julie nervously asked.

"If you want uninterrupted sleep," Ben replied, "yes. Besides," he deadpanned, "it's not the fall that'll kill you."

"It's not?" she frowned in all her naiveté.

"It's the sudden stop at the bottom," Noble answered, rolling his eyes. "Jeez. I can't believe you fell for that one. That lame joke is so old, I heard it when the Dead Sea was still sick."

Ben's face split into a grin. "I'll have to remember that one."

"Can we get going, please," Karl fussed.

As Ben led the way, Annabeth cast the spell on Dieter who didn't feel any different until he went over and placed a hand on the rocks and felt his hand stick like a magnet on a refrigerator. "I may want to use this again," he smiled.

"Any time, Dieter," Annabeth smiled back.

Thankfully the path to the cave was not far as Karl edged sideways along the stone wall, marveling at Ben's nonchalance as he traipsed down the rocky path to the cave's mouth.

The cave was large and dry, with a dirt floor probably blown in over the centuries. At least that would be the explanation IRL. Here in the game, it meant a developer had paid attention to detail.

Karl entered and took in the extent of the cave then decided to check on a friend. *Uafas. You OK?*

I'm fine. Obviously I'll need to find another place to rest.

Be careful. We'll head out again when night comes.

Good. That will give me time to find something to eat.

Be careful.

I always am.

Always? Karl chuckled. *Seems I remember a certain town…*

Yeah, yeah. Bring that up again. Aren't you supposed to be getting some sleep?

See ya later.

"You need to be careful even in here," Ben said. "The mouth of the cave can be seen from across the other side, so you need to stay in the shadows at all times."

"Orcs know about this cave?" Raquel asked.

"I suspect so," Ben replied, "but I've never seen evidence of them coming in here. I think the path is too narrow for them."

"Find a place and settle down," Karl told them. "Get some rest."

Julie came up next to him. "Where are you going to sleep?"

"Don't know yet. I'll wait for everyone else to get settled first."

"Then I'll wait too," she demurely stated.

"Hey Cinderella," Annabeth teased. "Why don't you come here and cuddle with your two stepsisters and leave the Viking alone in peace?"

"My name is not Cinderella," Julie imperiously replied, stamping her foot, and folding her arms.

"Whatever," Annabeth sighed with feigned boredom. "Leave the man alone so he can get some sleep."

"That's a good idea," Karl patiently urged. "Go find a place and get some rest. We've a long night ahead of us."

Not liking the option and with her lower lip protruding in a pout, Julie searched the cave for a suitable spot, picking a place where two could rest comfortably together.

While everyone found a spot and got comfortable, Karl walked over to Ben. "How do you know no one else has been here?"

"It's just like I left it," Ben replied. "I have little signs that I leave around the place to make sure. No one's been here since the last time I was here."

"We still need a watch," Karl commented.

"Why not use your wolf friend," Ben answered, stretching out on the ground, "if you're that concerned? I've been here a number of times and have had a great day's sleep."

"He needs rest too," Karl countered.

"Not as much as we do." Ben fidgeted a bit. "Go ahead and set up a watch if it makes you feel any better. As for me, I'm gonna get some sleep." He rolled over on his side and curled an arm under his head.

Karl glanced around the cave, noting that everyone had their eyes closed, working on getting to sleep, except Caryn who sat in watchful attention. He walked over to her.

"Go ahead and get some sleep. I'll take the first watch."

"What about them?" she asked, ticking her head at the others.

"They need their sleep. It's been tough on them."

"So do you," she pointed out. "Why not do what he suggested and let Uafas take the watch?"

"Like I said to him, Uafas needs sleep too."

Caryn studied him for a moment. He looked tired. "I'm too awake to sleep right now. Why don't you rest, and I'll wake you when it's time for me to catch some Z's. Between the two of us, we can let them get the sleep they need."

"Are you sure you're OK?"

Caryn stood. "Very. It's hard for me to sleep during the day. When the sun's up, my body says I'm supposed to be up too. I'll hit you up about noonish."

Karl nodded acceptance and found a place to stretch out, far enough away from Julie to be unmolested. His mind wandering, he drifted off and startled awake when he felt someone nudging him.

"What?" he blurted, bolting upright.

"It's just me," Caryn said. "I figure it's an hour or two past noon. I probably ought to try to get some sleep."

"Of course," he said, collecting himself and standing. "I've made this spot all cozy. You might as well use it."

"Thanks," she smiled and lay down on the warm ground.

Karl glanced around the cave. The others were deep in asleep, occasionally twitching to get comfortable. Even Ben was blissfully dozing, apparently unconcerned of the possibility they could be discovered.

Karl moved to the mouth of the cave, ensuring he stayed in the shadows, and gazed out across the canyon. The steep cliffs were crowned with a thick forest of pines and hardwoods, verdant and green. The scene reminded him of Cloudland Canyon in north Georgia.

Someone's coming, Uafas announced. *Orcs. They're moving like they're looking for something.*

How many?

Nine... ten... eleven. Eleven, heading your way.

As Karl turned to wake up the others, Annabeth eased next to him.

"You still awake?"

Karl held a finger to his lips then pointed above them and whispered, "Orcs."

"Wake the others?" she whispered back.

Pondering only a moment, he said, "Not yet," not wanting the possible commotion of the group to give them away.

They're directly above you.

Karl turned to Annabeth. "Do you have some sort of spell that can let us listen to what they're saying?"

Annabeth did a quick scroll through her skills then nodded. "Detect speech."

She cast the spell, closed her eyes and listened, whispering to Karl what she heard.

"Why are we here? This is stupid. Nobody's gonna come here. We're at the edge of the cliff. Only way of escape is back the way we come," an orc complained.

"We're here 'cause someone saw somethin' come this way," another orc replied with a firm tone.

"But the ear was on the road goin' the other way, towards Ozgul," the first orc stated.

"Besides," another complained, "just 'cause someone saw somethin' don't mean it's true. This ain't nothin' more than a fool's errand."

"Watch yer mouth," the one orc growled. "We got a job to do and we're gonna do it. There's a cave close by here we gotta check out. You, Fezrik, yer gonna check it out."

"Me?" Fezrik exclaimed. "Why me?"

"'Cause I said so. What's a matter? You scared?"

"Go to hell, Olnik. Just 'cause you was made leader of this patrol don't give you cause to act like you're somebody important."

"You disobeyin' my order, Fezrik? You hear that boys? Fezrik don't wanna obey my order 'cause he's a coward."

"Shut up, Olnik. Yer a damned liar and you know I ain't no coward."

"Then quit yer bellyachin' and do what he said," another orc chimed in.

"Aw hell," Fezrik spat, "I'll do it."

Karl narrowed his gaze at Annabeth. "You got anything else?"

With an impish grin, she cast a Banana Peel spell halfway up the path then sat back to listen.

A few moments later, there was a burst of alarm followed by a fading cry as the orc fell to his death on the rocks below.

"Damn," Olnik grunted.

Annabeth suppressed a snicker and whispered, "I've been wanting to do that ever since I saw I had that spell."

"You, Kurzgul," Olnik commanded, "go check out the cave."

"The hell with you, Olnik," Kurzgul snapped. "I ain't goin' down there. If yer so all fired up to see that cave, you do it."

"You scared, Kurzgul?" Olnik sneered.

"Damn right I am. You saw what happened to Fezrik. There ain't nuthin' in that cave anyway. I say we just leave it alone and go on back."

The others added their support as none had an urge to follow Fezrik's fate.

"Yer all yellow," Olnik mocked. "Just wait 'til we get back and I tell everyone what a bunch of cowards you are."

"Yer all talk," Kurzgul taunted.

"You shut yer yap," Olnik growled.

"Or what?" Kurzgul scoffed. "C'mon Olnik. Yer so brave. Show us how it's done."

"You just wait 'til we get back," Olnik bristled.

Silence followed as Olnik cautiously began his descent.

Karl leaned into Annabeth. "Cast that spell when I tell you." He then positioned himself within the shade of the mouth opposite the path.

"Damn," an orc said, "he's doin' it."

When Olnik was two meters from the mouth of the cave, Karl stepped into the open, whispering, "Now."

Just as the startled Olnik looked up to see the Viking wiggling his fingers 'bye', his foot stepped on the banana peel and his body lurched backwards in a violent spasm, his hands grabbing furiously at the smooth rock wall before he plummeted to the rocky bottom of the gorge.

A stunned silence settled above before Kurzgul said, "I told him that would happen, but he wouldn't listen. Didn't I tell him not to go down there?"

"What're we gonna do?" another orc nervously asked.

"Lemme think," Kurzgul replied. "OK. OK. This is what happened. We stopped a little ways from here. Fezrik said he had to take a leak. When he didn't come back, Olnik sent me to go look fer 'im. I couldn't find him, so Olnik went lookin' fer him. When he didn't come back, we all looked fer them and finally said we gotta get back before it gets too dark. Don't none of us know where either one is. Right?"

Grunts of agreement indicated unanimous support.

"I'm hungry," an orc complained.

"Yeah, me too," voiced another.

"Let's get outta here. Ain't nuthin' down in that cave anyway," a third voice commented.

The conversation continued as the voices faded.

"How'd you know there's a cave down there?"

"I don't. Olnik said there was."

"Olnik was a dumbass."

"Anybody know of a cave down there?"

"Fezrik was a dumbass to listen to Olnik."

Finally, Annabeth grinned and looked at Karl. "They're gone. That was fun."

"It was," he smiled back. "Is that banana peel still on the path?"

210

"I don't think so. It's supposed to work only once."

"Let's hope so," he replied. "Go back and get some sleep."

"Can't," she shrugged. "I'm too awake now."

They're heading back, Uafas said.

I know.

There are only nine of them now. Two may still be close by.

Those two are dead. They slipped off the path and fell to the rocks below.

Good. That's two less orcs to worry about.

We'll be leaving just before nightfall.

I'll be ready.

Karl glanced back at the others still asleep, wondering who it was that saw them to send a patrol here looking for them. They would have to be more careful. Hopefully this latest patrol would be convincing enough to keep attention on the road to Ozgul.

Looking at Ben, he was thankful that he decided to ignore his advice and post a watch. Who knows what would have happened had Olnik made it into the cave with them all asleep.

"You're awfully pensive," Annabeth observed.

"Just thinking about our friend there." He ticked his head at Ben. "For someone in the game as long as he has been, I'm surprised he's not on another island."

Annabeth leaned closer. "I don't think his elevator goes to the top floor. He may be good at killing orcs, but you see how he is, how he lives. The man ain't all there. What's the fascination with killing orcs, so much so that you choose to live among them?"

"But why leave him here? He doesn't even remember where his spawn spot is."

"And you want to take him with us?" She cocked an eyebrow at him.

"Maybe that's what he needs, interaction with people," Karl replied, "something more than living in the wild."

"Some people like living in the wild," she pointed out. "Remember all those mountain man stories?"

"Point taken. By the way, you're getting pretty good with all those spells."

"I guess," she said, shaking her head. "I don't see how gamers keep track of all the skills. I'm only a skill level two sorceress, and I have over 300 skills of various abjurations, conjurations, divinations, and other stuff. By the time I figure out what I should use, the situation's changed and I'm already behind the curve. The way I see it, I need to focus on a few things that I can do really well and add others as time goes on. I figure if we stay on this island for the next thousand years, I should be pretty good at being a sorceress." She smiled prettily at him.

By late afternoon, the team began to stir and Ben joined Karl and Annabeth at the entrance.

"Told you it was gonna be quiet," Ben said with a hint of self-assuredness.

"We had a visit from an orc patrol while you were asleep," Annabeth said. "They even came down the path to the cave."

Ben's eyes startled wide. "They did?"

"Look for yourself," Karl said, stepping to the edge and pointing down.

Ben edged over to the side and peered down at the two orcs in twisted death. "Damn. We were lucky they fell."

"Luck had nothing to do with it," Karl answered. "Be thankful we had a sorceress with us who used her magic spells to cause their deaths."

Ben regarded Annabeth with newfound respect and admiration. "I didn't hear a thing."

"Didn't need to," Karl replied. "Didn't see the sense of waking everyone up when the problem resolved itself, with a little help."

Ben glanced back over the edge. "Wonder if there's a way down?"

"I know what you're thinking," Karl gently admonished. "We don't have time."

"I know," Ben wistfully replied. "Just wanted a couple of ears, make up for the one I gave away to get here."

"What did I hear about orcs?" Caryn said, walking up.

"We had an orc patrol come by," Karl said, noting the rest of the group were now paying attention. He explained what happened, including some of the conversation. "Don't worry," he said to Ben. "I think you'll still be able to use this cave. I doubt any other orc patrols will want to try the path down here, especially after they find the two bodies and determine what happened."

"Do you know where we are?" Julie asked Ben.

"Yeah. We're a bit north of a small village called Braghurk. If all goes well, we should get to Mann in two more nights of travel."

Karl glanced out the cave at the setting sun. "Then we better get a move on. Watch your step as you make your way back to the top. You got your spider feet, Dieter?"

"I'm getting there," Annabeth chimed in, casting the Spider's Touch spell on Dieter.

Once clear of the cave and back above, Ben paused to warn them. "We'll be skirting orc towns on the way. The closer we get to the border, the more vigilant they are, so you need to be extra cautious." He then led the way towards Braghurk, keeping the canyon to the right as they traveled, Uafas acting as roaming security.

They came upon Braghurk two hours after sundown, giving it wide berth. Five hours more and several settlements later, Ben called a halt to confer with Karl.

"We're coming up on Righul Khar. The Broken Skull clan rules the area here and Righul Khar is their stronghold. We've got to pay attention. I've got a hiding place far enough away, but they send out patrols at all hours, night and day."

Karl nodded in understanding and passed the word to the rest of the team.

"You need to tell your wolf friend that they will hunt him down in the blink of an eye. He's not safe here."

Uafas?

Yes?

We're coming to an orc city where the natives are not very friendly, even more so than usual. Ben tells me that if they see you or discover that you are around, they will hunt you down. Perhaps it might be good for you to move on to the other side of the border. There's a wide river that separates the orcs from the kingdom of Mann. Wait for us on the other side of the river.

That assumes those on the other side of the river like giant wolves, Uafas pointed out.

I know. Still, I'd feel better if you were away from here.

I can take care of myself... as long as I don't have some wizard catch me unawares.

Have it your way. Stay close.

"Uafas is going to stay," Karl informed Ben. "He's a good ally to have," he added when he saw Ben's look of doubt.

Ben responded with a 'not-my-fault-if-something-goes-wrong' shrug.

Two hours later the forest grew thick and ominous, shutting out any moonlight, forcing them to tighten the gaps between them, almost stepping on each other's feet as they wove their way among the trees. Ben led them with sure purpose and though those following had long lost sense of direction, they trusted this odd man.

Finally Ben stopped and softly announced, "We're here."

"Where's here?" Sakura asked.

"Wait and see," Ben replied, mischief in his voice.

Leading them to a large oak, he unwound what appeared to be a vine from around the trunk. "One at a time. When I get to the top, I'll jiggle the rope." He then climbed up hand over hand disappearing into the darkness above.

Karl reached out for the vine, discovering that it was a thick rope, most likely of hemp.

It was longer than he liked before the rope jiggled and he cupped Elena by the elbow. "You're next, then Julie, then Dieter, Raquel, Annabeth, Sakura, Noble, Caryn then me."

As Elena began her ascent, Karl called out to the wolf. Uafas.

While I can't see you very well in this darkness, I can smell you well enough.

We're climbing up into the trees. You'll need to find a place to rest.

OK.

It was finally Karl's turn and he pulled himself up through the lower branches and then even more branches, surrounding him so tightly that he felt he was in a tunnel. He finally emerged out of the tunnel onto a platform with small green lights, reminding him of glow sticks, dimly lining both sides of a boarded walkway.

Standing beside him, Ben hauled up the rope while the rest of the team stood interspersed on the platform or the single rope bridge leading to another platform about twenty meters away.

"What is this place?" Karl asked, following the green lights past the other platform until they faded in the distance ahead.

"As far as I can tell it used to be an elven city," Ben replied, "though no one lives here anymore, except for squirrels and owls and such."

"How big is it?"

"Huge," Ben answered.

"How far does it go?"

"All the way to the border," he said in triumph.

Karl pulled up his screen map and was surprised to find it was indeed an elven city.

Ryath-sari, the ancient city of the elven Alari-dona clan, was the center of a far-reaching kingdom before the island wars caused them to abandon the city in favor of more remote security, removing themselves to another distant island. The wars forced the elves to abandon the city in haste, which caused them to leave behind many precious and valuable items. Few know about the city anymore, for as the orc armies spread across the island, the elves placed the entire city under a cloak of invisibility enchantment along with hidden dangers affecting those races inimical to the elven race. For good measure, they cast an aura of doom within the forest so that those entering the forest would feel the presence of evil. Yet any who claim elf as friend or fight against elven enemies will find comfort and welcome here.

"I've only explored a little of the city," Ben said. "The place still feels a little too creepy for me."

"But you are not an enemy of elves," Caryn said, gazing intently at him.

"Of course not," he replied with a frown. "But still… can't you feel it?"

Caryn turned to Karl. "I do feel something weird at the moment. It's almost as though I belong here, that I've been here before."

"Now that's weird," Noble scoffed, "especially as none of us has ever been this far in the game before."

"Say what you will," she shrugged. "I'm feeling something, like I'm supposed to be looking for something."

"We're safe now, so you can take all the time you want," Ben said, "but if you wait until daylight, you can see a whole lot better. Follow me. I've got a place close by to rest."

Ben led the way along the narrow boardwalk, the rest following behind at regular intervals as the bridge tended to sway. Once across, Ben led them a short distance along another swaying walkway, until they came to a wall of intertwined branches, in the center a stout thick wooden door that was ajar.

"This is an entrance to the city," Ben explained. "There's a place to stay close by."

Once inside through the long gateway and inside the city walls, Karl noted the abundance of green lights adorning walls and walkways, casting a dim luminescence, and giving soft shape to the dark buildings. They entered onto a street, solidly made of packed earth on top of boards. Tall buildings stood to their front and disappeared to their left and right.

Turning around, Karl saw that the homes on the wall side were built against the wall, adding strength to it.

"Come," Ben encouraged. "It's this house right here." He led them to a house three doors down against the wall.

Because it was dark inside, they stood in the doorway until Ben struck a flint and lit some kindling in the fireplace,

216

carefully nursing the flames until the fire provided enough light for them to see they were in what looked to be a large living room. A table surrounded by a dozen chairs stood in the center. Along the walls were several bureaus and cabinets, decked with candelabra, the candles still straight and full. Recessed doors in the two side walls led to adjoining rooms. The door opposite the main entrance led to the stairwell leading to the floors above.

Noble made a beeline to one of the cabinets and yanked open a drawer. His eyes lit up when he withdrew silver forks and knives. Jerking open the next drawer revealed silver and gold serving utensils.

"I'm rich," he uttered with joy, holding up a large ornately filigreed golden spoon. He twisted his head to stare at Ben. "You've known about this for how long and never thought to take any of this stuff?"

"Didn't see the use," Ben shrugged, turning back to nurse the fire. "Can only use one knife, fork, and spoon at a time. And besides, who was I gonna trade with?"

Noble stared at him, immediately accepting that the man was bona-fide crazy, and went back to plundering the cabinet drawers.

"Slow down, little man," Dieter gibed. "How you going to carry all that stuff?"

"We have unlimited storage, remember?" he replied with a triumphant grin.

"Find a place to settle," Karl interrupted.

"We don't all have to sleep in the same room, do we?" Sakura asked with a frown. "The city's supposed to be safe. If there aren't enough beds in this place, why not find a place next door to spread out."

"A good idea," Julie chimed in, scooting up next to Karl.

"How many bedrooms are in this house, Ben?" Karl asked.

"Four. I already lay claim to mine. You can have the other three."

"I'll find our room," Julie chirped, grabbing a candelabrum and lighting the three candles with a stick from the fire.

"Wait a minute," Karl admonished.

"We'll take the other two," Raquel interjected, speaking for herself and Annabeth.

"We'll see what's available next door," Caryn added. "I'll report back where everyone is."

Accepting that he had been out maneuvered, Karl simply nodded then watched as Caryn led the others outside, leaving Karl and Ben with the three ladies.

"There's a bedroom with a big enough bed for two upstairs to the right," Ben informed Julie before turning to Annabeth and Raquel. "My bed's big enough for two, too."

"That will give you plenty of space to spread out," Annabeth sweetly replied, patting his cheek.

"Can't blame a fella for trying," he grinned then added with a lascivious wink, "I figured you two was chummy enough to share a bed."

"Not tonight," Raquel sighed with feigned disappointment. "We both need our sleep. If we were to get frisky, we'd keep everyone up." She bit her lip to keep from laughing when she saw Julie's shocked face.

"I'll go check out our room," Julie said in a rush and hurried upstairs.

When the door closed behind her, Karl turned to Annabeth and Raquel. "You two are being rather generous tonight."

"Oh," Annabeth benevolently shrugged, "we figured she wouldn't have many more opportunities to have you to herself, especially after we get to Glenloch and those in charge learn why you're there."

"Speaking of that," Raquel said, "you have a plan?"

"Sort of," he hedged. "I figure we get a lay of the land and build up our forces as we proceed."

"Which means you're winging it," she chuckled. "Well… it's a strategy that's worked so far. No sense changing proverbial horses midstream."

"You forgot about a certain little vixen named Gwen," Annabeth corrected her.

"Oh yeah," Raquel nodded as though remembering. "That was a challenge."

"What happened?" Ben inquired, interested.

"We had to kidnap our own chief here," Raquel explained. "Got himself caught under the spell of a succubus."

"Gwen?" Ben said, surprised. When Raquel nodded, he shook his head. "I'd heard she was something to look at, but I stayed away. Didn't want to get bogged down in the city."

"How did you manage to get through there without being waylaid?" Karl asked.

Caryn pushed through the front door. "We've occupied the next two houses. Me, Sakura and Noble are in the house next door. Dieter and Elena are in the one next to us."

"Thanks," Karl replied. "Since we're relatively safe here, let everyone sleep as long as they want. We'll take the next day, or maybe two, to explore the city."

"Roger that," she answered with a smile. "Goodnight."

No sooner had the door closed behind Caryn that Julie entered the room. "I've got everything prepared," she said, anxious to get him upstairs before Annabeth and Raquel had a chance to influence the arrangements.

Yawning, Ben picked up a candelabrum, lit the candlesticks and waited while Annabeth and Raquel lit their own candles.

Julie led the way. At the top of the stairs, she took Karl's hand and led him to the last door on the right then turned around. "Your bedrooms are there," she said to Annabeth and Raquel, ticking her head at the two doors on the other side of the hallway.

Without waiting for a reply, Julie turned back around and thrust the door open to the bedroom, casting a nondescript "Goodnight" over her shoulder.

She had no sooner stepped into the room when Annabeth flicked her fingers at Karl and watched as he wobbled and staggered a few steps then slumped to the floor.

"O my God," Julie burst.

The others rushed into the room only to see Karl sound asleep on the floor.

"The poor man," Annabeth commiserated. "He was just so tired, he couldn't hold up any longer. Come. Let's get him to bed."

While Julie pouted with a mixture of frustration, disappointment, irritation, and helplessness, Annabeth, Raquel, and Ben managed to hoist Karl onto the bed where Julie had folded the covers aside in anticipation of a marvelous night with a tall handsome Viking.

"Do you want us to undress him?" Annabeth offered.

"No," Julie crisply replied. "I can do it."

"Very well," she said with a nod. "Sleep well then."

When they left, Julie stood at the side of the bed, hands jammed on her hips, staring down at the slumbering Karl. By the time the door closed behind Ben, she uttered a longsuffering sigh and leaned over to unbutton his shirt.

Outside the door, Ben tilted his head and frowned as he stared at the door to the bedroom. "Never seen a man drop off to sleep so sudden like that."

"Well," Annabeth explained, "he's been under a lot of pressure and now that we're in a safe place, he's free to just let go of all those troubles. He's barely had enough sleep these past several days. It's finally caught up with him."

"I suppose you're right," Ben said, the frown remaining. "Well. Goodnight."

He headed down to his bedroom then turned. "The offer still stands," he said with a hopeful grin.

"Goodnight Ben," Annabeth and Raquel replied in unison.

"Ah well," he chuckled and slipped into his room.

Raquel waited until the door closed before giggling. "You are so bad. Did you see the look on her face when she realized all she was going to do tonight was sleep?"

"Just trying to help her out," Annabeth smirked.

"How long is he going to be out?"

"The sleep spell lasts about an hour. I figure he was tired anyway and since it's bedtime, the way I see it is that he ought to be out the entire night."

Raquel laughed. "By the way, why didn't you just use some sort of spell and transport him to the bed?"

"Then my secret would have been revealed," she said with a wink. "This way our princess will never know."

Raquel snickered. "I guess we ought to follow our leader. Which bedroom you want?"

"Makes no difference to me. You're standing closer to this door, so this can be your room."

"OK." Raquel leaned in and kissed her on the cheek. "I'm so glad you're here. You make everything so much more fun."

Annabeth squeezed Raquel's hand. "The feeling is mutual."

They stood gazing affectionately into each other's eyes, before Raquel said, "G'night," and pushed open the door to her bedroom.

Annabeth remained rooted for a moment longer, staring at Raquel as the door closed behind her. Her gaze then shifted to the room where Julie was probably still yanking off the clothes of a comatose Viking. With a smirk, she turned and opened the door to her bedroom and was soon fast asleep.

Chapter 9

When Karl awoke, daylight illuminated the curtained windows. Blinking as he took in his surroundings, he frowned as he couldn't remember how he ended up in bed. It was then he realized he was alone. Propping himself on his elbows, he looked around the room.

It was a grand room, with a canopied bed where he now reposed, several tall wardrobes and lots of tall windows. There was another door on a side wall and he silently prayed that it led to a bathroom as he leaped out of bed, finding himself quite naked and again wondering how he got here.

Thankfully the door led to a bathroom complete with toilet and a tub big enough for two. By the time he emerged from the bathroom, Julie was standing beside the bed, a hot cup of coffee in hand. Her eyes lit up when she saw him, especially in his current naked state.

"Where did you find the coffee?" he said with heartfelt gratitude, accepting the mug and taking a savoring sip.

"Ben found it one of the times he was here before. I thought you might like a cup this morning."

"What time is it?"

"Don't know," she shrugged. "Sun's been up a couple of hours though."

"Guess I'd better get dressed."

"There's no rush," she said with an impish grin. "Remember? You said we were all to sleep as late as we wanted." She unbuttoned her blouse as she approached.

A knock on the door morphed her sensual come-on to overt irritation.

"What?" she snapped.

The door opened and Annabeth popped her head in. "Just wanted to see if our fearless leader wanted to accompany us as we explore the city." She smiled mischievously as she took in the nude Viking.

223

"We're busy at the moment," Julie huffed, striding back to the door, her blouse billowing to the sides, revealing her firm breasts.

"I can see that," Annabeth chuckled. "Gorgeous body by the way."

"Thank you," Julie replied, wrapping the blouse in front of her and covering up. "Now do you mind?"

"Not at all. I'd say take your time, but we're leaving in a few minutes."

Karl sniffed the air. "Is that breakfast I smell?"

"Yup," Annabeth answered. "Ben magically produced some eggs and sausage, though I think he had them here all along, something about coming here when we showed up. Still, I think his real magic was the coffee." She rolled her eyes in dreamy satisfaction. "And he makes a mean cup of coffee over the fire."

"I'll be right down," Karl said, his stomach grumbling.

"What?" Julie pouted.

"You may want to put on some clothes first," Annabeth teased. "While the guys might not be bothered, the ladies would be jumping your hot bod as soon as you walked through the door."

"What?" Julie fumed. "It was supposed to be my turn last night."

"No worries, Cinderella," Annabeth sweetly replied, "there will be other nights."

"Why do you keep calling me Cinderella?" she demanded.

"Cinderella was a fairytale princess," Annabeth explained, "just like you. She was a ravishing beauty, and everyone fell in love with her the moment they saw her."

"Really?" she said, flattered, turning to Karl who was in the process of tugging up his trousers.

"Uh… sure, something like that," he lamely replied. "It's been a long time since I read the story."

"So when I call you Cinderella," Annabeth continued, "it's a compliment."

"Thank you," Julie said, unsure whether she was either ready or willing to accept Annabeth and Raquel as trusted friends, let alone competitors for Karl's affection. Part of her liked the way the two women were so close that they willingly shared a man and had no jealousy or resentments. She wondered if that was something she could ever do. The other part of her said she was meant to be queen, which meant they would no longer have access to Karl. It was just a matter of time.

"Have you eaten?" Karl asked Julie.

"I had something to nibble on," she demurely replied.

"Nibble?" Annabeth scoffed. "She ate more than Dieter, and that's saying a lot."

"I did not," she fumed, stamping her foot.

"I'm just teasing," Annabeth soothed then turned to Karl. "She ate like a bird. You're going to have to force feed her if you want her to keep this luscious body of hers."

Though somewhat mollified, Julie wasn't sure she liked Annabeth or not, especially between the compliments and the teasing. Maybe she should try to tease back.

"I tied to eat more, but Annabeth kept stealing everyone's food."

Annabeth stared at her then started laughing. "I like you. When you tease, it sounds so innocent. You're good."

Julie blushed and smiled.

C'mon," Karl butted in, now fully dressed. "I'm hungry enough to eat for both of you."

Karl led the way downstairs and followed the smell of breakfast to the kitchen at the rear of the house where a plate of eggs and sausage lay on the counter near the stove. A coffee urn sat on the pot belly stove, the simmering fire inside the stove keeping the urn hot.

"Food's getting cold but the coffee's still hot," Ben said with a smile, pointing to the stove. He stood near a water basin, scrubbing dishes. "Don't like dirty dishes," he explained.

Elena stood to the side, drying the dishes with a small towel. She gave Karl a smile that said she tried to convince Ben to let her cook, but she failed.

"Where'd you get the eggs and meat?" Karl inquired.

Ben flashed a sly smile. "Killing orcs ain't the only thing I do. Orcs need food too. I just help myself to their bounty, a little here, a little there, nothing too much from one place. Sorta makes them think they miscounted."

"We appreciate your talents," Karl smiled, filling a plate with eggs and sausage. "Where is everybody?"

"Most likely still in the dining room," Annabeth volunteered, pointing to the door opposite.

When Karl pushed through the door, the conversation paused only for a moment before the teasing began.

"It's alive," Noble gibed.

"Good afternoon," Raquel said with an innocent smile.

Dieter said nothing, merely nodding and smiling

"Where's Caryn and Sakura?" Karl asked, scooting a chair out to sit.

"They took off to do some exploring," Raquel answered. "Said they'd be back by dinner time. They went off together," she added noting a flash of irritation cross his face.

Karl wasn't sure why it irritated him that the two had taken off without forewarning him. Caryn certainly knew how to take care of herself, and Sakura was just as capable. Perhaps it was the fact that he had a plan worked out to recon the city and their absence interfered with his plan. Further, if there was danger in the city, no matter the claim of friendship, the team was better able to handle a problem than just two of them. Still, there was nothing he could do about it now.

"What's the game plan, Boss?" Dieter asked.

"Once I finish eating, we go exploring." He smirked when he saw Noble's eager eyes. "I'm not sure you're going to be able to carry everything you find."

"I'll do my best," Noble grinned, flicking his eyebrows.

By the time Karl finished, Ben and Elena entered the dining room. Karl barely finished his last bite when Ben scooped up his plate and disappeared into the kitchen.

"Ben say anything more about the place?" Karl asked, swallowing the last of his coffee.

"Other than he's only explored about half the place," Raquel replied.

226

"Anything of note?"

"Not really," Ben replied, coming through the door. "Lots of house stuff, like furniture and things like that. If you're thinking of something made with elven magic…" he shook his head. "Doubt they leave something like that behind."

"Well," Karl said, "might as well get started then."

"One word of advice," Ben interrupted. "The tallest of the houses is only maybe four stories high, but spread out, so it's a big place. But most houses are three stories and jammed right next to each other. And then the streets wind and intersect, so that it's easy to get lost. What I'm saying here is that you can't just go to the top of a house and expect to see where you are. There are eight spots, or towers at certain locations in the city where you can see out over the entire place."

"How do you know that?" Noble asked.

"I've found one of them and climbed to the top. I saw the others."

"Did you find the others?" Annabeth asked.

"That's the problem," he replied. "This city is so convoluted with streets and alleys and back alleys that even working my way around the outside of the place took me far longer than I was comfortable with. So I used the old pebble routine."

"Pebble routine?" Elena frowned.

"Well, not pebbles per se" he sheepishly admitted. "I carried a bunch of dinner knives with me and anytime I came to an intersection, I placed the knife in the middle, with the blade pointing in the direction I came from. They're still there, at least I think they are."

Much to Ben's satisfaction, his knives were still there as he led the team through the streets of the city. Noble stopped at each house, wanting to explore and exploit any rich discoveries until Karl finally decided it was taking too long.

"Noble, either you keep up or find someone who is willing to dawdle with you and you can go at your own pace. I figure you'll only be about two streets away by the time we get back."

Noble's eyes brightened as he gazed at the others, searching for someone willing to stick with him, but he was quickly disappointed when no one offered an interest until Elena spoke, much to Dieter's surprise.

"I'll stay back with you." She hugged Dieter's arm and looked up at him. "I hope you don't mind, but I'd like to stay closer to the house here."

Gazing back at her, he noted her tired eyes and recognized she needed more rest. "I'll stay back too."

"No," she urged. "You go on. They might need you. I'll be OK. Noble will protect me."

Dieter cast an uncertain gaze at the thief who himself wasn't so sure this was a good idea. But Noble's desire for riches outweighed his logic and his hesitant look morphed to outward calm assurance.

"Make a decision," Karl urged. "We need to get a move on."

Dieter waffled a moment longer then nodded at his lover before turning a stern eye on the thief. "Take good care of her," he warned.

"You all go have fun," Noble said, flipping a hand at him. "We'll be fine. Just like Karl said, I don't expect to get very far." He rubbed his hands in glee. "C'mon," he said to Elena. "I didn't get a chance to finish the last house."

Dieter scowled as Noble led Elena back down the street. "I'm holding you responsible," he called after them.

"Chill, big guy. I got it all under control," Noble said over his shoulder as he and Elena disappeared around the corner.

"You gonna be OK?" Karl questioned.

"Yeah," Dieter grumbled.

It was midafternoon when Karl heard the shout behind them and turned to see Noble scurrying towards them.

"Where's Elena?" Dieter demanded.

"That's just it," Noble said, catching his breath. "I don't know. We were in the third house after you guys left and we were in the same room and when I looked up, she was gone."

"Where?" Dieter growled.

"I don't know," Noble answered, his face screwed up in worry. "I spent an hour looking for her. Even went back to the place we're staying at then retraced all my steps back to the last place she was with me."

"Damn it all," Dieter fumed and started back then jittered to a stop before turning back to Karl.

"Let's go," Karl replied, impressed that Dieter would wait until Karl gave approval.

They spent the rest of the afternoon searching and were back at the first house when Caryn and Sakura returned, their excitement overflowing until they saw the glum faces.

"What's going on?" Caryn asked.

"Elena's disappeared," Raquel responded.

"What happened?"

"She was with Noble not far from here and simply vanished," Raquel answered.

"It's not my fault," Noble whimpered.

"No one said it was," Raquel replied though Dieter's look said he still held the thief accountable.

"What are you two so excited about," Karl observed.

"Caryn found an Augury Stone," Sakura answered, as Caryn unwrapped a smooth solid black onyx stone about the size of a softball.

"What's an augury stone?" Julie asked, staring at the stone.

"It's a stone used for divination and omens and telling the future," Caryn explained.

"How does it work?" Julie frowned as she intently studied the stone. It looked like something some rich merchant would own, a bauble whose worth was inversely proportionate to its practicality.

"Here," Caryn said, shaking the ball. "Ask it a question."

"Like what?"

"Anything."

"Where is Elena?" Dieter asked.

"Uh… it can't be so specific like that," Caryn explained.

"Is Elena close by," Dieter tried again.

229

"Is Elena close by," Caryn repeated and then flipped the stone over to reveal a flat portion on the stone. As the others leaned in to look, the word 'Yes," appeared in white letters.

"My God," Raquel blurted. "That's just like the Magic 8 Ball toy my mother had when she was a kid."

"Magic eight ball?" Julie repeated with a frown.

"Yes," Raquel laughed. "It was made of plastic and when you asked it a question, you had to shake it and turn it over. It was filled with a liquid and there was multi-sided piece of plastic inside the liquid that would appear with the answer to your question."

"Plastic?" Julie's frown deepened. "What's plastic?"

"It's a… never mind," Raquel replied. "They don't use it anymore."

"Is this a toy?" Dieter asked, his hope wavering.

"I doubt it," Caryn responded. "I stumbled upon it in a large house in the middle of the city. As soon as I picked it up, I got the alert message telling me I've recovered the Augury Stone and that I could do all sorts of things with it, to include talking to other augury stones."

"Have you tired talking to other stones?" Karl asked, apprehension in his voice.

"No. I figured now was not the time, especially as we don't know who's at the other end. And besides, from what the instructions said, two or more stones have to be within proximity of each other, no more than a meter apart when the communications link is established." She shrugged. "It also says once a link is established, it is established forever."

"Better leave that alone for now," Karl advised.

"But you said Elena was close by," Dieter said, his hope improving.

"According to this, she is," Caryn said.

"Can I try it?"

"Sure." She handed him the ball. "Remember to turn it over and shake it before you ask the question."

Following her instructions, Dieter shook the stone. "Is Elena in the house where she and Noble were?" Flipping it over, he stared at it. "Nothing's happening."

"Try again," Caryn encouraged.

Dieter repeated the shaking and question to no avail. "It's still not saying anything."

"Here, let me try," Caryn said, taking the stone from him. Shaking it, she asked, "Is Elena in the house where she and Noble last were together?" She flipped it over and 'Yes,' appeared.

Dieter was out the door, dragging Noble with him, the others on their heels. Once inside the house Dieter ticked his head at Caryn.

"Ask it if she's here."

Caryn shook the stone. "Is Elena here?" Flipping it over, she nodded. "Yes."

"But we've searched this place from top to bottom," Nobel complained.

"Let's do it again," Karl ordered then abruptly stopped. "Noble's right. We've thoroughly searched this place, as least we think we have. Perhaps our lovely sorceress can assist." He peered intently at her. "Don't you have some sort of spell that allows you to see hidden or secret doors?"

"My God," she exclaimed. "I'd forgotten all about that. In all the excitement in searching for her, I didn't think that magic could be involved." Turning her back to them, she cast a Detect Hidden Doors spell. She then slowly turned around until facing the fireplace then saw the outline of a door to the right. "There," she pointed.

"There's nothing there," Noble objected.

Ignoring him, she crossed the room and touched her fingers to the ornate flower carved into the woodwork of the leg piece of the mantel. Upon twisting the flower, gaps in the wall appeared and the door swung open.

Dieter was by her in an instant, calling out, "Elena," as he entered the dark room.

"Dieter," came the faint plaintive cry. "Where are you?"

"Light," he shouted. "I need some light."

Annabeth grabbed a candelabrum off the mantel and cast an evocation spell of Radiance Glow, causing the entire candelabra to emit a bright light. "This only lasts for half an hour so make good use of it."

Grabbing the candelabra, Dieter held it aloft to reveal a small platform and a narrow descending set of stairs. The stairs, curling down in a spiral staircase, were planks of oak, well worn. No sooner had he taken the first step that lights, recessed into the intertwined branch walls emitted a soft glow.

Descending quickly, Dieter reached bottom and was immediately surrounded by five doors. "Not this again," he fumed before shouting, "Elena."

"Dieter," came the muffled desperate cry, but from where?

"Which door did you use?"

"The one in front."

"In front of the stairs?"

"I... I don't remember," Elena wailed.

Dieter whirled around and shouted up the stairs. "Caryn. I need you and bring that magic ball with you."

Caryn squeezed past Annabeth halfway down the stairs. "You might as well come too," she said.

Once at the bottom, she immediately saw Dieter's predicament. Stepping towards a door, she asked the Augury Stone, "Is Elena behind this door?"

The result of 'No' was repeated for the next two doors. On the fourth try, Dieter got the answer he wanted, but there was no handle on the door. Turning to Annabeth, he begged, "Open it."

Annabeth stared at the door a moment then cast a Knock-Knock spell.

The door opened and Elena burst out and into the loving and protective arm of the Berserker who swallowed her up in his grasp, one hand still gripping the candelabra.

"What spell did you use?" Caryn asked Annabeth.

"It's called a Knock-Knock spell. It unlocks and opens magically sealed doors."

Caryn gave her a warm smile. "You're pretty handy to have around."

"You ain't so bad yourself," Annabeth smiled back then turned to Dieter and Elena, still in a tight embrace, at the same time noting that wall lights in the stairwell had gone out. "Let's go you two before the candlelight goes out and we're all stuck down here."

Taking the candelabra from Dieter, Annabeth led the way back up.

Once upstairs, Karl gazed at the shaken Elena and asked, "What happened?"

"I was here with Noble and while he was in the dining room collecting the silverware, I saw the fireplace and thought how pretty it was. So I walked up to it and when I touched the flower, a door appeared to the side and I opened it and I saw there was a set of stairs and so I went in and the door closed behind me and I couldn't open it but there were lights on in the stairs and I thought maybe that might be a way out so I went down and then there were five doors and one door was still open so I went in and it was a wonderful room with all sorts of treasures."

"Treasures?" Noble perked up. "Which door?"

"Down boy," Annabeth chuckled.

"But after a bit," Elena continued, "the lights went out and I couldn't open the door and," she started tearing up as she cast woeful eyes at Dieter, "I was so scared that you'd never find me."

"Looks like everything worked out," Ben observed with an unaffected air then turned to Karl. "You want to keep exploring tomorrow or can I leave you here and head on back? Gotta get back and replenish my food supplies."

"I think we can handle it from here," Karl replied. "We owe you. You sure you don't want to come with us?"

Ben frowned in thought, tilted his head to the side then shook it. "Naw. I'm enjoying myself right now. One of these days, I suppose, but not yet. I'm having too much fun messing with the orcs."

"Suit yourself," Karl nodded. "Any time you decide to move on, you know you can count on our help."

"Much obliged," Ben said with an appreciative grin. "There's enough food in the house for dinner tonight and breakfast tomorrow. I'll be moving on then."

"You're leaving now?" Annabeth asked, surprised as evening was upon them.

"Night time's the best time to get where I'm going. Wanna come?" he asked, with a hopeful smile.

"I like my creature comforts," she replied with a shrug.

"I figured as much." His grin widened. "Well," he added turning to the rest of the group. "Stick to the outer streets along the wall and you'll eventually come to the other side of the city. You'll know you're there because there's a door just like the one here. There's only two main doors to the city, so you know you're at the right spot when you get there. There's lots of secret ways, but I'd steer clear of those 'cause they drop you straight down into the forest below. Now you might think that might not be such a bad idea, seeing as how it would take you straighter than working your way through the city. Problem is, though orcs usually steer clear of the place, doesn't mean they don't send patrols through, large patrols, meaning more than you all can handle at one time, if you get my drift."

"We do," Raquel said, ready for this odd and loquacious man to move on.

'Right," Ben replied then motioned Karl over for a private conversation. He shot a quick glance around then lowered his voice. "Me being gone means there's an extra bedroom. I'd appreciate it if you would let them know to leave it be. Don't like others in my bedroom or sleeping in my bed. It's sort of weird, others sleeping in my bed, if you get my drift."

Karl had the urge to point out that Ben was sleeping in someone else's bed but decided to leave it alone. "Of course. No problem. I think we're all content where we are."

"Appreciate it." Casting a wistful stare at Annabeth, he seemed indecisive. "I'd stick around and have dinner with you, but I gotta get back in time to do some pilfering and if I stick around any longer, I won't have enough time."

Karl followed his stare to where Annabeth was amiably chatting with Raquel and Caryn, looking more than fetching. "We're not going far, and hopefully we'll be back through here soon. She'll be around."

Ben's grin split his face. "Excellent. Well then. See you around."

"One more thing before you go," Karl interrupted. "I'd appreciate it if you wouldn't tell anyone else about this place."

"Why not?" Ben tilted his head and furrowed his brow.

"Because there may be players coming after us who might not be so... um, honest. What I mean is that there might be more players coming who are more interested in taking advantage of you and other players, to your own detriment."

Ben studied him for a moment. "You got someone in mind?"

"Yes," Karl admitted. "His name is Kevin. He's an assassin whose sole interest is himself. He's killed other players and he'll have no qualms killing you if it suits him."

Ben scratched his chin. "He the only one?"

"Doubt it. My guess is that if and when he ever crosses the bridge, he'll come with others of his kind. I'd give them wide berth if you can."

Ben slowly nodded in understanding. "Bad blood between you two?"

"Long story that I'd be happy to share another time when we get together. For now, let's hope he stays on the other island."

"Thanks for the heads up," Ben affably grinned. "Guess I'd better get going."

The rest of the team expressed their thanks with the women giving Ben a kiss on the cheek, except for Annabeth who kissed him on the forehead.

"That thing's gonna have to come off," she said, ruffling his beard, "before I kiss you anywhere else."

Ben's eyes brightened. "I can arrange that."

"Safe travels, Ben," she answered with an impish smile. "We'll see you soon enough."

"I'm looking forward to it."

Once Ben was out the door, Caryn said, "I'm hungry. Glad we rescued the cook. Otherwise, we'd all have to eat Karl's cooking."

"Who said I'd cook?" Karl parried, leading them back to the house.

Back at the house, Elena was glad to be in the kitchen where she surveyed what Ben had in the larder. An hour later, she brought out steaming rice and pulled pork then reemerged with several jars of mead.

"We're saved," Noble joked, holding up his stein.

Conversation initially slowed as they devoted their attention to the meal then picked up as their appetites were sated. When the meal ended and they settled down to nursing their mead and stretching out in thick cushioned chairs and sofas, Karl motioned Caryn to the side.

"Does that stone of yours give any answers other than 'yes' or 'no'?"

"I don't know," she replied with a smile. "Haven't had the chance to look at the directions."

Karl chuckled. "Keep a lid on it until you do figure it out. Don't want anyone else knowing we have it, so we need to warn the others. This isn't a toy."

"Roger that," she answered with an affirmative nod.

Julie sauntered up and slipped a hand around Karl's arm. "Annabeth and Raquel have been really sweet to me. They said since I didn't get my chance last night that I could have you to myself again tonight."

"That was kind of them," he said, looking past her shoulder to where Annabeth and Raquel stood together and waved at him, their faces betraying something else was behind their sudden generosity.

"I think we ought to adjourn for the evening," she lovingly, though firmly, said.

Karl was about to say he wasn't tired when he saw the look in her eyes that said she wasn't taking 'No' for an answer. "Alright. There's nothing more I can do here anyway." He glanced over to see that Dieter had gone into the kitchen to be with Elena.

Sensing the night was coming to an end, Noble stood up, mead mug in hand and turned to Sakura and Caryn. "I do believe there's still some wine in our house. Coming?"

"Sounds good," Caryn replied followed by a "Goodnight" to Karl and the others.

Soon, only Annabeth and Raquel remained.

"Might as well call it an evening," Annabeth said with a forced yawn.

"C'mon, my tall handsome Viking," Julie prodded, grabbing Karl's hand and leading him to the door leading to the upstairs.

Picking up a lit candelabrum, Annabeth followed behind, Raquel, who was doing her best not to snicker, in tow.

Julie led the way, wasting no time to get to the top of the stairs then down the hall to the last door on the right then turned around. "Goodnight," she said to two women before spinning back around and pushing Karl into the bedroom.

Karl was halfway through the doorway when Annabeth flicked her fingers at him and forcibly suppressed a giggle as he suddenly wavered then disappeared followed by a dull thump.

"O my God, not again," Julie exclaimed.

"Now what?" Annabeth frowned as she ambled over to the door, Raquel by her side. Peering in, she saw Karl sprawled out on the floor, fast asleep.

"Wow," Annabeth commiserated. "I didn't realize just how tired he was. I guess all the excitement of Elena's disappearance and then Ben leaving was just too much. He just couldn't hold up any longer. Here, let us help you get him to bed."

Julie's face was a mixture of anger, frustration, irritation, and suspicion. She narrowed her gaze at Annabeth as they lugged and pulled Karl onto the bed.

"Do you want us to undress him?" Annabeth offered.

"No," Julie snapped, glaring at Annabeth. "You did this."

"I did what?" Annabeth frowned in confusion.

"Made him fall asleep," she accused.

"How could I do that?" Annabeth protested. "If I could make everyone fall asleep whenever they wanted, we'd all be rested and wouldn't need to sleep at night. We could have had power naps whenever we wanted." She turned to Raquel. "Wouldn't that have come in handy all those times we had breaks in battle. A short power nap and we'd have been even more awesome."

"But... but," Julie retorted, "you're a sorceress. You have all sorts of magical powers."

"That I do," Annabeth admitted, "but I'm still learning them. Trust me, if I had a sleep spell, I'd be the first one to use it on myself."

"You can do that?" Raquel interrupted.

"I don't know," Annabeth shrugged. "Never thought of using a spell on myself, other than the usual spells that give me special powers."

By now, Julie was no part of the conversation as Annabeth and Raquel discussed the benefits of casting spells on oneself. Quickly realizing she was being ignored, she interrupted.

"Are you saying you didn't cast some sort of sleep spell on him?" she demanded.

"Why would I lie to you?" Annabeth replied with a hurt frown. "Look at him. The man's exhausted. All this responsibility is wearing him down. And you're not helping with your constant nagging."

"Me?" Julie sputtered.

"Yes you," Raquel answered. "Think about it. Annabeth and I leave him alone when we know he needs rest. You don't. It's as though he can't get any time to himself. You're always there, reminding him that he's going to be king and you're going to rule with him. We gotta get there first."

Julie suddenly felt guilty. "I never thought of that. Should we leave him here by himself? I could sleep in Ben's room."

"No," Raquel replied. "I think it might be nice if you stay with him, sort of like a protector. Even strong men need to be pampered now and then."

"OK," Julie said, needing no prompting.

"Goodnight then," Annabeth said.

Once outside the closed bedroom door, Raquel stifled a laugh and walked down to her bedroom door. "One of these days she's going to figure it out."

"Until then, we get to have some fun," Annabeth grinned in reply.

"I like the 'Why would I lie to you' comeback. You don't admit you're lying, though you are, and she never asks why you would lie. You'd make a good politician."

"Ouch," Annabeth winced, pretending she was poked. "Anything but a politician."

"So what happens when he wakes up in an hour?"

"Don't know," she shrugged. "I'm hoping she'll be asleep by then and he'll drift off again."

"Poor woman to be so close and not taste the fruits."

"You want her to romp around with him?" Annabeth frowned.

Raquel pondered for a moment. "Nah," she sniffed in disdain. "This is far more fun."

Annabeth looked back over her shoulder towards Julie's bedroom then back at Raquel. "I'm not sleepy yet. Wonder if there's more mead in the kitchen."

"Think I'll join you," Raquel said with a smile, holding out a hand.

Annabeth reached up and entwined her fingers with Raquel's then hand in hand they descended the stairs to discover there was a whole keg of mead in the larder.

Julie was not a happy camper in the morning, especially when she discovered that he was gone when she awoke. She was more put out when she discovered, during breakfast, that he had awoken just after she had drifted to sleep. She glared at Annabeth who had snorted a laugh then pretended to be choking on eggs.

Clueless as to her game with Julie, Karl frowned at Annabeth who shared an impish glance with Raquel causing him to wonder what mischief those two were planning. Knowing it was just a matter of time before he found out, he turned to more important matters and addressed the rest of the team.

"If you haven't done so yet, you need to change your respawn spot. Here would be an excellent location as it's relatively safe. With that in mind, I've decided we need to look around this city a bit more. I know Ben said he didn't find anything, but with Caryn finding the Augury Stone yesterday, there might be more here that we can use, especially if they've left a sword or two behind. We can cover more of the city if we pair off in twos. We use Ben's knife method for direction with the blade pointing back to this place."

"What are the teams?" Sakura asked.

"Dieter and Elena," Karl began, stating the obvious concerning those two, "Annabeth and Raquel, Sakura and Noble –"

"There's a powerful combination," Annabeth interrupted with a grin, "assassin and thief. Not sure I'd want to be a city burgomaster if I learned these two were in town."

In contrast to Noble's overt beaming, Sakura's face was impassive though Annabeth detected a hint of satisfaction at the recognition.

"I'll take Caryn and Julie," Karl concluded. "Take the entire day to explore. Remember,' he said staring pointedly at Noble, "we're looking for things that are useful, like weapons, maps, and such. Also, while this house is a good location for now, I don't like it as it's too close to the gate. We need a more secure area in case someone else discovers this city, some place where we can hide without anyone knowing we're here."

"How long we staying?" Noble asked, torn between moving on or staying and stacking up even more riches.

"Depends," Karl answered. "I don't want to dawdle, but at the same time, I don't want to miss opportunities."

"Wonder why we never find out about stuff until we're right on it," Raquel observed. "It's like we didn't even know this city existed until Ben showed it to us, and now it appears on our maps, at least it does on mine."

"Which begs the question of why can't we pull up a city map with all the streets?" Annabeth added.

Julie's face scrunched in confusion. "That's something I don't understand. Every now and then you all get this unfocused look in your eyes and wave your hands in the air." She mimicked them pulling up their individual screens and scrolling and pressing hyperlinks. "What are you doing?"

"We're looking at…" Annabeth began then stopped, realizing for the first time that she had never seen an NPC engaged in a personal screen. "Uh… somebody help me here."

"We're looking at individual information that is unique to players," Sakura said.

"Players?" Julie repeated.

"Players are unique people," Raquel answered, joining in the explanation. "How many people do you know like us: a Viking, a giant berserker, an elf, an assassin, or a gifted sorceress?"

"And thief," Noble interjected.

"And thief," Raquel added.

"I've never seen a Viking before," she admitted, "or an elf. But I have heard of sorceresses."

"Not like Annabeth," Raquel said with some pride. "She's not like the other sorceresses. Over time, she will become the most powerful sorceress on this island."

"Island?"

"I mean kingdom," Raquel hastily corrected. "But that aside, each of us has special talents and gifts not like anyone else. We can activate special screens… uh, special pages that can be seen by only very few."

"I don't understand," Julie frowned.

"When you see us do this," Raquel said, imitating the motions of activating a screen, "we are pulling up information that is invisible to everyone else except us. We can see all sorts of things and read all sorts of information." Though it wasn't completely true, it was enough to get the idea across.

Julie's eyes widened in wonder. "And all of you can do this?"

"Yes."

"I can't," Elena stated, feeling a bit left out.

"You don't need to," Dieter soothed, placing a tender hand on her neck. "You have me."

"Why don't we have these gifts?" Julie complained.

"I don't know," Karl answered. "Perhaps one day you will." Though he doubted it, one never knew what the developers might decide. "Anyway, all that's discussion for another time. We need to move out and conduct our recon. Meet back here for dinner. Remember to keep track of where you are."

"Yes, mother," Noble chuckled.

Karl slid his eyes to stare at Noble. "Are there any knives left now that you've absconded with the household silver?"

"I've only raided a couple of houses," Noble replied, holding up his hands in feigned self-defense then added with a twinkle in his greedy eyes, "There's got to be tons left."

Karl held back as the others began their searching, waiting until they disappeared around the corner.

"I'd like to work our way to the center," he said.

"Why?" Caryn asked.

"Don't know. Just a hunch really. I figure if we ever need a safe spot, this would be a good one. But too close to the gate opens up problems should someone else happen to stumble in. Better to be farther away. And then we need to figure a security system, a trip alarm that lets us know someone is here."

"Sounds like you're planning on staying."

"Not really," he smiled. "I've got a kingdom to rule after all. Still, I like having a sanctuary if needed. Anyway, you're the ranger, so I'll let you lead the way."

Chapter 10

For two days, Karl and the others scoured the city. Once he explained his sanctuary purpose for the city, Noble stopped collecting silverware after five houses yielded their abundance, deciding instead to find a suitable house to store all his prized goods, which he envisioned would include carpets, furniture, tapestries, and anything else of value.

Yet their search turned up two discoveries that made the stay worthwhile. The first was the city's citadel, which, in contrast to Ben's claims, rose above the rest of the houses by two stories and allowed an uninterrupted vista over the entire city. Though large in comparison to the other houses, it was not so grandiose as to demand awe and devotion.   It contained several large rooms, one of which was the throne room as the throne, or what remained of a throne, sat perched on a dais three steps high. There were the usual dining room, kitchen, larder, and buttery, which to everyone's amazement was still stocked with wines that likely were either well aged or had turned into vinegar.

As they gathered inside the buttery, agape at the stacks of wine casks, Noble, a wine enthusiast, cautioned against getting their hopes too high as to the likelihood of vinegar outweighed the possibility of great wines.

"But they're elven wines," Caryn reminded him. "And everyone knows elves live longer, so maybe their wines age better."

"We're talking grapes, not elves," Noble replied with a patronizing smile. "These vintages are hundreds of years old, if what the info in the database is to be believed."

"But the game isn't," Annabeth countered.   "Maybe these wines are only as old as the game."

"Now you're really messing with my mind," Noble complained.

"I guess there's only one way to find out," Raquel said, approaching a wine barrel covered with a thick layer of dust.

"I doubt the spigot still works," Noble said, shaking his head. "All the sediment probably clogged it up by now."

"We'll see," she answered with shrug. Retrieving a glass from the wine steward's shelf, she held it beneath the spigot then twisted the handle. A deep ruby colored liquid poured out, quickly filling the glass. She handed the glass to Noble. "You're the connoisseur."

Noble took the glass, swirled it then inhaled the bouquet. Frowning in surprise, he took a sip, savoring the flavor. "I don't believe it," he finally said. "This is good. It's like a cabernet sauvignon."

"I'm impressed," Annabeth teased.

The others needed no urging to sample the wine and would have indulged more had Karl not reminded them they still had something else to see.

Noble quickly gulped the rest of his wine, delighted to have finally found wine worthy of his attention, and followed the others tailing behind Karl and Caryn who led them back to the main anteroom then off into another short corridor to stand before a nondescript door with a silver handle.

Turning to face them, Karl said, "This is the only door Caryn and I couldn't open, no matter how hard we tried. We figured it was probably magic sealed, so we decided to call in the expert." He grinned at Annabeth.

Annabeth returned the smile and studied the door then cast a Knock Knock spell. Pressing on the handle, she felt a click and the door swung open to reveal the second discovery.

Sunlight slanted through two tall and wide barred windows of frosted glass, illuminating the armory, a large high-ceiling room filled with elven swords, bows, arrows, axes, helmets, armor, chainmail, and two large chests tucked against the far wall. They entered in hushed wonder at the largess and the amazement someone would leave such treasures behind.

Sakura gave voice to her thoughts. "I wonder if they were expecting to come back."

"Sure looks like it," Noble said, still marveling at the sheer volume of articles for battle. While the others approached the various weapons and statues adorned with armor, he wandered over to the two chests, prying the lid open on one.

"O my God," he burst, plunging his hands into the mass of gold coins, lifting handfuls and letting the coins spill out over his fingers. "We're billionaires."

Forgetting the weaponry for the moment, the others crowded around him as Dieter opened the lid to the other chest. It too was filled with gold coins.

"Forget the stinkin' silverware," Noble blurted as he began emptying his belt bags of forks, knives, and spoons.

"Hold on a minute," Karl warned as silverware clattered to the floor. "Let's not get carried away. The gold and everything in here belongs to all of us."

"I know, I know," Noble replied with a grim sigh.

"My point here is that we need to be wise about what we do with it. I, for one, will change my bind spot to here, as in this house, most likely one of the bedrooms. My bind spot will stay here from now on so that if something goes wrong and I have to respawn, it will be some place safe."

"Good idea," Caryn nodded, adding her support to his argument, though she and Karl had already decided upon their course of action.

"Which brings up another point," Karl said. "I want to repeat what I said earlier. No one else, and I mean no one," he gazed directly at Julie, "must know about this place."

"Why are you looking at me?" she whined.

"Because you are the only one who has other ties, other distractions," Raquel answered.

"You don't know that," she objected.

"Then why are we returning you to the House of Rhyeem?" Sakura asked.

"I don't know why," Julie pouted, locking her hurt eyes on Karl. "And I don't want any gold. You can have my share."

"That's not the point," Karl replied.

"I'll take her share," Noble said with a wink.

With a long-suffering sigh, Karl paused then said, "Listen, all of you. We need to think long term here. Right now we have a sanctuary that only Ben knows about."

"Yeah, but can he be trusted not to blab about this?" Noble countered.

"Who's he going to tell?" Raquel asked him. "He's happily living behind enemy lines. Not likely other players are going to go looking for him, especially since they don't even know he's here."

"Karl's right," Annabeth chimed in. "We all need a sanctuary we can come back to in case of danger. The fewer who know about it, the better."

"Thank you," Karl said, "which applies to all our bounty here. We try to take all of this with us and we're asking for trouble."

"And besides," Caryn said, staring at Noble, "suppose you take all your share with you and have the misfortune to get killed and have to respawn. You've just lost all your stuff and you got nothing left. On the other hand, if you leave most of your wealth here, you can think of it like a bank where no one's gonna touch it and you can use it when you want."

Noble blinked as he pondered the advice. "I like that idea."

"The same applies to weapons," Karl said. "Take only what you know you can use and leave the rest. That way we'll always have weapons and money to use whenever the time comes."

"I thought we were gonna rule a thousand years of peace," Julie said.

"A thousand years is a long time," Karl answered. "I don't have as much faith in mankind or game-kind as others do. I have a feeling things might not work out like they planned."

"Is the prophecy wrong then?" she asked with a worried frown.

"Not necessarily," Karl replied. "It's just that some people have a different idea of 'peace.'"

"I don't understand," she frowned.

"You will," he said, the tone indicating he was through with this discussion. "So, everyone, pick a weapon or two and grab a handful of gold."

"We're not going to divvy it up?" Noble asked, disappointed.

"Why?" Dieter said, peering intently at the thief. "What does it matter if someone gets an extra coin or two? There's more than enough in there for everyone... unless a certain thief has other ideas."

"Why you looking at me like that?" Noble bristled. "I may be a thief, but I'm not gonna screw my friends."

"Never said you would," Dieter intoned.

"What about the spell on the door?" Raquel asked. "Annabeth's the only one who can open it."

Karl turned to Annabeth. "Well? Is there something you can do?"

"Let me look," she replied. "Like I've said before, I'm still figuring out how a lot of my skills work."

"Take your time," he encouraged then smiled. "We leave tomorrow."

"We are?" Noble sputtered, his shoulder sagging in disappointment.

"We'll see," Karl answered then turned to Elena. "How we doing on food?"

"I've brought enough grain for bread for two more days. I left the eggs for Ben, but I did take some of the cheese."

"So we have enough food for two days," Karl reminded everyone. "We have two more days here then we need to move on. From what Caryn and I saw, there are enough bedrooms in this place so that everyone can have his or her own room."

"But I'm sharing a room with you," Julie emphasized.

"Not tonight, Cinderella," Annabeth corrected. "Tonight he's mine."

"And tomorrow night is my turn," Raquel added with firm intent.

"That's not fair," Julie loudly complained.

"Deal with it," Annabeth retorted before turning to Raquel. "You mind finding us bedrooms while I figure out what to do here?"

"I'm on it," she replied, heading out.

"Think I'll go visit the buttery again," Noble said with a grin.

While the others went off to find their rooms, Karl remained behind, watching Annabeth scrolling through her skills screen. Julie lingered in the room until Karl shooshed her out. Even then, Julie hovered outside the door.

"You not going to find a room?" she asked Karl, her attention on the entries.

"Caryn and I already selected our rooms."

Annabeth paused in her search to twist her head to stare at him. "You and the elf are pretty chummy. Anything Raquel and I should know about?"

"Jealous?" he teased.

"And possessive," she replied. "We don't mind sharing... if it's a good cause, but we want our fair share."

"Now you're sounding like Julie." He looked over his shoulder to see the hurt in Julie's eyes at the barbed comment. "I thought I told you to go find a room."

Julie turned and shuffled away, her sullen face edged with anger.

"That wasn't nice," Annabeth chided. "She's really a sweet, though deluded, girl."

Ignoring her, Karl ticked his head at her screen. "Anything?"

"I think I found something. It's called a Knock-Lock spell. All I have to do is program a knock sequence and the door will open for anyone who uses the sequence."

"Good. Tell everyone," he said then paused to walk to the door and poke his head out before walking and lowering his voice, "except Julie."

Annabeth was about to ask why, when the epiphany hit and she nodded. "You going to tell her?"

"Hopefully I won't have to. What's the knock code?"

Annabeth's face split into a mischievous grin. "How about 'Shave and a haircut, two bits.'"

Karl laughed. "I'm not sure some of them would know it. In fact, I'm surprised that you do."

"You do too," she teased.

"Yeah, but my mind is filled with all sorts of useless trivia."

When it came time all the team members were told and practiced the door code, only Elena and Noble didn't know the rhythm. Julie was kept away by Caryn and Raquel who consoled her regarding to Karl's brusque brushoff, reminding her that tomorrow was another day.

However, Julie's disappointment grew as the next two days were consumed with exploring the city. Nothing more of significance was discovered so after the second day, they left the safety of Ryath-sari and headed for Glenloch.

Leaving Uafas in the safety of the forest, Karl and company stood in the middle of the road on the knoll at the forest's edge and peered into the far distance at the majestic city atop a wide plateau. The city walls of Glenloch scintillated in the mid-morning sun. Tall spires rose at each of the wall's corners. In the valley between the city and the forest lay broad fields of grain interspersed with orchards of fruit trees. Farmers' and merchants' wagons plied the network of roads, the majority of traffic moving in and out of the main gates.

Karl glanced over to Julie whose nervousness bordered on apprehension.

"Does it look familiar?" he asked.

"I… I don't know," she answered, moving closer to him and clutching his hand. "It's like I've seen it before, but I don't know if it's just me thinking of one of my dreams."

'Guess we'll find out," Annabeth cheerily spoke up.

"Let's go." Karl said, forcibly removing his hand from Julie's grip.

The walk to the city gates was uneventful except for the growing number of stares they received, especially Caryn. The two guards originally manning the gate had suddenly multiplied to six, now led by a brawny sergeant who sized up the newcomers in a slow and unemotional gaze.

"Welcome strangers," the sergeant greeted them. "We've been awaiting your arrival."

"You have?" Karl cocked an eyebrow in surprise.

The sergeant regarded him with a lofty glance of superiority. "We are not all ignorant savages. We do know how to use our feathered friends. We began monitoring your progress two days ago when you crossed into our kingdom. As you were not orcs, we wondered how you managed to survive those vile creatures."

"So are we," Annabeth chuckled.

The humorless sergeant frowned at her before addressing Karl. "What is your purpose here?"

"We've business with the House of Rhyeem."

"I'm sure you do," the sergeant scoffed, "just like everyone else in the kingdom."

Pursing his lips at the arrogant man, Karl's first inclination was to whack him upside the head and be done with it. However, they weren't in the city yet and there were only eight of them against the entire city.

Pulling Julie close to him, he explained, "We rescued this woman in a place called Tarrytown and were given the quest to return her here to the House of Rhyeem."

The sergeant's arrogance diminished, and he narrowed his gaze at Julie then at Karl. "You better come with me." Without further explanation, he spun on his heels and led the way from the gates, the three additional guards joining them.

"Where are we going?" Raquel asked, returning a polite smile to the plethora of stares and pointing fingers.

"To see Lady Eleris," the sergeant replied over his shoulder.

"Who's she?" Annabeth inquired.

"She's the lord's bargrave for the city."

Instead of weaving in and out through side streets and back alleys, the sergeant led them up the main thoroughfare, finally stopping outside a colonnaded three story building of white marble.

"Nice place," Annabeth said, nodding with approval.

"What she like" Raquel asked the sergeant.

"You'll find out," he tersely responded and led them up the steps to the portico and into the building.

Karl casually glanced at the rest of the team as they mounted the steps, immediately sensing something wasn't quite right. It was then that he realized Nobel had somehow managed to detach himself on the way here. Shaking his head, he decided the thief would probably be caught and they'd have to rescue him. However, this was the last time, for the next time he saw him he would remind the little man that if it ever happened again, he was on his own.

Pushing through the doors, they stepped into a large wide wood-paneled room with a tall arched ceiling filled with skylights helping illuminate the activity below. A flurry of activity gave the impression of important business being conducted. But it was quiet, too quiet, despite the hurried activity of messengers sent away on various missions by a wizened bespectacled older man with wisps on white hair in disarray on his balding pate. He looked like he had just awoken.

The sergeant led them to the man.

"Good day to you, Sergeant Coyre," the man said, his dry voice broking no nonsense. "How may I help you? Just a moment, please." His eyes caught the inattention of a young male messenger who had winked at another messenger in passing, a comely lass who blushed with a smile. "You there. You've no time for flirtation. Be about your business."

Hiding his embarrassment, the young man hurried off while the old man returned his intense focus on the sergeant, pushing his glasses up the bridge of his nose.

"Good day, Proctor Shocan," the sergeant said with calm respect. "This is Karl the Viking."

Peering at Karl above the rim of his glasses, Shocan lifted an eyebrow in mild irritation. "We've been expecting you. However, the Lady is in conference at the moment. You all can take a seat over there. I'll let you know when she's available." He pointed to an area by the wall with four rows of ten chairs each, half of them filled with patiently waiting petitioners.

A pedestal podium stood at the font of the waiting area. On top was a small take-a-number dispenser made of wood and metal with a curved bar from which hung small wooden plaques with engraved numbers.

As Karl led the team to the waiting area, a plump matronly woman of long-suffering complexion waddled over, peered at the next number on the dispenser, flicked it to the rear and called out, "Thirty-four. Number thirty-four."

A young woman with two small children stood up.

"Follow me, please," the office woman monotoned.

"This is the second time –" the woman began before the other woman cut her off.

"Please wait until you are seated and in conference."

"But this is –"

"I'm not listening," the office woman, intoned, flipping her hand and marching off to another room, the young woman doing her best to corral the two youngsters and follow.

"This is like the DMV," Annabeth muttered, shaking her head.

Karl stopped, his expression growing colder before spinning around and marching back to Shocan's desk.

Perturbed at the obvious counter to his instructions, Shocan's head snapped up and he glared at Karl. "I told you to have a seat."

"I don't give a rat's ass what you *told* me," Karl snarled. "We're going to go find suitable lodging. When your lady has time, she can come find us." He turned to head for the door.

"But but…" Shocan bristled, "you can't do that. Hold it right there."

Karl saw him signal to the guards at the door. "I wouldn't do that if I were you," he threatened. "You forget who we are. We'll trash this place and kill everyone in it, you first."

Shocan swallowed as he sized up the tall Viking then the hulking berserker and the others who suddenly appeared far more threatening that he first surmised.

"If you'll wait there, I'll see if she is free." He scooted his chair back.

"You got thirty seconds," Raquel informed him. "If we're not speaking to her in thirty seconds, we're gone."

"Just a moment, please," he emphasized then shuffled towards a wide and tall ornately carved door as Raquel counted down the seconds. Slipping through the door, he reappeared just as Raquel was down to 'Five.'

"She will see you now," Shocan announced, resuming his air of superiority. "You may enter. However, you must leave your weapons here."

"Then we're not going in," Karl replied.

Shocan's face twisted in confusion. "Not going in? What do you mean, 'not going in?'"

"Just as I said," Karl spoke, his voice firm. "Our weapons go where we go. If she wants to speak with us, she sees us like we are. Otherwise, she can find us."

With a pained sigh, Shocan held up a hand. "Stay put. Let me see what her wishes are."

When the little man slipped back through the door, closing it behind him, Annabeth leaned over to Raquel. "This is painful. I'm getting hungry. I say we head out of here and find a place to stay and eat."

"You got my vote," Sakura said.

"He's got a couple of seconds left," Raquel nonchalantly replied.

The door opened and Shocan emerged, flustered and flushed. Karl guessed the little man just got a butt-chewing.

"She will see you," Shocan declared, none too pleased with the affront to his authority. "Follow me."

The room they entered was large, though not as large as the outer room, and the ceiling was lower. Massive fireplaces in opposite walls churned with roaring fires. Despite the heat generated from the fires, the room was chilly. Spaced at regular intervals, beginning at the door, guards stood impassively along the walls. Karl counted fourteen guards, all armed with crossbows, giving them a distinct weapons advantage if it came to a fight. Though they had Annabeth and her sorceress powers, he had the feeling there was something else in the room that more that counter-balanced Annabeth's talents.

At the rear of the room, on a raised dais, a woman sat.

Karl gained a clearer image of her as they approached, though unconsciously frowning as he puzzled the woman's name. *Eleris. Eleris. Where have I heard that name before?*

"M'Lady," Shocan intoned, "Viking Karl and his cohort." With a flourishing bow, he backed off to the side.

Eleris was willowy with long silky white hair and the milky skin of an albino. What Karl immediately noticed were her eyes, for they were cobalt blue, the color completely filling the eyes as though she had no iris or pupil. She wore a flowing white dress with long sleeves covering her slender arms.

She turned her face to Karl and smiled. "Welcome, Karl the Viking." Her voice had a sensual huskiness, reminding Karl of Lauren Bacall. She turned her face to look at Julie, though Karl had a hard time telling just where she was looking. "Is this the child in question?"

"Yes, m'Lady," Shocan said.

"Step forward, child," Eleris commanded.

Julie cast an anguished glance at Karl who urged her forward.

"Closer," Eleris urged then tilted her head to study Julie as she took another step. "She has the resemblance. Are we sure it's her?"

"No, m'Lady," Shocan answered, "we are not sure. I have not had a chance to interrogate... um, I mean *interview* her."

"No matter. Tell me child, what do you remember of your childhood?" She leaned forward, her eyebrows furrowed, her head dipping ever so slightly as the eyes studied Julie.

"I don't remember anything," Julie replied with a shrug. "My first memories are of Tarrytown."

Eleris nodded. "And dreams? Have you been here in your dreams?"

Julie hesitated.

"Well, answer me, child."

"If I say 'yes,' it just seems so silly. How could I dream this place?"

"Have you?"

Again Julie hesitated the quietly said, "Yes, even with the two fireplaces here, though I don't remember it being quite as cold. You are younger in my dreams, with blond hair and eyes the color of robin's eggs. A man sits where you now sit while you stand to his side. He has a scar on his left cheekbone."

Eleris jolted back. "By the gods, it is you." Twitching her head to gaze at Shocan, she said, "Fetch Gordyn. Tell him his daughter has returned."

While Shocan bustled out, Eleris addressed Julie. "You were kidnapped when you were very young, still nursing at your mother's breast. You and your mother were on the way here from Banvie when your carriages were attacked. Your mother was killed and no trace of you was found. After time passed without ransom demand, it was assumed you too were dead."

"Did you ever find out who attacked them?" Karl asked.

"No," she brusquely replied, ignoring him and focusing on Julie, "though we suspected those in Avnoch bore responsibility, we had no evidence to justify going to war."

Karl surreptitiously pulled up his screen and activated the map, which now showed more names of towns as well as the border for the next kingdom to the west, the Kingdom of Odryssa, with Avnoch as its capital. *Why the hell couldn't I have all this info in the beginning*, he grumbled to himself.

Closing the map and screen, he returned his focus to Eleris and Julie when the door burst open and an older man dressed as a common warrior barged in. His shoulder length hair was the color of salt and pepper. A thin scar ran the crest of his left cheekbone.

"Where is she?" he demanded.

"She's here," Eleris said, pointing to Julie.

"My God," the man gushed, eyes brimming with tears. "Is it true? Are you my daughter? Are you my Elspa?"

"I can answer for her," Eleris said, though not unkindly. "Yes."

"Elspa?" Julie repeated, taking a step backwards to the safety of Karl's presence. "My name is Julie."

"A name they bestowed upon you, no doubt when they kidnapped you," the man said, brushing away the significance. "If you prefer Julie, I'll call you Julie, though you will always be Elspa, no matter what name another has given you." He turned to Dieter.

"Are you the one I am to thank for returning my daughter?"

Dieter shook his head and jerked a thumb at Karl. "It was Karl who rescued her."

Gordyn turned a thankful gaze upon Karl. "Karl," he repeated, savoring the name. "The House of Mann owes you a debt that can never be fully repaid. But I will do my best to see that you are rewarded beyond your dreams, even up to half my kingdom."

"Thank you, m'Lord," Karl suavely replied.

"Is there anything you wish, anything at all?"

"Your army."

"My what?" the king choked.

"Your army. The orc kingdom lies between here and the rest of the island to the east. They grow stronger and unless they are dealt with now, the entire island is in danger of being overrun by orcs. I have the support of Strathwick and Beally in the east. With your army, we can defeat the orcs once and for all."

Gordyn shook his head in wonder then spoke to those in the room. "Here is a true man among men. He not only rescues and delivers my daughter to me, he now wishes to defeat my enemies. You shall have it."

"Is that wise, m'Lord," Eleris interrupted. "You know little of this man and yet you are willing for him to lead your armies?"

"Why not?"

"Those same armies he leads against the orc kingdom might be the same armies he leads again the Kingdom of Mann."

"So you're telling me the soldiers of this kingdom hate the king more than they love their own families?" Karl countered.

"You have a smooth tongue, Viking," Eleris smiled. "Yet you neglect to tell us that you wear the sword called Orc's Bane."

Gordyn stutter-stepped backwards. "My God, is it true?"

Karl paused, casting a suspicious eye at the woman on the dais, wondering how she knew. "Yes, it is true."

The king's eyes hardened. "You demand too much, Viking. Because you have rescued my daughter, I will not condemn you to death, but you are no longer welcome in my kingdom. Guards."

"A wise decision, m'Lord," Eleris cooed.

It was then Karl remembered the words of the old woman in Dinwahl, Elanda the white wizard. *I was defeated by the dark wizard Eleris, a beautiful woman. I nearly died but escaped to this town to gather my strength and powers. I need the Delf Stone to help me. Without it, I am condemned to spend my days here, brooding and waiting for a deliverer.*

"It was you," he blurted, staring intently at Eleris.

Eleris lowered her head to peer out at him, an evil smile curling her lips. "Take their weapons," she commanded the guards who had already leveled their crossbows at the team, "especially his."

"No," Julie pleaded. "He's not like that. He's a good man. I love him." She clutched at Karl's arm, refusing to be parted.

Karl motioned for the rest of the team to drop their weapons as he did his best to unhook his sword belt with Julie hanging on for dear life.

"You want this sword," Karl sniffed. "Here. Take it." He tossed it with a clang on the floor.

"Bring that one to me," the king commanded.

"No," Eleris countermanded. "Bring it to me."

Gordyn stiffened, giving Eleris a cold stare. "I am the king. I commanded that it be given to me."

"Yes you did," Eleris answered with a smooth wave of her hand like she was brushing dust off a mirror. "But you want me to have it."

Gordyn's irritation disappeared, and he relaxed and nodded. "That's right. I want you to have it."

"You want these newcomers taken to our deepest dungeons," she said with another wave of her hand.

"That's right," he said with determination. "Take them to the dungeon."

"But father," Julie wailed as two guards pried her away from Karl. "He saved me. You can't do this to him, to me. I love him."

"You're young," Eleris soothed. "This will pass." She waved a hand at Julie.

"Not it won't," she fumed, stamping her foot.

Startled, Eleris' brows dropped in a deep furrow, and she waved her hand again. "You have lost interest in the Viking. Go with your father."

"No," Julie snapped. "And you don't know what you're talking about if you think I've lost interest in him. He's my savior. He's going to rule for a thousand years and I'm going to be his queen."

"Get her out of here," Eleris exclaimed, shocked that her implant idea spell had no effect on Julie.

"It'll be OK," Karl mollified, patting Julie's hand still locked around his arm. "Go on with your father for now. It'll all work out."

"A wise answer," Eleris said, her warm voice hiding her seething anger. This Viking was going to ruin everything. "Listen to him."

"Promise you won't hurt him or any of the others," Julie demanded.

"They'll be taken care of," Eleris evasively answered.

"Promise."

"Of course I promise," Eleris reassured her. "They'll be taken good care of."

Julie turned to her father. "You'll make sure she keeps her word, won't you, father?"

Gordyn's expression softened. "Of course I will. Trust me. Everything will be fine."

"Then why does he have to go to the dungeons?"

"Because he wants to use our army to overthrow your father," Eleris tersely reminded her. "You yourself pointed out his treachery. Didn't you say he was going to rule a thousand years?"

"Yes, but…"

"Then you have condemned him yourself. Take her away."

"Put her in the guest apartment," Gordyn blithely instructed.

"Ensure she does not leave," Eleris intoned.

As they dragged Julie away, several guards collected the team's weapons. One of the guards bent down to pick up Karl's sword, eventually dropping to his knees and using two hands. Yet the sword would not budge.

"Pick it up," Eleris fussed.

"I can't m'Lady. It won't budge."

Eleris snapped her attention to Karl. "What trick is this?"

"No trick," Karl shrugged. "Your guard must be weak."

"Nonsense," she snapped. "You pick it up."

Karl bent down and easily retrieved the sword, holding it up with two fingers.

"Give it to me," Eleris demanded.

"Like I said before," Karl replied, placing it back on the floor. "You want it, come get it."

Eleris' lips tightened when she suddenly felt an overwhelming lethargy combined with the thought that she should let them go. Sleep. She wanted sleep. Yawning, she rubbed her eyes and gazed down at the Viking and his friends. Her eyes found Annabeth grinning at her and understanding burst.

"Nice try," she chuckled, nodding her head with admiration, casting an awakening spell to counteract. "You had me going there for a minute." Turning to the guards, she commanded, "Take them away. Place that one," she pointed to Annabeth, "in cell thirteen." She glanced back at Karl and then at the sword. "I'll solve this riddle without you."

As he was led away with the others, Karl suppressed a snicker when he heard Eleris snarl, "Damn it. Pick it up."

Chapter 11

Karl was half asleep when he heard the bolt securing his cell door slide open and dim flickering light from the hallway spill into the dark cell. The shapes of two guards hauling what looked to be a sack of grain with arms and legs, dragged it over to the wall in the recesses opposite him. Double checking to see that the Viking was still shackled, they turned and bolted the door behind them.

In the darkness of the cell, Karl heard rustling across from him followed by a chuckle.

"Hmmm," the voice spoke. "Why does this all seem so familiar?"

Karl blinked in surprise, staring at the hazy shape then shook his head and grinned. "Noble?"

"At your service."

"I was wondering where you took off to."

"I decided to scope out some of the finer establishments in the city while you were doing your business with whoever is in charge. I was in the process of ordering meat pie when I saw you and the others traipse by."

"So you got yourself arrested?

"I figured you might need some help."

"Uh," Karl replied, rethinking his recent resolution to jettison the thief the next time he saw him. Still, his hopes waffled as he remembered the last time they were in a cell. "Just how do you propose to help?"

"I tucked a lock pick in my boot," he chortled.

Karl's initial excitement vanished when he tried moving the chain that connected his wrists. When the right hand moved down, the left hand moved up, stopping at the grommet. Unfortunately, his right hand only came down to his waist. He had to stand on one leg and twist the other one up to reach a boot. The bottom line was that Noble would have to be a contortionist to get the pick from his boot.

He listened as Noble oomphed and grunted for a good twenty minutes before he heard a clink of the tool hitting the floor followed by a "Damn it."

"How's it going over there," Karl said, smirking despite his predicament.

"Fine," Noble muttered. "Be quiet so I can concentrate."

After another twenty minutes of Noble's efforts, punctuated with more than the occasional "Damn it," Karl sensed the efforts were hopeless.

"Not working, eh?"

"It's between my feet, but I can't pick it up. If I could get a boot off, I could scrunch my toes around it."

"Ah yes," Karl chuckled, "the primate in all of us."

"What?"

"Nothing." Karl glanced over at light beneath the door and saw an indistinct form scuttle across the light causing him to ponder a possibility.

Uafas? Can you hear me?

Yes. Where are you?

I'm in a bit of a problem right now.

I'm not surprised.

Yeah, thanks for that vote of confidence. Can you talk to Raquel or Caryn?

Probably.

They have talks-to-animal skills. Tell either one that we need a rat's help here fetching a key to give to our friend Noble here in the cell with me.

The small one is with you? Uafas chuckled. *I like him.*

Me too. Can you do that, please?

Of course.

Silence interposed for longer than Karl liked and just he was forming his thoughts, Uafas spoke.

Help is on the way.

Excellent. I owe you.

And I still owe you.

How about we call it even?

Not yet.

Have it your way. Karl fidgeted a bit then spoke to Noble as a rat scurried across the floor. "Help is on the way."

"What are you talking about? O my God it's a rat. He's at my feet. O my God. He's… he's picking up the pick. O my God, O my God, he's crawling up my leg."

Karl started giggling as he listened to Noble's squeamish response to a rat crawling up his body to deliver a lock pick.

"He gave me the pick," Noble sighed with relief as the rat scampered down to the floor and disappeared. "What are the odds of that ever happening in real life?"

In mere seconds, the shackles holding his wrists clattered to the floor and he crossed over to free Karl.

"Thanks." Karl nodded, rubbing his wrists.

"Now what do we do?"

"We free the others." Karl strode to the door, bending an ear close to listen. "I don't hear anything. Wonder what time it is."

"Haven't the faintest idea," Noble shrugged. "All I know is that I haven't heard much outside the door here since we were put in here. And what does it matter what time it is?"

"Shift change. Makes it easier to escape when nothing's going on. The problem is whether they do eight- or twelve-hour shifts."

As if answering his question, voices outside the door grew louder and more distinct.

"… goin' nowhere, so I left 'em alone. Whatcha got fer meals this time?"

"Got warm bread, roasted pork that'll melt in yer mouth, half a pumpkin pie, and the finest ale in the city."

"Damn. Yer ol' lady treats you good."

"Best damn cook in the…"

Karl strained to hear as the voices dwindled then disappeared. Holding a finger to his lips as a warning to Noble, he pointed to the door then whispered, "Can you open it?"

Noble studied the door for only a moment. "Nope. Don't have my tools. If I had a magnet, I might could do it like the last time. But I don't know where the bolt is."

Karl dipped his head in understanding. "Next time they come by, go back to your spot and call out like I'm hurting you."

"Got it."

With nothing else to do, they waited, Karl leaning against the wall by the door while Noble prowled around the dungeon cell, finally returning to stand next to Karl.

"This place is bigger than I realized," he whispered. "There's a whole nuther room around the side with all sorts of things that'll make you scream like a little girl."

"Torture devices?" Karl winced.

"Yup. Scary ones that I don't wanna find out how they work."

Karl was about to reply, "Me neither," when he heard heavy footsteps. "Get ready."

Noble hustled back to his place against the wall and waited for Karl's signal.

"Now."

"Stop it," Noble called out while rattling the chains. "Leave me alone. You're hurting me. Get off me. Stop it."

As Karl expected, the peephole door slid open. Noble's performance was convincing enough that the small door slid closed, and the bolt creaked followed by the guard yanking the door open.

Light from the hallway knifed into the room, illuminating Noble who stood facing the wall, part of the wrist chain in each hand.

"Hullo," he greeted the guard with an innocent smile.

"What the hell?" the guard fumed before receiving a breath-taking punch to the gut which doubled him over, followed by a powerful hit to the back of his head, rendering him unconscious.

"That was impressive," Noble remarked as Karl dragged the guard into the cell.

"Put the wrist shackles on him," Karl ordered as he positioned the man against the wall.

With the man secured in Noble's place, Karl took the guard's sword then headed to the open door and poked his head out, casting a quick glance up and down the stone hallway, lit with flickering wall torches.

"What happens when he wakes up?" Noble inquired, glad to be free.

"Hopefully it'll be long enough for us to get the rest and get out of here."

Stepping into the hallway, he took quick stock of the cell doors lining both sides of corridor. "Keep a listen while I find where the rest of them are." He pointed in the direction down the hall where the other guard was likely sitting at the guard desk then crisscrossed the corridor, sliding the peephole gates back.

Seeing a large shape in a cell two doors down, he yanked the bolt open and jerked the door wide. "Dieter?"

"Is that you, Boss?"

"You OK?"

"Yup. The others are in the cells next me."

Noble was already in the cell, jiggling the lock pick on the wrist shackles. Dieter was free in a matter of seconds.

"You're good," Dieter complimented.

"Thanks," Noble grinned, following Karl to the next cell.

In less than five minutes, the rest of the team was liberated, that is except for Annabeth in cell thirteen.

"What's the holdup?" Karl asked.

"I can't open the door," Noble fumed with frustration. "It's got some sort of spell on it."

Karl slid the peep door open. "You OK in there?" He jerked his head back when her face appeared on the other side.

"Yup. Doing just fine. Was wondering how long it was going to take before you got here."

"How'd you get free of the shackles?" he frowned.

"Used an acid splash conjuration on the locks. Suckers fell apart in no time."

"We can't get the door open. Noble thinks it's got a spell on it. You got anything to counter that?"

"I tired Knock-Lock already on it and it wouldn't budge."

Noble peered at the lock. "It's got runes on it."

"Ah," Annabeth nodded in understanding. "That explains it. Read me the runes."

"I don't know how to read runes," he complained.

"Here, let me," Raquel said, impatiently nudging Noble to the side. "It says 'open with the touch of a virgin.'"

"A virgin," Annabeth complained. "That pretty much leaves everyone here out. Where we going to find a virgin?"

There was a thick silence before Noble cleared his throat. "Uh... let me try again. And don't anyone say a damned thing. You hear me? Not... a... word."

He placed his fingers on the lock while Annabeth cast a Knock-Lock spell. A moment later, the outside bolt slid back, and the door opened.

"Ta-da." Annabeth stepped out and bowed. "Thank you, thank you. I'll be in town all week."

"C'mon, Houdini," Raquel smiled, touching Annabeth on the elbow, "we need to figure out how to get out of here." She was about to say something to Nobel when he shot a hand up.

"Not a word," he growled.

Avoiding eye contact with the thief, they stood in the hallway, rubbing their wrists and silently vowed revenge on those who had imprisoned them.

"All my potions are gone," Annabeth moaned.

"You still have your powers," Karl pointed out.

"Have you seen how many there are?" she complained. "There's over three hundred and fifty of them. How am I supposed to ever figure out what to use and when to use it? And that's just the first two levels of sorceress skills. There're seven more levels."

"Well pick one," Karl said, "to use on the guard. We need to get by him so we can get out of here."

"Gimme a second." Annabeth activated her screen and scrolled through her skills. "How about another sleep spell?"

"That'll work. How long does it last?"

"Same as on the orc. For a single character, he should be out for an hour."

"That's long enough." He looked at the other team members. "Questions?"

"Yes," Sakura said. "What are we going to do once we escape?"

"What do you think we're gonna do?" Karl replied, his lips tightening.

"I was afraid of that," she sighed with a smile.

"Besides," he growled, "they still have my sword."

Karl led the way down the hall, the others in single file behind. After two turns down long corridors, they approached the main guard post leading from the dungeon levels behind them to the next levels. As they approached, voices at the post told them there was more than one guard there.

"Do your best," Karl whispered to Annabeth.

Tiptoeing along the wall to the end of the corridor, Annabeth paused then cast a sleep spell. The conversation immediately stopped. Peering around the corner, she saw one guard slumped face down on the desk. On a chair next to him, another guard sat in a chair, his head back, mouth open, snoring.

"All clear," she called back in a whisper, waving the others forward.

"How long will they be out," Karl asked, seeing the two slumbering guards.

"There's two of them so probably half an hour."

"More than enough time. Let's more."

The process was repeated with each level until they were at the main door to the dungeons. Behind them, almost a dozen guards dozed in peaceful sleep, their weapons now in the hands of the escapees.

"We need a place to hide while we plan our next move," Karl warned, "outside the city would probably be the best. "

"That means opening the gate," Dieter pointed out. "If you think they're unhappy with us now, wait 'til they find us gone and the gate open."

"You got a better idea?"

"Just stating the obvious, Boss."

"Sorry," Karl apologized. "I'm a little testy. I'm getting tired of being thrown in jail. Let's get our things and get the hell out of this city. Anyone remember the way back to Eleris' place?"

"I do," Raquel and Caryn said in unison.

"What time is it?" Karl asked glancing around the room.

Elena pointed to a mantel clock above the hearth. "It's about two thirty in the morning."

"Good. Few folks should be out, other than thieves and guards."

"Hey," Noble objected.

"You're one of the good guys," Karl smiled, patting him on the shoulder. "Once we're outside," he continued, "Caryn takes point, Sakura has forward security, Raquel has flank and rear security. The rest of us are in the main body within sight of each other. We avoid contact unless discovered. If we are discovered, we eliminate the threat. If we get separated, the rally point is outside the front gate. Once we get into the building, we fan out and find our stuff. We have less than half an hour to get there, get our stuff and get out of the city. Questions?"

"Yeah," Noble said. "Why just half-an-hour? It's not gonna be light for another bunch of hours."

"The longer we take," Karl explained, "the less time we have to put distance between us and the city."

"And the more time for them to give chase," Raquel added.

"OK," Noble shrugged in defeat. "Just checking."

"Anyone else?" Karl asked. "If not, douse the lights and let's move out."

Once the torches were extinguished in the entrance hall, Karl opened the door, poked his head out to survey the surrounding area then opened the door wider.

"All clear. Let's go."

Caryn took the lead and in mere seconds, the entire team was out and heading for Eleris' residence. Caryn led with unerring efficiency and before long, they stood outside the building where hours ago they had been stripped of their weapons and possessions.

"How do we get in?" Dieter whispered, trying the front door.

"Same way Annabeth got out," Karl replied, motioning for her to work her magic.

Once the door opened, they silently entered, Karl closing and locking the door behind them. "Spread out," he whispered as he quietly headed to Eleris' reception room. Opening the door, he slipped in. The dying embers from the two hearths cast flickering dim light, enough light for him to see his sword on the floor close to Eleris' dais. Taking a step forward, he abruptly stopped when he saw what looked to be two red coals on the dais suddenly brighten.

Another step and the coals moved.

Still another step and the coals raised up and the hazy form of a creature began to coalesce as it stepped into the shadowy light.

It reminded Karl of a horned toad, a giant horned toad at least two heads taller than Karl and standing on two legs, holding a halberd. Its long tongue flicked out and Karl had enough sense to dodge the sticky appendage, rolling to the side as he gauged how far it was to his weapon.

The monster descended the steps and positioned itself over Karl's sword. Karl feinted left and dodged to the right, the creature easily following him. After several more attempts trying to get closer to the sword, Karl realized, despite its size, the creature was much too fast. Then, to a surprised Karl, the monster stepped away from the sword and spoke, its voice a throaty bass.

"Forget the sword and leave now and you will live. Take the sword and you must kill me if you wish to leave this room."

"Why not just let me take the sword?" Karl parried. "No one else can use it. It will stay there forever unless I take it."

"She knows that," the creature replied.

"Then why not let me take it?"

"Chose," the monster growled.

"You know that I can't leave without it," Karl answered.

"So be it." The monster took another step away from the sword, giving Karl ample room to make a mad dash for it were he quick enough to avoid the sticky tongue and the halberd.

"Are you allowing me to pick up my sword?" Karl inquired, edging closer.

Instead of replying, the monster stepped back again, allowing Karl to crouch down and retrieve the sword, all the while keeping a careful eye on the creature.

"There," the beast said. "Now you are armed, and we can face each other man to man."

"Man to man?" Karl chuckled. "How you figure that?"

"Defend yourself."

The monster thrust the halberd at Karl, but though the effort was strong, the movement slow and Karl easily parried the weapon, slicing it in half, the axe blade and spike clanging to the floor, leaving the beast holding the shaft.

"You have defeated me," it said. "Now you must kill me." It spread its arms wide, exposing its chest.

"Huh?" Karl frowned, puzzled. "You call that a fight?"

"Kill me," it demanded.

"This is crazy." Karl shook his head. "Why should I kill you?"

The monster leaped at him, and Karl instinctively raised his sword, impaling the creature in the chest as the massive body crashed upon him.

Karl oomphed as he pushed the creature off him and onto its back. Standing over it, he withdrew the sword and stared down. "Why?"

The creature's breaths were labored as it answered. "She can no longer torment me."

Then to Karl's amazement, the body began to transform, morphing from horned toad to that of a man, a young man once in his prime.

He slowly stretched a heavy hand towards Karl, motioning him to come closer.

Karl dropped to his knees to lift the man's head.

"She can be defeated," he gasped. "She has a weakness."

"What?"

The man inhaled deeply, pain wracking its body. "Her power lies in a stone, a small stone... plain appearance... incredible power."

Karl's eyes shot wide. "The Delf Stone?

"You know it?"

"I thought the orcs had it."

"They did... once."

"Where is it?"

"Her quarters, locked in a box in the wall... protected by spells."

"How do you know this?"

"I have seen it... I have seen its power. It is the reason you saw me as I was."

Karl stared down at the young man, wondering what he had done to deserve this fate. The man's body grew heavier. As the man's life ebbed away, Karl saw him weakly smile and faintly whisper, "Thank you," before his eyes glazed over and his head rolled to the side.

Gently placing the man's head back down, Karl stood and strode across the room, through the door and back into the outer room where Dieter and Elena stood quietly near Shocan's desk. They looked up as he approached.

"You the only ones back?" Karl said, stating the obvious.

"They're still collecting their stuff," Dieter replied. "It was all in a pile in that room over there." He pointed to a door to the right.

No sooner had he pointed that Annabeth opened the door, followed by Raquel and Sakura. Caryn emerged a moment later.

"Where's Noble?" Karl asked as they approached.

"I'm here," Noble announced as he slipped through a door by the waiting area, slipping a silver chalice into his tool satchel. He grinned mischievously as he walked up. "It was there begging me to take it."

Karl rolled his eyes yet smiled. "Let's go. Same formation to the gate. Sakura, I want you to roam farther forward in front of Caryn."

"Got it." She was gone in an instant.

"Wish I knew how she did that," Karl chuckled as the rest followed outside.

Raquel sidled up to him. "You don't trust me to take the lead?"

"I'm more afraid of what's behind us than in front," Karl soberly answered. "I need them to keep the way clear forward. It's behind us that I expect the most trouble, especially if anyone should stumble upon us as we leave."

Mollified, she took her place at the rear of the group.

Fortunately, other than the walking patrols there was no one out in the early morning and the escape to the main gate went unnoticed, that is until they came to the gatehouse that was blocked on both sides with thick metal sheathed doors barred with iron and a heavy portcullis in between.

Unbarring the doors was not a problem. Raising the portcullis was another matter, for it required winching the door open from inside the guard house. Dieter had already peered in through the door and held up two fingers indicating there were two guards inside.

"I don't want them hurt," Karl whispered as Raquel and Caryn lifted the cross bar away from the first set of gate doors.

Dieter nodded, pushed the door open, bowing down enough to enter.

A moment later Karl heard a loud, "Ow. What the hell?"

The door opened again, and Dieter popped his head out. "All set, Boss."

When Karl entered, the two guards sat on one cot, rubbing their heads where Dieter had wacked them with the flat of his dagger. They apprehensively stared at the berserker.

"We need to open the portcullis and need your help," Karl informed them.

"You can do it yerselves," one guard replied by way of explanation, shifting a fearful glance between Karl and Dieter. "Don't take nuthin' more'n workin' the winch."

"We know," Karl answered with a smile. "What we need is for you to close the gates and drop the portcullis after we're gone."

"Ah," the other guard nodded in understanding. "Why didn't ya say so in the first place?"

"Say," the first guard brightened when he recognized Karl. "Ain't you the fella with that one sword?"

"I am."

"It's him," the guard said to his partner. "He's the one Sergeant Coyre told us about." Turning back to Karl, he said, "We'd be happy to oblige you. And you can count on us to keep quiet."

Karl frowned. "Just what did Sergeant Coyre tell you about me?"

The guard glanced around then lowered his voice to a whisper. "He said you was the one's gonna get rid of the witch."

"Eleris?"

"Shhh, not so loud," he fussed. "She got ears everywhere."

"Sergeant Coyre's right," Karl reassured him, though wondering why Coyre was such an ardent supporter as he gave no indication when he led them to Eleris. "But we need to leave the city for a while to make plans. How often do you two guard the gate?"

"We're on night shift for the next month," the second guard answered.

"If we need to sneak back in," Karl whispered, "how can we do that without being seen? Can you two help us?"

The two guards exchanged a knowing glance.

Raquel popped her head in the doorway. "C'mon. We're wasting time."

"Just a moment," Karl answered.

The first guard curled a finger at Karl and pointed to a small bell on the wall with a thin rope attached to the top. "The other end of the cord on the top of the bell is on the wall outside, not far from the gate. All ya gotta do is pull the cord and it rings the bell inside here. But ya gotta do it a certain way: three pulls then two then one. Ya keep doin' it like that until the gates open or someone goes atop and tells ya to buzz off."

"Excellent," Karl nodded. "What are your names?"

"I'm Nergal," he answered then pointed to his partner, "and he's Sam."

"Sam?" Dieter chuckled.

"It's short for Samgard," Sam said, not happy with the berserker's mirth at his name.

Karl studied the two men for a moment. Nergal was a slender middle-aged man with smooth cheeks and close-cropped hair. Sam was about the same age, wiry and bald. He also had a scar across his collarbone near his throat.

"Let's get this gate open," Karl commanded.

With Dieter's help, the portcullis flew into the gatehouse recesses, the screeches not as loud as Karl had feared. Once outside the gates, Karl turned to the two guards.

"Keep this quiet as long as you can without getting yourselves into trouble. If they discover we left this way, tell them we threatened to kill you if you interfered. Think about your story and make sure it matches each other."

Nergal nodded and nudged Sam. "We're good at tellin' whoppers. C'mere." He led the way a few steps along the wall and pointed to a small piece of rope dangling about a hand's length out from the wall. "Here's the other end of the cord."

"Thank you."

"Sorry about the whack on the head," Dieter apologized.

"It's OK," Sam reluctantly said. "Ya didn't know."

"We need to move," Raquel urged.

"Same formation," Karl said. *Uafas? Can you hear me?*

Yes. I've heard you for some time.

Where are you?

South of the city. There's a small farmhouse not far from the bridge over the river. You better hurry. They're not going to be happy when they discover one of their tasty hogs is missing.

We're on our way.

"Head south, Caryn. Stay on the main road. We travel in over-watch at a jog until we connect up with Uafas."

As Caryn took the lead, Karl looked behind him to see Nergal and Sam closing the gates.

Dawn spread across the sky while Karl and company sped their way south and west. By the time they stopped for their first rest, it was mid-morning, and they were at least six hours gone from Glenloch.

"What's the plan, Boss?" Dieter sat on a fallen tree, poking leaves on the ground with a stick.

Elena wandered close by, picking berries and digging mushrooms. The rest of the team was spread out in a perimeter, keeping careful watch.

Karl stood up in the center. "Now's as good a time as any to discuss our future."

"I think we've already been through this," Annabeth cheerfully replied. "You're supposed to become king of this island and rule for a thousand years. We're going to help you do it and we're going to run this place with you."

"But to do it," Raquel joined in, "we're going to have to eliminate everyone in the way, which means we're going to have to come back and defeat the witch and the soon-to-be former king."

"What do we know about the Kingdom of Odryssa?" Caryn asked.

"Just what's listed in the files," Sakura answered, "which is pretty much nothing. I've looked. Other than the usual brief background history, all it says was that the two kingdoms are neither friendly nor unfriendly towards each other. They trade at the borders, but pretty much leave each other alone."

"We have some support already in the city," Dieter pointed out.

"Defeating Eleris might be a problem," Annabeth said. "She's a level 20 wizard, but her powers seem far stronger."

That's because she has the Delf Stone," Karl answered.

"Delf Stone?" Raquel and Caryn replied at the same time.

"It supposedly adds to her powers," Karl said.

"How'd you know about that?"

Karl explained about Elanda and his encounter with the horned lizard in Eleris' reception room and both mentioning the Delf Stone.

"So he wanted you to kill him," Raquel said, melancholy in her voice. "How sad, especially for someone so young. Wonder what he did to earn her displeasure?"

"Don't know if we'll ever find out," Karl replied. "Point is, we need the stone to defeat Eleris."

"So how we going to get it?" Sakura asked.

"We need a talented thief," Karl said, shifting a sly glance at Noble.

"Me?" Noble squeaked. "You saw what happened to me in Tarrytown. You need a professional, someone with genuine skills. I'm still an amateur, a newbie."

"And a thief," Karl reminded him.

"But why me?" he whined.

"Because you're the only one we have and trust. But it's not like we're going to send you in there with no plan or help."

"So what *is* the plan?"

"We need time to recoup and recover. Obviously we can't do that here in Mann. She'll be looking for us. We can't go back, so the only logical thing to do is head over to Odryssa."

"Wonder what happened to Julie," Annabeth said. "I kinda miss her."

"You just miss teasing her," Raquel quipped.

"But I did like her," Annabeth replied, "even if she was too full of herself."

"Not our problem right now," Karl said.

"There's one thing I don't understand," Dieter interrupted. "Returning Julie to the House of Rhyeem supposedly brought us eternal thanks and enduring friendship with them. So why did we get thrown in prison?"

"Good question," Sakura agreed.

"Maybe we still have their friendship," Caryn said. "Maybe it's because Eleris is in control now. You saw how everyone obeys her, even the king. We get rid of her then the rest will fall into place."

"Sounds easy." Annabeth grinned at Noble.

"For you, maybe," he sourly replied.

"Let's focus on the moment," Karl asserted. "Everyone pull up your maps. We're southwest of Glenloch. We need to head directly to Odryssa, specifically the capital city, Avnoch. Let's get a measure of our reception there. We're going to need them if we're going to win this island."

"OK, Boss," Dieter cheerfully replied, closing his map.

"Let's change up the order a little," Karl said, "Uafas up front as usual along with Caryn, Raquel in the rear and Sakura roaming security. One more thing," he said staring at Annabeth and the two Rangers. "We again need to move in secrecy. I suspect Eleris will expect us to head to Odryssa. She'll use whatever means she can to find us, including animals and birds. You three will need to be on watch for any suspicious activity."

"For example?" Annabeth asked.

"Birds flying overhead," Raquel answered. "He makes a valid point. We're going to have to stay off the road system to avoid being spotted. But there are still forest animals that can track us."

"All the more reason for you three to make use of whatever skills you have to keep us safe and secure," Karl said.

Felix stood at the window, mindlessly staring across the river thinking that, lately, he tended to spend much of his days standing here gazing across the river. When not standing here, he took to wandering the hallways now almost devoid of human interaction. There were still some essential personnel and of course Gerard was still around, complaining that he had nothing to do and threatening to immerse whether ITL liked it or not.

"You've decided on a game?" Felix had asked, standing in the same spot as today when Gerard barged in and announced he was bored.

"I've nothing left to do," Gerard fumed. "I'm the last one of my department. Everyone else is already immersed." He flopped down into a chair and scowled like a petulant child, his arms folded across his chest. "Why can't I immerse?"

"So you *have* decided on a game," Felix said, repeating the question as a statement.

"I don't see what's so important that I have to hang around here anymore," Gerard moped, ignoring Felix's question.

Felix's first inclination was to tell him the truth - "Because I like tormenting you," but decided that might not be the best answer at the moment. Instead, he again stated his question. "What game have you chosen?"

Heaving a longsuffering sigh, Gerard said, "The Maze King."

"The Maze King," Felix repeated with a slow nod. "Is that the one where you create games within the game and try to outsmart each other?"

"Yeah," Gerard said. "It's more of an intellectual game, not like those fools who think something like golf is a real challenge."

I know," Felix agreed, ignoring the dig. "It's so much better being trapped in a maze because you're not clever enough to unravel the clues. So how does one level up again?"

Oblivious to the oblique taunt, Gerard explained, "Each player develops a game, a sort of maze. To level up, you have to complete another player's maze. But you can only accept a maze challenge no more than two levels higher than you already are. That's to keep players from getting too deep and lost. There are all sorts of clues, the higher the level the more complex and the fewer clues. It's a real mind-bender."

Felix already knew the intricacies of the game and like Gerard, it too bored him. "Tell you what," Felix said with a forced smile. "I'll talk to Landon and see if we can accelerate your immersion."

"I'd really appreciate that," Gerard said, standing.

"In the meantime," Felix added, "how about telling those fools in maintenance to quit joy-riding across the front lawn."

"They were just celebrating," Gerard grinned. "And besides, what does it matter? It's not like anyone's going to care anymore."

"I care," Felix tartly answered. "They are still ITL employees, and I expect them to behave. Do you have anything specific for me? If not, I've a call with Landon in a few minutes."

"Anything I should know about?" Gerard asked, wanting to appear needed and necessary.

"Just the routine daily check-in," Felix answered. "Close the door behind you please."

Disappointed he was not part of what was now Landon's inner circle, which as far as he could tell consisted only of Felix, Gerard shuffled out of the office, closing the door behind him.

A moment later Felix's computer screen beeped, and Landon appeared on the screen.

"Good morning, Felix."

"Good morning, Sir," Felix replied with a smile.

"Anything interesting in your neck of the woods?"

Felix chuckled. The more he got to know Mister Landon, the more he liked the man and his idiosyncrasies, especially his penchant for archaic expressions.

"Our favorite whiner was here again this morning," Felix said, rolling his eyes. "I've been giving some thought to his status. My recommendation is to let him immerse then yank him out every so often on some lame pretext, especially when it looks like he might succeed in a certain quest."

Landon's smile widened. "Has he chosen a game?"

"The Maze King."

Landon mused for a moment, slowly nodding. "That would be most amusing, especially if he was pulled out just as he was about to solve a maze."

"My thoughts exactly."

Landon chuckled. "Let's do it."

Chapter 12

They remained hidden at the edge of the small encampment, watching soldiers cleaning weapons, and chatting amiably. The scent of meat cooked over an open fire in the center of the bivouac site rose with the smoke and floated towards them. There were a few individual tents, simple affairs of canvas made from hemp, held up by two ridge poles and staked down, but most of the soldiers slept in bedrolls in the open, which meant the encampment was temporary.

Karl counted thirty-three soldiers in the bivouac area, not counting the perimeter guards. The perimeter guard posted close by spent more time looking over his shoulder at the campsite than out into the woods. It was when he saw another soldier approaching the guard that Karl understood why the man kept looking over his shoulder.

"Supper 'bout ready?" the guard asked.

"Almost," the other man said, coming up beside him. "Anything out there?"

"'Course not," the guard sniffed in disdain. "Don't know why we even bother. Hell, we're at the edge of the kingdom. Who's gonna look for us here?"

"Yeah, I know" the man agreed.

"What's fer supper?"

"The usual," the man sighed.

"We need to find ourselves a cook," the guard complained. "I'm gettin' mighty tired of burnt venison."

"I'd kill for some hot bread and cheese."

"And ale," the guard added, his mouth watering, "cold ale."

"You ever had the ale in Fyrdon's place in Talbet?"

"The Rusted Nail?"

"Yup."

281

"Yup, I have.   Good ale at a good price," the guard sighed contentedly.   "Mebbe Evnan will let us hit the town on the way to wherever."

The man frowned in response.   "This is getting' old."

"It got old the day we left Contyn," the guard replied. "Don't see much sense to runnin' away to fight another day when the odds are stacked against us."

The man looked back over his shoulder.   "Probably shouldn't be so loud. Someone might hear us."

"Yeah, well too bad.   Evnan needs to think about our future too."

Karl listened to the two men commiserate, thinking it never changes in any army, the right of the enlisted soldier to complain.   Yet he listened to learn what was happening in the kingdom.   It was when the man replaced the first guard that he decided his course of action.   Signaling to Annabeth to put the guard to sleep, he cautioned the rest to be ready.

Uafas. Stay out of sight for the moment. I'll call you at the right time.

As you wish. Don't be too long; that deer smells good.

As the guard dropped to the ground, Karl stepped out of hiding and scooped him up, whispering over his shoulder to the others, "Follow me. Stay alert."

The first guard approached the center of the camp, unaware of the procession following not too far behind him. The guard whirled around when one of the soldiers cleaning her sword looked past him and exclaimed, "Alarm."

The surrounding soldiers leaped to action, weapons drawn, bows ready.   An older yet sturdy man scrambled out from one of the tents, sword in hand.

"Hold your place," the man commanded when he saw Karl approach, carrying the slumbering man in his arms. He then gazed past Karl to see the hulking Dieter, ax in hand, cold death in his eyes.   His gaze traveled to Raquel then Caryn with her elf ears then Annabeth and the others. He startled when he felt a stiletto blade at his throat and a soft voice in his ear.

"Don't make any sudden moves," Sakura ordered.

Karl walked to the center near the cooking fire, placing the man down outside ring of fire stones. "Don't worry. He's not hurt. He's merely asleep, put there by a sorceress' enchantment."

The words caused an immediate reaction as the soldiers flinched in nervous anticipation of more spells.

"And the big man there is Dieter, our berserker. Irritate him at your own peril, you and all those around you for once the rage is upon him, none of you are safe." He turned to the man with Sakura's blade at his throat.

"Well done, Sakura," Karl complimented with a nod, indicating she could let the man go. "This is Sakura the assassin, the deadliest unseen and unheard enemy you will ever face. We have one more we'd like to introduce."

Uafas. Ready.

Ready.

C'mon in.

In an overt display of raucous malevolence, Uafas leaped out of the forest and planted himself close to Karl, emitting a terrifying howl that sent the soldiers clamoring and tripping backwards over themselves.

"You must be Evnan," Karl nonchalantly said to the man.

Evnan's eyes blinked wide. "How'd you know who I am?" Evnan was probably in his early 50's, solidly built, with short salt and pepper hair and a beard neatly trimmed. He carried himself as one used to being obeyed.

"I listen," he smiled, staring intently at the man. "Now if you all would put down your weapons, we can all be friends."

They instantly obeyed, especially when Uafas emitted a low-throated growl.

"Are there anymore of you besides what's here?" Karl asked Evnan.

"Just a two-man patrol scouting towards Abynee," he replied, still staring at the monstrous beast.

A soldier close by gaped at Karl then blurted and pointed at the sword on Karl's hip, "M'Lord look."

Evnan looked down at the sword then furrowed his brow. "Who are you?"

"I am Karl the Viking," Karl announced with a bit of flair, immediately disappointed when no one reacted.

"The sword you wear," Evnan said. "It seems unusual for a man of war."

Karl withdrew the sword and handed it to Evnan. "I find it more than suitable. Try it yourself."

Evnan hesitated then reached for the sword, instantly dropping to his knees by the immense weight, vainly struggling to budge it once it lay on the ground. He jerked his head up when Karl casually bent over and picked it up with two fingers and placed it back in the scabbard.

"My God," Evnan sputtered. "It's you. The prophecy said that the king would return wielding a fabulous sword and commanding large wondrous beasts and even gnomes like this one."

"Hey," Noble fumed. "I'm not a gnome. I'm a thief, and a damned good one."

"Yes," Karl replied, suppressing a snicker at Noble's indignation, "I am he."

Evnan raised himself to one knee and bowed, presenting his sword to Karl in an act of obeisance. "My Lord."

Immediately the rest of the men and women under Evnan's command likewise dropped to their knees and bowed.

Karl reached down and took Evnan's hand to help lift him to standing. "Arise, my friend and tell me what's going on." He motioned for the rest to likewise stand.

"We are at war, m'Lord," Evnan said. "The kingdom is torn in a civil war between the House of York and the House of Lancaster."

"The War of the Roses?" Karl blurted, cocking an eyebrow. "You're serious?"

"Yes, m'Lord," Evnan said with a frown at Karl's obvious surprise.

"Looks like the developers had a sense of humor," Raquel said with a smile.

"Or ran out of ideas," Annabeth added.

"Are you not from this kingdom?" Evnan asked.

"We began our journey at the far corner of this island," Karl answered.

"Island?"

"Uh, what I mean is that we began our journey here on the other side of the Kingdom of Mann, beyond the borders of the orc kingdom and even farther beyond the independent cities of the Black Forest.

Evnan stared at him with wonder. "You truly are the promised one if you survived the orc kingdom. We have heard only tales and stories all evil."

"They're probably all true," Karl chuckled. He then sniffed the air. "I'd say your meal is over-done."

Evnan inhaled the smell of singed and burnt meat. "The gods damn you Barclef," he growled. "That's the third meal you've ruined."

"I never said I could cook, m'Lord," Barclef whined. Barclef was a painfully slender man with a hooked nose who eyes betrayed a certain vacuity.

"Is there game close by?" Karl asked.

"Plenty of it," Evnan sighed. "I would have brought my cook with me if she were up to it."

"We have a cook with us."

"You do?" Evnan marveled.

Karl motioned and the beautiful Elena stepped forward, much to the appreciation of a number of the men until they saw her sidle up to Dieter and his menacing glare.

"Elena is a superb cook. If you will send some of your warriors to find some game, I'm sure our Elena can satisfy your hunger."

Elena preened when Karl said 'our' for it denoted a total acceptance that she was an integral member of the team.

"I will send some hunters to get dinner," Evnan said, grimacing at Barclef.

Uafas. Do you want them to get you something?

The lazy part of me says 'yes.' Still, I prefer my meat warm. I'll hunt on my own. The wolf rose and with a single bound disappeared into the forest, much to the relief of those in the camp.

"He's going to find his own dinner," Karl explained. "Now," he said, looking around for a suitable place to sit and have a conversation, "tell me about the civil war. To what house do you and yours belong?"

"We are of the House Lancaster."

"The red rose," Caryn added.

"Yes," Evnan replied, curious that an elf would know of the war.

Sitting near the fire pit as Barclef tossed out the charred meat, Karl pulled up his map and was awarded with a summary of the war. *Why do they wait until the last moment to tell you anything?*

The Kingdom of Odryssa is has been torn asunder by two rival houses laying claim to the throne: the House of Lancaster, whose symbol is a red rose, and the House of York, whose symbol is a white rose. The House of Lancaster, centered in Statmyr, is ruled by Fraster, the half-brother of Conall (former king, now deceased), while the House of York, centered in Contyn, is ruled by Kerr, nephew of Baldur (brother to Conall, also deceased). The War of the Roses has taken its toll on the kingdom, both economically and physically, with trade unions taxed beyond their capabilities to fund the war, nobles compelled to provide more soldiers, and the common people caught in the middle.

The war started when Conall failed to produce a male heir, subsequently dying under suspicious circumstances. Fraster's claim was challenged by Baldur who accused Fraster of treachery and complicity in Conall's death.

Presently, neither House has made any substantial gains, either militarily or via alliances with the lesser houses.

Karl finished reading the summary, noting the location of each of the houses then closed the screen.

"You're a long way from home if you're part of Lancaster," Karl said.

"Though my loyalty is to Lancaster, my domain is here in the York realm. The city of Talbet is my home. When the war started, I was forced to flee."

"How long have you been on the run?"

"Almost two months."

Karl glanced around the camp. "Doesn't look like you have much of an army."

"This is just one group of my army. They're spread out in different parts of the domain so that we can be more effective. They act independently for most of the time, conducting hit and run operations then joining together for larger battles when necessary."

"What's your relation to Fraster?"

"He is my brother-in-law," Evnan said.

"You are nobility?

"Yes," he replied with a smile, "but of more importance is that my sister is of unsurpassed beauty."

Karl nodded in understanding. "How many men do you have?"

"I have almost 300 men and women at arms."

"How many here?"

"Forty-one."

"Are you in communication with Fraster?"

"Almost daily."

For the next hour, Karl interrogated Evnan, during which time, hunters returned with two deer, butchering them then standing back to watch Elena work her talents.

It was when the savory bouquet of roasting meat wafted across the encampment that Karl interrupted his questioning. It was then he also noted the unusual attention Caryn received.

Evnan saw his puzzlement. "We know about elves, m'Lord. We've just never seen one, especially one so fair."

"Be advised," Karl warned, "she may be beautiful, but she's a deadly warrior, fearless and ruthless when necessary."

"Point taken, m'Lord." Evnan saw his warriors lining up for the feast, some with extra pewter plates to take to those on guard. Karl's team started for the rear when they were politely, though awkwardly, repositioned at the head of the line, much to their own self-consciousness. Caryn stood aloof, waving away requests to get in line.

"Shall we, m'Lord?" Evnan said, indicating for them to head to the front of the line.

"I'll wait until everyone else has been served," Karl matter-of-factly replied, quietly studying the soldiers of Evnan's force.

"My Lord?" Evnan frowned in surprise. "With the way my ravenous vultures eat, there might not be anything left."

"Then I'll find something else," he shrugged, still unaware of Evnan's amazement that a nobleman, the future king, would not be first in line.

"But my Lord…" Evnan again broached the issue. "You must maintain your strength."

"So must they," Karl replied, ticking his head at those in line. "A good leader always makes sure his people are taken care of first."

Evnan stared at him, blinking dumbly. He was even more surprised when Elena began dishing out the meal without waiting for Karl's permission to start.

"Forgive me, my Lord, but I've never before seen a king or nobleman defer to the people before his own desires."

"You included?" Karl chuckled.

"Sadly, yes," Evnan admitted, "me included." He noted that Caryn still remained aloof, waiting. "Is she nobility also?"

"She's a leader," Karl stated, "a good one."

Karl studied Caryn as though seeing her for the first time. Yes, she was very attractive, especially with the elf ears. But she also knew what it meant to be a good leader. It dawned on him that he had been depending on her as though she was his second in command when that position had always gone to Raquel. He wondered if Raquel felt she was being shunted aside then recalled the several times she questioned her position in a formation or role in an operation. Yet she never hesitated to obey.

He was further surprised when he saw Raquel holding two plates then carrying one over to Caryn. They both sat on the ground, chatting amiably.

Annabeth walked over carrying two plates, handing one to Karl. "There's plenty to go around, so you don't have to wait until the end." She turned to Evnan, smiled cheerfully, and handed him the other plate. Without a word, she turned and walked to the end of the line.

The others watching what she had done, immediately motioned for her to resume her place up front. One agile and handsome warrior leaped to block her way to the back, escorting her to the front.

Evnan watched in awe as his own warriors solicitously ensured the newcomers were taken care of. "You seem to have a good influence already, m'Lord."

"Let's hope it stays that way," he said with a smile.

Evnan cut a piece of meat and placed it in his mouth, his whole body settling in peace at the savor of properly roasted venison. "I haven't had this good a meal since I left Talbet. This is every bit as good as my own cook, and your cook has done in it under these conditions."

He glanced over to see Dieter hovering close by. "The giant and the cook are united?"

"Yes," Karl answered. "They're very protective of each other."

"Does it not cause concern that their affection may impact operations?"

"At first, I thought it might, but as time went on, Elena has proven herself every bit as necessary as the rest of the team. That she and Dieter are pledged to each other actually works for the better as he prefers to remain alive and thus is unlikely to do anything foolish."

"And if something should happen to her?"

Karl shrugged. "Life happens."

Evnan nodded, accepting that fate can sometimes be cruel. "What are your plans, m'Lord, if I may ask?"

"The first thing we need to do is stop this civil war. I need a united Odryssa if I am to unite the land."

"That will be difficult, m'Lord. Kerr has sworn that nothing but Fraster's death will stop his quest for the throne."

"Then we'll just have to change his mind. How large is his army?"

"About the same as Fraster's, probably a little over 3000," Evnan said. "Like Fraster, Kerr's forces are divided among his domains, much like me here. That is one reason why we have not had a protracted battle to end it all. Fraster and Kerr are careful not to consolidate too many forces in one place for fear of the other sending his forces to the rear and attacking, especially his capital."

"If you were in charge, where would you attack?"

"I'd send a force to threaten Contyn while consolidating the remaining forces to conduct a full-scale attack throughout Kerr's realm."

"Wouldn't that leave your own realm undefended?"

"For a time, m'Lord. What I would do is to pull back all the people and food as far away as possible so that Kerr's army could not resupply itself."

"That would take time," Karl observed.

"Time is what we have plenty of, m'Lord," Evnan commented. "Neither army commits, yet there are enough skirmishes to place the entire kingdom off balance. It is affecting everything from farmers to guilds. No one is safe anymore as there is an increase in highwaymen as they are quite content to rob without repercussion as the soldiers required for the safety of the towns and citizens are obligated to the war."

"Why are you not in Talbet?"

"Because I am in the half of Kerr's realm ruled by Neacul, his cousin, who commands half of Kerr's army. As Neacul has a larger army, I was forced to retreat. Like I said, I conduct small operations to keep Neacul off-balance, but not enough to wage a full-scale battle. I don't have the manpower."

"Then the first thing we must do is defeat Neacul," Karl mused.

"How, m'Lord?"   Evnan looked askance at the suggestion.

"How large is Neacul's army?"

"Probably close to 1500."

"But you said they are not consolidated in one spot."

"Yes, m'Lord."

"How long would it take to consolidate them?"

"They're spread out and he would have to leave some to defend the various castles," Evnan said, wondering what Karl had in mind. "Thus, it would take a while, depending on the urgency."

"Where is Neacul's capital?"

"In Abynee, about three days journey, unimpeded, from Talbet."

"How long would it take you to gather your army?"

"Not long at all."

"Then do it," Karl commanded. "Here is what I have in mind. My team and I will harass Abynee on the way to Contyn, forcing Neacul to withdraw forces to defend it, while you attack and secure Talbet."

"That's suicidal, m'Lord. While it might put Neacul off balance, Kerr has far more soldiers in Contyn that he doesn't need to withdraw other resources."

Giving him a patronizing smile, Karl said, "You forget who he's dealing with. See that beautiful woman with the long raven hair, the one who brought me my meal?"

"Yes."

"She's a powerful sorceress."

Evnan nearly choked on his meal. "My God. I thought she might be but did not wish to give in to my hopes. She will be a huge asset, especially when it comes to combatting Kerr's sorceress."

Karl cocked his head and then an eyebrow. "You didn't mention that Kerr has a sorceress."

"My apologies, m'Lord," he shrugged. "I assumed that you would know."

"Does Fraster have a sorceress?"

"Yes, m'Lord."

Karl pondered a moment then said, "They sort of cancel each other out, don't they."

"Exactly, m'Lord. They are sisters of different fathers."

"Good Lord, not again." Karl rolled his eyes and groaned.

"M'Lord?" Evnan frowned.

"Long story," Karl replied brushing him off. "I take it these sisters have no love lost between them."

"None at all."

"What level are they?"

"Level?"

"Yes," Karl frowned, "what level? Like you. You're a level 5 aristocrat. What level are they?"

"Ah, yes," he bobbed his head, "I understand. They are both level 16 sorceresses."

Karl raised an eyebrow. "They're not succubi, are they?"

"Not that I know of," Evnan responded, curious at the question.

"Does Neacul have a sorceress?"

"No," Evnan replied with a shake of his head. "There are only two sorceresses in the kingdom at the moment. However, there are rumors that druids abound yet remain out of sight until the time is ripe."

Evnan shifted his eyes around the campsite then back to Karl. "There is one more thing, m'Lord that you should know. Neacul has a beast he keeps contained in his castle. I have seen it with my own eyes. It has human form almost your size, but with the head of a jackal. It is cruel and powerful… and gives unyielding obedience to Neacul."

"Do Fraster and Kerr have their own beasts?"

Evnan averted his eyes then heaved a sigh. "Sadly, m'Lord, Fraster does. His too is… or rather was a human man, a warrior of some renown before he died in battle. Fraster's sorceress resurrected him."

"Why doesn't Kerr have a beast?"

Evnan shrugged. "I think he believes his sorceress can provide him with what he needs when he needs it without having to deal with a problematic beast."

"Anything else?" Karl asked, wondering what he had wandered into.

"Not that comes to mind."

"Then the mission still stands. My company and I will head out to Abynee tomorrow morning. Alert Fraster to what you are doing."

"Is that wise, m'Lord?" He gently touched Karl on the arm.

"Why not?"

"Fraster wants to be king, just like Kerr. If he discovers the true king is here, what's to stop him from joining forces with Kerr to defeat you?"

Karl furrowed his brow in thought, slowly nodding. "What an excellent idea."

"M'Lord?" Evnan replied, eyes widening.

"If you had to choose between Fraster and me, who would it be?"

"You of course," he replied, the answer obvious.

"Why?"

"Because you are the true king, m'Lord."

"How do you know?"

"The sword," he answered solemnly. "All who know the prophecy know that only one person can wield the sword. I would be a fool to deny it."

"How many others do you think would feel the same way?"

Epiphany hit Evnan and he answered, "Anyone who knows the prophecy, which is just about everyone these days as citizens are tired of this civil war and the hope of a true king and lasting peace swirls in everyone's heart... though they are careful not to express it too loudly especially in the presence of Fraster and Kerr."

"Regardless of House?"

"Yes, m'Lord, regardless of York or Lancaster. The ones who would fight you are Fraster and Kerr... and their loyalists, those most affected by their side losing their place."

"But why should anyone lose their place? We need to convince those integral to Fraster's and Kerr's success that their own success lies elsewhere.... specifically with me."

"Easier said than done, m'Lord... but not impossible."

"The first thing to do is spread the word. Send your friends and spies out to tell all that the prophesied king has arrived and that the war will end soon." Karl motioned for Caryn to come over.

"But that might not necessarily be true," Evnan pointed out.

"We know that," Karl winked, "but what better way to spread the news than to promise relief from pain and anxiety?"

"Yes?" Caryn said, as she squatted down next to them.

"We've come up with a plan," Karl announced. "I want you to hear it to tell me what you think."

"OK," she replied, flattered that Karl selected her instead of Raquel or Annabeth or one of the others.

Karl explained his concept while Caryn patiently listened, occasionally interjecting a question. "Well?" he said when finished.

"The only proverbial fly in the ointment is dealing with Fraster and Kerr and their devoted followers, which include, by the way two monsters and two sorceresses. Still, it's a lot better than trying to use guerilla tactics and whittle them down. At least this way you get a larger loyal following from the get-go."

"They'll be loyal as long as we win and keep winning," Karl observed. "You know how fickle support can be."

"We need time to let word spread," Evnan added. "We start in Talbet and send word with merchants and all other travelers."

"We can also start by clearing the roads of highwaymen," Karl stated, "again, beginning in Talbet. While word spreads, we start clearing the vermin out of the realm."

The camp was up early the next morning, just as dawn was breaking. Elena had sent several of Evnan's soldiers to find eggs so that by the time the camp was almost packed to move, the bouquet of scrambled eggs, roasted venison, and coffee filled the air. Even Uafas settled in for a quick breakfast. Though accepting his presence, Evnan's soldiers kept a respectful distance, all except one, a younger warrior still in his teens, fascinated by the huge beast. Asking permission, he sat next to Uafas, chatting happily. His joy was made complete when Uafas allowed him to scratch the giant wolf's chin.

I like him, he said to Karl. *A bit chatty happy, but a kind soul nevertheless.*

Remember our mission from here on out. Your job is to terrify and impress. No eating people unless I say so.

Spoil sport.

Karl snickered. *You're in luck though. We're on a search and destroy mission of highwaymen. You'll be our roaming security. Alert us so we can deal with them. You can have your pick when we're through.*

Works for me.

"How good are your scouts?" Karl asked Evnan.

"I've two very good ones. The others are still learning."

"I've two topnotch scouts of unequalled talent, both Rangers," Karl said. "You won't find any better."

"I defer to you, m'Lord," he said with a respectful dip of his head.

Moving to the front of the assembled groups, Karl spoke in a commanding voice. "Do you know who I am?"

There was a moment of silence before the young man who took a shine to Uafas said in a loud voice, "You are the king, the promised one."

"Do you believe that?"

"Yes, m'Lord," the young man quickly replied.

"What about the rest of you? Do you believe it? Will you submit to me being your king?"

Sakura leaned in to Annabeth and whispered, "I didn't realize this was up for discussion."

Raquel heard her and shot her a stern stare. "He's making them commit," she whispered in explanation. "Once you verbally agree to something, it's harder to go back on your word."

"Whatever," Sakura shrugged, ready to get going.

This time more voices spoke their fealty until the rest of Evnan's men and women spoke their claim.

"It is time to unify the kingdom. This is our beginning. You all here are the foundation of our future. Our mission today is to begin unification by cleaning out the rabble who infect our land, the highwaymen and other bandits. We head back towards Talbet, cleaning up along the way. My two

Rangers will act as point. Lord Evnan will select scouts for flank security. Uafas, my friend wolf, will act as roving security. There is a chance he will discover our prey before we do. If so, we prepare to surprise them and destroy them. Once we get to Talbet, we take a short rest to gather more forces. But every one of you must be ready to move on a moment's notice. Questions?"

There was a brief silence until a voice asked, "Where do we march from Talbet?"

"That depends," Karl answered, "on what forces we gather. But know this, the final goal is Avnoch." Without waiting for further questions, Karl turned to Evnan. "Ready?"

"Yes, m'Lord."

"Let's move out."

A little more than an hour later, Uafas discovered an abandoned woodcutter's mill not far from the road leading to Talbot. The once flowing river that had turned the saw wheel had turned to a trickle, ankle deep and an easy hop across due to the fickleness of ancient rivers that sometimes change their course. What remained of the mill was still sound and the present occupants had shored up the structure and rethatched the roof. The center roof beam protruded about a meter beyond the roof line, an old pulley still attached. Whoever lived there had even planted a small vegetable garden.

Karl pulled up his personal screen and was rewarded with a prompt.

You have discovered a highwayman hideout.

Expecting something about quest or reward or some other perk, he scowled at the paucity of information.

"That's it?" he grumbled, irritably flicking the screen away. "Why do I bother?"

His attention returned to the mill. So confident in the remoteness of their safe house, the bandits neglected to post security.

Karl's forces surrounded the mill and settled down to wait and watch. As Karl had anticipated, the bandits had grown lax in both security and daily activities, which meant sleeping late. Thankfully their waiting was not long as the door opened and a man emerged, yawned and stretched and ambled towards the river to relieve himself. He was in the process of untying his trousers when Karl gave the signal and Raquel's arrow penetrated his chest, causing him to crash backwards, his hands still on the trouser cord. He writhed a moment or two then lay still.

The door opened again, and two men stepped out, one rubbing his eyes in the sunlight.

"I'm hungry," the other one said. He was a lean man in his early 30s. "Think I'll make m'own breakfast."

"What're ya gonna fix?" the first one asked. He was younger, probably in his late teens.

"Same as usual," the older man grunted, "eggs and sausage."

"If I make the coffee," the younger man said, "you fix me a mess of eggs and sausage?"

"Sure," the older man nodded with a smile. "You make the best coffee anyway. Gotta take a piss first or I'm gonna explode."

He led the way around the mill but before they were midway past the building, two arrows flew from behind and rammed through their backs, the tip of one arrow protruding through the older man's chest. They both fell forward, contorting in the dirt until the older one lay motionless, followed a bit later by the younger one.

An upstairs shutter pushed open and an older man with grizzled beard poked his head out, inhaling the morning air with a smug satisfaction. He looked down and burst a shout of warning. Before he had a chance to poke his head back in, several arrows found their mark and he fell backwards into the mill.

"You in the mill," Karl called out. "You are surrounded. We can do this one of two ways. We can burn the mill down and you inside it, or you can give yourselves up. You've got thirty seconds to decide before we torch the place."

Fifteen seconds passed when the front door thrust open and six men and two women cautiously paraded out, their hands high in the air.

"Tie them up," Karl commanded. "Evnan, send a team in to clear out the inside of the mill."

Quick to respond, Evnan sent five experienced warriors to check the mill while the bandits outside had their hands bound behind them.

Karl strode over to a tall man who stared at the two bodies of his compatriots, an arrow shaft rising out of their backs. "Who's in charge?"

The man turned his focus to Karl. "He's dead." He ticked his head back towards the mill. "He's the one you shot through the window."

Two warriors of the clearing team pushed through the door, clutching a woman by her arms, and propelling her forward to stand in front of Karl.

"We found her hiding behind the grain sacks," one warrior, a well-built man in his late twenties said.

Karl saw a subtle exchange between the woman and the prisoners.

"I was kidnapped," the woman wailed, clasping her hands and falling to her knees. "I'm not with them."

Karl stared down at her. She was an attractive woman, slender, with high cheekbones and an oval face with hazel eyes. Her hair was strawberry blond, thick and shoulder length. Under different circumstances, she could have been mistaken for an aristocrat's younger wife. She wore a man's leggings, boots that came up to mid-calf, and a blouse with puffed sleeves

A warrior stood in the doorway and beckoned Karl. "M'Lord."

"Tie her up," Karl commanded as he strode over to investigate.

"But I was kidnapped," she cried out. "I'm innocent."

Ignoring her, Karl stepped inside. He was surprised as the interior had been remodeled into a large dining/living room with separate rooms along the side for storage. A spiral stairwell led to the second-floor bedrooms. It was obvious that a skilled carpenter accomplished the change.

"This way, m'Lord," the warrior said, leading the way to a storage room. Above them, the other two warriors continued their search.

The warrior stopped at a door at the back of the room and opened it. Inside were shelves lined with silver and gold goblets, plates and serving ware. Three large, locked chests were positioned against the walls.

"Fetch the one called Noble," Karl said, holding his hand waist high, indicating a short individual, "and the sorceress."

"Yes, m'Lord."

When the warrior disappeared, Karl surveyed the room thinking that these bandits and Noble had a lot in common. How could he justify punishing them while turning a blind eye to Noble's activities? Was it that Noble only robbed from the rich while these folks preyed on anyone who happened by?

When Noble and Annabeth stepped into the room, Karl was still ruminating as he examined a golden goblet studded with rubies.

"Looks like they've been busy," Noble observed, a gleam in his eyes.

"I need you to open these locks." Karl pointed to the chests.

Noble briefly studied the locks. "No problem. They're simple key activated locks."

Pulling out his set of locksmith tools, Noble popped all three locks in less than fifteen seconds, much to the amazement of the watching warrior.

Karl and Annabeth yanked open the lids revealing chests full of coins, precious stones, and jewelry.

"Wonder how long they've been at this," Annabeth commented.

"From the looks of all this, either quite a while or someone's been helping them," Karl replied. "And my guess is that someone's been helping them." Turning to Annabeth, he said, "Can you lock these again?"

"Of course," she smiled, casting a Lock-It spell. Immediately the three locks clicked shut.

"Put something else on them so that no one else can open them."

"As you wish, my handsome Lord," she replied with a twinkle in her eyes.

Smirking, Karl shook his head and turned to the warrior. "Leave everything in this room for now. Secure it as best you can."

"Yes, m'Lord."

The other two warriors descended the stairs and approached.

"There's nothing up there except sleeping quarters," one guard said. "Although, given enough time, my guess is that there are probably hiding spots in each one."

"No doubt you are right," Karl acknowledged, "but we don't have time for that now. Come with me."

Back outside, Karl headed over to where the captives were seated in a circle.

"You," he said to the attractive woman claiming to be a kidnap victim. "How long have you been here?"

"I've been here more than a month," she answered, her voice pleading her innocence as she stood.

"Have they mistreated you?"

"Horribly at first, but then they treated me with simple contempt." She sneered at those seated on the ground.

"Were you bound or chained?"

"At first I was then I was allowed to move but always with a rope around my ankle."

"But you were able to hear all the conversations that went on in the mill," Karl said.

"Oh yes," she nodded. "I listened to them all."

"Excellent. Who else was involved with your raids?"

"Pardon?"

"I asked," Karl calmly said, "who else was involved in the raiding?"

"I don't know," she waffled.

"Don't know? Surely you must have heard a name or two," Karl said with a frown then abruptly turned to Evnan.

"I think we need to administer some justice. Make a noose. Wonder if that old pulley still works?"

His words had the desired effect as the outlaws cast terrified glances up at the pulley.

"We'll start with you." Karl peered intently at the tall man who swallowed hard as two warriors jerked him to standing. "You have two options. First option is that you truthfully answer my questions after which we take you to the nearest city and hand you over to the constabulary. The other option, which is a lot more gruesome I might add, is that we hang you here and now." He shifted his stern gaze to the others. "The same offer applies to all of you. Answer my questions truthfully or hang."

Turning back to the tall man, Karl asked, "Who is your leader?"

The man hesitated, licking his suddenly dry lips as he lifted his head to see a young nimble warrior out on the thick ridge-board, threading a thick rope through the pulley.

"I will only ask this once more," Karl threatened, "then you'll be the first to test the effectiveness of the pulley. Who is your leader?"

"Tell 'em Bogle, or I will," a man sitting on the ground cried out.

When the tall man hesitated again, Karl jerked his thumb to the gallows.

"She is," the tall man spouted, jerking his head at the woman standing next to Karl.

"Too late," Karl coldly replied.

"But I'm telling the truth," he exclaimed, struggling as he was dragged to the gallows and the noose slipped over his head and tightened.

Turning his back to the prisoners, Karl folded his arms and commanded, "Hang him."

It took three warriors heaving with all their might to yank the kicking man off his feet. They secured the rope to an outside fence post then turned to watch with morbid fascination as the man twisted and bucked then slowed to a stop, his body slowly spinning in the wind, his eyes protruding, and his tongue thrust out.

Turning around, Karl pointed at the man who had offered to tell. He was a middle-aged man with a bent nose. The two warriors jerked him to his feet and pushed him over to stand before Karl.

"Who is your leader?" Karl asked.

"She is," the man answered without hesitation.

"He's a liar," she clamored.

"Shush," Karl impatiently ordered. "Can't you see the man's trying to tell me something?" Turning back to the man, he asked, "What's her name?"

"Her name's Leri."

Karl looked at the woman. "Is your name Leri? Now remember my rules about telling me the truth."

The woman scowled then admitted, "Yes."

"Ah," Karl smiled. "Now we're getting somewhere." He directed his attention back to the man and his seated compatriots. "Do you all know this woman?"

The response was brisk nods mixed with the overt "Yes."

"Is she your leader?"

The response was the same.

Karl turned to Leri. "I'm so disappointed in you. You lied to me. You know what happens when you lie to me."

By now, the man on the gallows had been lowered, the noose removed from around his neck, and the body dragged off to the side.

"You can't do this," Leri loudly objected. "You have no right to barge in here and act like you're judge and jury."

Karl stared at her a moment then burst a laugh. "A moment ago, you said you were innocent and merely a victim of these people. Now you want a lawyer? Sort of implies your guilt. I might reconsider your fate if you tell me who is supplying you with all your loot."

Leri narrowed a gaze of cold hatred at him then repeated, "I was kidnapped by these vile people. I –"

"You hear that?" Karl interrupted, his attention on the bandits. "Not only is she willing to sacrifice you to save her own skin, she insults you in the process." He shifted his focus to the man standing before him. "You look like a smart man. Who's supplying you with the extra loot?"

The man hesitated only a moment before blurting, "Lord Kerr."

"He's lying," Leri accused.

"You be quiet, or I'll have you gagged," Karl threatened then shifted his eyes to the gallows, "permanently." Glancing back at the man, he asked, "Why?"

The man shrugged. "Don't know."

"I do," a woman captive volunteered. She was young with the clear complexion and smooth pale skin of someone who had never done a day of hard work in her life, someone who had grown up in a life of privilege, the kind of child who rebelled against her parents to join some cause only to become disillusioned. Of course, who knew if any of that was true, at least it sounded good.

"Go on," Karl urged.

"Shut up Ina. You can't believe her," Leri again interrupted. "She's only trying to save herself."

"You mean like you?" Karl intoned then nodded for the young woman to continue.

"Lord Kerr lowered taxes to gain the support of the people," she explained. "But he still needs money to pay for his army, so he has us rob from the rich and uses the money to pay the army. We get a cut and everyone's happy… well, except the rich. We prefer coin because it's easier to use and you can't trace where it came from. All the other stuff, the jewelry and things like that, we ransom back to the owners at a low enough cost to make it worth their while."

"Excellent report," Karl said with a smile then turned to the three men at the gallows rope. "Hang that one." He pointed to Leri.

"You're making a big mistake," Leri yelled as the men grabbed and dragged her to the rope. "I'm innocent."

The rope was around Leri's neck when Karl held up his hand to stop them. He turned to the other bandits. "You do realize that if you are even remotely lying to me a worse fate awaits you than hanging." *Uafas.*

Yes.

How about a loud piercing howl and growl?

A loud angry growl split the air, causing the bandits to huddle closer together.

Now I need you to make an impressive entrance.

The growling grew louder and burst when Uafas leaped into the clearing causing even those who knew he was there to jitter backwards.

"This is Uafas, my friend," Karl said. "He has a penchant for warm meat. He's tried orc, but they don't taste all that good. His preference is human, especially young women." He paused to give Ina a hard knowing stare. "So be wise in your answers to me."

Uafas trotted up to glare malevolently at the cowering Ina. He moved close enough to sniff her then slowly lowered his head to lock his eyes on hers.

How am I doing?

Wonderful. Karl suppressed a smirk.

"It's the truth," Ina wailed. "I swear on all the gods in the entire universe. Please don't let him eat me."

Karl turned to the warriors surrounding Leri. "Continue."

"Wait," Leri begged. "I'll tell you everything."

"Too late," Karl said with an indifferent shrug.

"But I know who else is involved," she clamored.

Karl waited until they moved to yank on the rope. "Hold on a moment."

The warriors paused, patiently waiting for Karl's command.

"Who else is involved?" Karl asked.

"Take the rope off my neck?" Leri bartered.

"Let's hear what you have to say first," Karl replied. "If I like what I hear, then I'll consider it. If not…" He shrugged and splayed his hands. "So make it good. You got ten seconds to convince me your life is worth saving."

"Ten… Nine… Eight," Raquel counted out loud.

"Kerr and Fraster are in this together," Leri said in a rush.

"What?" Evnan startled. "Impossible."

"Four… three… two…"

"It's true," Leri exclaimed.

"One... zero."

"It's true, it's true," Leri pleaded.

Karl twisted his head to narrow his gaze at Ina. "Is it true?"

"I don't know, m'Lord," she answered. "We weren't privy to all that. We always stayed here whenever she went to meet Lord Kerr."

Karl turned back to the warriors surrounding Leri. "Keep the noose on her while I talk with Lord Evnan." Stepping closer to Evnan, he asked, "Well?"

"My first instinct is that the charge is impossible," Evnan replied, "especially my own brother-in-law. But then, my sister wasn't known for her intellectual strengths, or her attention to the affairs of the kingdom. She wanted someone to feed her extravagant lifestyle. Fraster could do that, and he was a prince as well. But when I consider how long this war has been going on between Fraster and Kerr and suddenly the accusation gains credence. I always thought that neither made gains because of the parity of their forces. But now...?" He shook his head. "Sadly, it makes sense, though I don't want to believe it."

"How well do you know Fraster?"

"Well enough to have second thoughts as to the woman's accusation," Evnan replied, peering past Karl's shoulder to stare at Leri with the noose around her neck. "We may need her, m'Lord," he quietly said, "if we are to prove the truth."

"I was thinking the same thing," Karl acknowledged then tilted his head as an idea emerged. He glanced over his shoulder at his team, focusing on the human ranger. "Raquel."

Raquel strode over to stand next to Karl and Evnan.

"I need the brains of a marketing expert," Karl said with a smile. "How can we exploit this to our advantage?"

"What do you want to accomplish?" she asked. "In other words, define the mission."

"We need to convince everyone that Kerr and Fraster are in this together, undermine their positions and authority. Connect them with the highwaymen and the discord in the kingdom."

Raquel nodded. "Believe it or not," she replied with a grin, "I was thinking the same thing. Regardless of environment, rumors spread amazingly fast, even back in the world of technology and instant information. In this present environment, we need to unleash the rumor monster. That means sending as many individuals as possible at once to as many locations as we can – with the same story. Then we let rumor control take over."

"What story?" Evnan asked, impressed with her approach.

"First," Raquel answered, holding up a finger, "we connect Fraster and Kerr to the robberies. Second, we connect Fraster and Kerr together, that they are one team acting to make themselves rich at the expense of the kingdom. Third, we announce the true king is here, the one who wields Orc's Bane, the fulfilment of prophecy, the one who will save the kingdom. Fourth, if anyone doubts, the king has captured one of the bandit leaders who will testify the truth."

"I like the idea," Evnan said, "but how do we accomplish it? All my warriors come from my domain."

Karl turned his head to give the bandits a curious glance. "Where are you all from?"

"Different places, m'Lord," Ina answered. "I'm from outside Abynee, while Bogle here is from near Kinlich. Don't think none of us is from the same town."

Karl turned back to Evnan, a sly smile gracing his face.

"You would use them, m'Lord?" Evnan sputtered.

"Why not? They know their game is up. What better way to use them than to employ them in defeating their bosses. Raquel?"

"Can you trust them?" she wondered.

"We'll see," he grinned. Turning to the warriors surrounding Leri, he commanded, "Blindfold her then take the others inside the mill."

"I'm telling the truth," she implored, "I swear."

While a warrior ripped a length of fabric from a dead man's shirt and wrapped it around Leri's eyes, the others were marched inside the mill and seated on the floor. Karl motioned for Caryn to come along as he led Raquel and Evnan into the mill. "Wonder why she gets to go," Sakura observed.

"Good question," Annabeth said, not a little put out that Caryn seemed to be replacing her in Karl's inner circle. "One I'm sure we'll learn when they emerge." She looked over to see that the young warrior enamored with Uafas had managed to work his way close to the wolf and was tenderly petting him and scratching his cheek.

Inside the mill, Karl towered over the prisoners, his arms folded. "Part of me wants to simply hang you and be done with it, a fitting punishment for your crimes." He noted with satisfaction the fear mixed with desperate hope on their faces. "And then another part of me says you might still have a place in our kingdom. I've discussed your future with Lord Evnan, and we've decided your fate."

Evnan noted the 'we' of Karl's statement and was surprised he would elevate him with that much authority.

"Here is the situation," Karl explained. "I am going to release each of you."

"You're letting us go?" Ina said, eyes wide at the reprieve.

"With conditions," Karl stated. "First, if any of you ever return to robbing our citizens again, trust me, I will find you and you won't hang. I will feed you to my wolf. Understand?"

There was a furious nodding of heads as they realized they were not going to be hanged.

"Secondly, I expect each of you to become productive citizens. How long have you been in the robbing business?"

"'bout a year and a half, m'Lord," Bogle answered.

"I assume you all have accumulated a nice little nest egg during this time," Karl said.

"Nest egg?" Bogle frowned.

"Savings,' Karl explained.

"Actually, not much, m'Lord," Ina joined in. "Leri divided the profits with us, but we all had to contribute for food and other things."

"What other things?"

307

"She called 'em future operations," Bogle said with a scowl. "None of us understood it, but she kept part of our money. Don't none of us know how much."

"But you all have some money," Evnan interrupted.

"Yes, m'Lord," Bogle replied, "but probably only enough to live on for a couple o' months."

"We complained," Ina added, "but our share never got too much. It all went to Kerr."

"And Leri, if you ask me," the other woman glumly spoke. "Never did trust her."

"Leri is not your problem anymore," Karl stated. "She will be dealt with. In exchange for your freedom and joining society as productive members, here is what I will do. I will give each of you fifty gold pieces."

"Fifty," Bogle blurted, stunned.

"There is one other thing," Karl smiled. "Ranger Raquel will explain."

Raquel stepped forward and detailed what was expected of them in spreading the rumor. While she explained, Evnan leaned in towards Karl.

"Where do we get 350 pieces of gold, m'Lord?"

Karl answered with a sly grin. "We... um 'borrow' it from the pile in the room back there." He ticked his head towards the room with the stolen loot.

Evnan was about to object that the money and everything in the room belonged to someone else, when he realized there was no possibility of ever determining whose money it was. Chuckling at the simplicity, he pondered what Karl was going to do with it all.

Once satisfied they understood their mission, Raquel stepped back and gave Karl a nod that said she was finished.

"Before you leave, you will give your name and destination to one of the warriors," Karl said. "After that, I except to hear great things about you."

"Thank you, m'Lord," Ina said with heartfelt thanks. Her future looked far better than it did with Leri.

Evnan had the guards free the prisoners while Karl went to the door and popped his head out.

"Annabeth. I need you."

"Of course you do," she sweetly replied.

"In this instance," Karl said, returning the smile when she entered, "I need you to open the treasure boxes."

"How boring," she said with a wink.

It wasn't until the last bandit had been released and departed that the noose was removed from Leri's neck, and the blindfold untied.

As she blinked in the sunlight, Karl informed her, "Here is your fate. You will accompany us all the way to Avnoch where you will give testimony of Fraster and Kerr's duplicity. After that, your future depends on my mood. If I believe I can trust you, I will free you. If not... I will feed you to my wolf friend."

Chapter 13

The journey from the mill to Talbet turned out to be uneventful and they were a bit disappointed that they had not come upon any more highwaymen. Still, all along the way, in each village and town, they made sure the tale of Kerr and Fraster's deception and corruption was firmly implanted, the captured bandit leader adding her part in the affair. Then Karl was presented as the prophesied king. Doubters were encouraged to pick up his sword, which added to the narrative.

Karl was impressed with the reception Evnan received at each place. "I thought you said you were on the run from Kerr?"

"I was," Evnan replied, likewise surprised that they had not encountered any resistance from Kerr's forces.

Evnan was even more surprised when they reached Talbet to discover a bored messenger from Kerr waiting for him to return.

"How long have you been here?" Evnan asked.

"A week, m'Lord," the messenger replied, relieved that he could finally deliver his message and be on his way. For all the attention, food, and ale that Evnan's servants provided, he was still forced to sit and wait... and wait.

"What's the message?"

"M'Lord Kerr wishes to hold a parley with you, at your earliest convenience."

"About what?"

"I'm not privy to that, m'Lord," he shrugged. "Will you convey your answer now, m'Lord?"

"Yes, yes," Evnan brusquely answered. "Tell him, I've just returned to Talbet and I need a day or two to check on things. I'll leave for Contyn day after tomorrow."

"Very good, m'Lord." The messenger bowed.

311

After he had departed, Evnan turned to Karl. "Odd. Wonder why now?"

"Perhaps he wants to entice you into the activities of a certain lady thief," Annabeth suggested, shifting a glance at the bound Leri.

"Regardless," Raquel interrupted, "now would not be a good time to go see him."

"Why?" Karl and Evnan asked in unison.

"First, we need more time for word to spread of Fraser and Kerr's crimes, as well as the arrival of the king. Secondly, if word of Karl's presence has already reached Contyn, you would be walking into a trap."

"Makes sense to me," Karl nodded.

"What do you wish me to do?" Evnan asked.

Karl turned to Raquel who answered, "Put him off for a week. That will give more time for the story to spread. Likewise, once Kerr finds out that Karl is here, my guess is that he's not going to like it and will move against you."

"He has a ten to one advantage in soldiers," Evnan fretted.

"Maybe not," Raquel countered. "Once the news spreads, who knows who will stay with him?"

"And who knows how many will join us?" Annabeth added.

Though still not liking the odds, Evnan knew his fate was linked to Karl. "I have a guest house on the other side of the gardens that will accommodate you and your team, m'Lord."

Annabeth looked at Raquel. "I've lost track of whose turn it is."

"Me too," Raquel replied. "But in all fairness, you can have him tonight."

"That was sweet," Annabeth said, squeezing Raquel's hand, "but I think it's your turn."

Evnan frowned at Karl who rolled his eyes and shook his head.

"How about we just let the Viking have a night to himself," Karl ventured.

"Now, now," Annabeth replied, sweetly patting his cheek, "let's not get carried away. If we can't decide, you just might have to have both of us."

"I can help," Noble exclaimed, raising his hand.

Ignoring him, Annabeth said to Karl, "You just carry on your conversation while my colleague and I work out the details." Taking Raquel's hand, she led her away in a leisurely stroll towards the doors leading to the gardens.

Seeing Evnan's curious look, Karl lifted a hand and shook his head once again. "I'd say it's complicated, but it's not. How about you show us where we can stay."

Two days later, Karl emerged onto the portico of the main house and saw Annabeth and Raquel standing at the far end of the garden by the guest house and Elena in the middle about thirty meters away, standing on the path between the guest housed and the main house.

Annabeth and Raquel were talking quietly when Elena announced, "Yes, I can feel it." Annabeth flipped a hand like she was pushing her away causing Elena to take a large step backwards.

Annabeth and Raquel resumed their conversation until Elena again said, "Yes, I can feel it," followed by another step backwards. This continued until Elena was almost at the steps leading up to the portico of the Main house.

"What are you doing?" Karl asked with a curious smile.

"Annabeth's practicing casting a sleeping spell without looking," she explained, "and she's seeing how far she can cast it."

"And you're the guinea pig?"

"Yes," she replied with a sheepish smile.

"Don't let me interrupt," he chuckled. "Have you seen Caryn?"

"I think she's in the guest house."

"Thanks," he replied, descending the steps. When he approached Annabeth, he said, "There's a reason you're doing this?"

"Yes," she answered. "I realized that every time I cast a spell upon another sorceress, I give myself away because I'm

313

smiling at them. You saw what happened with Eleris when we were in Glenloch. I almost had her, but when she saw me, she counteracted the spell. I figure that if I can cast a spell without them knowing it, I'll have a greater chance of success, just like Kamdyn."

Karl remembered the sorceress' succubus powers and frowned.

"Don't worry," Annabeth said, noting the look. "I'm not a succubus." She waited until he passed by and smirked, "Yet."

When Karl disappeared inside the guest house, Raquel glanced at her friend. "Can you do that?"

"Become a succubus? I don't know," she shrugged. "I think you have to have that as a characteristic from the start. Wish I would've known. I could've had lots of fun."

"You've had lots of fun already," Raquel observed with an impish smile. She turned when, out the corner of her eye, she saw Darren, Evnan's steward, erupt past Elena.

"Where is the king?" Darren burst.

"He's inside." Raquel hooked a thumb towards the door. "What's the problem?"

"Neacul is on his way here with his army," he burbled, pushing through the door.

Five seconds later, Karl bustled through the door, Caryn and the others on his heels. "War council in Evnan's office. Now."

When they arrived, Evnan was bent over a map, the scout who brought the news at his side. They looked up when Karl and company entered.

"He's a day's march away," Evnan said, his face grim.

"How many does he have with him?" Karl asked the scout.

"Don't know, m'Lord," the scout replied. He was a wiry young man with bright eyes. "As soon as I saw the lead scouts, I rushed here to tell Lord Evnan. But they've stopped for the –"

"How many do we have here with you?" Karl interrupted.

"I haven't had enough time to consolidate my forces," Evnan said by way of justification.

"I know that," Karl cut him off. "How many?"

"150 perhaps."

Karl looked over his shoulder at Raquel. "Apparently word has spread far enough that Kerr knows I'm here. That was fast. How'd he get word to Neacul so quickly?"

"Bird messenger," Evnan answered. "He knows he can't respond quickly enough, especially with Fraster on his border. Neacul is close enough to handle the problem."

Karl turned back and leaned over to stare at the map. "If we were going to set up an ambush, where would the ideal spot be?"

Evnan studied it a moment then placed a finger on the map not far from where the lumber mill was where they had captured the bandits. "The forest here provides excellent terrain and concealment."

"Good. Get everyone ready, we move out in an hour."

"M'Lord?" Evnan sputtered. "But –"

"We don't have time to debate this," Karl snapped. "We take the battle to them." He turned to his team. "You all ready."

"We're always ready," Caryn answered for the group.

"Elena stays here," Karl said to Dieter.

"Of course, Boss. Wouldn't have it any other way."

Karl whirled back to Evnan. "C'mon man. Time's a wasting."

By the time they were ready to move out, Karl discovered that Evnan's 150 turned out to be 134, though another 27 townsmen and women armed with pitchforks and scythes also showed up.

Separating the soldiers from the townsfolks, Karl stood before the citizens group who had the distinct feeling they were going to be told to go home. They were happily surprised when Karl selected a leader then spent the next ten minutes outlining a plan for the defense of the town, which included barriers, perimeter security, early warning, choke points and more. The more Karl talked, the more overwhelmed they became with their responsibility.

"You all will need to enlist the help of the rest of the city," Karl advised. "Defenses need to be set up and finished no later than this evening. I'll establish contact once we're in position." Leaving them to take care of the city, Karl and company and the rest of Evnan's soldiers headed out the road towards Abynee.

It was late afternoon when they arrived at the ambush point. Once perimeter security was established, Karl called in his team and Evnan to discuss the ambush.

"You and your men," he said to Evnan, "will hold here." He swept his hand at the forest on both sides of the road. "Me and my team, along with Uafas, will head far enough up the road so that the tail end will pass us. When you hear Uafas howl, launch your attack."

"How will we know when they approach?" Evnan asked, scoping out the surroundings.

"You'll know," Karl said with a chuckle. "You'll hear them. If, not, I'll send Sakura to alert you."

While Evnan set up his forces, Karl collected his team and moved up the road a bit then stopped to discuss their plans.

"I want your input," he told them. "We don't know how many soldiers Neacul has, which means," he turned to Sakura, "I'll need you to scope out the enemy."

"Tonight?" she asked, her impassive face hinting a smile.

"Yes." He then addressed the others. "Part of me wants to let Sakura have a field day in their camp, but at the same time I don't want to alert them to our presence. Neacul has access to nearly 1500 soldiers to our paltry 100+. The only way we're going to offset that imbalance is to terrify them."

"I'm surprised more of the city folk aren't here with us," Noble said.

"You have to look at it from their perspective," Caryn answered. "They're merchants and farmers and bankers and such. They're not fighters."

"I wasn't either," Noble lamented, "until I started hanging out with you all. They gotta learn some time."

"Now's not the time," Karl said. "Back to the issue. Do we let Sakura work her magic or do we wait until they come here?"

"We do have Uafas," Noble reminded them.

"We wait until we find out how many there are," Caryn said. "I doubt Neacul would send his entire army down here, knowing that Evnan has so few forces. He's probably sent a token force, one large enough to send Evnan back to hiding."

"Point taken," Karl said. "Then what?"

"Once we see how large a force it is, we decide then. My guess is that he's probably sent 300 plus. If that's the case, then we unleash the assassin and let her wreak havoc."

"I like it," Sakura smiled.

"Other input?" Karl asked, looking at the others.

"Why not do it together," Annabeth asked, "like we did in Westhaven? We destroyed a good chunk of the bad guys before the battle even started."

"She has a point," Raquel said. "I think descending on their camp when they don't expect it will create more havoc than one assassin."

Karl looked up at the berserker. "Dieter?"

"I agree with them, especially with Uafas joining in the mayhem."

"Besides," Annabeth grinned, "I've got a bunch of spells I've been wanting to try out."

"Then it's settled," Karl said. "Once Sakura returns, we make our decision."

Sakura waited until dusk then disappeared. It was dark when she returned two hours later.

"I counted about 350," she said. They've got security set up, but it's not very alert. I easily got past them."

"Yeah, but you're an expert assassin," Noble sourly noted.

"How far away are they?" Karl asked.

"About an hour."

Karl mused for a moment then said, "I like the idea of surprise. Where's Evnan?"

"Here, m'Lord," Evnan answered, walking up.

"There's been a slight change of plans," Karl said. "You and your force will remain in place while I and my team will create enough of a disturbance to force them this way."

"They still outnumber us, m'Lord," Evnan pointed out.

"By the time they get here," Karl smiled, "it'll be more than a fair fight. My team and I will move out a little before midnight. Annabeth has some nice touches we can use." *You getting all this Uafas?*

Yes. Just to repeat, which way did you want to send those escaping?

Towards Evnan's soldiers. We don't want them going home to regroup. Better to destroy them here.

Sounds like fun.

"M'Lord," Evnan ventured. "Not that I doubt the power of Lady Annabeth, but they are still 350 strong, far more than a single sorceress can handle."

"You haven't seen our sorceress in action," Karl grinned. "I'll let her explain some of what she has in mind that will help us."

"I've got some spells I've been wanting to experiment with," she said, making no effort to hide her excitement. "First, I've got a Magic Booby Trap spell that I'll set up between them and you."

"Like what," Noble asked, "and how will we know not to fall into it?"

"Stay with me and we'll make sure you're safe. It's going to be a long narrow ditch with spikes in it. The spell lasts for only an hour, so we're gonna have to make sure we make a big impact to send them running. It'll be the last spell I conjure before we begin. Second, along with the booby trap, I've got a Trap Ivy spell that will snare any and all who come close to it. I'll place that on both sides of the booby trap.

"How long does that last?" Sakura asked.

"An hour to creep and hold and another hour before it releases."

"Why not use that at the beginning?" Sakura said. "Send the ivy in to trap them where they are."

"I thought about that, but the ivy doesn't discriminate. If you get too close, it'll take you too."

"Ah," Sakura nodded in understanding. "What else ya got?"

"I can cast a Night Vision spell on two people. I figure you didn't need it as you're an assassin and can pretty much move unnoticed regardless of day or night." She turned to Karl. "I thought I'd give night vision to the two Rangers. That way they can use their bow and arrows and hit their targets."

"That makes sense," Karl agreed.

"Got anything for me?" Noble asked.

"How about Spider's Touch?" Annabeth replied. "That way you can move around the trees and descend when and where you want."

"Not sure what I'd do with it, but I'll take it," Noble said with a shrug.

"I've got a couple more things I want to try," Annabeth continued. "One's called Fireworks Burst. It's like the 4th of July gone bad. Another is –"

"We get the point," Sakura wryly interrupted. "Anything that dazzles comes from you."

"Pretty much," Annabeth grinned.

Karl turned to Evnan. "You were saying?"

Evnan shook his head. "While I do understand magic, I don't understand much of what she has in mind, m'Lord, but I have a feeling it will be a sight to behold. I'll go alert my soldiers."

"Figure it'll be two to three hours before they get here. When they do, capture as many as you can. Otherwise, you know what to do with the rest."

"Yes, m'Lord."

As Evnan hurried away, Caryn turned to Annabeth. "That fireworks thingy you got. What does it do?"

"According to the instructions, it lights up the night so bright, it looks like the middle of the day."

"That's it?"

"Pretty much," she shrugged.

Caryn twisted her head to look at Karl. "When Uafas lets out his howl, wait a little for them to jump out of their tents then let Annabeth toss her fireworks."

"It'll kill their night vision," Karl said, completing her thought. "Perfect. Everyone understand? When Uafas lets out his growl, everyone shut and protect your eyes. Wait until the light fades and then go to work."

It was an hour before midnight when Uafas led them around the enemy encampment, leaving Sakura to protect Annabeth as she cast her Booby Trap and Trap Ivy spells, while Karl set up the rest of his team in pairs at points surrounding the bivouac. When the sorceress and assassin returned, he paired Noble with Annabeth and let Sakura, as usual, to operate alone. Once everyone was in position, Karl silently called out to Uafas.

Ready?

Ready and waiting.

It'll be a little bit, but I want another grand entrance like you did at the wood cutters mill.

With pleasure.

Karl and company settled down to let Annabeth's ivy begin its work.

Half an hour later, they heard a perimeter guard burst, "What the hell," followed by violent slashing as the guard hacked away at the ivy twisting itself around his leg.

Uafas.

Yes.

Let 'er rip.

A thundering angry howl ripped through the stillness of night. At the same time another perimeter guard cried out, "Somebody help me," as ivy twisted around his torso.

The camp erupted as soldiers grabbed their swords, bows and other weapons and scrambled out of their tents. Suddenly the night was lit up with a blinding brightness as though a mini nova had exploded on the encampment.

When the dazzling glare finally subsided, Karl and company went to work. As the enemy staggered about, Dieter cut a swath right through the center of the camp, his double-bladed ax swinging left and right. Raquel and Caryn, aided by their enhanced night vision, dropped soldier after soldier, their arrows penetrating chests and backs. Karl worked alongside Dieter, stopping in the middle to dispatch the commander, a tall strong warrior who blindly called out commands to terrified soldiers.

Karl almost felt guilty when he separated the man's head from his shoulders. Every now and then he came upon a soldier with his or her throat cut, the work of Sakura. Others were wrapped in flames, courtesy of Annabeth's fire bolts. Many more were dismembered, torn apart, the unfortunates who caught the attention of a giant wolf.

Halfway through the other side of the encampment, they heard the anguished and pained cries of fleeing soldiers falling into Annabeth's booby trap. Other plaintive pleas for help of those wrapped in ivy overlapped the dying in the trap.

Karl grabbed Dieter's arm to stop him from going too far. He ducked just as Dieter's ax swung around and narrowly missed his head.

"It's me, damn it," Karl burst then immediately recognized he shouldn't have grabbed the hulking man when the berserker rage was upon him. "Stop here. There's a trap ahead. Remember?"

Dieter glared at him a moment then understanding swept though and he nodded.

"C'mon. Let's work the rest of the camp." Karl led the way, discovering there weren't many left who offered any resistance. Those who remained now either kneeled with their hands in the air or cowered in abject fear, praying their fate would result in life.

Raquel and Caryn began collecting survivors and consolidating them in the center of the bivouac near the cooking fire pit. The others swept through the remaining tents, poking and prodding, finding the occasional occupant who decided that hiding was better than dying.

Sakura came up to Karl who stood with Dieter near the fire pit. "What's the plan?"

"Head out the road to Abynee and see if we missed anyone. Take Uafas with you." *You copy that Uafas?*

Yes. You know I can go faster than she can.

I know but let her go. In fact, let her ride. It'll go much faster.

You do realize having someone riding me not only slows me down, but it's embarrassing.

You have a better idea?

Like I said. Let me go alone. I can do what you need quicker than I can having to keep tabs on her.

She goes, Karl huffed. *You two work it out. I don't care how you do it, but I want it done.*

Uafas sighed. *As you wish.*

"He coming?" Sakura began when Uafas invaded her thoughts. "Thanks all the same, but I'd rather go at my own pace. Why don't you take the forest and I'll head up the road." With that she headed out of the camp towards the road that led to Abynee. Uafas paused a moment then bounded after her.

Nautical dawn was just beginning when Sakura and Uafas returned, Sakura riding atop the massive wolf.

I thought you said – Karl began

It was faster getting back this way. Besides, it's dark and no one can see us. Anyway, I like this one.

Whatever. Karl waited until Sakura slide off, surprising him when she gave Uafas an uncharacteristic hug. "Well?"

"We found three more," she said. "They won't be going home."

"Good job."

"What now?"

He saw that her adrenaline was still up. "I need you to head down to Evnan and tell him to bring his forces up here. Take Uafas." *You OK with that?*

No problem. She's an excellent conversationalist, quite a breadth of knowledge.

OK... Karl replied, cocking an eyebrow.

Yes, Uafas cheerily replied. *We were discussing Nietzsche's concept of the Ubermench when we found the first victim... um, I mean, the first soldier who escaped.*

Karl frowned over blinking eyes. Some gaming developer must have really gotten carried away. An NPC

322

who knew history and philosophy… and was a giant wolf. His head ached trying to make the connection as well as understand the reason. Instead, he shook his head.

Yeah, well… that's nice. See you when you get back.

Once Sakura and Uafas departed, Karl returned his attention to the others at the campsite, surprised at the number of survivors who now kneeled in orderly rows. "How many we got left?" he asked Caryn.

"Far more than I expected," she answered. "I counted a hundred and eighty-one."

Karl walked over to stand before them. They were a motley mix of men and women warriors, many of them young and obviously inexperienced, their faces advertising their fear.

"Do you know who I am?" he asked, his voice strong with authority.

Many shook their heads; others gave voice to their answer. "No."

"Do you know why you marched on to Talbet?"

Silence ensued before a woman's voice said, "We were told that there were rebels in Talbet and we going to defeat them."

Karl nodded as though musing. "Do any of you know the prophecy of Orc's Bane?"

"Yes," the same woman answered. "The one who wields the sword called Orc's Bane is the true king of Odryssa."

Karl withdrew his sword and held it high. "Then behold Orc's Bane." He tossed it amongst the captured soldiers. "Go ahead. Pick it up."

"If it is Orc's Bane, no one can pick it up other than the king," the woman replied.

"See for yourself," Karl replied, folding is arms.

The woman stood up. She was lithe and athletic with short, cropped hair. Approaching the sword, she reached down to pick it up then dropped to her knees. "My God," she blurted then turned to a warrior next to her. "You try it."

The man grabbed the handle, first with one hand then with two. "I can't budge it."

"You try it," the woman commanded another close by.

The results were the same. After four more tried, Karl calmly walked among them, stopped by the sword, then with one finger, hooked the handle and raised the sword, placing it back in the scabbard.

"My God," the woman gasped. "It's you. You're the king."

"I am." He repositioned himself at the front of the group. "How many soldiers did you have here," he said to the woman who appeared to have some authority.

"There were three companies, m'Lord," she answered. "All told, 330."

"Do you know how many I have with me, who defeated you?"

"No, m'Lord."

"There are seven of us, plus my wolf friend."

"By the gods," a man's voice blurted. "It took only seven to defeat 300 of us. It is magic."

"Yes," Karl admitted with a smile. "There was some magic. But know this, had we wished, we could have killed you all for the magic used was just a small bit of our sorceress' power."

"Lord Kerr has a sorceress," the man said. "Is yours stronger than his?"

Karl sensed the doubt in the man's tone. "Stand up." When the man hesitated, Karl commanded, "I will say it only once more. Stand up or we destroy all of you."

That was all it took for the others to drag the man to his feet.

"Look about you," Karl said. "While my sorceress is more powerful than Kerr's or Fraster's, this was not done only by sorcery. You failed to take the measure of the others, like him for instance." He ticked his head at Dieter. "Or them," he said turning to Raquel and Caryn.

He took measure of the man and recognized the type, a man who could not be trusted. Turning instead to the woman, he asked, "What is your name?"

"Annys, m'Lord."

"What is your place in the company?"

"I am a platoon sergeant, m'Lord."

Karl addressed the group. "Is there anyone else amongst you who outranks Sergeant Annys?"

Two raised their hands.

"Stand," Karl commanded.

Two men stood.

Karl stared at one man, a middle-aged man, fit, though beginning to go soft. "You."

"I too am a platoon sergeant, m'Lord, but I have been a sergeant longer and therefore outrank her."

"And you?" Karl said to the other man, a younger man, trim and muscular with a subtle arrogance in his demeanor.

"I am a lieutenant, a platoon commander."

"You are the senior person here," Karl said, firmness in his tone, "a leader who should have taken command, yet you let this subordinate speak for you instead."

"I hadn't had time yet to appraise the situation," he haughtily argued.

"How much time did you need?"

Before the man could answer, Annys spoke. "What's to become of us, m'Lord?"

"That depends," Karl replied, "on whether you are ready to unite this kingdom or continue in this present course of killing each other."

"Ask them about Kerr and Fraster," Raquel cut in.

Karl nodded then asked, "Have you heard about Lords Kerr and Fraster and their roles with the highwaymen?"

"I have, m'Lord," another woman's voice spoke as she stood up. She was a younger woman built much like Annys.

"What is your name?"

"Maelona, m'Lord."

"What have you heard, Maelona?"

"That the two Lords was in cahoots and jippin' the people outta their earnin's. But he was payin' the army folks pretty good. That's why I joined up."

"That's right," Karl acknowledged. "For the rest of you, listen up. Lords Kerr and Fraster only pretended to be at war. Have you ever wondered why neither side ever wins, and all the battles are mere skirmishes? That's because they operated their scheme together. Yes, they lowered your axes, but they also financed the highwaymen to rob you of the very taxes they gave back to you." He went on to explain what Leri had told him.

He paused, their rapt attention focused on him. "Is that what you really want?"

"But m'Lord," Annys replied. "All of that no longer matters. I mean, it does, but it doesn't because you are the rightful king." She pushed her way through the captives and kneeled before him. "I swear by all the gods above and below, I will follow only you as king."

Surprised and touched by the woman's obeisance, Karl reached a hand down and gently raised her to standing then looked past her to the others.

"What about the rest of you? Will you follow me and restore this kingdom?"

For many, there was no hesitation. Only a few vacillated and Caryn marked those, curling a finger at them and separating them from the others, Dieter acting as enforcer. When the last soldier professed fealty, there were four men standing next to Caryn, among them was the lieutenant.

Narrowing his gaze at Annys, Karl said, "Secure those four to a suitable tree. We'll come back for them."

"How dare you," the lieutenant sputtered. "I've done nothing wrong."

"Too late," Dieter growled.

"What's your name?" Karl demanded.

The lieutenant hesitated then replied, "Lomen."

"Well, Lomen, you seem to think you're someone special."

"He's Neacul's nephew, m'Lord," voice from the group sneered.

"You're going to rue the day you ever came up here," Lomen threatened, glaring at Karl. "When my uncle finds out what's going on, you'll wish you'd never been born."

Ignoring him, Karl turned again to Annys. "Choose two soldiers you know you can trust and get me a body count."

"Yes, m'Lord."

By the time the four men were secured, their backs to a large tree and their wrists tied to the man next to him, dawn was beginning to spread its light upon the sky. Karl collected his team and called Annys over.

"How many soldiers does Neacul have back at Abynee?" he asked.

"About another 400," Annys answered, "but most of them are home guards."

"Home guards?" Caryn repeated.

"They're soldiers who are past the age of battle but are still under enlistment bond."

Hearing the discussion, Maelona urged, "Tell 'im about the jackal."

"Lord Neacul has a monster he keeps locked up," Annys explained. "He has the body of a man, but the head of a jackal. He's big, though not as big as he is." She twisted her head to look at Dieter then back to Karl. "Probably more your size."

"Have you seen him fight?"

"Yes, m'Lord," Annys replied. "Lord Neacul brings him out once a month at the coliseum to fight, usually against captured warriors from Fraster's army or if there are none then he sends one of the convicts from the prison."

"It's not much of a fight," Maelona added. "The monster's powerful strong. He carries a pole axe that's got a spike at the end, a blade on one side and a hammer on the other."

"And he will destroy you," Lieutenant Lomen taunted.

Ignoring him, Karl walked over to stand before the captured soldiers who were still seated.

"Effective immediately, Annys is your commander. She will choose her own subordinates. Those of you selected, do not disappoint me."

Uafas came bounding up, causing an immediate tremor of fear to ripple among those seated.

Where's Sakura?

She's coming. Had to make a nature call, if you know what I mean.

Karl chuckled, thinking it quite un-assassin like. *What's the status of Evnan's force?*

They should be here any moment.

Karl felt a presence and cocked his head to the right to see Sakura standing next to him. Shaking his head, he asked, "What's Evnan's status?"

"They didn't see any action," she replied. "Needless to say, they're a bit shocked that it's all over."

"Thanks."

As Sakura walked over to chat with Uafas, the two soldiers conducting the body count approached, Annys along with them.

"Report," Karl commanded.

"We counted 88 dead in the encampment," the man answered, "another 30 at the south end and 25 choked in vines." The last was said with a frown of fear.

Annys did a quick tally. "We're missing three, m'Lord."

"They've been accounted for," Sakura said.

Evnan arrived, took a quick glance around and strode up to Karl. "When Sakura and the wolf arrived with their tale, I couldn't believe it. But I will doubt no more."

"We've another 187 soldiers to add to our forces," Karl said then called Annys over. "This is Annys, the new commander of the Abynee forces. And this," he said to Annys, "is Lord Evnan, Lord of Talbet."

"Lord Evnan," she said, giving him a respectful bow.

"What is your plan, Sire?" Evnan asked.

"We march on Abynee."

During the march to Abynee, they intercepted two runners sent by Neacul to ascertain his army's progress, absorbing both into their growing numbers. Annabeth, Raquel, and Caryn cast a wide sweep using animals and birds, enlisting their aid in preventing Neacul from discovering their approach and managed to intervene with several messenger pigeons, which were subsequently brought down.

Yet some of Neacul's former soldiers expressed concern for their futures should Karl be defeated. More than once,

Karl had to stop the march and remind them of who he was. Still, it was with some trepidation that Annys approached him just as they were breaking camp to begin the final trek to attack the city.

"How many?" Karl asked.

"Three, m'Lord. They left during the march."

"What happened to our perimeter security?"

"It was one of the perimeter guards who took off," she said, her lips tight.

Karl read the body language, knowing she was more than angry that any of her soldiers would desert.

"I'm sorry, m'Lord.   There goes our element of surprise."

"We'll deal with it," he said. "Get your troops ready to move out."

As Annys bowed then spun around on her heels and barked commands at her subordinates, Evnan said, "This is going to make it harder. Though Neacul does not have the forces for open combat, this gives him time to prepare defenses."

"We'll see," Karl cryptically replied.

So it was with some amusement that when Karl and his army arrived at Abynee, the gates were shuttered and barred. Neacul stood between the merlons of the battlement above the gatehouse, haughtily staring down at Karl. Beside him, between other merlons, the city's leaders likewise surveyed the army arrayed outside the walls. The rest of the battlements were packed with merchants, soldiers, and the curious.

Though Annys and others had described the Lord of Abynee, Karl was surprised at the man's corpulence for the man reminded him of a baby elephant without the trunk and ears.

Seeing his former soldiers among the army, Neacul sneered at Karl, "I see you have traitors among you. Be watchful. Just as they abandoned me, they will abandon you."

Ignoring the jab, Karl spoke with a commanding voice. "I have come to accept the surrender of the city. Open the gates and spare these good people a prolonged suffering."

Neacul barked a laugh. "Surrender? Oh, I agree about surrender, but it is you who will surrender to me."

The gates pushed open and Neacul's monster emerged, a buckler in one hand and a claymore in the other. Karl was impressed for its appearance caused an audible sucking in of fearful breaths from his soldiers.

The monster was much like Annys and the others described. He was tall and muscular, bare-chested, and wore knee length leggings of cowhide, and calf-high leather boots. He cast a cold look across the field and strode out to the middle.

"Defeat him and the city is yours," Neacul jeered.

An arrow flew across the open space, smacking into the monster's chest... and bounced off.

In a sudden lurch, the monster leaped forward, raising his sword.

Dieter nudged Karl to the side and ran out to meet it. Swinging his massive axe, he smashed it down on the buckler, propelling the monster backwards who then rolled and jumped up, sword at the ready. For the next several minutes they traded blows, Dieter blocking the claymore with his axe. Yet every time Dieter landed a blow, the monster was hurled back only to pop up, seemingly fresh and ready.

Karl knew it was only a matter of time before the berserker rage left him and Dieter would tire. "Annabeth," he said out the side of his mouth.

"Yes."

"We could use some help here."

Annabeth cast a quick sleep spell, but nothing happened. Nothing that Dieter's blows were landing with less force, she frantically searched her spells. Still nothing worked.

"You're doomed," Neacul taunted. "You've signed your own death warrant and all of your followers too."

Finally, as Dieter began to weaken and yield to the monster's attack, she cast a fireball spell that caught the monster's trousers on fire. Yet it still attacked, impervious to the flames spreading across his legs.

Soon the pants burned away, falling off onto the ground, but now the skin and flesh were burning. And still the monster fought on. The flames engulfed its chest and it looked to be one large ball of flame, flailing a broadsword at Dieter who backed away and swung around, the monster easily following him.

Soon enough, the skin and flesh had burned away, leaving a charred skeleton that continued the battle.

Raquel was the first to notice it. "The heel. Look at his heel."

Karl saw it, the thin lead casing surrounding the heel bone. "I don't believe it," he muttered. "Achilles' heel? This is absurd." Shaking his head in frustration, he called out, "Dieter, take out his left heel."

Dieter looked down, saw the lead casing, feinted left then rolled right, and swung his great axe and sliced through the ankle bones.

The monster toppled backwards and lay still, its hand still gripping the claymore. Suddenly it rolled over and pushed to its knees and began crawling to retrieve the heel. Dieter picked the bone up and pried the lead casing away, flinging the heel bone towards Annabeth who snatched it up and placed it on a rock in the field. Quickly finding another rock, she smashed it against the bone until it was pulverized.

As soon as Annabeth's first strike cracked the bone, the monster froze and wavered, the sword dropped from its hand. With each succeeding blow upon the heel, the monster's skeleton quivered until in collapsed into a heap.

A stunned hush filled the battlements as cheers erupted behind Karl.

Walking over to gaze down at the dead monster, Karl shot a quick glance at Caryn and Raquel and nodded. In that instant, two arrows sped their way to where a shocked Neacul leaned forward to gape down at his fallen champion.

The arrowheads impacted into the man's throat. Before he had a chance to gurgle his dying breaths, two more arrows imbedded then disappeared into his swollen stomach.

Karl looked up to see Neacul fall backwards and disappear.

"Will you open the gates now," Karl called out, "or must we attack?"

A thick silence settled, and Karl was about to call out again when the front gates creaked open wide and a man wearing the robes and chain of a burgomaster burst out, followed by half a dozen leading citizens.

"Welcome m'Lord," the man gushed. Though not as obese as the now deceased Neacul, he was a plump man used to good food and wine. His hair was meticulously coifed, and his clothing bespoke a man of wealth.

"Welcome to Abynee," he continued. "I am Graer, the burgomaster. And these," he added, sweeping his hand at the others with him, "are the city council. We welcome you to our humble city."

Karl gave him a level stare. "Do you know who I am?"

"I... um..." Graer vacillated. He had expected Neacul's death would elevate him to the role as Lord of the domain. With this newcomer, the future wasn't quite so sure.

Karl shot him a malevolent glare. "Are you that stupid?"

"M'Lord?" Graer sputtered, eyes wide.

Karl turned around and in a loud commanding voice, said, "Who am I?"

His army responded in bellowing unison with, "You are the king."

Karl turned back around to face Graer. "These men and women, though many not having the advantage of your education, know who I am, yet you don't?"

"Well... I mean, m'Lord –"

Karl cut him off with a raised hand. Looking past him, he spotted one of the city council not as opulently dressed as the others. She was a slender matronly woman with hair just beginning to grey. Her eyes were bright with excitement.

"What is your name?" Karl asked.

"Brin, Sire," she said with a respectful bow.

"What do you do and how long have you been on the council?"

"I am an ale merchant, Sire. I have been on the council for a little more than a year."

"Are you native to this city?"

"Yes, Sire."

"Then you know what needs to be done to make this city prosper. You," Karl said turning to Graer. "Take off your chain of office."

"Bu… but, I'm the burgomaster," he argued, bowing up.

"Do it before I separate your head from your shoulders," Karl threatened.

With indignation in his eyes, Graer reluctantly slipped the chain over his head though retaining it with a tight grip.

"Now give it to her," Karl commanded.

"Her," Graer answered. It was almost a sneer. He twisted around to glare at her. "She's but a merchant, a peddler of brews, hardly a fitting candidate for office. How she got elected to the council is beyond me." Suddenly he felt the prick of a sword tip at his throat.

"I will not ask again," Karl growled.

Graer thrust out the chain and medal.

Holding the sword to Graer's throat, Karl addressed Brin. "You are now the burgomaster of Abynee."

"Yes, Sire. Thank you. I will serve you well." She took the chain and placed it over her head, much to the consternation of the other council members.

"Your immediate fealty is to Lord Evnan," Karl said. "He will be ruling this portion of the kingdom in place of Kerr."

Evnan's eyes blinked in surprise as this was the first he had heard of Karl's plan.

"Yes, Sire," Brin politely nodded at Evnan, giving him a winning smile.

"Secondly, you will hold elections to replace the other remaining members of the council."

"What?" they burst in anger.

"Shut up," Karl snarled. "When I want your opinion, I'll beat it out of you."

Their mouths snapped shut, though their faces gave away their emotions, a mixture of anger and fear.

"You are not bound by the council size," Karl said. "If you want fewer or more, it is up to you." He glanced back over his shoulder and called out, "Annys."

"Coming, Sire," she replied, jogging over to where he stood.

Addressing Brin, he said, "Until I decide otherwise, Annys is the commander of the garrison here, as well as those spread out among the domain."

"Excellent choice, Sire." Brin nodded with approval, noting Annys' surprise.

"Good. Now, let's get down to business."

Chapter 14

What ensued surprised even the most skeptical of Karl's team, for in the next few weeks word spread like a grassfire that the promised king had returned. Karl collected the rest of Neacul's army and marched on Contyn, collecting volunteers along the way. By the time he arrived at the city gates, his army had swelled to over 3000. Having heard what happened to Neacul, Kerr met Karl with open arms.

"Welcome, m'Lord," Kerr expansively greeted him.

Karl noted that Kerr called him 'Lord' and not 'Sire.' Deposing Kerr from his exalted position was going to be a pleasure.

Karl publicly accused Kerr of his crimes then brought out Leri to verify the accusation. The outcry against Kerr was so great that Karl had to sequester him away in the gaol for his own safety.

Kerr's sorceress fared much better. Annabeth took a shine to her and the two became fast friends, which left Raquel momentarily alone until Caryn filled in for the absent Annabeth.

With Kerr's domain secure, Karl turned his attention to Fraster's part of the kingdom. Imagine his surprise when two days into planning, a wagon showed up, escorted by a dozen of Fraster's elite warriors. Trussed and gagged in the back of the cart was Lord Fraster.

Karl suppressed a grin seeing the once proud lord bound like a common criminal. The captain of the escort group approached Karl then dropped to one knee.

"M'Lord King," he said. "When we received word that the king had returned, we determined that your rule should not be impeded. Not wanting to take justice into our hands, we have brought Lord Fraster to you."

"Stand," Karl commanded. "What is your name?"

"I am Gilmyr, Sire, captain of the garrison of Statmyr."

Karl studied the man. He was medium height but well-proportioned and had the air of calm authority.

"Who is the commander of Fraster's army?"

Gilmyr hesitated then replied, "Lord Fraster's son, Sire."

"His son? Does he have experience? Is he a proven warrior or leader?"

Several of the guards cleared their throats, a gesture Karl fully understood.

Gilmyr again hesitated until one of the guards urged, "Go ahead and tell him, Captain. Tell him the truth."

"That's a wise answer," Karl agreed. "The truth always works best."

Gilmyr glanced at the shackled Lord Fraster then took a deep breath. "He's incompetent, Sire. He has no experience, no leadership qualities, nothing that would engender any loyalty amongst the soldiers. He spends his time in taverns or whoring. I could go on, but I think you understand."

"Thank you. Effective immediately, you will assume command of the forces in that part of the kingdom. When I have appointed a regent to rule that area, you will report to him or her. Until that time, you report directly to me."

"Yes, Sire," the man replied, thrilled though cautious in this new role.

"What of the sorceress?" Karl asked.

"She remains in Statmyr, Sire, unsure of her welcome here. Otherwise, she would have accompanied us."

"Once I have dealt with lords Kerr and Fraster, I want her at Avnoch."

"Yes, Sire. I will send word."

"Good," Karl answered with a smile. "Now then, let's get down to the business of consolidating a kingdom."

Felix reveled in the attention and personal interest Mister Landon showered on him, especially the daily invitation to dinner, for it allowed him the excuse of arriving early to spend five to ten minutes talking with Alyson who appeared open to conversation.

One Friday he was caught pleasantly off guard when he mentioned that he had contemplated immersing into the Green Jacket Golf Pro game.

"I've never played golf," she said with that captivating smile that caused Felix to feel like he was an awkward teenager.

"You'll have to play with me some time." He blushed when he saw her hide a smirk and realized what he had said. As he struggled to think of something clever to cover his stupidity, she smiled at him.

"I would like that."

"I'll be playing tomorrow and Sunday if you're free," he said, hope rising within.

"How about tomorrow?"

"Tomorrow it is then," he replied, forcibly stifling his euphoria so it wasn't too obvious.

"What time?"

"Back in the day, I used to get up early," he said, rolling his eyes, "but these days anytime of the day is fine. Whatever is convenient for you."

"Ten?"

"Ten it is then."

"Where shall I meet you?"

"We can do it one of two ways," he said, doing his best to be gallant. "The Moccasin Bend Golf Course is an easy course with nice views of the river and the mountains. I can either meet you there, or I can pick you up, whichever you prefer."

"If it's not too much of an inconvenience," she began.

"Not at all," he interjected, thrilled to have even more time with her.

Her hand went to the earpiece in her right ear then down to scribble on a piece of paper. "Yes, Mister Landon, he's here. Thank you. Yes, Sir. You have a good weekend too. Good night." Tapping off, she smiled at Felix and handed him the paper with her address and phone number. "He's waiting for you. See you tomorrow."

Felix remembered little of the dinner and conversation with Mister Landon and the restless night at home other than time seemed to drag on until he was finally able to head over to Alyson's house. She lived in a high rise overlooking the river and he was impressed to note that she lived on one of the upper floors.

When she answered the door, he sucked in his breath, overwhelmed at her beauty and sensuality. She wore a cream-colored polo shirt that fit snugly across her ample bosom, and tan hiking shorts that revealed toned and shapely legs. Her long hair was tied in a ponytail that protruded out the rear gap of a New York Yankees baseball cap. She had the aura of the girl next door mixed with the dreams of fantasy.

"Do I look OK?" she frowned, seeing his reaction.

"OK?" he sputtered. "My God, you're gorgeous." He winced as he silently berated himself for such a stupid overt comment. "I'm sorry, I didn't mean –"

"You didn't mean I'm gorgeous?" Her frown deepened and she gave him a hard stare.

"Well yes you're gorgeous, I mean, but I didn't mean it like –" he fumbled until he saw her grinning at him.

"That was sweet," she said patting his cheek. Grabbing a shoulder bag, she announced, "I'm ready."

Felix marveled at the woman's ability. She was a natural at golf.

"You sure you've never played before?" he asked after she sank a long 30-foot putt.

"This is the first time ever," she sweetly smiled. "The only reason I'm doing better than average because I have such an awesome teacher."

"Better than average?" he chuckled. "You could have been on the Tour."

"There you go again with the compliments," she said, staring intently at him. "Are you always like this?"

Felix shrugged. "Never thought about it."

"I like that in a person," she replied. "No games. What you see is what you get. Far too few people like that."

The day went by much too quickly and after the last putt, Felix desperately wanted the time with her to continue. "If you're not obligated for the rest of the day, I know a little place that still serves food. It's probably the last restaurant open in Chattanooga, but it serves good food."

"I would like that," she smiled, "But you'll have to let me at least get a shower before dinner."

"Pick you up at seven?"

"Perfect."

Time again raced by and too soon they were standing outside her door at the end of the evening. Wanting to be the quintessential gentleman, he dipped his head in a respectful bow.

"Thank you for spending so much time with me. This has been truly wonderful."

She hesitated and he thought she might invite him in. Not wanting to spoil his anticipation, he preempted her invitation.

"If you are available tomorrow, I thought we might see what boats are available and take a ride on the river."

Her eyes brightened. "I would love that."

"Tomorrow then. Same time?"

"Make it eleven. I'll bring a lunch."

"Eleven it is."

He was about to turn away when she stepped towards him and gave him a quick kiss on the lips.

"Thank you," she whispered and unlocked her door.

All the way home, Felix floated in bliss. Being one of the last men on earth had its advantages.

Except for those nights Felix dined with Landon, Felix and Alyson spent their time together, finally culminating in the overnight stay at her apartment. Felix was not disappointed for she was more than an exquisite and sensual lover, she was caring and compassionate... and he was head over heels beyond infatuation... he was in love.

So it was with frantic concern that late Friday evening after dinner with Landon when he arrived at her apartment, and no one was home. The repeated knocking was met with silence and his first reaction was fear that she had lost interest, that she had found someone else. He called her phone and received the voicemail prompt. He tried again, leaving a voicemail this time.

Travelling back down to the lobby, he waited in the echoed silence of the vast colonnaded room, sitting in an overstuffed chair facing the doors. When noon the next day came and went and his stomach growled its need for food, he sighed and shuffled home, ate a quick meager meal and returned to the lobby, this time with a book. At midnight and after repeated phone calls and messages, he went home to a sleepless night.

Sunday, he took to wandering the empty streets in hope he might catch a glimpse of her. His meanderings invariably brought him back to her apartment, to knocks on the door and to disappointment then trudging back to the elevator then out the lobby to once again roam the silent streets.

Thus it was with a heavy heart that he arrived at work Monday morning, walking down the empty corridors, past the vacant offices and cubicles, glaring reminders that he was alone… again. He was fixing a cup of coffee when Landon called him.

"Yes, Sir?"

"I need you to come over here."

"I'm on my way."

Leaving the steaming coffee mug on the counter, he bustled down the stairs and out to his car in the now packed lots filled with cars of immersion travelers who simply left their vehicles with the keys in them. When all the spots were filled, they had taken to parking on the lawn. The same occurred throughout Chattanooga. All the parking garages, street spaces and anywhere else an auto or pickup could fit were filled with cars that would never move again. Some locked their cars out of habit. Others simply tossed the keys on the front seat and walked away forever.

Navigating his way to Landon's office, Felix mused at the silence of the city. The once bustling and humming city was a ghost town. Yet still they came for immersion. ITL had set up a bus service so that immersion seekers could park as far away as the malls at Northgate and Hamilton Place.

But downtown Chattanooga was desolate, a wilderness of buildings and cars.

Entering the parking garage, he was crestfallen to see Alyson's car parked in her spot, which meant she had spent the weekend avoiding him. His heart breaking at the thought that she had spent the weekend with another, he strode through the hallways, rehearsing what he was going to say to her.

He was more than surprised when he entered Landon's outer office for Alyson was not at her place and the doors to Landon's inner sanctum were open with Mister Landon himself standing in the doorway.

"Good. Glad you're here," Landon said, his tone all business. "You need to see this." He led the way to his office and motioned Felix to come around to look at the computer screen. "I know you and Miss Whitmer have been spending quite a bit of time together and I thought it puzzling that she had not arrived at work at her customary hour. Never in the entire time of her employment here has she ever missed a day or been even a minute late. Initially I thought you might have been responsible."

"Me?" Felix choked.

"That was my initial thought, though I should have known better. The two of you would not have allowed your personal lives to interfere with your professionalism. So I decided to take a look at the security cameras, and this is what I discovered."

He adjusted the screen so that Felix could see the split screen of the security cameras in the lower parking garage.

"Notice she was down in the garage at seven fifteen. That would have been right after you came here for dinner. See? She's walking to her car."

What happened next shocked and enraged Felix, for out of the shadows, two figures emerged a younger man and an older man. In that instant, the older man pointed the taser at her and pressed the trigger.

The darts shot out and the jolt just about lifted Alyson off the ground before crumbling in a heap. The younger man kneeled beside her and duct-taped her wrists while the older man removed the darts.

After lifting her into the passenger seat of her car, the young man climbed into the driver's side while the older man walked away.

"O my God," Felix blurted. "I've got to find her."

Yet he felt helpless. Who could they call to help? Besides the Police having their hands full with immersion crowd control, their own numbers had drastically dwindled due to immersion. The military? It was not their jurisdiction. The FBI? They suffered the same personnel reductions the police did.

"I've called in some favors, and we're connected to all the cameras along all the roads leading in and out of the city. Look here."

He flipped the screens and Felix watched as the pickup truck burst out of the parking garage and down side streets and main thoroughfares until it was on I-75 heading towards Cleveland. It was easy to track as it was the only vehicle on the road heading away from the city. They followed the truck via camera as it turned off the interstate on Exit 20 to take the bypass around Cleveland.

Felix watched with growing anxiety. The kidnappers, or killers, or whoever they were had a two days head start.

The cameras caught the truck as it circled Cleveland and exited on Route 74 towards Ocoee. Several cameras later, they watched the truck exit south onto Route 411, heading towards the Georgia border.

They watched a bit more until Landon heaved a heavy sigh and pointed to the screen. "We lost them here in Cisco when they turned off the main road and headed into the Cohutta Wilderness area."

"Damn it," Felix muttered. "What are we going to do?"

"We need someone to go get her," Landon said then hastily added, "not you," when he saw the look in Felix's eyes.

"Why not me?"

"Let's be realistic, Felix. The kind of men we're dealing with here are not the kind we're used to. You and I live in a world of technology and luxuries. How good are you with a gun?"

"A gun?" Felix's lips tightened, knowing full well he had no experience with guns other than in a video game when he was younger.

"These men are holdouts, most likely looking for women to stay back with them, start civilization all over again and all that. We're going to need someone with the skills to flush them out and rescue your fair maiden."

Felix thought for a moment then cocked his head. "Karl?"

"Exactly."

"He's probably going to need help," Felix replied, immediately liking the idea, "someone with the same level of skills. The only one like that who has real world experience is Caryn."

"Then we bring them both out."

"What do we tell the others?"

"We tell them what they need to know, that they need to stay behind and keep things status quo until Karl and Caryn return. What's their status now?"

"Karl's consolidated power in Odryssa and has set himself up as king. The rest of the team is there with him, planning their next mission, which is to attack the Kingdom of Mann," Felix said. "From the looks of things, Karl has sufficient force to subjugate the Kingdom of Mann, though the sorceress there will still be a significant problem."

"They're going to have to put that on hold until we can get the Alyson situation settled."

"Thank you," Felix said, breathing a sigh of relief. He thought again of Karl and Caryn's resurrection. "What do we tell them?"

"The truth."

"They're not going to be happy," Felix observed, "especially when we tell them there's nothing wrong with them."

"We'll cross that bridge when we come to it," Landon said then chuckled. "Gives a whole new meaning to the game of Bridge Quest."

"I know who we can send to deliver the message," Felix said with a sly grin.

Landon returned the grin. "I was thinking the same thing."

Karl cocked an eyebrow at the man who entered the rear of the throne room in the castle at Avnoch and eased along the back wall, vainly trying not to get noticed. It seemed a foolish objective as the man stuck out like the proverbial sore thumb for he wore nice jeans, polo shirt and penny loafers.

Their eyes met and the man gave him a frustrated half smile, pointed at Karl then himself then tapped his fingers and thumb together intimating talking. Karl motioned him forward.

Noting the strange man approaching, Raquel excused herself from the conversations and tucked in behind the man who was unaware he was being followed. Caryn likewise noted the man and joined with Raquel.

By now, those present became aware of the man and his strange dress and conversation stopped as eyes and attention followed his progress across the room, people stepping back to let him pass. Realizing he had made an impact, the man stepped boldly to stand before Karl.

"Good day to you, *Lord* Karl," the man said with grandiloquent emphasis that hinted of patronage.

"Good day to you too," Karl replied. "Who are you?"

"My name is Gerard. I have a message for you."

"Yes?"

Gerard hesitated, casting a quick glance around the still silent room. "It is for your ears alone."

Karl leveled a hard stare at him. "Be thankful I'm in a good mood. Otherwise, I'd have you dragged away to the dungeons."

Instead of cowering, the man merely shook his head.

"Your threats have no impact on me," Gerard smugly countered.

"Really?" Karl turned to the guards. "Take him to the dungeons. Make him uncomfortable."

Gerard's smugness evaporated and he held up his hands. "Just a minute, just a minute," he pleaded as two burly guards lifted him up by his armpits and began dragging him away. "They want you to go back... to real life."

"Wait a moment," Karl commanded, halting the guards. "They found a cure?"

"That's not what I said," Gerard replied in a huff.

"Release him. Let him approach."

Demonstrably straightening his clothes, Gerard walked defiantly up to stand in front of Karl. "You are to go back."

"You've said that already. Why?"

"I don't know why specifically," Gerard sniffed. "They have a mission for you."

"Suppose I don't want to go back."

"You don't have a choice."

Karl's heart sank. Why the hell couldn't they just leave him alone? He was happy here. He didn't want to go back. How could he make them understand that he wanted to stay here?'

"When?" Raquel asked, her countenance hard.

"I don't know exactly when," Gerard bristled. "I'm just the messenger, but most likely very soon." He shifted a disdainful glance at Caryn. "And the same message is for you too."

"They found a cure already?" she asked, shocked.

"Again," he intoned, shaking his head, "that's not what I said. I am simply to tell you and Karl that your services are needed, urgently."

"I don't understand," Karl fumed.

"They'll explain it all when you go back."

"Will Caryn and I return here?"

"Yes," Gerard nodded. "There. You know as much about what's going on as I do and now that I've delivered the message, I expect to be returned at any moment."

"That's it?" Raquel demanded. "What about the rest of us?"

"You're to remain here and keep things under control until they return."

"How long will that be?" she challenged.

"Good god you people," Gerard chafed. "Get a grip, will you. I've delivered my message. Now stand clear while I go back to my own game." He folded his arms, shaking his head and muttering, "I'll be glad to be rid of these newbie fools."

Karl looked at each of his team members. "Raquel is in charge while I'm gone. But you know the rules. We're a team, a family. We live or die as one. I don't know what's going on, but I'll do my damnest to get back as soon as I can. The same for Caryn. Let Evnan know and the subordinate commanders that we've been detained elsewhere. Establish a workable chain of command."

And then it happened, before Karl had finished giving his instructions, he and Caryn fizzled away. A smug Gerard stood to the side, arms folded, confidently waiting for his own return.

Yet nothing happened. The longer he stood there, the more his confidence wavered until Raquel flatly stated, "Get him out of here."

Karl's first awareness was that his body felt heavy, thick, like wading through chest deep mud. The second perception was his heartbeat. *If it stops that means I'm dead.* The coalescing of light and distinction of shape invaded the fixation on his heartbeat, and he blinked his eyes to focus, yet nothing looked familiar. He felt cold and he shivered.

"Give yourself a minute or two to wake up," a voice said.

Feeling reached down to his fingers and he lifted a stiff arm, seeing the electrodes on the tips of his fingers. Understanding swept through him and he twisted his head, the electrodes falling away as life returned to his body.

It took another ten minutes for Karl to fully recover and sit up. His mouth felt dry, and he licked his lips as he stared at the two strangers then down to discover his only article of clothing was spandex tight shorts. "Water."

"Of course," one man replied, handing him a large plastic mug with a straw. He looked to be in his early 40's, trim and fit, with short wavy auburn hair. He wore vest and slacks of a three-piece dark grey suit, the sleeves of his mauve shirt rolled up.

As Karl sucked down the liquid, he looked around the large room filled with immersion tables. "Where am I?"

"Back in Chattanooga," the man answered. "I'm Felix Hubach and this is Mister Landon."

Karl twisted his head to stare at the man next to Felix. He was in his early 50s, slim, average height, with short auburn hair and a pencil moustache. "I've heard of you. You're the one who owns this whole affair."

"Guilty as charged," Landon replied with a smile then turned to Felix and ticked his head towards the adjacent table where Caryn was reviving.

Karl's eyes followed Felix as he moved away and over to help Caryn sit up. Karl frowned as he studied the woman. He knew it was Caryn, but it didn't look like Caryn. This Caryn didn't have the pointed ears of an elf.

Still, this Caryn was rather attractive, sitting in her shorts and loose t-shirt, her legs dangling over the side of the bed. She had shoulder length thick blond hair, blues eyes on an oval shaped face, and well-defined arms and legs as she scratched her head and ran her fingers through her hair.

"Welcome," Felix greeted her.

"Why are we here?" Karl asked, his throat raw from disuse.

"A rather existential question," Landon deadpanned, "but in this instance, we need you two to rescue my secretary."

"Your secretary?" Karl repeated.

"Yes," Felix chimed in. "She's been kidnapped, and we need your help."

"You're serious," Caryn said, cocking an eyebrow.

"Very."

"And the cure for our condition?" Karl demanded.

"Well… um…" Felix vacillated.

A thick silence settled for only a moment before Karl exploded. "You brought us back into bodies that are about to expire at any moment just to rescue your secretary? What the hell is wrong with you? Is this some kind of goddamned sick joke?"

"It's not as bad as you think," Landon soothed.

"It's not?" Karl retorted.

"You're not really sick," Felix blurted.

Karl snapped his head back round to glare at Felix. "What did you just say?"

He held up his hands in a defensive gesture. "It was all just a ruse, a trick. Neither of you are ill."

"What?" Karl burst, pushing himself off the table.

Felix and Landon instinctively stepped back.

Grim faced and clenching his fists, Karl glared at them. "This better be good."

"You were never sick," Felix began then explained the concept of an assassination team. "The only way we could get you into the game was to convince you that you were dying."

"You bastards," Caryn spat. "You robbed me of my life just to use me."

"It's not as bad as you think, really," Landon placated. "The world has changed in the year you've been gone."

"A year?" Karl sniffed in disgust. "We've been gone for what, a month two months maybe?"

"Game time and real life time don't match," Felix said. "It's like time dilation, the correlation between traveling in space and living here, except it's reverse in game time."

Still seething, Karl turned back to Landon. "So what's different?"

"The world isn't here anymore. Most of mankind is immersed in a game. When you step outside these walls, you'll be in a kind of twilight zone. The world once inhabited by the teaming masses of mankind is now a world of tumbleweeds and silence."

Karl leaned against the immersion table, shaking his head, torn between ripping their heads off or keeping his mouth shut because he needed them to get back into the game. "How many games are there?"

"Thousands upon thousands," Landon answered, "one for every interest and passion."

"So why the need for an assassination team?" Caryn asked, walking up to stand next to Karl. She was about half-a-head shorter.

Karl looked down at her. "Hey."

"Hey," she replied with a smile.

"You look good."

"So do you."

"There is no need, per se, anymore," Landon acknowledged, interrupting them. "We initially determined the need to compete with the Russians and Chinese in the elimination of potential threats to our programs. But then the demand for immersion exceeded all expectations and the need for assassination personnel all but disappeared."

Karl turned to Landon. "So who were we to have assassinated, had the need arose?"

"Mostly individuals whose positions influenced people's decisions, like some in the media and government."

"As well as some of the religious leaders," Felix added. "You know how rabid some religious devotees can be."

"Were any of these people eliminated?" Caryn asked.

"Oh yes," Landon cavalierly asserted. "The problem we faced was that we had no home-grown gaming assassination teams, so we had to hire out from the Russians and that was getting expensive. Still, they made quite a dent in the media. Took out several big names in the major networks."

"Roland Prime of Prime Time with Prime," Caryn said. "I remember that one. They did it live on TV, complete with fireworks behind him. Not very subtle, but quite effective."

"That was you?" Karl said, impressed.

"Actually, it was our Russian friends," Landon admitted. "Still, it did the job. The marketing traction we got on that one was amazing as there was an immediate spike in immersion applications."

"So what about us now," Karl asked. "You no longer have a need for assassination teams. What happens to us?"

"Don't confuse perceived irrelevance with need," Landon corrected. "There will always be a need for an enforcement team. At some point in time, humans will no longer roam the earth."

"Everyone immersed in a game?" Caryn interrupted, wide eyed.

"Exactly."

"Who controls the games?" she asked.

"Artificial Intelligence, programmed to take care of everything," he replied.

"You're kidding, right?" Karl furrowed his brows.

"Not at all," Landon said.

"If everyone is in a game, then why even have a hit team?" Caryn asked.

"Because at some point there will be a last man standing."

"What do you mean?"

"ITL is not the only immersion company in the world. There are at least a dozen major companies and scores of lesser ones. We all will need insurance to ensure we remain operational."

"I still don't understand," Karl huffed. "Are you saying that you want us to screw up the competition when everyone's immersed?"

"Yes and no," Landon chuckled. "What we need is to ensure that *we* are not screwed up, to use your colloquialism. At the same time, we may want to subvert competition when necessary or appropriate."

"You need computer geeks to do that," Karl dismissively replied. "That's not us."

"You misunderstand," Landon smiled. "We have the computer geeks to do that already in place. What we need is a team who can function here on the outside that can survive in the wilds and still accomplish its mission. Once you leave here, you'll understand. You two are already trained soldiers who can survive in the wilderness. The average human can't. They've been given everything they needed to survive. Food? Go to the grocery store. Move from one location to another? Get in a car and drive, stopping at a fuel station to fill up."

"Or sit in specially designed chairs," Felix added, "wear specially designed helmets and spend your life playing video games."

Landon folded his arms, his smile widening. "Think of the average human being, used to sitting on his butt and watching TV or playing video games. How many of them have actually survived in the cold, hunting and killing food?"

"My body will die at some point in time," Karl reminded him.

"Ah," Landon nodded with respect. "You get to the heart of the matter. That is why these next few years are critical, though in truth, the patient enemy waits until all are asleep. We have plans in place to solve the permanent need for human bodies. It's merely a matter of insemination and controlled growth. By the time you two are near your end, your new bodies will be ready."

"Does that mean we are permanently on the outside now?" Caryn asked, her disappointment obvious.

"No," Landon reassured her. "You were retrieved for a specific mission. Once the mission is complete, you return to your game in the exact spot you left it."

"But not necessarily the same conditions when we left," Karl reminded him.

Landon gave Karl a look of respect. "Once again you have surmised the difficulties. But, I fear we digress too long. At this very moment, my secretary, also his girlfriend," he slid his eyes at Felix, "is being held captive somewhere in the Cohutta Wilderness to the southeast of here. We need you two to rescue her."

"Suppose we don't want to play your game outside here?" Caryn asked, leveling an intense stare at Landon.

Landon returned her gaze with an equally hard stare. "You're in no position to barter. You refuse and the two of you are on your own, stuck in the outside."

"We'll just find another immersion company," she retorted.

Felix chuckled. "Yes you can, but you won't get back into Bridge Quest with your friends. Bridge Quest is exclusively ours. So, yes, you can immerse with someone else. Just think of all the new friends you'll make in a game that's not designed for you."

"What do you mean?" she asked, her heart sinking.

"What gaming skills did you have before you entered Bridge Quest?"

"None," she replied. "I'd never been a gamer."

"Neither had any of your other friends or any of the players in Bridge Quest. The game was designed for people like you, total newbies." Felix grinned at his use of the word, as though he were some expert gamer.

Understanding swept through her and she grimaced. "You bastards."

"Now, now, not so angry," Landon reproached. "We've provided you with an opportunity of a lifetime… and longer. What we ask for in return is your cooperation."

"Was it just Karl and me or was everyone else perfectly healthy too?" she scowled.

Felix hesitated then quietly said, "None of you were sick," then hastily added, "But remember, that was the only way we could get you into the game."

Karl titled his head and stared at Felix. "Raquel has two kids who believe their mother is dying. You destroyed her family because what you wanted was more important than her life."

"That was a mistake," Felix said, holding up his hands in defense. "We discovered that too late."

"Bullshit," Caryn retorted. "You could just have easily pulled her back out of the game, pretended there was a cure and sent her back to be with those she loved."

"No we couldn't," Landon interrupted. "She knew all about Bridge Quest."

"So what?" Caryn sneered.

"For obvious reasons, Bridge Quest was, and I remind you - still is, a restricted and classified game known to a select few. Releasing her to the public domain would have compromised the game."

"You're telling me that with all the research you clowns did on each of us that you managed to miss two kids?" Karl demanded. "Are you really that inept?"

"Even the best efforts can have a weak link," Landon replied. "We discovered too late that the one responsible for Raquel's background check had it in for her. He was a former jilted lover, and this was his way of getting back at her."

"He's been dealt with," Felix stated.

"What," Karl sneered, "a slap on the wrist?"

"He was placed in the Drug Lord game."

"You placed him in a game?" Caryn shook her head in disbelief. "How is that punishment?"

"You can't respawn," Felix intoned, "and they torture informants."

"Ouch," Karl winced, understanding the man's fate. Realizing he and Caryn we going nowhere until they accomplished their mission, Karl heaved a loud sigh and looked at Landon. "What do we know about the kidnapping?"

"We have it on camera," Landon replied. "I can show you."

As they started to move away from the tables and headed to the doors, Karl twisted his head to gaze at Landon. "I have a one more little question."

"Yes?"

"Suppose we get injured or killed while we're out of the game? It's not like we can respawn."

Landon and Felix exchanged a look before Felix shrugged and said, "Just don't get killed or injured."

Chapter 15

Dressed in a set of their old clothes, Karl and Caryn stood in Felix's office watching the recording of the security cameras remoted from the brightly lit basement garage of the Landon Building. The camera, pointed to the glass entrance doors to the elevators, showed the doors and the parking spaces on either side. Two cars, a silver 2010 Koenigsegg Trivita parked in a wide parking spot edged with metal barriers, and next to it, a blue Audi R8 e-tron were parked to one side of the doors. The remaining spots were empty.

"This was this past Friday evening," Felix stated.

"I know," Karl answered in a monotone. "It says so right there on the screen." He shifted his gaze to Caryn who wore hiking shorts and a polo shirt, apparently with no bra beneath for the two points where her nipples pushed the fabric caused him to shake his head and remind himself to stay focused.

"And it wasn't until Monday that you discovered it?" Caryn challenged.

"Opinions to the contrary," Landon remarked with a frown, "I don't spend my weekends watching the security cameras in the parking garage. You'll note that the garage is almost empty. Except for myself, Miss Whitmer, and a few remaining immersion specialists, the parking garage, and the building itself is oppressively quiet."

"There she is now," Felix interrupted, pointing at the screen.

A tall curvaceous beauty walked out through the doors. The pinstriped business suit, though professional, could not hide the large firm breasts, narrow waist, long legs, and long thick black hair cascading over her shoulders.

"She's undone her hair," Landon observed with an interested frown as though seeing the woman in a new perspective. "She looks very pretty that way.

355

To Karl, she reminded him of the gorgeous women in the game and he silently chuckled, wondering if there was a connection.

She keyed the remote in her hand as she walked over to the Audi and the car lights flashed telling all that the car was unlocked. Abruptly she paused and turned her head as a man approached from the left. He was middle-aged and almost as tall as Alyson. It was obvious that he didn't work there by his jeans and oil-stained t-shirt that didn't quite fit over his protruding belly. He wore a battered and stained baseball cap with a John Deere logo that shaded most of his face, except for the long grey and black beard. He held something in his hand.

She jerked her head to the right as another man approached, a younger man though dressed much like the older man. Karl watched as the older man pointed the taser at her and pressed the trigger.

The darts shot out and the jolt knocked Alyson to the ground. The younger man hustled to kneel beside her to retrieve her car keys and duct-tape her wrists while the older man yanked the darts out.

"That animal," Felix growled.

After the two men lifted her into the passenger seat of her car, the young man casually glanced around the garage before climbing into the driver's side. Soon, Alyson's Audi headed towards the exit.

"Here's the next camera," Landon said as the screen shifted to the Audi driving out of the garage, following an older model gasoline powered, faded silver Dodge pickup, the requisite dents in the body and tailgate.

"We were able to track them via road cameras to Cleveland then Ocoee then down to Conasauga. They turned off the main road just before Conasauga and headed east on Ball Play Road. We lost them after that."

"Map?" Karl spoke.

Felix pulled up satellite imagery on an adjacent computer screen and drilled down to Conasauga.

"Pull back," Karl ordered, and the resolution lessened so that Karl could see Conasauga in relation to Chattanooga and the surrounding area.

"He's in the Cohutta Wilderness," Karl observed.

"Do you know it?" Felix asked.

"No," Karl shrugged, "but I can read a map."

"I know it," Caryn interjected. "Used to hike the Jack's River trail down to the falls a lot when I was in college in Kennesaw."

"Excellent," Landon nodded then saw the steely determination in Karl's eyes. "What do you need?"

"I want 1:25000 topo maps, satellite comms, night vision optics, drones –"

"Unlimited access to weaponry," Caryn chimed in, "and clothing and supplies as needed or required."

"The city is yours to plunder," Landon grinned.

"Gun stores close by?" Karl asked.

"None close by within walking distance," Felix said, pulling up a computer map showing locations, "so you'll have to drive."

"There are plenty of unlocked cars with the keys still in them," Landon added. "Take your pick."

"We'll need to set up a command-and-control center," Karl said. "Don't care where, but we'll need you two to man it."

"We can use my office," Landon said, smiling at Felix. "We'll take shifts."

"Where's your office?" Caryn queried.

"Downtown at Cameron Hill Circle," he answered, "where the old medical insurance facility used to be."

"We'll find it," Karl said. "We'll need a pic of her before we launch. We'll get our supplies then meet you back at your place." He then turned to Caryn. "You ready?"

"Yup."

"Here," Felix interrupted. "Take this." He handed him a computer tablet. "Makes the search easier."

"Thanks."

"And this," Landon said, holding out two cellphones. "Our numbers are already programmed into the phones."

"Thanks, again."

Watching them stride through the doors, Felix said, "Think they'll be successful?"

"We placed them in the game because they were better than good," Landon answered. "They were among the best. If anything, their motivation to succeed is greater now because both want to get back into the game."

"And when they see how lonely the world has become, they'll want to get back even faster," Felix observed.

Walking down the empty hallway, Karl listened to the echoing of their footsteps as he occasionally peered into vacant offices and cubicles.

"This is straight out of Twilight Zone," he said.

"It is kind of weird," Caryn agreed, casting a sideways glance at Karl the no-longer-a-Viking. He was tall, though not as tall as when he was a Viking, with short wavy brown hair. Still, he was rather handsome, with chiseled face and broad muscular shoulders and arms and chest and legs and her mind wandered off to the bedroom, wondering if real life sex was better than gaming sex.

Her memories wandered to her former boyfriend. Frank had been fun in the beginning, attentive and excellent in the bedroom. But as time went on, she realized he was linear deep, a one trick pony rooted in his self-arrogance that believed he knew what was best for everyone… which likewise translated into his bedroom performance. She started calling him Mister Vanilla, afraid to even think of anything outside his comfort zone.

"What?" she asked, realizing Karl had just asked her a question.

"I said, where do you want to start first?"

"Weapons," she replied. "The rest isn't as necessary."

"Agreed. Let's go find us some transportation."

Riding the elevator down to the main floor, Karl slid his eyes to take in the woman next to him. She was very pretty with shoulder length blond hair shaped around her oval face. She also had the body of an athlete: well defined arms and legs, flat tummy, and firm breasts that bounced when she walked, which reminded him that she wore nothing beneath the shirt, which caused him to wonder what she looked like naked, which caused a flash of guilt when he remembered Raquel and Annabeth, which he immediately suppressed and tucked away in a forgotten corner of his mind. *After all, we're here and they're not.*

"What do you think of them bringing us out of a game to track down this guy's girlfriend?" he asked.

"I think it's bullshit," she snipped. "Not only did they lie to us about us dying, they stick us into a game where we now have brand new lives only to be yanked back out at someone's whim. What's to stop this from happening any time someone gets a wild hair up his ass?"

Karl stared at her and deadpanned, "Don't sugarcoat it. Tell me how you really feel?"

Caryn grinned despite her irritation. "At least I'm out here with you. You know what you're doing."

"So do you," he said, returning the compliment.

The doors opened and they stepped out into the wide foyer, walking past the vacant receptionist counter and guard desks. They paused once through the outer doors. It was a glorious late spring day of sunny blue sky and warm gentle breeze.

Karl scrunched his face. "It's too quiet." He then took in the broad parking lot packed with cars. Even the once manicured grass and tended greenspaces overflowed with cars.

"Pick anything for now," he said. "We'll decide what we want and find an auto dealer later."

The search ended at the first car, a late model Ford electric with a baby seat in the back. Tossing out the baby seat, he slid into the passenger side.

"I figure you probably know your way around here better than I do. You drive and I'll navigate."

"Yes, Sir," she grinned.

Karl typed in a search for gun stores. "There's a place close by off of Ashland Terrace. Head north a quarter mile then take the right to go across the bridge."

As she edged out of the parking lot, checking for traffic, she shook her head before heading north on Amnicola Highway. While no other cars were on the road, the sides of the highway close to ITL were lined with cars on both sides of the road, ceasing only when they turned onto the exit ramp for the bridge.

"This feels so weird," she commented. "I feel like it's holiday traffic, but there's absolutely no one out."

"And no one at home," Karl remarked.

Ten minutes later they pulled into the parking lot of the Gunner's Club with its barred windows and door.

"How we getting in?" Caryn frowned.

"Good question," he replied, getting out of the car. With his hands on his hips, he studied the iron bars on the windows and door. "We're going to need something to pry those things off the building."

"Why not just get one of those earth moving machines and crash it into the building?" Caryn suggested.

Karl slowly nodded. "Think I'll try the front door first."

"Why bother?" Caryn replied shaking her head.

Karl walked over to the door and grabbed the doorknob, followed by a laugh. "It's open."

"You're kidding," she scoffed then blinked in surprise as he opened the door and walked in, flicking on the lights.

Caryn hustled in behind him. "I'm surprised the lights still work."

"Maybe he was a later traveler," Karl distractedly replied as he gazed at the various shotguns, rifles, and handguns. His eyes lit up when he saw a rifle in the display case. "How good are your sniper skills?"

"Pretty good still. Why?"

"He's got an M24-A2," he said and pointed.

"We going to snipe them?" She frowned as she went around the handgun display case.

"I'd like the option of taking them out as far away as possible," he replied, noting the M24-A2 case was locked.

"What handgun do you want?" she asked, pulling out a Glock.

"Either a Glock or SIG Sauer, nine-millimeter," he answered, deciding he didn't need to be gentle prying open the display case and smashing the glass with the butt of a pistol. "But I'm open to whatever you want. Either way, we both take the same caliber weapon so we can use the same ammo. What rifle you want?"

Caryn looked up at the wall display and grinned when she saw the Russian AK47. "Gimme the AK there. That way we can use the same ammo for the AK and the M24."

By the time they loaded up the car, they had two rifles and three handguns apiece, four scopes, various knives, and six cases of ammo.

"We need a vehicle," Karl said, doing a search for ATV dealerships, "that can haul ATVs."

"Why not two vehicles with an ATV each," she countered.

"Excellent idea." He leaned over so that their shoulders touched and showed her the locations of dealers.

She leaned in so that her head gently touched his.

At the same time, they slowly turned to face each other, their noses almost touching. Gazing into each other's eyes, understanding passed between them and their heads tilted as their lips pressed in a kiss.

Finally pulling back, Caryn smiled. "I've been wanting to do that since the first time I saw you in Strathwick."

"Why didn't you?"

She chuckled at his obtuseness. "Julie?"

"Yeah, but –"

"No buts," Caryn replied. "She had the hots for you, and you returned the interest, no matter how little emotionally involved you were with her. Raquel and Annabeth are another matter. What you three have going is a little beyond me. I've often wondered why the three of you just don't room together."

Karl sat back. "To be honest, I don't quite understand it either."

"I don't see you complaining," Caryn said, her blue eyes staring intently at him.

"Not sure it would do anything," he mumbled.

361

"You always have a choice," she objected.

Karl returned the gaze. "Yes, I do have a choice. And you won't hear me complain because the truth is that I rather enjoy the personal attention."

"What will you do when you become king and one of them wants to be queen?"

"Maybe I'll have two queens… or three," he added.

Caryn shook her head. "I don't play well with others, and I won't stand in line waiting to be noticed."

Karl studied her then said, "It's all rather moot at the moment. We're here and they're not. Besides, we have a mission to do and like Felix said, try not to get killed."

"Live for the moment, eh?" she slyly grinned.

"It's my life's motto," he answered. "No one knows what's going to happen an hour from now, let alone tomorrow or the next day."

"Oh," she calmly replied, "I know exactly what's going to happen later today."

"You do?" He frowned then saw the impish grin and wink. "I'm tempted to move that adventure up to right now, but," he said, flapping his shirt, "one of us needs a shower."

"Besides," she teased, pulling her shirt down enough to reveal cleavage, "anticipation is half the fun."

It was dark by the time they returned to the Landon parking garage, driving two trucks with trailers loaded with ATVs, drones, satellite comms, food supplies, clothing, and anything else that caught their fancy. Cases of ammo filled the truck beds.

While they rode the elevator up, Landon lowered the door barriers, effectively sealing off the parking garage.

"Your search was successful?" Landon asked when they walked into his office.

"Not bad," Karl answered, walking over to Landon's desk computer and pulling up an area map showing Chattanooga and the surrounding area all the way to Blue Ridge, Georgia. "Let's get down to business. We know from the cameras that the bad guys exited in the Cohutta Wilderness just before they got to Conasauga. Cohutta and

Big Frog Wilderness connect for about 45,000 acres of wilderness, all surrounded by paved road. What we need for you two to do," he looked directly at Felix and Landon, "is to find a way to monitor all the cameras on the roads."

"My God," Felix blurted. "That has to be over 100 miles of road."

"You're right," Karl replied, unfazed, "but we need a way to ensure they're still in the area. You know what the truck looks like and it's not like there's a lot of traffic to monitor."

"We'll take care of it," Landon assured him.

"Caryn and I will start operations at the last known point." He then went on to explain drone searching and subsequent rescue plans once the villains were found.

"How long will this take," Felix fretted.

"Haven't the faintest idea," Karl admitted, "but it's the best we got with what we've got. If I had a battalion of soldiers, I could do it quicker. But there's only four of us. Unless you want to get more folks involved, be happy with what you got."

"Everything's   fine,"   Landon   placated.   "Please continue."

"Caryn and I will head out first thing tomorrow morning and set up our HQ in Conasauga. In addition to monitoring the roads, I want to know where all the grocery stores and gas stations are. Unless they're pumping and refining their own oil, milking their cows, and growing coffee beans, they've got to get that stuff from somewhere."

"You got it," Landon replied, excited to be a part of this unique adventure.

"Good. Now all we need is a hot meal and place to sleep."

"Dinner is ready," Landon answered, pointing to the doors leading to his apartment "and there is a bedroom for each of you upstairs."

Karl and Caryn exchanged a knowing glance and smiled, which did not go unnoticed by Landon who quietly smirked.

It was a little after eight the next morning when Karl pulled out of the parking garage, Caryn following behind. His attention focused on direction, it wasn't until he navigated the exchange to I-24 east then onto I-75 east towards Cleveland that he relaxed enough to let his mind wander.

Last night's meal of roasted pork loin, sautéed asparagus, and twice-baked potatoes was excellent, especially along with the vintage Pinot Noir, yet he pondered whether he could tell the difference between real life food and gaming food. Some of the meals he had in the game were exquisite, as were the wines and ales.

The dinner had been an intimate affair, the four of them sitting at one end of the long table in Landon's dining room, Landon and Felix seated across from him and Caryn. Karl wore clothing he had picked up earlier that day: slacks, Ralph Lauren polo shirt, and dock siders. Landon remarked that he looked the quintessential upper crust blueblood.

Their heads turned when Caryn entered. She wore tight black slacks, stiletto heeled shoes, and a not quite sheer white blouse atop a lace black bra.

Karl wondered why women did that, for it naturally drew attention to the breasts, not that he was complaining, especially when one was as fetching as Caryn, but it did make it difficult to divert his eyes from wandering over her body.

His reverie drifted to the after-dinner delights when he and Caryn excused themselves for the night. Recognizing the obvious, Landon and Felix bid them goodnight and wandered to the living room for a brandy.

Pausing outside Karl's bedroom door, Caryn gently tapped him on the arm. "I'll be right there. Just need to change and freshen up. Don't go away."

"Wouldn't dream of it," he winked and walked into his room.

Ten minutes later the door opened, and Caryn walked in. She wore the same pants and blouse. The difference was no bra.

Karl's arousal increased as she sensually sauntered over to him and whispered, "Guess what?"

"What?"

She paused and slid her eyes to gaze around the room then huskily said, "I'm not wearing any underwear."

Karl chuckled as he drove past Hamilton Place Mall, looking in the side mirror to see her driving behind him. Theirs were the only vehicles on the road. In fact, he was hard pressed to see any cars other than those at the few auto dealer lots they passed. He knew there were still holdouts, the 'Refusals' as Landon called them. They were few but determined not to be swept away into technology... which meant they were dangerous, which reminded him that he was glad he had Caryn with him.

Caryn was quite an interesting anomaly: a beautiful woman, an exceptional lover, and a professional killer. What surprised him was that he had learned more about her in the brief time here than all the time they had been together in the game.

Caryn was a captain in the Highland Scouts, a company commander of an elite unit much like the Widowmakers. Though perhaps not quite as ruthless as the Widowmakers, the Highlander Scouts had earned the reputation of an aggressive devastating force, one that took no prisoners and left no trace other than a single calling card – a Scottish Highlander in kilt, holding a claymore in one hand and a severed head in the other.

The realization hit Karl that when they returned to the game, Caryn was the logical choice for second in command. He frowned thinking of how he was going to navigate that conundrum, once Raquel realized she had been replaced.

His mind then wandered to visions of being king of an island. Would he have a queen? If he was supposed to have kids – can they do that in a game? – he'd have to have a wife. Could he have more than one wife?

He grinned at the thought. While it sounded appealing, the personalities were too strong for that to happen. And what about Julie? The last he remembered her was when the guards hauled her out of Eleris' chamber while she wailed her undying love for him.

"Exit 20, three miles ahead," the GPS voice announced, interrupting his reverie. "Turn right, going east, onto bypass U.S. Route 74."

Focusing on the task at hand, he took in the surroundings, shaking his head when he saw the tall billboard advertising immersion with ITL.

"Turn right, one half mile ahead, Exit 20," the GPS stated.

Karl glanced down at the dashboard, wondering how he could turn off the annoying GPS. He knew where he was going and didn't need to be reminded.

It wasn't until they were off the interstate and around Cleveland and onto US 74 heading towards Ocoee that they saw the remnants of civilization close up. Fast food restaurants, gas stations, small businesses, schools, and even churches all stood empty, the occasional abandoned car or truck sitting forlorn in the parking lot.

Karl now kept a careful watch of the surrounding area, still surprised at the absence of human beings. Turning south at Ocoee, he headed down to Conasauga, noting Ball Play Road as he passed then across the Conasauga River and into the tiny hamlet of Conasauga, pulling up in the Conasauga River Baptist Church parking lot.

"We'll set up here," Karl said as Caryn exited her truck. "We'll use the church as our CP. Park the vehicles behind and out of the way so no one knows were here."

"Except for Felix and Landon, no one *does* know we're here," she grinned.

He tossed her the keys to his truck. "Go ahead and pull the vehicles around while I rearrange the inside of the church. I'll help unload once I get space."

While she went back to her truck, Karl pulled out a cordless drill and walked up the steps to the front doors, which were unsurprisingly unlocked. Pushing the doors open revealed a small sanctuary filled with pews that were screwed down to the floor. Up front raised up three steps was the preacher's pulpit with the choir folding chairs to the side.

He was still unscrewing pews when Caryn walked in carrying their gear and setting it next to the pulpit. An hour later, they had the pews pushed aside, folding tables set up, and a work board tacked with pictures of the truck, the villains and Alyson, in the center, and coffee brewing in the church kitchen… and weapons neatly laid out where the choir used to sit.

"Let's see how well these things work," Karl said, unpacking a drone box. It was a small drone, about half a meter wide with the blades unfolded. Noting map sheets spread out on the table, he pointed to Ball Play Road. "We'll start here. Where the road splits, you head north and I'll head east."

"Roger that," she nodded. "I'll go set up the antenna remotes." Grabbing two compact antenna dishes, she attached them to her belt and headed towards the front of the church where the bell ropes dangled. Gently pulling down one of the thick ropes until she heard a dull clung of the clapper, she shimmied up the rope and into the belfry. Ten minutes later she was back standing beside Karl who had two computers connected to two large screens each, with the computers data linked to the drones. The result was that they could fly the drones from the comfort of inside the church.

For two days, they piloted their drones in two-hour blocks of searching then returning to change batteries and resume the search. Though spotting abundant wildlife, including several black bears, the results were disappointing.

"This is mind-numbing," Caryn remarked, stretching her back and arms. "I've been sitting on my ass for two days. I've got to move."

"I know," Karl agreed, frustrated that after all the action in the game, he was stuck here sitting at a console, joy-sticking a drone searching for someone who could be hundreds of miles away. "At least the coffee's good," he sighed, scooting back from the table, coffee mug in hand.

"Just the coffee?" she deadpanned with a frown.

Karl flashed a grin. "That part is beyond good."

"So say it," she teased.

"I just did. You want some more?" He held up the mug and grinned. "Coffee, that is?"

"We got movement." Felix's excited face appeared on another computer screen.

"Where?" Caryn asked, ignoring Felix and focusing on the map on the table.

"Coming out at Cisco, heading south towards Chatsworth. It's the same truck."

"Can you see inside the truck?" Karl asked

"Gimme a minute," Felix replied. An impatient silence ruled the room until Felix came back with, "Just one person. Can't get too clear a picture, but it looks like the older man."

"Keep a tail on him while we search up road from where he came out," Karl said. "I want to know when he comes back."

"If he comes back," Felix worried.

"He'll be back," Karl reassured him. "Let me know whenever he stops."

"Got it."

"He's too far to chase," Caryn said. "I say we load up the drones in the ATVs and head south to Cisco."

"Agreed," he replied with a contented smile, knowing she was every bit as capable as he was in making the right decisions.

While they packed up their gear, Felix kept them appraised.

"He's getting gas at the Victory Fuels station. I can get a better look at him now. He looks to be mid-50s, long beard, still wearing that same t-shirt and jeans. He's got a gut on him. He keeps looking around but doesn't seem to be in too much of a rush. He's wearing that same John Deere baseball hat. I wonder if he sleeps in that thing... He's finished now. Getting in the truck. He's driving off."

Thirty minutes later, Karl and Caryn were in Cisco, set up in one of the abandoned outbuildings behind the gas station across the street from the Baptist Church. Their prey was still inside the Bi-Lo grocery store in Chatsworth.

"He's coming out now," Felix intoned over the earpiece stuck in Karl's ear. "He's got a shopping cart full of stuff, food I'd guess." A minute later, he announced, "he's heading back your way."

"OK," Karl said. "Unless he goes somewhere other than turning right at Cisco, stay off the comms."

"OK."

Karl turned to Caryn and nodded. "He's headed this way. I figure it's around 25 k's between there and here, so we got a couple of minutes. Though he's confident enough to be out in the open here and now, he's still antsy. He has to know someone's looking for him. My guess is that when he turns right here, he'll still be looking around for other traffic, more out of habit than on purpose. That said, we need to make sure he doesn't see us."

"I think I can handle that," she said, staring at him.

"Sorry," he said with an awkward shrug. "Old habit. I know you could have done this all by yourself. You already know all this stuff."

"It's OK," she smiled. "It's a lot more fun with you."

They heard the distant sound of an engine and stepped back into the shadows of the building. Up the road came the pickup, a beat-up Dodge at least 20 years old. The vehicle slowed as it approached the turn before the church. The man in the truck had the windows down, an arm nonchalantly resting on the window frame.

Like Karl expected, as the man braked to make the turn, he glanced around, his gaze passing quickly over where they stood hidden within the shadows of the abandoned buildings. Once the truck made the turn, their drones were in the air, following high above as the man headed east on Old Highway 2.

"There's another church to the right on the road," Caryn said, waiting until the truck rounded a bend before zipping down to get a better look. "It's called Mount Sumac Church."

"Road's splitting," Karl said. "He's going right. Catch up." A moment later he added, "paved road ends. It's dirt now."

The two drones followed the truck as the road curved and bent, snaking its way northward, past empty houses and yet another church.

"Good God," Caryn blurted. "Why is this church here, stuck it the middle of nowhere?"

A half-mile later, the truck slowed then turned left up a dirt driveway shaded in trees for about 100 meters before opening up to a long narrow pasture area with a house and barn at the far end. Alyson's Audi and another pickup truck were parked in front. Four barking dogs bounded down the rutted driveway to greet him.

"See if you can get a closer view without being seen," Karl said.

Caryn expertly maneuvered the drone along the edge of the pasture, dipping in among the trees for cover, while Karl pulled his back and out of sight then up above the treetops, zipping in a straight line due west until he came to the pavement of US Route 411. In short order, he had the drone back, changed the batteries and headed back to resume the watch, alternately watching his and Caryn's monitor.

"You're pretty good with that thing," he complimented.

"I played with them when I had the chance," she replied, focused on the task. "Used to set up competitions in the command."

Karl half smiled, knowing the answer. "Never lost, did you."

"Nope."

As she positioned the drone closer to the house, they watched the man unload the groceries and haul them into the house, a two-story Victorian affair with wide front porch. In contrast to the occupants and their vehicles, the house appeared well tended, which caused Karl to think they were not the owners.

When the last of the groceries were inside, the man reappeared and sat in a rocking chair on the porch, a shotgun across his lap. He turned his head to the door and yelled something. A moment later the screen door opened, and the younger man came halfway out. There was a brief conversation between the two with the younger man occasionally looking back into the house before finally disappearing back inside.

Karl and Caryn watched the older man rock contentedly. Two dogs settled at his feet while the other two romped around in the yard. A half hour later, the man ticked his head towards the door then got up and went inside.

Nothing changed for the next half hour.

"We're gonna have to pull back and recharge pretty soon," Caryn reminded him.

Karl checked his remaining battery time. "Another ten minutes."

Another ten minutes passed in silence. Just as Karl was about to call it quits, the door opened and the older man emerged, smoking a cigarette, shot gun in his left hand. A moment later, the younger man came out, tapping a cigarette out of the pack.

"I'm pulling back," Caryn stated. "We're running out of time."

"One more second," Karl said, focusing on the younger man who jerked a thumb towards the door and said something that caused the older man to laugh. "OK."

Caryn expertly withdrew the drone to the back of the house then to the tops of the trees to circle back to where Karl's drone hovered on the road.

"Here," he said handing her the controls to his drone. "Take over while I bring yours back to change batteries."

The hand off complete, Karl marveled as he snatched glimpses of Caryn's drone working its way around trees towards the back of the house.

For the next hour and a half, Karl and Caryn exchanged controls while Karl changed batteries then sped the recharged drones to Caryn who maneuvered them between views of the back and front of the house. Several times, the younger man would go inside while the older man contentedly rocked and cradled the shotgun. At one point, with the two men on the porch, the back door opened briefly, but whoever it was remained unseen in the doorway.

"That's good for now," Karl said. "It'll be dark soon."

Nodding, Caryn brought the drone back through the woods to the dirt road then back to their hiding spot in Cisco.

"We know at least one other person is in the house," Karl observed, "but we don't know for sure it's her."

"Who else would it be?" she asked, replacing the batteries in the drone.

Karl shrugged. "Let's assume it is her. The dogs there present a problem, effectively undermining our element of surprise. We'll have to get them away from the house."

"I have an idea," she said with a smile.

"Thought you might," he grinned back. "Let's compare notes."

For four days, they watched the house, only once catching a glimpse of a person coming to the front door. When Felix found out they had discovered the hideout, he wanted action.

"Go in and get her," he demanded.

"You want her dead or alive?" Karl calmly replied.

"Pardon?" Felix choked on his coffee.

"If they were willing to knock her out to bring her back here, I've no doubt they're quite willing that if they can't have her then no one will."

Thereafter, Felix held his tongue except to complain, "What's taking so long?"

"Patience," Karl sagely answered. "You brought us here to do a job, now let us do it."

On the fifth day since their arrival at Cisco, Karl nudged Caryn awake. "He's on the move. Get ready."

Caryn was up in an instant, brushing the sleep from her eyes as she climbed the ladder to the top of the roof of the storage shed, two sniper rifles slung over her shoulder. She was in her prone position when Karl's voice came over her earpiece.

"He's just passed Mount Sumac Church. We take him as soon as he makes the turn."

Two minutes later, the truck appeared, slowing down for the stop sign though not stopping, again heading south towards Chatsworth. As soon as he made the turn, Caryn

372

fired two quick shots, the silencer muffling the sound. The result was two flat tires, front and rear right side. As the truck slowed to a stop, Caryn changed rifles to a smaller .22 caliber with long range bullets.

The man got out of the truck, cussing up the proverbial storm. Coming around the bed of the truck, he stood there angrily denouncing the gods of mankind when she fired a single shot to the knee.

He dropped like a Georgia pine in a tornado. Before he had chance to understand what was happening, something thick and heavy impaled his back forcing him onto his stomach while a burlap sack jammed over his head. His arms were yanked and tied behind him with zip ties. He felt hands rummaging through his pockets and his phone liberated.

Momentarily forgetting the pain, he heard a man's voice say, "Help me get him up." Deciding to let them struggle, he let the dead weight of his corpulent body hang. After only a moment, he heard the menace in the man's voice and the tighter grip on his arm. "You. Stand up or I shoot you in the other knee."

The man struggled to stand then felt himself pushed down to sitting followed by movement and the sound of an engine. They didn't travel far, and he was helped to a chair, his wrists zip tied to the arms of the chair. The pain in his knee throbbed.

"What do you want," he pleaded. "I ain't got nuthin worth stealin'."

Inside a nearby shed, Karl sat opposite him, saying nothing, sipping a freshly brewed cup of coffee while Caryn busied herself checking and cleaning her weapons. He watched the man twitching his head, straining to listen for sounds.

"Hullo?" He cocked his head and listened. "I know you're there you sons o' bitches. Say somethin'."

"You have something we want," Karl said, picking up a rubber baton.

"Who are you?"

"You have a woman," Karl replied, ignoring the question. "We want her."

"I don't know what cher talkin' 'bout." He shifted and the pain in his knee spiked. "Damn it all. Why'd ya shoot me?"

Karl wacked the baton on the man's bad knee causing the man to howl.

"We want the woman."

"Go to hell," the man shot back, his breath labored.

"Where is she?"

"Don't know what cher talkin' 'bout. Don't know nuthin' 'bout no woman."

"That's a double negative," Karl said, "which means you do know something about the woman."

"Huh?"

"Where is she."

When the man did not reply, Karl wacked him again on the knee.

"God damn you," the man yelped, squirming in anguish.

"I can play this game all day," Karl reminded him. "The sooner you tell us, the sooner you can get back to your pitiful life, and the sooner you can get that knee looked at. It looks pretty bad. Might get infected… gangrene sets in. It's not pretty when you have to cut off an arm or a leg."

"Go to hell."

"Have it your way." Karl stood up and let loose a crushing blow on the man's knee.

The man doubled over in pain causing the chair to nearly tumble over had not Karl caught it. When the pain subsided and the man caught his breath, Karl repeated the blow.

"Where's the woman?"

"I don't know any woman," the man bellowed.

Once again Karl struck.

"O God, O God, stop," the man begged, tears streaming down his face inside the burlap sack. "Why you think I got a woman?"

"Because we saw you when you drove by us in Cleveland," Karl lied. "Saw you in the pickup with another car behind you, probably driven by your son. The woman was in the seat next to him."

"Why you want her?"

"That's none of your business. Let's just say we're looking out for our future. Now where is she?" The man paused and Karl gave the knee a light tap with the baton.

"OK, OK," the man blurted. "She's back at the house."

"Where's that?"

"Just up the road from the church."

"How far?"

"'Bout two miles up. Keep to the left when road splits."

"What about your son. Who else is there?"

"Just him."

"Dogs?"

"No."

Karl glanced over at Caryn who shook her head with a grin. "She still OK?"

"Yup."

Karl stood up and patted the man's cheek, outside the burlap. "See? That wasn't so hard."

"Take this thing off m'head and gimme a cigarette."

"Not yet," Karl smoothly replied. "We're going to check your story first. If it's not true, I'll be back to shoot your other knee.

"Did I say 'left' at the split?" the man exclaimed. "I meant go right, when you came to the split. Don't go left."

"An easy mistake to make," Karl said with an indulgent smile. "We'll be back."

Once outside, Caryn lowered her voice. "What're we going to do with him?"

"Leave him for now. Where'd you park his truck?"

"Across the tracks behind the post office," she replied. "We just going to leave him here?"

"For the time being," he answered. "I want him alive if we need him. After that, we can decide what to do with him. What's your bet as to how long it will be before junior comes out looking for him?"

"Two days."

"I'll say by this time tomorrow, he'll be out in the other pickup, Alyson beside him, her hands tied."

They were both wrong.

Three days later, Junior made his move.

In between that time, the older man was left alone, his pleas for help growing less and less with each passing day as his body weakened from lack of food and water.

His phone buzzed incessantly the first day. By the third day, the phone lay silent.

"Why don't we just put him out of his misery," Caryn argued.

"Not yet," Karl responded. "We may still need him if things don't work out like I want."

Caryn looked back at the shed where the older man sat, bag over his head, which hung down on his chest, his pants wet from urinating on himself the first day. "It stinks in there. Let's hope Junior gets a set and comes out to find him."

"He will," Karl reassured her.

Three days later, during Caryn's morning watch, she announced, "There they are."

Karl glanced over at the screen to watch Junior escort Alyson, her hands tied in front, down the steps to his truck, his hand gripping her arm. She looked tired, but defiant.

"I'll take over," he said. "You go get ready."

Caryn took only one rifle this time, no suppressor attached and climbed atop the gas station roof to get a better shot.

"They're on the way," Karl informed her via her earpiece.

Setting up the tripod, she lowered herself to prone position and shouldered the rifle.

"They're passing Mount Sumac Church. Get ready."

Caryn waited until Junior got to the intersection. Unlike his father, Junior came to a complete stop, looking both ways before the crack of a high-powered rifle sent the lead through the windshield and into his forehead.

The truck started rolling forward as Karl zoomed out an ATV and placed it in the path of the truck, effectively stopping it.

Leaping out of the ATV, he came around to the passenger side of the truck. "Alyson? Are you OK?"

Alyson's color was beginning to return to her face. Beside her, Junior's lifeless body slumped to the side, one hand still on the steering wheel. She inhaled a sigh of relief when Karl announced, "Felix sent us."

Then she started crying.

"It's OK," Karl soothed, opening the door and cutting the rope binding her wrists. "It's over. Time for you to go home."

"Thank you," she gushed, scooting out of the truck as she wiped her tears. She then wrapped her arms around him and hugged him tight, much to Caryn's annoyance.

Felix barely contained his joy when Karl, Caryn, and Alyson walked into Landon's office. Alyson fell into his arms and started crying again, while Landon looked on like a pleased father whose wife just gave birth.

"Well done," Landon praised. "Any problems?"

"None," Karl replied.

"It was easy," Caryn chuckled. "They hadn't a clue we were there."

"They're both dead?"

"Yes," Caryn replied, explaining how they captured the old man and then finished him off shortly after they rescued Alyson.

"Gruesome," Landon grimaced, "but it had to be done. Thank you."

Alyson stopped crying and apologized for her behavior while brushing away the dampness on her cheeks.

"Did they harm you?" Landon asked.

"No" she said with a deep breath of relief, "not yet. They were supposedly trying to act like gentlemen, but they were nothing more than crude scum whose concept of class was moonshine and a Hostess Twinkie." She shivered at the memories.

"Did they ever tell you why they kidnapped you?" Felix asked.

"Something about escaping to where no one would find us and recreating mankind," she replied. "They saw immersion as from the devil and the whole world had gone to hell and it was up to them to save humanity. It was no use discussing anything with them as they were convinced their mission was holy. I was merely the first woman captured in their scheme. The plan was to capture at least twenty more."

"Let me guess," Karl smiled, shaking his head. "Those two would be the only men in this whole arrangement."

"Bingo," Alyson nodded.

"Almost sounds like someone else I know," Caryn muttered, shifting a glance at Karl.

"What?" Landon frowned.

"Nothing," she grinned then fluffed her shirt. "I think I could use a long hot bath."

"O God, me too," Alyson moaned.

"Mi casa es su casa," Landon expansively said, spreading his hands. Make yourselves at home."

"If it's all the same to you," Alyson said, "I'd rather go home to clean up." She turned to Felix. "Will you come with me?"

"Of course," Felix said.

"Then dinner at least," Landon said, "at seven."

Caryn leaned into Karl and batted her eyes. "Hey sailor. Want to join me?"

Landon surprised them at dinner that evening when a gorgeous redhead arrived just before seven.

"Everyone, I'd like to introduce Meghan."

Meghan was a slender buxom woman with bright emerald green eyes that seemed captivated with everything she saw.

"Meghan and I share a passion in things antique and ancient," he explained. "I would have introduced her sooner, had we not been involved in our recent project."

"You'll have to tell me about that," she said, her voice warm and soft.

Karl noticed the interaction, immediately recognizing Meghan knew far more than she let on.

With dinner served, the conversation turned to immersion. Sipping his wine, Landon turned to Karl and Caryn.

"I imagine you're ready to get back to your adventures."

"Not quite yet," Caryn quickly answered.

"Oh?" He cocked an eyebrow in surprise.

"We'd like a few days exploring around here before we get back to the grind," she said with a knowing smile, "sort of a mini vacation before we have to go back to work."

"An excellent idea," he complimented. "There's lots to do without the inconvenience of standing in lines now that no one is here."

The evening ended early as the stress of captivity caught up with Alyson and she asked to go home shortly after dessert was served, Felix leaping up to act as escort and guard. Karl and Caryn likewise excused themselves and headed upstairs, leaving Landon and Meghan who were quite content to have the time to themselves.

For five days, Karl and Caryn roamed Chattanooga and the surrounding area, still marveling at the absence of humanity. The forbidden delight of rummaging through stores and taking whatever caught their fancy began to wane by the fourth day as they stood amongst various toys, cars, clothing, and oddities. Even the yacht they had tied up on the river lacked the enticement it once had.

Each evening they returned to dinner with the others, settling into a routine of dinner with friends and then off to their own enjoyments in the evenings, though Caryn managed to find other locations for sexual romps, including a frolic in the lobby of the Chattanooga Choo Choo hotel. Karl mentioned more than once the desire to return to the game, but Caryn's persuasive powers managed to distract him.

On day six, they decided to head down to Atlanta and were near the Georgia border when Felix called.

"You need to come back."

"What's up?" Karl asked.

"I'll explain when you arrive."

Landon was in Felix's office when Karl and Caryn walked through the doors.

"Sorry," Landon said, "but we're going to have to cut your vacation short, that is unless you want to go into another game, which you are free to do."

"What's going on?" Caryn asked.

"Your friends have been imprisoned," Felix said. "With your absence, another has claimed the throne for himself. If you want to save your kingdom, you need to return now."

"So who's in charge now?" Karl asked.

"You'll find out when you get back," Felix said, waving away Karl's question.

"You can't tell us?" Karl frowned.

"I've already told you too much," he evasively answered.

"But you do have options," Landon quickly reminded them. "You can choose to enter another game if you wish. If we need to find you, the AI knows where you're at and can retrieve you when and if necessary."

"But not everything is equal," Felix interrupted. "Remember, your gaming skills are still elementary. Bridge Quest was designed with your skills in mind. It was developed so that you wouldn't have to keep track of attributes and skills while at the same time allowing you to progress as if in a normal game. My point here is that should you choose to enter another game, you will have to become a true gamer."

"I don't want to go into another game," Karl admonished. "I was happy where I was."

"Me too," Caryn chimed in then turned to Karl. "Will you still want me when I'm an elf?"

Karl smirked. "I've never had sex with an elf."

Landon shook his head and smiled, spreading his hands. "T-M-I… too much information."

"Let's get you down to the immersion room," Felix said, redirecting their attention. "By the way," he continued as they head out, "the AI assumes your completion of the quest here is within the construct of the game and has rewarded both of you with a significant increase in levels. You're both now level 25, which is the max a player can have on this island before being required to cross the bridge to the next island."

"Level 25?" Caryn marveled. "That's quite a jump, almost double what I was before. Why?"

Felix shrugged. "I think the AI determined the quest exceeded the bounds of gaming constraints. In other words, since you had no magic or potions or anything else to use to aid you in your quest, you were rewarded accordingly."

Caryn chuckled. "It wasn't all that hard."

"You complaining?" Felix replied with a wry smile.

"What about the prophecy?" Karl frowned. "I'm supposed –"

"- to rule for a 1000 years," Felix interrupted. "Yes, I know. As far as I can tell, the prophecy still holds."

"What about me?" Caryn demanded.

"What about you?" Felix replied.

"Do I have to move on, or can I stay on the island?"

Felix impatiently shrugged. "I don't know."

Caryn curved a thumb at Karl. "Why does he get to stay and I'm forced to cross to the next island?"

"Like I said," Felix huffed, "I don't know yet. I've got one of the remaining techs looking into it."

"Why can't he just fix it?" Karl queried.

"It's not as easy as it sounds," Landon answered as they walked into the immersion room. "Once the game is set up and the AI in control, the permutations become exponential and human control is eliminated."

"Can't he just override it?" Caryn asked.

"Again, it's not that easy," Landon said. "There are safeguards built into the AI to prevent overrides. Protocols have to be written and introduced into the program that dovetail with established parameters. In other words, the AI has to sense that the attempted input commands are in accord with its directives."

Karl's lips tightened and he jabbed a finger at Felix. "Fix it. Tell your technician to tell the AI that I can't rule for 1000 years without her. She is integral to the prophecy."

"I understand," he placated. "I'm working on it. Now unless you two want to hang around some more, I suggest you get on the immersion tables."

"Where are we immersing?" Karl asked as he went to the designated table.

"The AI will put you in a place that will be of most benefit," Felix answered.

"That's not very reassuring," Karl said.

"I guess you'll find out when you get there."

Karl and Caryn shared a last look and settled on their respective table and with the electrodes in place, they were soon on their way. This time the floor traps stayed closed and instead of their bodies sliding off the tables down into conveyor belts leading to the incinerator, lifeless Karl and Caryn were shunted off to cold storage.

"That was quick thinking," Landon complimented.

"It was the best I could do at the moment," Felix sighed.

Landon folded his arms and stared at the empty room. "Wonder what their reaction would be if they knew we have no techs left, that you and I and Alyson are the last remaining employees of Landon Limited."

OTHER BOOKS

I write GameLit, Space Opera, Steampunk, Dystopian, Literary, and even poetry, and you can find my books in numerous eBook stores. You can check out my website for more information about my books, upcoming projects, and events I'll be attending where you can visit with me and even get signed books.

Thank you for choosing to read this story! If you enjoyed it, I'd appreciate your feedback in the form of a review.

Thanks for reading!

-pdmac

WEBSITE: www.pdmac-author.com

FACEBOOK: www.facebook.com/pdmacauthor/

Bridge Quest: A GameLit Adventure Series

Bridge Quest

Orc's Bane

Lord of Innis Torr

The Wyvern Master Chronicles

The Sixth Kingdom

A Spy in the Court

Raising the Dead

Wizard King

Steampunk Western: Tombstone Trilogy

Fool's Gold

An Ounce of Lead

The Devil's Disciple (Coming soon)

A Dystopian Novel:

Rebirth of Angels

A Time Travel Novella

Ctrl Z: The Do Over Stone

Poetry

a young man no more